Caleb, Caleb, Caleb

guy carey jr.

PUBLISH AMERICA

PublishAmerica
Baltimore

First printing

All characters appearing in this work are fictitious. Any resemblance to real persons, living or dead, is purely coincidental.

ISBN: 1-4241-6594-6
PUBLISHED BY PUBLISHAMERICA, LLLP
www.publishamerica.com
Baltimore

Printed in the United States of America

This book is dedicated to the friends, families and work companions who have been sharing their stories with me as we are traveling along life's path.

To all the people who asked for a continuation of Caleb's story, my sincere appreciation. My thanks also go to my family for their support and encouragement. To my daughter-in-law Lynn Carey a very special thanks for her expertise in making my writings readable.

PROLOGUE

The book, *The Town Barn Isn't There Anymore*, was a coming of age story about Caleb Carney growing up in a small New England town in a large family, during 1930s and 40s. The story was written from the memories of an older Caleb when he returned to that town in retirement.

This book, *Caleb, Caleb, Caleb*, is a story of Caleb's struggles with the transformation from his youth to the realities of adulthood and its responsibilities.

There is a third book outlined, so far unnamed, that will bring Caleb back to where *The Town Barn Isn't There Anymore*, began.

CHAPTER ONE

So this is Oklahoma, I thought as Eunice met me at the train station. Wow! I used to think that Oscin was a big town, but the city of Lotus, Oklahoma, made Oscin look like a cow path by comparison. Eunice helped me collect my luggage and we loaded it in the car.

Noticing my awe she said, "What did you expect, Caleb? Sterling is far from being the whole world."

"I know, Eunice," I replied trying to cover my fear. "We went through many places like this on the train ride, but this is the first time I actually set foot in a town bigger than Oscin."

Eunice laughed and said, "It's okay, Caleb. I was pretty awestruck myself when I first left Sterling. You will come to realize that places like Lotus are called cities, not towns. I suppose the reason for that is it takes so much more management to oversee places this big."

As we drove through the city with its big buildings dwarfing the cars on the street, I felt the fear creeping in, much like the day when I first went to work at the milk barn. What was it Josh used to say? When you are faced with doubt about how things are going to be, try recalling when you felt that way before and how it ended up. This thinking helped me to become comfortable with my position at the barn after I had been there a while. So thinking of that gave me hope that I would be as comfortable here after I become used to it.

We left the city and entered a suburb where, even though the houses were too close together, there weren't many tall buildings around.

Eunice turned into the last house on Walnut Street announcing, "Here we are, Caleb, at your home away from home for the next four years. Hey, you look like you've been hit by a brick, Caleb! Talk to me! Are you all right?"

"I'm okay, Eunice, but this is a lot to adjust to in such a short time; you have to remember that I am just a country boy lost in a new world," I said, "I'll find my way around eventually, though."

The house was a big old farmhouse. I imagined it must have been here before they started building all those row houses we had just passed along on Walnut Street. The big barn was still there but it had been converted to a garage and workshop and there were many of Harry's tools and his motorcycle stored there.

Eunice took me on a tour of the house ending up at a big room upstairs saying, "This is your room, Caleb. Now here is something new for you—an inside toilet and a room of your own. I bet you'll like that. I have to go down and get some bids of Harry's ready to mail. You get unpacked and explore on your own for a while."

After unpacking the clothes I sat down on the bed wanting to cry. Eunice had Harry and her new life with him but all those dear and close to me were gone. Even though it had been some time since we had lost Josh, being here made me farther away than ever from him. I did not have Josh, or even Homer who in many ways had taken Josh's place in my life, to run to or lean on. Nor was Edgar in my life to listen to my tales of woe and offer his Indian perspective on the situation. Taking the medallion that he had given me, I sat fingering the etchings wishing I were back there with Molly and Roxy the horses.

I was sitting there engrossed in my misery when I heard a truck pull into the yard.

Someone came slamming into the house, shouting, "Where's that Caleb? Caleb! Get your butt down here, and let's take that old Indian out for a spin before it gets too dark, so I can show you the neighborhood."

"Now, you hold on there, Harry; I don't want you rushing in here yelling for Caleb and forgetting I'm here," Eunice shouted.

Harry laughed, giving Eunice a hug, saying, "I could never forget the little country girl who I got to follow me out into this big old world. I'm just anxious to get reacquainted with our hero of the Sterling barn crew!"

Hearing Harry's voice again shook me out of my doldrums, and I ran down stairs to see him. "Hello, Harry, I saw the Indian in the barn, and I was hoping I would be getting to ride on it, but I didn't think it would be this soon."

"Well, Caleb, as soon as I pacify your sister here, we can get it on the road. It has been sitting there too long without giving anyone a ride. Eunice hasn't let me strap Little Harry on behind me yet, and we seldom have anyone to watch him so she can go with me. That poor old Indian has just been rusting away in the barn."

In my fear and confusion I had completely forgotten that they had a baby to care for.

Eunice said, "Okay, you two bums go for your ride while I go get little Harry at the babysitters."

Harry and I went to the barn. Harry grabbed a cloth and went about wiping the dust off from his bike saying, "I'm glad you're here, Caleb. Now I'll have an excuse to ride my bike more often. I have been so busy with the business that when I'm home Eunice needs me to spend my time with her and Harry. Now Eunice can ride again, too, while you watch little Harry for us sometimes."

It was great being on the bike again but riding around the town and seeing how different things were here, brought my thoughts back to how far I was from home. Though I was glad that Harry thought I was mature enough to watch Little Harry, I thought this trip was about a job and college, not about bikes and babysitting. I really enjoyed riding behind Harry, although the thrill of having all my friends see me on a bike was sorely missing here, cruising around Harry's town of Lynbrook.

After our ride, we roared back to the house and put the bike back in the barn. It was nice to see how respectful Harry treated his bike by carefully checking for dirt or oil streaks before we went in to the house. Eunice had dinner ready with Little Harry running around the kitchen floor.

Harry said, "Come over here, Hank, and see your old daddy."

Hearing Harry's voice Hank lit up and came running across the floor. Harry gathered him up in his arms and it was easy to see the love they had for one another. Though our father had been much apart of our lives, I never remembered him ever showing that kind of affection.

Eunice, noticing me watching this scene said, "Caleb, look! I remembered and made your favorite meal, roast pork with lots of garlic."

Harry, laughing, said, "See, Caleb? What a gift your being here is to me! This is one of my favorite dinners too."

After Harry said grace and thanked God for my safe trip, we enjoyed a sumptuous meal with a wonderful chocolate pie for desert. After dinner Eunice and Harry did the dishes while I became acquainted with Hank. I had imagined Hank as a little baby. It didn't seem possible that he was already over four years old. It had been a while since Francis or Nellie was this small, but playing with Hank reminded me of the fun I had when they were. I remember imagining what they would be like when they became adults. Now that Francis and Nellie are older I realize how far off my imagination had been, but still I found myself now imagining what Hank would be like when he grew up. After dishes were done and Hank was tucked safely in his bed, Harry said, "Well, Caleb, are you ready to go to work in the construction world? I have a big job back in Lotus doing the steel work on an eight-story building that's well under way, and I could use another man or two."

"I dunno, Harry, that I'll be much help right away. I don't have any experiences in building projects. Remember, I've only worked as a barn boy and a teamster. I do know that Dad wanted me to work with you for the summer. He thought that I should have experience in a number of jobs. He doesn't think that working as a writer is very promising."

Harry laughed and said, "Caleb, we all have started new jobs with some trepidation, and there are times we find out that some jobs aren't for us. Still, as long as we are willing to give our best effort, things have a way of taking care of themselves. Nobody is going to expect you to be able to compete with our experienced workers only to learn from them. After all, you had to learn how to milk cows and to handle a team of horses. You will sign on as an apprentice and be upgraded as your skills increase; no one will expect you to be an expert in anything in the beginning. If you don't have any questions, Caleb, we better hit the bunks. I have to be on the job at six in the morning."

As I headed up to my room I starting asking myself questions. *What happened to the all the excitement I felt when we first planned this? Why do I feel so scared and lonely? Eunice is family, and I have always liked Harry, but everything here is so strange. I suppose with Eunice being so much older, she and I never developed the closeness that was between us younger Carneys.* As I finally fell into a fitful sleep, I dreamed of Josh. He was writing poetry, and as he left he handed me a paper with what he was working on. He had written:

It isn't how strong you can lift
Or how much strength you feel
It's knowing you have given your all,
That makes a man of steel.

I shouted, "Josh, Josh, don't go! I need you; I need you!"

I woke with Eunice shaking me, saying, "Wake up, Caleb; you're having a bad dream. I guess you might as well stay awake now, it is almost time for breakfast anyway."

After Eunice went downstairs and my fog started to lift, I realized where I was and all my doubts and fears of my new adventure returned. Still remembering my dream about Josh, I got dressed and headed down to the kitchen thinking that even though Josh was dead he still was watching over me.

Harry was at the table eating his breakfast and hardly acknowledged I was there as I sat down to eat, except to say, "We'll be leaving in fifteen minutes, so hurry up and eat."

As Harry left for the barn to load some tools, Eunice said, "You'll get used to Harry's morning stupor, Caleb. It takes him an hour or so in the morning to get his mojo going. It took me a while to get used to his morning moods, but it is just the way he is, so don't take offense at anything that happens with him the first hour or so in the morning."

I went to join Harry to see if I could help with the loading, but he was finished and ready to leave as soon as I came out. After his curt, "Climb in, Caleb," we drove silently to the job site in Lotus.

There wasn't anyone at the site yet and Harry silently went about checking the work that had been done the day before, leaving me by the truck. About twenty minutes after we arrived, cars and trucks started pulling into the site. I noticed that many of them were Indians or had some Indian blood, which was no surprise because the majority of those who had been working in Oscin had Indian blood like Harry. The men gathered around Harry's truck and started joshing me about being Harry's protégé.

One of them, who looked younger than the rest, came over and took my hand and said, "Hey, Caleb, we been hearing a lot about you and how you started working at a farm when you were only nine years old. My name's Shaquille, but every one calls me Shag or Shack. I guess you'll be working with me while you learn the ropes around here."

I was just going to try to say something to Shag, when one of the other men hollered, "Hey, Harry is it safe to talk to you yet?"

Harry answered, "I'm not sure if you want to talk to me, Kale. I found two welds that I am not satisfied with, so get your equipment and redo the ones that I marked, and maybe by then I'll be in a better mood."

The man called Kale laughed and said, "Only two bad ones today, Harry! I must be getting better. Maybe I should put in for a raise."

"You'll get a raise all right," Harry answered, "but it will be with the point of my boot if I keep finding faulty welds every day."

The whole crew started laughing and teasing Kale. He just laughed with them and said, "You know, Harry, if you didn't work us so long and hard that I keep falling asleep welding, I would have a perfect score every morning. Isn't that right, Willy?"

Willy said, "I don't think so, Kale. Maybe if Harry checked at night, you would stand a better chance, but you know nothing is ever right the first thing in the morning with Harry."

Shaq came over and said, "Get used to this, Caleb, Harry is hell on wheels in the morning, but he comes around quick."

I said, "I know, Shaq; my sister tried to warn me this morning about his 'stupor,' as she called it. Does this go on every day?"

"Pretty much, Caleb, but it doesn't mean anything; by coffee break you wouldn't know he was the same Harry."

Harry called out, "Quit your bull over there, and let's get this building going up."

The men separated; taking their tools they started positioning themselves around the building. They were already up to the third floor with the steel skeleton of the building. Many of the men went climbing to the top and took up positions on the beams there.

Shag said, "I guess you are going to work with me, Caleb. What we are going to be doing is hooking the next beams to the cables from the crane and holding the guide ropes so they won't swing and knock somebody off up there."

Shaq showed me how to identify the different beams by the numbers on them. Some of the beams were uprights and some were cross beams and because the building was being built in a trapezoid shape there were different length cross beams. Sending the wrong one up would waste time and Harry would be sure to blow up about that.

Shaq said, "Mel, the man who operated the crane is pretty grouchy most of the time, so we have to be precise in how we hitch the cables so he can suspend the beams exactly in their proper place while they are bolted and welded. When he can't place one where the climbers want it, he always blames the ground men for the way they hitched up."

After we had hooked the first beam up, Shaq showed me how to lean back against the ropes while watching the signals from the climbers, not Mel in the crane. Sometimes when they had a hard time up on top Mel would yell at us, but Shaq said not to listen to him, just to the monkeys up top.

The first couple of hours went by fast; there was so much to learn about how the different ways of hooking beams would make them fit right when they were placed between two uprights. It blew my mind to see the monkeys, as the men up top were called, walk out onto beams swinging on the cables and ride them into place. And then after unhitching the cable, walking those beams without railings or any hand holds. I thought, *I sure hope Harry doesn't expect me to ever do anything like that; I get dizzy sometimes looking out a window if I am above three stories in a building.* When we weren't hitching beams or holding guide ropes, our job was to sort the various bolts needed to bolt the beams together and tie them in a net that we sent up for each new beam.

Shaq said that it was too dangerous to store them up top because anything loose up there might get knock off seriously hurting the ground crew. Suddenly a whistle blast echoed through the building and all work stopped. A van with a big coffee cup and donut painted on its side pulled in to the site. The monkeys climbed down from the top and all the men gathered around the van ordering.

Shaq said, "Come on, Caleb, time for a coffee break. I'll introduce you to the gang. Listen up, crew. For all of you who weren't completely awake earlier, this here is Caleb Carney, Harry's brother-in-law. Caleb, these are the three monkeys: Sunny, the one with the two donuts, Karly is the one with two coffees, and the last one over there by himself is Shawn. The welder Kale and his helper Willy you heard from this morning, and last, our friend, Mel, the crane operator."

In unison they yelled, "Welcome, Caleb, how do you like it so far?"

Before I could answer Harry came up and said, "Don't let these monkeys get you on the wrong track, Caleb. Keep in mind all the tricks the barn crew used to pull, and stay on guard."

Harry seemed more like himself so I answered, "Don't worry, Harry, I think my initiation back then has made me a little smarter in more ways than one, so I'll be careful here. I was beginning to think earlier that I had more to fear from you than them."

"You tell him, Caleb; he has us all shaking in our boots every morning. My wife has to push me out the door every morning because I'm so scared to come here," Kale shouted, laughing. "Maybe being a family member you can save us poor working stiffs from such abuse."

15

Harry patted me on the shoulder laughing and said, "I guess I was worried about nothing. You've already become just another one of the bums who work for me. Okay, crew, ten minutes and then let's get back at it."

Back at work I asked Shaq what he thought made Harry so moody in the morning.

Shaq said, "There is much talk about that, especially when we get a new member. Still I have studied on it the little time I've been here. I asked Willy one day what he thought, and he said he thought that Harry's success frightens him sometimes, and that each new day he deals with that. You know he feels extremely lucky that someone like your sister loved him, and he is always striving to make good for her. This is his first big job with him being responsible for everything. Story is, he was born on a reservation. His mother was mixed blood and his father had mostly Indian blood. His father was a ne'er-do-well who drank too much and whose mother left him and moved off the reservation when Harry was about ten or twelve. Harry's mother fought to get him a good education, but when he was in the last year of high school he started working in steel and never finished his education. He made such a good name for himself as a foreman and an overseer on different steel construction jobs that he was offered jobs on his own. Though he has worked on many jobs before, this one is the biggest he has tackled by himself. Most of this crew have worked with him on one job or another over the years, and they all put up with his moods in good humor. They are more concerned about him than angry about it."

Working for Harry the first couple of weeks was much like when I started working sticking lumber with Dad. Get up early and come home so tired that after playing a little each day with Hank and discussing things with Eunice I crawled into bed early. A couple of times Harry and I rode around on his Indian and if it was a warm evening I would stay with Hank so Eunice could go with him. I suppose it was from working with cables and ropes that I used muscles that I hadn't been using, but after awhile I wasn't as worn out at the end of the day.

One Friday at work Shaq said, "Caleb, it's about time you saw some of Lynbrook beyond the streets that Harry takes you riding on. My sister and I go to a club that caters to the young people in town; would you like to join us?"

"I'm not sure, Shaq. My sister would have a fit if she heard I was going to a club."

"Oh! Caleb I am not talking about a barroom. It's a place where young people can gather without booze to tempt them. They only have soda and

16

snacks and a jukebox to dance to. They have a donation box so you can leave them a couple of bucks if you can afford to."

"You know, Shaq, that sounds a lot like how they closed off the bar at the Inn back home for the younger group once a week; I think I would like to go."

That night after supper, Harry said, "You know, Caleb, your Massachusetts license is good for the first six months you're here, so if you want you can take the pickup tonight."

I thanked Harry and left right after eating, not sure I could find Shaq's house if it got too dark. I found Elliot Street much easier than I thought and pulled into Shaq's yard a little earlier than we had planned. Shaq hollered out, "We'll be out in a few minutes, Caleb." Looking around, I thought it was strange he didn't invite me in. The neighborhood looked fairly prosperous, and the yards around were well kept. Finally Shaq came out and climbed in the truck saying Etta would be with us in a few minutes.

He said, "You know how girls are, don't you, Caleb? I hear you have other sisters."

I was about to answer him when out of the house came a stunning vision of a girl. She had dark hair and skin, and as the boys would say, she was built. She glided down the path in a sensuous walk that about took my breath away. I noticed Shaq giving me a look, so I tried to erase my thoughts, saying, "Yeah, sisters can be a problem sometimes."

When she reached the truck Shaq said, "Caleb, this is my twin sister, Shaquieta, but everyone calls her Etta. Etta, this is Harry's brother-in-law, Caleb. I told you about him when he came here a couple of weeks ago."

After getting into the truck Etta took my hand and said, "Pleased to finally meet you, Caleb. This is a surprise; Shaq usually doesn't want me even talking to his friends, or at least the ones that are boys. Couldn't you boys find a little better chariot to pick Cinderella up in?"

Shaq said, "Knock it off, Etta; he's not here to date you. I'm just trying to get him acquainted with some of the people in town his age. He will be here all summer, and I imagine even a lot of the time after he starts college."

"Oh, wow!" Etta exclaimed, "That's why I'm allowed to talk to him! He's going to be a college boy."

We had just left the driveway when Shaq shouted, "Stop the truck, Caleb! I'm not going to have my night ruined by her crazy antics again. Stop and let her out."

Not knowing what else to do I pulled over.

Etta said, "If you leave me here, Shaq, I have a little information I'm sure mother would be amazed to hear about you. Now don't be a jerk and I'll behave myself tonight if only for Caleb's sake."

Shaq seemed subdued by this and said, "Drive on, Caleb."

Following Shaq's directions we made our way to the Youth Club he had described. The dance floor was on the second floor and was a big square room, not like the long hall we had in Sterling. Shaq introduced me to a couple at the door as Miles and his sister June.

June said, "Well, Caleb, I heard that Harry was bringing in a relative to work the summer with him. Little did I dream he would be as handsome as you! Want to dance?"

"Too bad, June" Etta said, "Caleb has his dance card all filled up, isn't that so, Caleb?"

"Well! I dunno about all filled up. I've promised Etta the first few dances, June, but I'm sure she will let me dance with you after her toes get sore enough."

After giving her brother a haughty look, Etta whirled me out onto the floor. I said, "Etta, you have to understand that your brother has been more than good to me since I've been here, and I don't want to have him be angry with me."

Etta said, "Come on, Caleb; it's just a sister-brother thing. I won't get you in any trouble with him."

Etta danced with the same ease and abandon as Jennie had the first time I took her to dance night in Sterling. After a couple of dances I begged off after doing one of the bump and grind dances. She was getting to a part of me that sure as hell was going to cause trouble.

We sat down at the soda bar and when I asked what she would like she said, "Give us a vanilla coke and two straws."

I thought, O *man, this isn't going to be good.* As the girl at the counter served up the coke, June appeared saying, "C'mon, Caleb. My turn now," taking my elbow.

I said, "I guess I've caught my breath enough for one dance, June; let's go."

After we danced a couple of dances I went back looking for Etta, but she was gone. The girl tending the bar said, "Etta said to save this for you," sliding me our soda.

The vanilla soda was half finished with one of the straws broken in two hanging on the glass.

Shaq came and joined me and said, "Caleb, I was sure I could handle my sister's crazy ways; I'm sorry if she is a bother to you."

"She isn't a bother, Shaq," I answered. "Remember, I have sisters, too, and I know as a brother what a pain in the neck they can be."

I knew it would be a mistake if Shaq knew just how his sister was bothering me; luckily some girl came and dragged him off to dance. I saw Etta out on the dance floor dancing wildly. Her partner looked somewhat like Harry with the wide shoulders and a tall slim build but he was somewhat darker than Harry and looked younger than even Shaq. He sure seemed to enjoy dancing with Etta. I looked around for June but she already had another partner.

One of the girls standing on the side gave me a smile so I walked over and said, "Hi. I'm Caleb, would you care to dance?"

She smiled and said, "Caleb is it? We had you down as Etta's toy for the night. How did you get away from her? My name is Loraine, and I would be pleased to dance with you."

As we eased out to the floor, someone had punched in a slow waltz, so I said, "Etta's toy, huh? I hardly know her. I happen to work with her brother, and he invited me here tonight, and she came with us. I am not anyone's toy, just a stranger trying to find my way around in a strange place."

Loraine laughed, throwing back her head saying, "Well, stranger, you sure picked a hell of a way of looking lost, carousing around with the likes of Etta. Every boy in town wants to date her, and all the girls hate her for her beauty and haughty ways. You're lucky that June likes to challenge her, and I have enough self esteem so I can ignore her, or right now you would be sitting in the corner licking your wounds."

"Oh, c'mon, Loraine; don't you think you're laying it on a little thick? I didn't even know there was an Etta until a couple of hours ago. I'm sure that she doesn't care if I'm here or not."

"Wait a little, stranger; just wait." Loraine said as she walked me off the floor.

"What's up, Loraine? Afraid to dance any longer with this stranger?" I asked as she started towards the door.

"No, no Caleb. It's not that, but someone just came in, and I promised him I would be watching for him. Catch me later, and we'll dance again, that is, if Etta lets you," she said as she hurried to the boy by the door.

I went back to the bar and ordered another soda. June came and sat beside me and said, "Can I get a straw and join you, Caleb?"

"Hell, June, let me buy you a coke. I'm not broke."

"Oh, I didn't mean to insult you Caleb, I just like to bust Etta. I thought, wouldn't it burn her if I was over here with her squeeze, drinking out of the same glass?" she said, laughing.

19

"Dammit, why does everyone think I belong to Etta? I was just telling Loraine that I only met her when I picked up her brother on the way here. If I belong to any girl, it's one who is far away from here, and she won't see us, so get your damn straw and join me."

"Okay, Caleb." June said, "Now here is the way we do this here. We both bend over the glass and drink from our straws together."

I did what June said and was thinking, *She sure smells good,* when our glass went flying off the bar and crashed to the floor with a bang. Whirling around I was face to face with Etta. She had fire in her eyes, but she never said a word. She just turned and walked out the door.

Shaq came running over and said, "What happened, Caleb? What the hell did you do?"

"Whoa, Shaq," June shouted. "Caleb didn't do anything. He was just sitting here sharing a coke with me, and Etta came over and slammed it to the floor."

"I'm sorry, Caleb," Shaq said, "but lately she has been lashing out more and more. I'll go and find her."

June laughed and said, "Boy, that turned out better than I could have hoped for. Let's dance, Caleb."

Bewildered, I allowed June to lead me to the dance floor asking, "What gives here, June, anyway? Why is it fun for you to upset Etta?"

"Well, it's like this, Caleb. I had a boyfriend, and we had been together since kindergarten. One night here at the dance he danced with Etta several times. The next time I came here, he came in with Etta and completely ignored me. I went to see him the next day, and he told me he was helplessly in love with her. They went together for a couple of weeks, and then she dumped him, and he hasn't come to any event in town since. Now you see what makes me do what I do?"

"Oh, I see, June, but I don't want to be used as your weapon any more than I wanted to be called Etta's squeeze," I said, leaving her on the dance floor.

I started for the door but ran into Loraine who asked, "Ready for my dance, Caleb?"

I was going to shrug her off, but then I wondered if she could help me understand what was going on any better, so I said, "I was looking for you, Loraine."

She laughed her throaty laugh again and said, "Is that why you dumped poor June out on the floor? It's okay; Caleb, I'll dance with you, but you have to promise not to leave me stranded like that."

"Don't worry, Loraine; I am not about to get a third girl mad at me in one night. It's just that June used me, and it made me angry. Still, I know I shouldn't have walked off on her. I'll seek her out later and apologize, let's dance."

As we danced I asked, "Loraine, what the devil is it that makes everyone so crazy here tonight?"

"Hold on there, Caleb. Not everyone here is crazy. It's just you got yourself mixed up in a hornets' nest when you got between Etta and June. June has been out to get Etta for weeks now, and it seems that somehow you helped her do it. I understand June's problem, but Etta has us all puzzled. She was just a normal, teenage, boy-crazy girl until about two or three months ago when she became the vindictive angry person we saw tonight. I feel sorry for Shaq. He is a wonderful person, but lately he has been spending all his time trying to keep Etta out of trouble."

As we danced over by the door, Shaq was motioning to me so we danced over to him. He said, "Caleb, would you mind leaving a little early? I have a little problem."

"No, I'll be with you after this dance. I promised Loraine I wouldn't leave her stranded on the floor."

Loraine said, "That's okay, Caleb. For Shaq, I'll let you go."

Shaq leaned over and gave her a little kiss on the cheek, saying, "You're a sweetheart, Loraine."

Loraine said as she left us, "Watch that, Shaq, or I might not let you go."

Shaq said, "Sorry to break up your evening, Caleb, but I have to get Etta out of here before she causes more trouble."

When we got back to the truck Etta was already inside, Shaq asked her to let him in the middle but she wouldn't budge so he got in beside her with a sigh.

I said, "What's up, Etta? Didn't you enjoy the dance?"

She just said, "Shaq, make him shut up."

Shaq said, "Best to leave it alone, Caleb; her trouble is beyond me."

When we got to their house Shaq climbed out saying, "I'm sorry, Caleb, about tonight."

I said, "Hell, Shaq you don't have anything to be sorry about; I had a wild time."

At that Etta threw her arms around me

Shaq was hollering, "Etta cut that out this minute."

She just held me tighter, kissing and rubbing against me. If the steering wheel hadn't been in her way I think she would have been right on top of me.

Just as Shaq started to get in the truck to pull her off, she let go, jumped out, and said, "Bet it wasn't as wild as that, was it, Caleb?"

I drove slowly back to Harry's place thinking, *Man, it was a good thing Shaq was there. I'm not sure that I could have managed to stay a gentleman if we had been alone. I wonder what the devil possessed her. Anyway she is just about the most beautiful girl I have ever seen, but she sure is scary.*

We had the next day, Sunday, off, and Harry said, "Caleb, I have to go over to the job site. Want to ride over on the Indian?"

As we were getting the bike ready I asked Harry, "What gives with Shaq's sister? She sure acted strange last night."

"I'm not sure what the trouble is there, Caleb, but from what I've heard you better steer clear of her. Seems that something happened in the family a month or two ago, and she has been acting strange ever since."

We rode to the job site, and Harry spent some time checking out our tool chest. Seems some of the monkeys had been complaining about the condition of some of the wrenches. Most of these tools were strange to me. A lot of the wrenches had long tapered handles. I knew from watching the monkeys that they were used to line up the holes in the beams so they could bolt them. Harry found a few that had broken or bent handles, he made a list and said, "I guess that's it, Caleb; let's take a ride around the city."

I still liked riding the bike and there were some interesting sites in the city but it wasn't the same thrill as riding around Sterling where everybody knew me.

After we got back I sat with Little Hank while Eunice went for a ride and when they returned Eunice had picked up some brochures and catalogs from the college. After supper I went to my room to study them, it brought my mind back to why I was here and brought back some of my old fears about leaving Sterling.

Next morning it was back to work. Shaq was very quiet at first but after the coffee break he said, "Caleb, I'm real sorry about my sister. She has been acting strange lately, and I thought that maybe going dancing with us it would be different."

"Don't feel bad about me, Shaq. Remember, I have sisters too."

"God, Caleb! I hope none of your sisters act as crazy as that."

"Maybe not, Shaq, but they still could be a pain in the butt. Harry tells me that Etta wasn't always like that. What happened to her anyway? It must have been something that caused her strangeness."

"I have never told anyone, Caleb, but maybe I can trust you. At least you didn't blow up at her antics last night. Etta had been going with the same boy since grammar school. Right before she graduated mother caught her and him doing some heavy necking and read Etta the riot act. That didn't seem to do the trick, because mother saw them necking in the car one night when he brought her home from a date. My father has been gone for a long time now, and mother has raised us alone. She was so upset about this she talked to her brother. Mother has mostly Indian blood, and her brother is a wheel on the reservation. I heard he had a talk with Etta's boyfriend right after he graduated from high school. Seems that he left right after that, and Etta hasn't heard from him since. She was so distressed she spent weeks in her room. Mother got so worried that she asked her brother to come talk to her. The story is, he told her boyfriend that the Indian way of dealing with any man who messed up a female relative was to hold him down and skin the inside of his legs, and if that didn't stop him, he was castrated."

"Wow! No wonder he ran, Shaq! I sure would've if I had been him," I said, thinking, *Boy, now I'm really glad I wasn't alone with Etta when I brought her home.*

"Hell, Caleb, that's not really the Indian way, though they can be brutal sometimes. It was just my uncle's way of putting the fear of God in him."

Now that I knew the ropes of working the ground crew, work was becoming the tedious same-old, same-old every day, and I was beginning to see the wisdom of getting an education. Then one day right after the coffee break, somehow a beam swung into Shawn, one of the monkeys, and badly shattered his left leg.

Mel started swearing at Shaq and me, saying, "If you two paid half as much attention to your job as those girls you're always talking about, this wouldn't have happened."

I wasn't sure who was at fault, but Harry came roaring over and said, "Cut the crap all of you. Let's get together and lower him down. The ambulance is on its way."

We lowered Shawn, and they loaded him in the ambulance and sped off. Harry said, "All right, boys, everyone take a deep breath and then let's get back to work. I'll go up top and take Shawn's place for the afternoon."

That evening at the supper table Harry said, "Caleb, how would you like to take Shawn's place and work up top? It pays considerably more than what you're doing, and it would help you develop another talent."

23

Eunice said, "No, Harry, Caleb isn't ready for that at his age."

"Eunice!" Harry replied rather curtly, "Caleb is nineteen years old now; you can't keep seeing him as a little boy."

"I don't know, Harry," I broke in, "I have a little trouble with heights sometimes. I'm sure if I had to I could overcome it in time, but I would probably slow your job down too much to try it now."

"Well, is that the old Caleb talking sense to me, or is it Caleb outsmarting me?" Harry said laughing, "You're right that I can't afford to lose any more time on this job, so I guess I'll have to find someone else."

The next day on the job Shaq began working as a monkey, and Harry hired a new boy named John to work with me, simply saying, "You can show him the ropes, Caleb."

John already had a good understanding of the job from other construction work he had done and was very easy to work with. Shaq was happy to finally get a promotion and a raise and the news about Shawn was good, he wouldn't be working for six months or so but his prognosis was good.

Work was becoming old hat and I began enjoying living with Harry and Eunice. Little Hank and I had become buddies and he looked forward to our times of rough housing together. On Fridays I had been going to the youth dances and dancing with June, Loraine and some of the other girls there. Shaq and Etta hadn't been back since the first night I came. One Friday during our coffee break Shaq asked me if I was going to the dance that night, I told him I hadn't given it much thought, but I probably would.

He said, "I wouldn't ask this of anyone else I know, Caleb, but Etta wants to know if you will pick her up tonight, too?"

"Let me think about it for a while, Shaq, I'll let you know."

Oh, wow, going to the dance with Etta! It just got so that she wasn't the topic of every discussion I had with the girls when I went there dancing there. I thought about how Josh would have handled this and knew immediately that he would do it, if he thought he could help a friend. I guess that didn't really leave me any choice except to say yes.

Later when Shaq and I talked I said, "Okay, Shaq, but tell her we have to have a few ground rules. One, I don't belong to anyone, and two, I need to be free to dance or talk with other girls. Maybe, Shaq, if I could have a few minutes alone with her when I come, it would be best."

"Whoa, Caleb, I saw the way she kissed you when she left you the first time, remember? You're not getting ideas, are you?"

"Not on your life, Shaq! I am not about to have my legs peeled or worse for any girl. I just want a chance to talk to her by myself for a few minutes, okay?"

"Well, I guess it's okay, Caleb, as long as you stay in the dooryard with her. I feel that I can trust you. I still don't know how she'll act, and you might need to be rescued from her. After all I'm familiar with what antics like hers can sometimes do to a man."

That night when I drove into Shaq's yard, Etta came out right away. Again as she came down the walk, it struck me what a beautiful, desirable girl she was.

After settling herself in the seat beside me she said, "Shaq tells me we have to talk, and that I owe you an apology."

"No, Etta, I don't need an apology from you," I said as I caught my breath. "But I would like to talk with you. Shaq has told me a little about what you have been going through, and I want to help."

Etta's face was getting red, and her body tensed up like she was about to pounce. I quickly added, "Etta if you don't want to talk to me, then let's just go to the dance as friends and forget it."

She said, "Good idea, Cale; maybe it would be best. Blow the horn for Shaq. Isn't that supposed to be your signal if I get out of hand?"

I said, "Okay, Etta. I only wanted to help if I could, but it's no big deal."

As I was reaching for the horn Etta grabbed me. At first I struggled to reach it but she said, "Wait, wait, Caleb, let's talk. I'm not going do anything foolish."

"I dunno, Etta. I had an idea maybe talking would help, but you have to want to be helped before anyone can help you."

"Caleb, I am not sure any more of what I want, except for the hurt to go out of my life."

"Look, Etta, I'm no expert in emotional affairs, but I have lived through a few of them and have learned that life goes on. When my brother was killed in the war, I was in a purple funk forever. The one thing that stood out in my mind after I had it under control was what a waste of my life it had been. I should have understood it as something beyond my control in the beginning and dealt with it sooner."

"Caleb, you said Shaq had told you a little about my boyfriend and me and about how my family had driven him away. I have been holding hands with him since we were in grammar school. I couldn't imagine living without him. I thought he would never be able to leave me. Now I am alone in the world."

"You're far from being alone, Etta," I answered, "There is a whole world out there waiting for you to rejoin them. Not in anger but as part of wonder, because as a girl, you are a marvelous example. And as for your boyfriend and your family, there was a similar situation in my family. My father kicked Harry off our property and threatened to kill him if he ever came back. Still, Harry was strong enough to persist, and Eunice and he got married, and she left with him. Even though my father disowned Eunice, Harry didn't quit; he kept working on the situation until he and Eunice could get back together with our family. To me that is love and respect. He could have just as well ignored the situation and never brought Eunice back. Now, not knowing your boyfriend, it's hard for me to evaluate him, but it seems to me if he had loved you like Harry loved Eunice, he would still be here in the picture. I have found that sometimes bad happenings end up with the better results. So if he couldn't handle this situation, maybe that means there is someone better suited for you out there."

Etta just said, "Blow the horn, Caleb, it's time to go dancing."

Shaq came out, and we went to the dance. After a couple of dances with Etta she said, "Time for you to find another partner, friend."

I located Loraine and asked her to dance. She laughed and said, "I don't know if it is safe, Caleb, considering who you came with. What's up, you a sucker for punishment or are you another boy stricken by her looks?"

"Oh, c'mon Loraine," I said as we waltzed out onto the floor, "Her brother is a good friend of mine, and he asked if she could come tonight; besides she seems to need a friend herself."

"She sure has a damn funny way of showing it lately, Caleb, though it's true that she didn't mix much before except with her steady squeeze. You know how she is of mixed blood? That never was a problem for most of us, but her good looks and haughty ways sure caused a lot of envy. I expect she really doesn't have a close friend to talk things out with."

"How about you, Loraine?" I asked, "Seems that you have a little hankering for her brother."

Loraine slapped me lightly across the face and said, "Don't go there, Caleb, or I might be the one who throws things tonight."

"Okay, okay, Loraine, I get it. My lips are sealed on the subject," I said with a little laugh.

After dancing with Loraine and once with June I got a coke and sat down. Shortly after, Etta came and asked if she could join me. Looking at her and thinking how breathtakingly beautiful she was, I said, "Certainly, friend, come and join me, would you like a coke?"

She laughed and said; "I heard that it was safer here to have separate cokes than one with two straws, so maybe you should buy me one."

Shaq came and joined us asking, "Is she behaving, Caleb?"

"Like an angel Shaq, like an angel."

The three of us sat there talking for some time, and Etta said, "Caleb, I have been thinking about all you said, and it seems to be making some sense to me. Can we talk more sometime?"

I said, "It would be my pleasure, Etta, any time you're willing to hear my sad tale of woe I'm available."

Shaq hit me lightly on the shoulder saying, "Don't you two get any ideas without including me."

Just then Loraine came over and said, "What's up, Caleb? Too tired to dance? Don't I get one more before you go?"

Etta said, "Tell you what, Loraine, dance this one with Shaq, and let me borrow Caleb back for a couple."

Shaq said, "Sounds good to me, Etta," as he danced off with Loraine.

As Etta and I made our way to the dance floor I again marveled at what a beauty she was, thinking that if all this wasn't so complicated I could have easily been smitten by her.

As we danced Etta said, "Caleb, I have been thinking about what you said about my Henry not having a love strong enough for a lifetime commitment. You may be right, but this just creates a different type of pain for me."

"I believe that is about where my thoughts about losing Josh were, when I decided that I had to deal with that pain myself instead of blaming the rest of the world. I know it is not an easy path, Etta, but it is heading in the right direction."

"Caleb, I need someone like you in my life right now. Can you commit to that?"

"Etta I would be more than happy to help you, but with the understanding that it isn't a boyfriend-girlfriend commitment, just a commitment of friends," I answered, thinking of Jennie's and my final arrangement.

Etta held me close saying, "I already feel that you are a very close friend, Caleb, and I will behave myself from now on, but I can't promise you my emotions won't grow beyond friendship over time. I am so glad you were brave enough to allow me to come with you tonight."

As we were finishing the dance June came over and asked if she was entitled to at least one more dance before closing. I saw the fire start in Etta's eye, but she shrugged, and laughing said, "Thanks for rescuing me, June; I need to rest my feet for a while after his dancing all over them."

June whirled me out on the floor asking, "What's up, Caleb? You and Shaq got her on tranquilizers? She sure isn't the Etta we are used seeing the last four or five months."

"No, June, she isn't on anything, but she is working to recover from a bad experience," I said, thinking that June had been more cordial to Etta than before.

Well, as mother always said: one hand washes the other. Maybe June and Etta could forgive each other. I should keep that in mind if the subject comes up in talking with Etta.

After one more dance with Etta it was closing time and we went with Shaq to the truck. On the way Shaq said, "I was so pleased with tonight, Etta; I hope you had fun too."

"You know, Shaq, I was thinking as I was listening to Caleb, how much of what he said was like you have been trying to tell me, but somehow Caleb's version penetrated more. Thank you for loving me enough, Shaq, to stay the course this long."

"Hell! Sis, I'm not just your brother, you know. We are twins. Too bad, though, you got all the looks," Shaq said with a laugh.

"Oh, I don't know, Shaq," I chimed in. "I got the opinion that Loraine thinks your looks are pretty special."

Shaq kind of blushed and said, "Loraine and I have been fairly close before, but it kind of wore out."

"Jeez," Etta exclaimed, "If what I saw was kind of close, then close would have to be inside each other's skin."

Shaq half heartedly smacked Etta as we were turning into their yard. He said as he got out, "You two take a minute or two, but I'll be watching."

Etta held my hand and said, "Caleb I'm a long way from being over my 'madness,' as Shaq calls it, but I do feel as though I have taken a step in the right direction. I hope you meant it when you said you would be there so we could keep on talking."

"Etta, like I told you I am not an expert, who has all the answers, but I know from experience how important it is to have someone of the opposite sex that you can confide in," I said, as I thought about what Jennie and I had all those years.

"Is it okay if I call you, Caleb, sometime to see if you're free? Maybe we can talk on some week nights for an hour or so."

"That would be great, Etta; my time at Harry's does get boring sometimes in the middle of the week," I said, as she leaned over and kissed me good night. Her kiss was a little longer than friendly, and even without the body pressing of last time it excited me. We said goodnight, and I drove out without waiting to watch her walk her up the path thinking, *Man, this is going to be a trial.*

Harry's job was nearing completion and Eunice had been keeping me in contact with the college. All the paper work was ready except for the signing. Eunice had decided that since I had full tuition money including for rooming, it would be better for me to live at the college. That way I wouldn't need a car or have to depend on her for transportation.

Etta had been making arrangements for us to be together a couple of times a week and she was making great progress in her thinking. I believe my comparing her Henry to Eunice's Harry had struck a cord that made sense to her. Shaq told me that she was getting out on her own more now and she had even been on a couple of shopping trips with Loraine. It had been over a month since we had our first talk although sometimes my mind wandered deliciously during our talks. I have been able to keep my desires under control and felt that Josh would have approved of what I had accomplished.

One afternoon a week before I was scheduled to enter college Eunice got a telephone call from Mother. Dad had been in a terrible accident, the bedding collapsed on one of the lumber piles that they were working on and Dad got caught between it and the wagon. He was very seriously mangled when the team reared and pulled the wagon out.

When Harry and I got home and heard the news, Harry made a couple of calls so his crew would be able to continue without him and began getting ready to leave for Sterling right then.

Eunice said, "Harry how about Hank? We have to think about him, too."

"Don't worry. Hank will be all right. If he comes with us, he can sleep while we are driving, and if we take turns we can drive right through and get there in less than three days."

My mind couldn't fathom my father with all his virility being mangled. The news brought back the horrors of Josh and his hospital stay. Harry was telephoning while Eunice and I packed a few things, and in less than an hour after getting back to Harry's house I was on my way back home to Sterling, loaded with more fears than I had when I arrived in Oklahoma.

CHAPTER TWO

While Eunice packed some clothes and snacks, Harry went to check out the car, making sure that all the fluid levels were full. Hank had a car bed already in the car, and Eunice brought enough food for him to last through the trip.

We hadn't been home from work much over an hour before we were on our way back to Sterling. With one of us sleeping and one keeping the driver company and keeping him alert, we drove almost continuously for almost four days, with only pit stops for our relief and gas.

As we pulled into our yard in Sterling, it was about three in the morning. We were just trying to decide what to do when the lights came on inside and Mother came out on the porch. Eunice and I both rushed out, hugging her. There were tears in her eyes. Harry dealt with little Hank, lugging him in with his car bed.

Eunice said, "How is Dad, Mother? We've been worried sick all the way here."

"We are not sure yet how he's going to be; the doctors are hopeful, but he goes in and out of a coma. Today they told us that most of his internal organs are starting to function properly, and they hope they will be able to operate on his leg soon. So far they have fixed his arm and stitched up most of the places he was bleeding. They said they really couldn't tell yet how much he will recover." Mother sighed and sat down as she spoke. It was a shock at how much she had aged since I left.

I sat beside her and said, "Mother, we are here now. Eunice and Harry and I will help you take care of things. Maybe if we asked God for help for Dad and the doctors, Dad would come out of this all right."

Eunice who was wiping tears from her face exclaimed, "Like he helped with Josh, huh, Caleb? A lot of good it did us then."

Harry said, "Now, now, Eunice we're all too tired to get into a discussion like this. Let's get some rest before allowing ourselves to imagine things worse than what they are. Caleb, I think that you could be right. It sure can't do any harm for each of us to talk to the God of our understanding in our own way."

Mother said, "Caleb, you go bunk with the boys. Eunice, you and Harry can use Clem and Caleb's room. Clem is staying in a shanty at the job site."

There were still three beds in the boy's room, and one of them was empty, so I crawled in and despite all that was on my mind, I feel right to sleep. I guess the long drive had taken a lot out of me. I woke up about ten o'clock with Jason and Francis jumping all over me.

Jason said, "We would've gotten you up earlier but Mother came in and told us to let you sleep. I hope you've come home to help, Caleb. Everybody is worried about what's going to happen to us because Dad isn't going to be able to work, maybe never ever again."

As I dreamily became conscious of the situation again, I held both Jason and Francis and said, "Not to worry, boys; I'm not sure what is going to happen, but rest assured, we will find a way to keep our family together."

Downstairs Mother, Eunice, and Harry were at the kitchen table eating and talking.

Harry said, "I'm not sure, Mother Carney, how long I can stay, but if it will help, Eunice can stay awhile. We'll have to talk over Caleb's situation; it's pretty complicated."

I jumped right in saying, "My situation is that I have to stay here and take care of the family. There is nothing very complicated about that."

"Whoa, little man," Harry said, putting his hand on my shoulder. "We all agree that as the oldest boy you have a responsibility, but there are a few different options on how this can be done. I was just suggesting that we study all of them before making any decisions. We'll be looking for ways how each of us in the family can work together to keep things as they have been. Eunice and I are going to drive Mother to the hospital, and we are asking you to watch

Hank and the children. You'll have to be very alert with Hank. He's never been around farm life before, and we don't want him getting into trouble with his curiosity about new things."

I really wanted to shout, "No, I'm going to Dad, too." But I knew Harry was right, and even if he wasn't, I would lose any argument about it with him. So I said, "That's okay, Harry. Jason, Francis, Nellie, and I will watch him every minute."

Hank and I followed Jason while he was doing the chores. The cow amazed Hank and when Jason squirted some milk at him from her utter, he squealed with delight and tried to do it himself. The pigs were almost full-grown now, and that, along with their smell that was enough for Hank who said, "Dirty, go away!"

The chickens were a different story. There were a few running loose, and Hank was beside himself with laughter watching them run and flutter when he tried to catch them. Watching Hank enjoying the farm so much brought back the old yearning to once again be a part of all this.

Muldon's truck pulled into the yard, and Homer came flying out, and like to knock me down as he came running to me, shouting, "Caleb, Caleb, Caleb! Am I glad to see you! I would've woken you this morning except Mother warned me not to. Are you going to stay, Caleb? I'm scared to death about Dad and what's going to happen to the family. I've taken more hours with the Muldons, but even if I quit school, I wouldn't make enough to keep all the bills paid. I wanted to go and work with Clem, but Mother said I am not going to quit school to do that. I've saved some money, and I gave it to Mom, but it wasn't much. You know, Caleb, I wanted to be able to go to college too, so I could go somewhere else in the world besides little Sterling to make my life."

Damn, there it is again. All I want is to come back here to be comfortable, and he talks about escaping.

"Don't worry, Homer. We haven't worked out any exact plan yet, but I'm sure there'll be a way that you can escape Sterling someday. Right now let's concentrate on getting Dad back."

"Oh, Caleb, I'm sorry. I didn't mean it to sound like I wasn't thinking about Dad. It's just that I've had a couple of days since the accident to mull over the many possibilities, and it scares me. I pray every night with Jason and Francis that Dad will recover, not for me but for himself. You know, without you around anymore, I'm expected to be the big brother, and I really don't like being that responsible. When you were here and things went wrong, it always seemed to be on your shoulders, but now it's mine."

Remembering some past experiences like the Travis' court case and Uncle Louis having to shoot old Tom the horse, I said, "I know it sometimes seems unfair, Homer, but it's only a part of growing up, and it'll seem like such an unimportant part of your life someday."

Just then Harry drove in the yard and we all rushed over to get the news. Mother said, "There is good news today, children; your dad has regained consciousness and was able to recognize us all today. The doctors think they'll be able to operate on his leg soon. He's still in a lot of pain and says things that you don't want to put much store in. You shouldn't mention how he looks or what he says if you get to see him."

Harry asked, "How's Hank been doing, boys? I hope he hasn't been playing in the manure pile. Eunice will have a fit if he gets dirty."

"I don't know about manure, Harry," Jason laughed, "but he is pretty dirty. He's been having a time trying to milk the cow, and he fell a couple of times chasing the chickens. He couldn't catch them, but he had a ball collecting eggs. Good thing we don't have Big Red anymore, huh, Caleb?"

Harry said, "We'll let Eunice decide what to do about you wild Carney boys, but I'm glad he's had a chance to see how his uncles live."

As the boys and Nellie took Hank to tell his Mother about his escapades I said, "Harry, what is this about not taking stock in what Dad has to say?"

Harry scratched his head and said, "Well, Caleb, your dad is in real bad shape, and the chances of him coming out of this a whole man are pretty slim, and he talked about that. What he said to me was, 'Harry, I want you to promise me that if I can't come out of this whole, you will convince the family to let me die.'"

"Damn, Harry, I hope you didn't tell him you would do it, did you?"

"Well, Caleb, there are times when it is best to promise what someone wants to hear even if you are against it. No matter what the outcome is with your dad, right now he has the peace of knowing I am on his side. The truth be known, Caleb, I can see that sometimes death is not the hardest thing to face, and our beliefs, no matter what they are, are unimportant."

Thinking about what Harry said, I remembered Uncle Louis talking when he was in his cups about death. He would say death seemed like such a common thing when he was in the trenches in France during WW I. It seemed strange that Uncle Louis wasn't here anymore. Mother had written that he had taken a sawyer's job in northern Vermont. Seems as though he had run into an old-time friend of his who owned a sawmill there. Mother said he was required to swear he would not drink before his friend would hire him. She said from all reports he was staying sober and was a different man now.

Everyone was gathered around in the house discussing different things that could be done. Mother talked about Hester and Emma and the money they could contribute, along with Homer's earnings. The talk went around and around about different plans. No one came right out and mentioned that I could stay and work in Dad's place, but I know it was on everyone's mind.

So I said, "Look, I can take Dad's place and keep his business going so everything financially could stay the same."

There was a lot of, "No, no, Caleb, you have to go to college."

I drowned that out with, "We all know there isn't another solution that makes as much sense. If I can keep Dad's business afloat and the rest of the family kicks in some of their earnings, I'm sure we can pay for Dad's care and survive."

Mother said, "Okay, enough talk for a while. You boys see to the chores. Harry has some telephone calls to make back home, and Eunice and I will start getting supper ready. Even if nothing else gets settled we still have to eat."

Jason asked Eunice if Hank could go with him to milk the cow.

Eunice said, "I guess he can't get any dirtier. What's up, Jason? You training new help for the Muldons?"

"No, it's not that, Eunice. It's just he was so interested when we squirted milk at him before, that I thought it would be fun to have him see what milking was really like," Jason said, grabbing a pail as he and Hank headed for the barn.

I went out and started splitting some of the wood that was dumped in front of the woodshed. I could hear Hank squealing with delight in the barn with Jason. When they had finished milking, and were coming out of the barn, a car came up, and Hester and Emma got out. Hester came and hugged me like I was a lost lover, crying softly on my shoulder.

Emma ran to Little Hank shouting, "Come here, little nephew! Come see Aunt Emma."

Hank, frightened, hid behind Jason.

Jason put down the milk pail and held Hank, saying, "I don't blame you, Hank, she scares me half to death sometimes too. It's only at first glance, though. She's really a pussycat. Look, she will even let you pull her hair and tweak her nose. Here you try it, Hank."

Emma didn't have any recourse so she let Hank and Jason plague her and kept on smiling. I guess it worked, because Hank took her hand on the way to the house.

Hester said, "Caleb, I feel so much better now that you're here. Are you going to stay?"

"I think so, Hester; I think it's the only answer."

"I'm so glad. Caleb, I need you to talk to. Emma is still the boy-crazy, free soul she has always been, and she does not always understand. I met this wonderful man several months ago. He's an engineer that works for an outside outfit that's been working off an on at the Stuart factory in Oscin. He's been here to meet Mom and Dad several times, and things went well. He's being reassigned to Japan in a month or so, and he has asked me to marry him and go with him. Mother and I discussed it the day before Dad got hurt, so we never had a chance to approach Dad about it. Now I feel like I can't go and leave Mother with all the trouble the family is in now. And I could never involve Dad now. I'm not expecting you to have the answer for me, Caleb. I just need someone close who I can talk to."

"I'll try to be there for you, Hester, and maybe if you could talk to Eunice about it before she leaves, it would be a help to both of us," I said, thinking, *Man, if my life isn't messed up enough with Dad hurt, now this! I wonder if it is going to be safe for me to catch up with the rest of the family and their lives.*

After supper Harry said, "Mother Carney I hate to rush you, but I am not going to be able to stay too long, and I need to understand your financial picture. Maybe if we let the rest of the crew clean up and watch Hank, you and I and Eunice could go over your financial situation. I know Eunice and I are in a position to help some; maybe that will give us a better picture on how to do that."

Jason had gone to Muldon's barn, so Emma, Jason, and I cleaned up and did the dishes while Nellie played with Hank.

Jason said, "It will be like old times, Caleb, having you back again."

"I don't know about that, Jason," Emma cut in. "Caleb can't be too thrilled at having to leave college and the big city, to be back in this burg, right, Caleb?"

"To tell you the truth Emma, I don't know what to think yet. There are so many things that have to be considered I couldn't tell you exactly what I'm going to do, except that I'll do what is best to keep us a family."

Homer came home from the barn saying, "Hey, Caleb! Everyone at the barn wants to know if you are going to come visit them, although outside of John and Arty, most of the crew you worked with are gone. Jennie still works in the milk house, though, and fills in at the barn sometimes."

Mother, Eunice and Harry had been going over the family finances. Harry called me over and said, "Caleb you should study this budget sheet we have worked out so you'll understand what is needed here. We haven't made any decisions yet on a method that is satisfactory. There was a thought that occurred to me as we scanned these figures. Now remember, it's just a thought to be perused, not a final decision. Your dad's business doesn't clear much more than a good week's pay after feeding the horses and buying needed equipment. My thoughts were, that if you have to give up college and go to work, your mother could sell your dad's business. Then she would have money in the bank to back her and the family up. My accountant told me when I called that I won two of the contracts I bid on, and I could pay you at least as much as you could earn running your dad's operation. You can stay with Eunice and me rent-free so you'd still have some money for hell raising after sending the bulk home. Clem has offered to try and find the money to buy the business if the family decides to sell."

"You know, Harry, my mind is so full of all that is happening I'm going to need time to assimilate everything that has come up. I am glad you are here to help, Harry. I know from working for you that you are good at planning."

The next morning I joined Homer and went to the barn with him. As we entered the barn, Old Golly Moses was coming out.

He said, "Caleb, I want you to know that the Muldons will help your family in any way we can. By Golly, Moses, Henry Carney is a good man, and he deserves to be helped. Mr. Banner has started a collection at the Inn to help with the hospital bills. Frank Butler said he was giving the profit from the logs he bought from me up by the Coors barn. This is a good town, Caleb, and we will all be there for you, no matter what happens."

Homer said, "I'll give this town that much Caleb. The town is always there for anyone who gets hurt. Look at the way they backed up Glenn's father all those years, after he lost his arm."

"Damn! Homer, don't even think like that! I can't imagine what Dad would be like if he lost a limb."

Jennie saw us coming into the barn and came over and gave me a big hug saying, "Caleb, we were so sorry about your father. Are you going to have to give up college and come back home?"

"I don't know yet, Jennie. We have several options that we're discussing, but I think Sterling might have to be putting up with me again."

Jennie said, "Oh, Caleb, all of Sterling misses you."

"Ya!" John cut in, "especially Jennie; she's been pining ever since you left. How are you, Caleb? Long time no see. Truth is, Caleb, life around here has been kinda boring without all the little escapades you used to get us into. We haven't had a good party since you left."

It was good to hear the old banter, but the barn seemed strange without Arthur and Leonard there. I said, "I don't have a lot of time, fellows, but I couldn't be in Sterling without visiting the old barn crew. I'll try to get back again soon."

As I walked out, Jennie joined me saying, "Hope you don't mind if I walk a ways with you?"

Though I had ridden down on my bike, I wanted to talk with Jennie so I left it.

"Caleb," Jennie began as she took my hand, "How was it with all those big-city girls? Bet you had yourself some flings, huh?

"No, Jennie, I was so busy with my new life there that I didn't have much time to get that acquainted with the girls there except one who was beyond this poor country-boy's reach."

She laughed and said, "I find that improbable, Caleb. As I remember it, you never minded cuddling all that time with Joan and then using Beverly and me to satisfy the desires she caused."

"Oh, damn! Jennie, it wasn't like that. My time with you has been among my sweetest memories, even after we became just friends. I still hear the tone of your voice saying, 'Careful, Caleb, about tying your heart to a stone that's too big.' I am not completely sure what you meant, but it's been a warning that keeps haunting me."

"I sure didn't mean to haunt you, Caleb. I have been watching you and Joan for years and I never thought your relationship had the legs to last into adulthood. Maybe back when I had that big crush on Josh, what you and Joan had made me jealous, because Josh only saw me as a little girl."

"Jennie, Jennie, you're tearing at my heart, and I so want it to continue talking to you; can we meet later and continue this talk?" I said turning back to get my bike.

"Sure, Caleb," she replied, laughing, "But if I'm tearing at anything besides your heart, remember, just as friends, not lovers. Call me or have Homer let me know when you're free."

When I arrived home Mother said, "Caleb, I need to talk with you. I know what Harry said about selling out, probably makes the most sense of anything we can do. Still I don't want to do that to Dad in his present state. You know how much of himself he's put into the business, and how proud it has made him since it succeeded. Harry's plan makes a lot of sense money wise, but we have to consider Dad in whatever we do. I thought that maybe Clem could hire someone to work with him instead. I know there wouldn't be much left over after paying two wages and cost. Still if you could contribute the heft of your pay working with Harry for a while we would survive."

"Don't you worry, Mother. I'll always have Dad in the forefront of whatever is decided. I agree with Harry that we should pursue every avenue before committing to a plan. Right now I am trying to keep everything straight in my mind. One thing you can count on, Mother, is that I won't make any decision that hurts you or Dad. Hester has talked to me and told me all about her boy and his proposal. Is there any thing we can do to help her?"

"Eunice has suggested that if Dad seems strong enough today we should mention it to him, at least the proposal. I want you to go with us today. Harry agreed to stay here with Hank and the children."

Later at the hospital we had to wait while they were changing Dad's bandages. The nurse came and said, "You may go in now. I think you will be pleased by how much he has improved since yesterday."

I don't know about improvement. Dad had bandages on one side of his head and all over his body and his left leg was hitched up to some weights and pulleys. Still he tried a smile and whispered, "Good to see you, Caleb. Did you come home to rescue your old man?"

"Well, I don't know about me rescuing you, Dad, but I am sure going to keep after the doctors to get that done. The family and I have been trying to figure out how anyone can go about temporarily replacing the toughest man we ever knew."

"Hell, son, why do you think I taught you how to be tough? This was always my plan to be able to sit around and let you carry on for me. Still, you better make the most of the short time you're going to have to play at being me and enjoy it."

I laughed at that and felt much better about the situation now that I could see and hear him.

Mother kissed Dad on his good cheek and said, "Now, Henry, let's not over do it the first day you begin feeling better."

Eunice said, "I can't believe how much better you seem today, Dad."

"Well, Eunice, to tell you the truth I wouldn't have given myself much shift the last few days, but today I am beginning to have hope. The doctors say I am recovering from the shock of it all, and they can start putting me back together soon."

Mother said, "Henry, we have some great news. Remember the young man that Hester has been bringing home? He has asked her to marry him, and she wants your blessing before she answers."

At first I thought Dad was going to take it bad, but he said, "Oh! You mean that Richard she has at the house all the time? You know, I liked him. You tell Hester she has my blessings and to bring him in. Of course if she is in a hurry, I guess there is another daughter I won't get to walk down the aisle. Not that I'm faulting you, Eunice; you picked a good man, and I am the one who lost out, not you."

The nurse came in and asked everyone except Mother to leave while she checked some of his dressings. Out in the hall a doctor approached us asking, "Are you members of the Carney family?"

Eunice answered, "I'm his oldest daughter Eunice; Caleb here is his oldest living son."

"Good, I need to inform the family about what to expect. Your dad has shown good improvement. All of his internal organs are now functioning near normal, and we have been able to increase his pain medication. These are the reasons you see him so much better today. Still, he has compound fractures of his left arm, several broken ribs, and a badly mangled left leg. We were able to return the blood flow to the lower leg, but it will be touch and go trying to save it. He has to go through several operations that are going to be a shock to his system, and for a while he will seem more like he was the last few days than he is today. We have great confidence that eventually we can bring everything except the leg back to normal. There will be times when he will be in much pain and very discouraged. I'm depending on the family to help him over this hump while we repair his body. Any questions?"

"God, Doc, you're not telling us he is going to lose his leg, are you?" I exclaimed.

"I'm trying to tell you that we have hope of saving it, but no guarantees, son," he answered.

Mother came out and said, "Go say goodbye to your dad. The nurse said he should rest now."

On the way home we discussed what the doctor said with Mother. "She said we should contact Hester. Maybe it would be best if she and Richard saw him before these operations start."

"It's okay, Mother," Eunice answered, "Hester said she was going to call to see if she could visit Dad before she came home tonight, and maybe Richard could be with her."

Later that night Hester and Richard showed up at the house all smiles, "Well," Mother said, "looks like it went well with you and your father, Hester."

"Oh, Mother! I was so afraid about this, but Dad seemed happy for us. He said he thought Richard and I had a great future together, and he wished us the best. He even suggested that we not wait for him. Richard told him he might be shipped to Japan for a year and wondered if he would object to us being married before. Dad smiled and said, 'They damn well better be married if they were planning something like that.'"

After all the talk died down Richard said, "Caleb, I think you and I should have a discussion about what this all means to the family. Hester and I made some decisions on the way here that you should be aware of as temporary head of the household. First, the marriage. I don't have any immediate family except my mother, and she is too elderly to be able to travel from Washington State for the wedding, so if the family agrees, we would like to get married right here on the farm. I only have a little over a month before I leave, so we thought we would leave right after the wedding and use the trip as our honeymoon. The good thing about that is it will be an all-expenses-paid honeymoon.

"Now about finances," he continued, "I make a substantial salary and can well afford to help out while your dad is laid up. Hester had saved up money for the wedding, and we would like to contribute that to your dad's hospital bill. We know that is going to be a burden for a few years for the family. Hester doesn't need to work, but she thought if she could get a clerical job with my company she could send her pay home. I would prefer she didn't work at all, but she says that if she does you would be able to go to college like you planned. Now, I know this is a lot to assimilate all at once, and it might seem selfish of us considering the family's situation, but we are open to any changes the family thinks are needed."

"I don't know, Richard, about this head of the family bit. Mother is still the boss here. I don't think you two are being selfish. In fact, you seem willing to offer an awful lot for someone who is just joining the family," I answered, my head awhirl with all the possibilities his talk opened up.

After Homer came in I suggested the family all gather together and listen to Richard and Hester's plans. Mother was hesitant about another daughter getting married without a proper wedding celebration, but agreed that most of what was planned made sense. She was insistent that we could survive without taking money from them. Harry was just as insistent that when you're a part of a family, it is a duty to help when you have the resources.

Harry told us that he would have to leave in a day or two because his business called. Eunice talked about staying behind but Mother told her that since she would be back soon for the wedding, it would be better if she went back. All eyes turned to me asking me my decision.

My mind was awash with all that had been talked about so I said, "I still have a day or so before Harry leaves. I'll have a decision before then." Meanwhile, I thought, *Oh, Josh, Josh, why did we lose you? I am so lost and scared about all of this.*

The next day I rode my bike into town and started walking around some of my old haunts. I was just coming down from the school swings when I saw Beverly coming out of the library.

She shouted, "Caleb, Caleb! Great to see you boy, or is it man now? I heard you were back and that you might be staying. Is that true? We miss you around here; we were all sorry about your dad and that you might not be able to go to college now. How's your dad doing now? Any improvement over what I been hearing?"

"Man, Bev, you sure are full of questions. Dad seems to be out of the woods so to speak, but he will be laid up for a long time. I'm still pondering the college bit; I just thought walking old haunts would clear my mind."

John Muldon was coming down the street, turning the air blue with his cussing as he tried to lead a cow that was giving him a hard time. He hollered, "Hey, Caleb, how about a hand? I have to take this bitch of a bovine up to the bull! Get behind her with a stick and help out."

"Looks like fun," Beverly said, "Let's go, Caleb."

What the hell, I thought as I said, "I guess going to the bull pen is one of my old haunts. It'll give John and me a chance to catch up on what's been going on with the barn boys since I left."

Beverly and I got behind the cow with a switch, and it didn't take much convincing to get the cow to follow John.   John said, "You know what, Caleb? We really meant it when we said that you were sorely missed since you left. Why, we hardly ever have a party since you went away, and we sure wanted to try out your uncle's wine again. I think losing you was one of the reasons all the girls quit at the barn. You know, it sure made it more enjoyable during the milking when they were there, even though they would only go home with you."

"Sorry about that, John," Beverly chimed in, "But you and the other boys never held a candle to the Carney boys."

"What the hell, Bev? What's this Carney boy stuff? Don't tell me you have Homer playing your little games?" I exclaimed without thinking.

"Watch it, Caleb, or you'll be giving yourself away. You don't think we believed that you and those girls were always playing marbles, do you?" John laughed

41

"Now, now, John, don't be picking on Sterling's only adult virgin." Beverly said laughing.

When we had reached the Coors barn where the bullpen was, John led the cow in and opened the gate for the bull. It was all over in a flash. I had always been amazed at how little time it took the bull to breed a cow.

As John brought the cow out she took off, dragging him swearing and yelling down the street.

"He'll be all right now," Beverly said, "She'll go right back to the barn with him. Man! Was that bull fast! How are you doing in that department with your big city girls?" Beverly asked, putting her arm around me.

"Oh, Bev, to tell the truth I haven't done anything like that since leaving Sterling, but don't pass that around."

"Caleb, you know I keep your secrets real well," she said, laughing and holding me closer.

As much as being there with Beverly and watching the bull had affected my libido I kept remembering what Jennie said about me using Beverly and her to quench the desires Joan caused.

"What do you think, Caleb?" Beverly teased, "Think we should check out the hay in the barn?"

"C'mon, Bev! We aren't kids anymore. It could be more dangerous for us now."

Beverly laughed, saying, "Like you said, Caleb, 'We're not kids anymore,' but even when we were I could have gotten pregnant if I hadn't been careful."

"I wasn't thinking of only that Bev; it's just that I'm beginning to think that there should be more of a commitment than just animal desire involved in sex."

"Commitment? Have I ever asked you for a commitment, Caleb? You know that I went after you just for the hell of it in the beginning. There isn't any doubt that I care for you, Caleb, but I am not asking you for a commitment, only a little roll in the hay for old times sake," she said holding me, running her hand up and down my leg.

Suddenly all the pent up desire that I had locked away with Etta and Jennie came rushing through my veins, so I said, "What the hell, Bev, you win! Let's go!"

We climbed into the haymow where we had the wildest sex I had ever experienced. Beverly held me close for a few minutes then jumped up and said, "Let's go, Caleb. We wouldn't want John to come back and find the virgin of Sterling rolling in the hay with me, would we?"

Just like our first time, here I couldn't get over how unaffected she seemed about what we had done. I joined her climbing down the ladder and said, "Bev, how is it you seem so cool when we do this, and I always feel like I'm paving my way to hell?"

"Well, Caleb, I guess the best way to explain it is to say that boys aren't alone in craving sex. Some of us girls get just as horny as you boys. It is just that with boys, it's okay because, 'Boys will be boys,' but with girls, it's scandalous; we're called sluts, so we have to hide it."

Beverly and I walked back to town. I found that I really did enjoy her company once my ardor was defused. We talked about old times and Karl, who had married his nurse and moved to Maine. She said she had always felt that Karl and she had too much history to have ever made it as husband and wife, so she hadn't been too depressed about what happened. She said she's had other boyfriends but it was always hard for her to keep her libido under control, and that wasn't what she wanted a relationship to be.

"Hell, Bev, someday you are going to make some man very happy," I said as we approached the Town Common.

"Like I just did you, huh, Caleb?" she said as she left to go back to the library.

It was afternoon by the time I got back home, and Nellie was sitting out in the yard looking like she was in deep thought. I said, " What's my little girl pondering about today, Nellie?"

"I have been waiting for you, Caleb. I think it's time you and I went for a hike up Mount Fay so we can have a little talk."

"I think that is a fine idea, Nellie. Let me check in at the house first, and then we'll bike down and climb the mountain."

After letting Mother know where we were going I went back got my bike and joined Nellie. Nellie was very quiet as we started hiking. She seemed preoccupied, so I didn't speak. It was good to be back on the mountain again. The memories were so vivid when I came here. The end of school trips to the tower, camping over night, first with Karl then with Jake. How Karl and I had run for our lives when we had spied on Bob and Katie. The days I spent here seeking solace when we lost Josh. How it had been the last time I was here with Joan and how exhilarated we had become about life that day. *Oh, Josh, you were right—this will always belong to us. How did you put it?*

As a babe I stood at the foot of her trails
Gazing at her beauty with awe

43

As a young boy I clambered her sides
Exploring these wonders I saw
Many days I spent in her heights
Her lessons and wisdom to share
Studying the flowers and fauna
The wild beauty, which God had put there
Again and again I return
Her wonder and beauty to see
She may not be much on the maps of the world
BUT MOUNT FAY IS MY MOUNTAIN TO ME

I must have mumbled some of the verses out loud because Nellie said, "You're still pretty lost without Josh aren't you, Caleb? It was nice when you could always count on him for all the answers, wasn't it? Tell me, Caleb, what's it going to be, college, back to work for Harry, or back to the sawmill in Dad's place? You know, Clem needs an answer because his helper is going back to school in a week. Harry needs to know so he can hire a replacement if you don't go back. Richard and Hester need to know. In fact, Caleb, the whole damn family is in limbo until you decide, and it has to be today. Is your answer up here in the mountain or with your friends in Sterling, or is it in your real fear of really having to leave all this and go out and face the world?"

"Damn, Nellie that's quite a mouthful, and from the youngest Carney at that."

"I'm sorry, Caleb, but don't you remember our last time here, when I told you that sometimes it's like I can read your thoughts and how it scared me? You told me then not to be afraid of it, but to only use it for good. Well, it was like I could feel how confused and incapable you felt, so I thought maybe if I spelled it out it would be helpful to you."

"Thank you, Nellie. I think talking to you could be the help I need. Still, in a way, I feel that the answer is here on the mountain and maybe you're just the messenger. Look, I believe that the only solution for both the family and me for is to take Dad's place and stay here. Maybe some of the other options will make more sense later, and most of them won't go away."

"What about college, Caleb? Won't you lose what Hanna has left you?"

"No, I called attorney Welch's office yesterday, and he said not to worry, that I had up until six years after high school to use those funds. He thought right now I belonged with the family and probably Hanna would too. Let's climb to the tower, Nellie; I want to have a look over Sterling and holler, 'I'm back,' even if it is only for a little while."

After we had reached the top, and I did my shouting, Nellie asked, "You really do have a love affair with Sterling, don't you, Caleb? I do, too, but Homer talks all the time about getting out of here and making something of himself. He makes me angry when he talks like that, because I feel so comfortable with Sterling, especially when I am on our mountain."

I gave Nellie a big long hug and said, "Let's race to the bottom," and off we went.

Nellie beat me easily to the bottom, and I was surprised at how much harder I was breathing than she was. She laughed and said, "What happened, Caleb? City life soften you up?"

I hugged her again and we walked hand in hand back to our bikes. By the time we arrived back home everyone was just sitting down to supper. Nellie said, "Listen up, everyone; Caleb has an announcement to make."

"I know everyone has been waiting for me to make up my mind, and I assure you that I am sure for now at least, my only place is here with Mother, Dad, and the family. College can wait; the money will still be there for me. Harry can easily replace me, but I am the one needed here at least until we see how everything goes with Dad. I know everybody wants to help, and most of you still can, just the way you all have offered, and with a family like all of you behind me, I know we won't fail."

There were questions, a few, "Are you sure, Caleb's?" but on the whole I felt as though this was the plan they all wanted to hear, and after all, it did keep me in Sterling. At least for as long as Dad needed me.

Later that night, tossing in my sleep, I dreamed again of Josh. He was writing. I couldn't see it all, just the words he wrote, and just the job well done, at the end of a poem he was working on.

I must have been talking to Josh in my sleep because Homer was shaking me awake, saying, "Damn Caleb, that's something we didn't miss while you were gone, you and your damn nightmares."

I mumbled, "I'm sorry, Homer," thinking sleepily, *I'm really back in Sterling.*

CHAPTER THREE

Eunice and Harry left with Hank a couple of days after Nellie and I had been up on the mountain. Dad already had one operation on his leg and the doctors were still skeptical about saving it but said they were making some progress. Going to see Dad after the operations was hard because he was either out of it or in too much pain to talk much. Since Harry's car was gone, it was harder to arrange transportation to the hospital every day. We only owned the old truck, which Clem had at the job site. Richard and Hester were able to take us most evenings but during the day we had to depend on townspeople. As usual Mr. Banner the innkeeper was insistent that we contact him anytime we needed a ride. Mother was adamant that she be there almost every day, she was worried that Dad would get depressed. I was amazed that Dad was able to take it as well as he was. It was hard to imagine him as docile as he had become. Mother said it was the medication and his realization that his chances of being whole again were slim. I believe that was why Mother thought she had to be there for as much time as she could to keep him fighting.

I borrowed Muldon's pickup, and Homer and I went to the job site to get Dad's truck back home. Clem was upset that he was losing it and said we would have to bring him hay and feed for the weekend as well as pick him up some groceries. We were taking a chance with Homer driving the truck back because he wasn't licensed to drive yet. I wasn't worried about his driving as long as he didn't get stopped. He had been driving Muldon's trucks and farm equipment for some time now. We got back to Sterling without any trouble. I asked Homer to tell Jennie that I would be taking a trip back with the feed for Clem and to ask her if she could go with me.

"One thing for sure, Caleb, all your confusion about everything else doesn't seem to hold as far as girls are concerned. I heard you were seen walking Beverly back from the Coors barn the other day, and didn't you go walking once with Jennie already? When is it going to be Joan's turn? Or are you working your way back to that? Man, I thought I had it made with my kissing games. Looks like big brother needs to coach me a little," Homer said as he grabbed his bike and headed for the milk barn.

"You watch what you say Homer!" I hollered at him as he rode off.

"Don't worry; Beverly's virgin," he shouted back as he rode out of sight.

Damn! Homer was almost as bad as Nellie in knowing how I feel. I *had* thought about Joan, and even though I heard she was leaving for college soon, I had been avoiding seeing her. I am not sure why, but I think it might be the way she feels when she's in love. With her, it's like being in love is being owned, and that is really scary to me. I have deep feelings for Joan, and our life together has been important to me, but I don't believe I could ever be anybody's slave to love.

Jason came around the barn and said, "Caleb, I'm glad you're here! Come help me. The damn pigs got out. I have the pen all fixed, but I can't get them back in alone."

Jason and I spent the next half hour wrestling with those hogs before we got them penned up again; by that time we both smelled like pig manure.

Laughing, I said, "You know what, Jason? I think we smell almost as bad as the day I caught my snipe."

"Maybe so, Caleb. I hope this washes off better, though, or Mother will be washing us with bleach and tomato soup. Man, that was funny seeing you up in the haymow smelling of skunk piss. One thing that taught me was never to go snipe hunting with a gunny sack."

We got some strong soap and water and went out to the shed to wash up, with Mother threatening to let us starve if we didn't smell any better before we came in.

Mother had been to see Dad that day and said he was in good humor for a change but the doctors said that they needed to operate again in the morning because part of one rib needed to be either taken out or reattached, it was a danger to his lungs.

Homer told me Jennie wanted to go with me tomorrow but she wouldn't be done at the milk house until eleven and to meet her there, if I could wait. I had to pick up some groceries and hay in the morning so I arrived at the barn a little after ten thirty the next morning.

Jennie hollered out from the milk house. "Glad you could make it, Caleb; be with you in ten!"

Driving off we were both quiet at first. Being alone with Jennie again got me thinking about how she had been so good for me while I was dealing with losing Josh. So I said, "You know, Jennie I want you to know how much you being my friend has meant to me. I know that you think all of us boys only think of sex when it comes to girls. I have often thought about how much fun we had when we went dancing and how you consoled me during my funk about Josh. I want you to know how important our relationship has been to me. It may be true we aren't meant to be lovers, but sometimes I'm not as sure about that as you are."

"Caleb, Caleb, Caleb, you will always have that little boy way of thinking, won't you? I suppose it's a part of what makes you so charming to us girls. I think about you, too, Caleb, and know if I had got as close to any other boy in town as I did you, they would have been bragging about it all over town. Regardless, I believe most of the boy's believe it's true when they call you Beverly's *Little Virgin*. Damned if I know how you do it. You even seem to have Beverly, with all her faults, on your side. Then there's Joan, I know there've been times when you two seem to have split, but you always end up together again. If rumors are right, you spent your last day before you left with her. Josh always said that it was a little boy little girl thing back when you were sneaking around having ice cream together every week. I wonder what he would say now that you two are still an item at nineteen. Oh, I'm sorry I talked about Josh, Caleb," she said, as she slid over closer to me.

"Don't be sorry, Jennie. As long as we can talk about Josh that means that we haven't entirely lost him. I think of Josh often and his quotes about life's situations. I remember a poem he read to me about searching for happiness.

Who am I? I wish I knew
And could really get it right
I know from history, that I'm different now
From what I'll be tonight

It's not the heights or depth of what I've been
Or what I might someday be
I'll know today I've been a success
If I am happy, being me

"You know, Jennie, I am not always happy being me; sometimes I'm scared at what life is handing me. That's why I am so lucky to have someone like you, who I can talk to about my fears. You have a way of helping me see that there's life beyond the problem at hand. That was Josh's forte."

"Whoa, Caleb, don't mistake me for Josh; I'm Jennie, remember?"

I laughed and said, "After all we've been through together, that's not likely to be a problem. I was only saying you have a way of getting to the crux of the problem, and because of that you will always have a place in my heart."

Jennie gave me a little kiss on the cheek saying, "I like the thought of being in your heart, Caleb as long as you can keep me out of your carnal thoughts."

"I'm not sure I ever can stop thinking about that, Jennie, but I can and will stop asking. Fair enough?" I asked

"Well, I guess seeing as you were one of 'those barn boys' for so many years it would be asking the impossible." Jennie said, laughing, as we were pulling in by the barn just below Clem's shanty.

I unloaded the hay and feed for the horses and went up to the shanty with Clem's groceries. I could hear him talking and was surprised there was someone there, as I hadn't seen another vehicle around.

I rapped on the door and Clem shouted angrily, "Just a minute, Caleb, I didn't expect you until later today."

When he opened the door I could see his company was a woman. He said, "Just put the grub down, Caleb; I'll be right out to talk to you."

I went back to the truck with Jennie and waited for Clem to come out. There was a heated discussion going on in the shanty, but from where we were we couldn't make it out what was being said.

Clem came out, and you could see he was in an angry mood. He said, "Damn it, Caleb; something has to be done if I'm going to stay on here. I can't be left way up here without any transportation. I want to do what's right with your dad but I can't afford a vehicle on what he's paying."

I was kind of surprised at Clem's belligerent attitude. Noticing the quizzical look on Jennie's face, I said, "Hold on Clem; don't climb all over me. I am just starting to try and take over for Dad. What's your problem? Everything is just the way it was before Dad got hurt; you didn't have the truck then. I know Dad was using it to travel back and forth."

"Things are different now, Caleb," he shouted. "I am not going to stay on here if I don't have wheels available."

"Look, Clem," I shouted back, "We were counting on you being there for us, but if you can't stay then give me a week so I can see about replacing you."

Clem marched back to the shanty muttering. Jennie said, "I guess you're not such a little boy after all, Caleb; you handled that well. He certainly isn't the Clem I thought he was. I understood he and your father were great friends."

"I dunno, Jennie; this is sure a surprise to me. I guess I better check on the horses," I said as I turned towards the barn.

Roxie and Molly seemed well cared for. Clem at least was taking good care of them. I patted the horses and talked to them like Dad had taught me, and it was amazing that even after all the time I had been away from them, they seemed to recognize and respond to my voice.

Jennie said, "You know, Caleb, it's like you belong to them, the way they looked you over and listened to you. I thought animals didn't have memories, but those two sure seemed to remember you."

"I guess, Jennie, it is more that Dad has taught me how to use my voice and actions to communicate with horses, than it is that they actually remember. Still it's nice to think that I had some past input in their response."

As we were talking a woman came out of Clem's shanty and hailed us. She said, "If you two are going anywhere near Braskin on your way back, could I catch a ride?"

I said, "Sure, we go right through there. If you don't mind riding in a beat-up old truck we would be glad to take you."

She laughed a kind of lilting laugh and said, "That looks like a chariot compared to some of the things I've ridden in."

I puttered around the barn for about ten minutes hoping Clem would come out and give some explanation. Realizing finally that he wasn't going to show I decided to leave.

Jennie asked the woman, "I suppose from the hollering you already know this is Caleb? I'm Caleb's friend, Jennie; he invited me along for the ride, but he didn't tell me about the side show."

She answered, "My name is Virginia, someone who tried to be Clem's friend, but I guess I failed." As we started down the road she said, " I guess you deserve some kind of an explanation. I met Clem in a bar one night, and he was so drunk I drove him home, in this truck by the way. I stayed with him, and he took me back the next day. He poured his heart out to me that night. I was so concerned about him. I had a buddy of mine drop me off here this morning. I thought he still had the truck and would be able to take me back. When you showed up he blew his top at both of us, and has been in a rage ever since. I probably shouldn't tell you this, but Clem needs help. He told me all about the Dear John letter he received from his wife when he was overseas. Still, what really has caused him to fall apart this time is that he blames himself for what happened to your dad. Seems your dad was always telling him that he needed to build the beddings that they put the lumber piles on better. He said many times your dad would do some of them over. One time when your dad was doing that Clem got mad and asked him, if he wasn't satisfied with his work why didn't he fire him? After that your dad didn't say anything more about the bedding to him. When your dad got pinned by that lumber pile it was because the bedding collapsed. Clem has had nightmares about it ever since. I thought I might be some help to him, but I guess he is your problem now, Caleb."

Virginia asked to get off about half way down the main street of Braskin saying, "Thanks, kids, and good luck with Clem, Caleb. It looks like you're going to need it."

Jennie and I were both quiet for a while after we had let Virginia off. Finally Jennie broke the silence saying, "Caleb you don't think she was, ah—you know, a woman of the night—do you?"

I wanted to respond with the usual know-it-all, barn-boy bravado, but there was something about Virginia that had gotten to me, and besides I was with Jennie. So I answered, "I don't know, Jennie, but I don't believe that just because they met in a bar makes her a hooker. I wish she had been more successful with Clem, though. I am going to have enough of a time handling my own feelings without having to deal with his."

"I don't think you have to worry, Caleb; you seem to have been capable enough when Clem confronted you at the shanty. Still, I was thinking when Clem was hollering at you how it always seems that you have more than your share of problems. Josh used to say he sometimes thought his main profession in life was hauling you out of trouble."

"Man, Jennie, I wish he were here now to help with a little hauling; he always seemed to know what to do. Me, I sometimes feel like a scared rabbit looking for a hole to hide in."

Jennie put her arm around me saying, "None of that, Caleb; no more black holes in your life, remember what a waste that was last time? And no matter what you do, our friendship pact always stays in place, we will never be the same people again we were then."

Laughing I said, "Don't worry, Jennie, I don't have any intentions of falling back there. Your arm around me reminds me that there were some good things about when I was that way."

Jennie pulled her arm back saying, "Caleb, you'd better remember your promise."

"Don't worry, I'll keep it. I know how much I'm going to need a friend like you that I can trust to tell me the truth about myself," I said, just as we were pulling into Sterling. Jennie had asked to be left at the library. Pulling up there, I gave Jennie a little kiss and said, "But it's going to be hard."

She climbed out of the truck. "What the hell, Caleb? There is always Beverly and the Coors barn," she said as she went running into the library.

That's twice I heard about the Coors barn and Beverly. I wondered as I drove back to the house if Beverly had said anything . The thought kind of scared me, but then I recalled Homer's *Beverly's virgin* retort, so I guess I didn't have to worry about that.

When I arrived home Mr. Banner had just brought Mother back from the hospital and she was all smiles when I walked in.

She said, "Caleb, I'm glad you're back! There's good news! Your father is so much better today than he's been and the doctors are more hopeful about his leg every day. He is hell-bent on coming home, so after discussing it with the doctors, I told him that the doctors are afraid he might lose his leg, and that the only chance he had of saving it is staying there. He held my hand and said, 'I know, Helen, but we will never be able to pay all these bills.' The doctor came in while he was talking and said 'You know, Mr. Carney, you will be in much better condition to pay these bills with two legs than you will with one, so give us a chance.' I told him about Richard and Hester's plan of getting married at the house, and about Hester using her trousseau money towards the bill. He accepted that a lot better than I expected, saying Hester sure has picked a good one there."

Mom had forgotten to tell Hester that she was going to the hospital with Mr. Banner, so she and Richard came to the house to pick her up. Mother apologized, but Richard said no apology was needed.

Hester said, "I think Richard and I should go anyway."

"May I go, too?" I asked, "I need to talk with Dad about the job if he is as well as Mother said."

Mother said, "Now, Caleb, we still have to be careful how much we lean on your father until he is much better."

"I know Mother, I just thought it would be good for him to hear how things are going. I won't trouble him with anything," I said, thinking that I didn't want to mention Clem's strange behavior, even to her, because she was so happy after seeing Dad.

Richard put his arm on my shoulder and said, "I'm glad you're going with us; it will give us a better chance to get acquainted."

On the drive to the hospital they talked about their wedding plans, but Hester was very upset about something. Richard turned to me and said, "Caleb, I have to let you in on a fact that isn't well known in your family, and I am going to trust you to be man enough to come to me and me only if you have a lot of trouble with it."

I said, "Okay, Richard," thinking, *Man, I thought Hester's trouble had been all settled.*

Turning to me Richard said, "This is the problem. Hester and I had planned to have your local pastor marry us at the house. We already have the wedding license and our blood test, but he wanted us to come and have a counseling session with him before he would marry us. After he had gone over our papers and discovered I was a divorced man, he has refused to marry us. Hester had decided that we should keep that fact from your family until they got to know me better. Now with the wedding only a couple of weeks away, our decision has come back to haunt us. We have decided that come hell or high water we are going to get married anyway, so she can go to Japan with me. If you have any advice on how we can handle this with the family, we would appreciate it. Hester is scared that everything is going to blow up in our face."

"Wow! Richard, when you said I would get to know you better I never expected anything like this. I guess we had better let all this roll around in my head for a while before I answer," I replied.

We were already at the hospital so I was saved from having to say anything until after our visit. One thing for sure was this was something that we couldn't let Dad know about, at least until after he was back home and at work.

Mother was right, Dad seemed much more his old self than I had seen him. He smiled as we came in, saying, "What's this about a wedding at my castle and nobody has invited me?"

Hester gave him a little hug and said, "Oh, Dad, if you want we'll get married right here in this room with you. Richard and I are so sorry that we are rushing getting married at this time, but I don't want to wait until he gets home from Japan. He is not even sure how long he will be there. It might be a couple of years, and I'll end up being an old maid."

Dad's smile broadened as he said, "I believe that your Richard is a good man, Hester, but I doubt you would end up being an old maid. Richard should be the one who's worried about someone else scoffing you up while he was gone."

Richard said, "You're right, Mister Carney, that is what was foremost on my mind when I rushed this marriage."

Dad said, "Call me Henry or Dad, Richard. I feel old enough lying here without my daughter's intended calling me, 'Mister.' How about you, Caleb, have you got everything ready to take over for me?"

"I've been working at it, Dad; I went and got the truck back from Clem. He felt bad about not having any wheels, but I guess I can work it out with him. I took hay and feed up to the shanty barn and checked out the gear and the horses. Everything looks fine. I feel real confident that Clem and I can handle everything all right."

Dad said, "Keep and eye on his beddings, Caleb, he's a little careless sometimes in how he builds them. I've tried and tried to make him better at it, but he is adamant that what he does is right."

The nurse came in and said, "Ten minutes to the end of visiting time."

Hester gave Dad a kiss on his cheek and said, "We mean it, Dad, we are willing to get married right here if that's what you want."

Dad said, "Hester, I want you and Richard to be successful in whatever you do, but I don't think that getting married in a hospital room is a good omen. You know it might be possible for me to be home for the wedding even if I can't stay. The doctors are making me do some strength exercises already and who knows how far I'll be along in two more weeks?"

We all left the hospital feeling better about Dad than we ever had. As we were driving away Richard said, "What about it, Caleb? Have you come up with a brilliant plan for your sister and me?"

"I've been thinking, Richard; right now the only thing I know for sure is you are going to have to tell Mother. She is your only chance of convincing our pastor to marry you two. I know that if you bring in another pastor, Mother is going to have to know why, and our pastor won't lie to her. So you see that telling her is the first thing we'll have to do. I'll stay with you when you do if you want me to, but I don't know if I'll be any help."

Hester said, "He's right, Richard, we have to tell Mother right away, but I'm not sure we want her to know we discussed this with Caleb first. It is going to be bad enough that we hid it from her this long."

Richard said, "Okay, that's the plan. We'll tell her tonight. By the way,

Caleb, I heard what you said to your dad about the truck and Clem. You know, I have to dump this old Chevrolet somewhere when we leave, so why don't you take it over? When I came back to Oscin to work there were three of us using one company car, but when I started courting your sister I had to get some wheels of my own. I won't have a need for it in Japan, and I was just going to sell it for whatever I could get quick for it."

"I don't know, Richard; our money situation is so uncertain right now I wouldn't want to spend money for a car."

"Hell, Caleb, I wasn't talking about your buying it. I would just leave it for you. If it bothers you as a gift, think of it as just keeping it for me until I get back."

I thought, *Man, Dad was right; Richard does seem like a good man for Hester—he is already putting the family first in the way he thinks.* I didn't say anything more about the car. Hester and Richard got busy making plans on how they would approach Mother the rest of the way home.

At home Hester and Richard asked Mother for a few minutes in private and they went into the parlor and closed the door. I had an ear tuned and heard Mother s gasp as she was told about Richard. They were in that room over a half an hour before Hester came out and asked me to come in.

Mother said, "Caleb I have just been informed that Richard is a divorcé, and as much as I have grown to admire him, I find this very disturbing."

I wasn't sure how to answer because I didn't know what Hester had told them.

While I was standing there trying to formulate something, Richard said, "Mother, if I may still call you that, we informed Caleb on the way to the hospital, and his reply was, 'We have to talk this over with Mother.' Mrs. Carney, you have to believe us, we had no intention of hiding this from the family. Hester said it would be best if the family got to know me first. She was so afraid that we could end up like Harry and Eunice that she wanted Dad's approval before she married me. Now with Dad so bad off, and my having to leave the country, we thought it better for everyone to wait until after we came back. I guess that God and your pastor have shown us that that was a mistake."

"Hester you need to clear something up for me," Mother said frowning. "Neither one of you seemed to even give any thought to postponing the wedding. Is that true?"

"Mother you don't understand." she stuttered.

Mother cut her off with, "All I want is a yes or no answer, Hester."

"No, Mother," she said shakily, "we have thought about it, but it not only doesn't work for us, it isn't going to benefit the family if we wait."

I could see where this was heading so I jumped in with, "You know, Mother, Hester is planning on going to work for Richard's company and sending her pay home, so I can go back to college. I told her that was a dumb idea, but Richard told me that his paycheck was living proof of how important it was to have a good education. Especially when I'm getting mine free of cost. He said it took him some time after he graduated to pay for his."

Mother sat for a few minutes holding her head, then said, "Okay, now here's what we will do for now. We won't say anything about Richard being a divorcé to anyone. I'll have a talk with our pastor. If he can't perform the ceremony then he can at least keep quiet as to why. I believe it won't be any trouble finding a pastor who is willing to marry you. Now get out of here, all of you, before I change my mind."

It was after eight o'clock but I thought I might be able to catch some of the boys in the center of town so I said to Richard, "If you are going to be here for a while, can I try out my new car?"

Richard laughed and said, "I guess you earned it, Caleb, but don't be long. I don't want your mother thinking I'm staying here too late, especially tonight."

Starting the car I thought this might seem old to Richard, but a '41 Chevy was the last model Chevrolet built before the war, and was like brand new to me. The boys had all left the barn by the time I arrived there, so I cruised around to all of my old haunts. When I swung into the school yard, someone was sitting in one of the swings. Thinking this would be someone to talk to about my getting my own car I shut off the engine and got out. After I was out of the car I could see it was Joan.

Not knowing what else to say I said, "Joan, I'm glad you're here, I was thinking about going to your house, but I thought it was too late."

"Oh! I bet, Caleb, you were looking for me. I saw that car pull in down at the barn before circling around by the library. Did you think I would be at the barn? Or were you hoping you would find Beverly or Jennie?" she said, getting up to leave.

"Whoa, Joan! My life right now is confusing enough without my ice-cream-eating girlfriend turning on me," I said, putting my arm on her shoulder.

She turned and slapped me, and then threw her arms around me crying, "How could you, Caleb? When you left that day after we were on the mountain I felt so close to you. You've been home over a week, and you haven't even tried to see me."

"Oh, Joan," I said holding her close. "Things have been so hectic since I came back. Dad's in the hospital badly injured; all of us have been trying to come up with a plan that will keep the family together. I just haven't had time for visiting."

Joan leaned back and slapped me again, saying, "The way I hear it you had time to visit with Beverly and spent the day with Jennie. If we have anything between us, why wasn't it me you called to go riding with you?"

I pinned her arms and held her tight, kissing the tears off her cheek. I said, "Joan, Joan, do you think with all I have suffered with your mother I was going to pull up to your house with Dad's old, beat-up truck and ask you to go out? I'm involved in enough trauma without going out looking for it."

I kissed her tears again working my kisses down the side of her neck, she started relaxing and becoming less tense in my arms, when suddenly she pulled away from me. She shouted, as she ran towards home, "I need more from you than your damn barn girls do, so maybe it's the right thing that you don't come see me."

I ran after her shouting, "Joan, Joan! Don't go. Let me explain." I stopped running, thinking, *Just maybe she is right.* As much as I felt for her, I wasn't ready to make the commitment she wanted. It was true that I had put off meeting her. *Damn, I wish I understood all of this. Josh, oh, Josh, why did God have to take you?*

I went back to the car and sat there, wondering why it always seemed so tough for me with Joan. I was just going to leave when someone hollered, "Caleb, is that really you?" It was Jake. I hadn't seen him since I left for Oklahoma.

"Jake, Jake, man, it's good to see you. I was hoping we would be able to get together before you left for college."

"Caleb, I heard about your father and thought you would be home. You're going back in time to enter college, aren't you, Caleb?" Jake asked

"No, I'm afraid I won't be going, Jake, at least not this year. I checked with attorney Welch and he said it would be all right. Hanna's will allowed me six years before I would lose the money. I'm sorry that we won't be together, Jake, but my family needs me now, and it has to be family first."

"Too bad, Caleb, I had figured that by the time I got to Oklahoma you would be a big-city boy and could show me the ropes," Jake said laughing. "What's with the car, Caleb? Did you strike it rich in Oklahoma?"

"No, I just borrowed Hester's intended's car, though he has talked about leaving it with me when they go to Japan. I am not sure how I feel about all this, Jake. Oklahoma was all right, but I was never near as comfortable there as I am here in Sterling. Maybe I'm just not cut out to be a writer or journalist, Jake. Sometimes I think what I really want out of life is right here for me."

"Come on, Caleb!" Jake shouted, "Don't you realize that we are the luckiest dumbbells alive? Why if old Hanna hadn't selected us, we might have been destined to live this life forever. I know Sterling is a great little town to grow up in, and maybe even to retire to, but what kind of professional opportunities are here for young families? Even if your writing talent doesn't pan out for you, an education opens up many paths to a successful life. Caleb, we've been friends forever, and as your friend I beg you not to waste the gift that Hanna left us."

Jake sounded so upset that I said, "Hell, Jake, I didn't mean that I wasn't going to ever go back; it's just, my life seems to have so many ups and downs, I get to thinking how easy it was just fishing and hiking with you, Karl, and the kids in town than it is to have all these decisions I have to make all the time now."

"I have to be getting home, Caleb. How about giving me a ride so I can tell everyone I got to ride in Caleb's new chariot?" Jake asked

On the ride home Jake talked excitedly about all he had learned working for the paper, and as he got out at his house he said, "Caleb, you have to promise me that if it ever enters your head to not go to college, you will come and talk to me first," he started to the house then he came back, yelling, "Wait, Caleb! Give me your hand." I held out my hand and he nicked my thumb with his knife, then pushing his own, already bleeding thumb to mine, said, "Now you; it's a blood oath, and friends don't forget those."

I left Jake's house with my mind full of conflict. I had not really meant that I wasn't going to go back to college, but it was true it kept popping up as an alternative.

Remembering that Richard needed the car to go back to Oscin I drove back home, thinking, *Jake was a good friend.* Life is funny, if Hanna hadn't put us together writing, we probably wouldn't have become this friendly.

The next day was Friday and the last day Clem's helper would be working, as he wanted a week off before he went back to school. So I decided I would go to the job site and get reacquainted with the job. I arrived about ten in the morning when the men were at their coffee break. Most of the mill crew was new to me; this was still Jocklin's Mill but run by his son and a much younger crew than when I worked here a year ago. The site they were cutting was mostly hemlock with some pine, and all of it was being sawn square edge, not the box pine that they cut when I worked here.

I told Don, Clem's helper, that I wanted to do a couple of loads with Clem as they went back to work. I was a little clumsy with the lumber at first but it was coming back to me. Clem wasn't as easy to swing lumber with as Dad had been. It seemed that instead of us being in time, he was trying to be ahead of me all the time. He managed to pinch my fingers a couple of times before I caught on to him. The pace was much slower than it was when we were sticking box lumber. It was much more work for the mill, when they had to square up everything. I worked a couple of loads with Clem in the field. It was different too; every load had several different cuts of lumber, meaning we had to stop at different piles while unloading the lumber.

After I had done a couple of loads, I realized that I wasn't going to have to work anywhere near as hard as I had before, though it was plain to see that working with Clem wasn't going to be any picnic. As I was leaving, Clem said, "What's the matter, Caleb? The job too much for you?"

"No, Clem," I answered. In fact I was thinking how much easier this was than when I worked with Dad. "I need to get back so I can take Mother to the hospital to see Dad." I was back at the truck when I remembered about Richard and the Chevy, so I went back and said, "Clem, I almost forgot the good news. Richard, Hester's intended, is going to leave his car with me when they leave for Japan. So I'll be able to leave the truck here for you after that."

"Damn good thing for you," Clem sneered, "I was already talking to Leclat about driving team for him. That job pays more than this one."

I drove back to Sterling thinking it might be a good thing if Clem did get another job. I was sure I could get someone to replace him. Funny how much he had changed since the war. Uncle Louis said it was more losing his wife than the war because he didn't really see any action; he was a part of our force that occupied Japan after the war had ended.

Mother was waiting when I got home, and we left for the hospital. Mother said, "I had a long talk with the pastor. He still isn't going to perform the wedding, but he has agreed not to tell anyone why; not that I care at this stage. How do you feel about Richard being a divorcé, Caleb?"

"To tell you the truth, Mother, with all that has been going on since I got home, I haven't given it much thought. I only know that Hester is all right with it, and I believe that we have to trust her judgment. I like what I have seen of Richard, and when they are together he treats her like a queen. I also like the idea that he is financially secure enough so we don't have to worry about how Hester will have to live."

We had arrived at the hospital. As I helped Mother down from the truck she said, "You know Caleb, they operated on Dad's leg day before yesterday, and he hasn't been very pleasant to visit since. The doctors have tried a new procedure in trying to get blood flowing properly to his foot, and they seemed discouraged with the results. Your father has been under pretty heavy medication so don't be shocked at what you see."

Dad looked much worse than he had the last time I came, but he was conscious and seemed really glad to see us, saying, "So it's back to the old saw mill for you, huh, Caleb? Do you think you'll enjoy that as much as all those college girls and books you had planned on? I have been talking it over with Mother, and it seems that the family is all gathering behind you to make sure you get your college education. I don't plan on being this helpless for too long, Caleb, and when I'm better you can go back to your college life."

"You don't have to even think about that, Dad," I answered, "Hanna's will gives me up to six years after high school to use that money, so we have plenty of time."

Mother said, "Now, come on, you two, let's not get into the work area today. Caleb still has the weekend before he has to start."

"You know, Mother, work is the thing us men talk about best. I bet you Hester and Richard have bored him to death with all the plans I been hearing about the wedding next week. I want Dad to know that I am on top of the job, and he probably needs to hear that," I said with a little laugh.

Dad laughed too and said, "I don't know about being bored about the wedding, Caleb. What has upset me is listening to your mother brag about how capable you are in taking my place. A man doesn't want to think he can be replaced so easily. So if you want to do me a favor, make the job look a little harder."

At first Mother looked a little taken aback, but she smiled and said, "I can't help but feel proud of all my children. Caleb not only leaves Oklahoma and college, but without a whimper he goes about figuring what's best for the family. I know that we would have found another way to survive if we had to, but now we can keep everything just the way it was until you get back. We both have a right to brag about our children."

"Well, Caleb," Dad asked, "Have you checked the job out yet?"

"Yes, Dad, I went over today and worked with Clem for a couple of loads.

I'm sure everything is going to be fine. Richard is leaving his car with me, so I will be able to let Clem use the truck. He was real happy to hear that. Clem did talk about looking for a better-paying job, but he said he wouldn't leave unless we had a good replacement. I don't think it would be a problem to train a new man on that job, Dad; the pace is really slow compared to the way we had to work when I was with you."

"I know Caleb, I think I underbid that job a little. I had intended to pay Clem a little more, but we can't afford more than what he gets on this job. I thought that the mill would be more productive than it has been. The logs are a poorer quality than I was told. Next time I will be smart enough to check a lot out before I bid, if I ever get to bid another job," Dad answered.

Mother said, "That's enough job talk for today, Henry. Let's not hear any more talk about not getting back to work. There isn't any doubt that you have a ways to go, but we all know you will be back driving your horses in the end."

A nurse came in and said, "I'm sorry, but you'll have to leave now. Mr. Carney has to go for therapy."

Driving back in the truck Mother was quiet for a long time, then she said, "What are we going to do, Caleb, if he isn't able to do that kind of work again? He's never done anything for work except work in the woods. I try not to think like that, but the doctors have been talking more, lately, about how he could be fitted with an artificial leg. I asked them not to talk to him about it until he is stronger, and they agreed for now. They think that the leg is holding his recovery back, and that it is slowly becoming a case of where he might be better off without it. I'm sorry, Caleb, I don't mean to burden you, but with Hester's wedding and Eunice gone, that leaves you and Emma as the only ones in the family old enough to talk with."

"It's okay, Mother," I answered with a knot building in my stomach. "One of the reasons I'm staying is I know you need help getting through this, too. I don't want to think about Dad losing that leg, but it is something we should at least consider might happen. There are some books in the library that might be of help if we have to talk to Dad about how well other people have managed after losing a leg. There are jobs that he could do even in the woods. Look at Mr. Phelps. He went back into the woods after he lost his arm, and if I remember right Mr. Jocklin told about having a one-legged roller working in his mill for years. I'm sure if the worst comes, Dad can find a way to continue working."

Mother said, "It seems funny, Caleb, hearing you discuss things like such an adult. I didn't want you to know how badly I needed you to stay home, and I was so relieved when you made that decision yourself."

"It wasn't that hard a decision for me, Mother, beyond it being my duty I am much more comfortable home in Sterling than I am out in the world."

"I hope that doesn't mean that you're giving up on college, Caleb," Mother said as we drove into the yard.

"No, Mother, not giving up—just postponing for a while. The best way for me to handle this is just to put college out of my mind until it's time to address it again," I answered as we drove in the yard.

It was just about six, so I said, "Mother, if you don't mind, I want to go down to the barn and talk to Homer and the boys."

With Mother's okay, I drove to the milk barn. I just stepped into the door when Homer hollered, "Glad you came down, Caleb. I ran into Joan this afternoon, and she wanted me to tell you she is leaving day after tomorrow for college. I asked her if there was anything else she wanted me to tell you but she said, 'No!' Just that. What did you do to little Miss Prissy? Now, did she catch you with Beverly?"

"Knock it off, Homer! Don't I have enough trouble at home without you spreading tales about me?" I answered sharply

"O, c'mon," John chimed in, "don't tell me Beverly's Little Virgin is afraid we'll hurt his reputation? I know I'd be ashamed of mine if someone like Beverly called me her Little Virgin."

Muttering, "To hell with you guys," I went back to the truck and left the barn thinking, *Now what?* The way Joan left me the other night I figured she didn't want anything to do with me.

Being a little angry, I decided to drive up to Joan's house—truck or no truck. I knocked at the door, and her mother answered saying, "I'm sorry, Caleb, but Joan is too busy getting ready for college to have any company. Sorry to hear that you're not going to be able to go to college now. I'll tell Joan you called."

I went back to the truck wondering how come that woman could always make me feel like a piece of crap. I had just started the truck when Joan came running out shouting, "Caleb, Caleb! Please don't go."

I waited and Joan got in the truck and said, "Let's get out of here."

I drove off saying, "Where to, my little ice-cream queen? Where would you like to be seen in this fine chariot?"

"Caleb!" she shouted, "you stop it this minute! I know I left you in a huff when I saw you by the swings the other night, but it's just you made me so mad when you didn't even bother to come see me when you came home. Now don't give me any of your excuses. Let's just pretend it didn't happen. I need to talk to you. I really don't have much time tonight because I am sorting clothes and packing, but I wondered if we could walk up the mountain tomorrow. I can squeeze out a half a day if you want me to be with you at all before I go."

Even though Joan's possessive ways always scared me, I loved being with her, and it was always good to be able to talk to her about my fears. So I said, "I think it will be all right, Joan, unless Mother needs me. We're very concerned about Dad's condition, and she likes to go to the hospital as much as she can. I'm glad you ran into Homer because I didn't want you going off to college with the other night being our last contact."

We parked by the swings at the schoolhouse and as I put my arms around her she snuggled up close saying, "I really missed you, Caleb. You know there has never been another boy in my life."

I laughed without thinking. I said, "With your mother's ways and your father's bullwhip, I'm not surprised; are you?"

Joan stiffened but didn't pull away, saying, "Caleb, let's not go there tonight. I want it to be just us," She kissed me softly at first, then squeezing me tighter, her kisses became more and more passionate. Finally just when I thought I was going to lose it, she pulled away and said, "Take me home, Caleb, before I give my father cause to use his bullwhip."

Man, that wasn't what I had in mind right then; but I said laughing, "For future reference, Joan, in a case like this who would get the whipping, you or me?"

"You know, Caleb, with my mother urging him on, he would probably tie us both to the same stake and then burn us after the whipping," Joan said, laughing.

I drove Joan home, and once she was where she felt safe, she held me and kissed me so passionately I had to push her away. She jumped out of the truck saying, "Tomorrow at ten, Caleb, okay?"

"Will I be safe then, Joan?" I asked

She laughed and said, "Of course, Beverly's Little Virgin," as she ran into the house.

When I got home I accosted Homer, "What the hell are you trying to do to me; are you mad because I came back home or what?"

Homer looking slightly aghast said, "What in the world are you talking about, Caleb? I'm as glad that you are staying as Mother is. What the devil do you think I have done that has you so upset?"

"You damn well know, Homer. The last thing Joan said to me tonight was,

'Beverly's Little Virgin.' You were the one who talked to her today, so I know that had to come from you."

"Whoa, whoa, whoa! Caleb, I had hoped you had more respect and faith in me than to think I would have done that. It was John; he was with me when I met Joan, and when she asked me to tell you about her leaving, John asked her what she wanted with Beverly's Little Virgin."

"I'm sorry, Homer; I don't know why I would even think it was you. It's just that my situation with Joan is becoming so perplexing. Sometimes I don't think straight after I've been with her. Forgive me." I asked.

"Ah, it's okay, Caleb. I know you have a lot on your mind, but if I was you I think I would cut and run as far as Joan is concerned. Why would you want to suffer her mother's crap anyway? Now that you aren't a college boy, she'll just make it harder and harder for you two. Bets around town are that you two will never end up together anyhow," Homer said, turning away.

"Wait, wait, wait, Homer! Don't tell me that people are betting on who will end up with who now?"

"Oh, c'mon, Caleb. It's just gutter talk from the barn. You should remember how it was; I'm going to bed," he said, turning away again.

Emma was in the next room reading and must have heard us talking, because as I walked by she said, "What's the matter, Caleb? Are your boyhood flings starting to catch up with you? You know there is some wisdom in what Homer tried to tell you. Joan gets a steady diet of how unworthy you are for her from her mother every day. My guess is even if you two ended up getting married, when things got tough you would hear about it over and over."

"Hell, Emma, marriage is the furthest thing from my mind right now. All I want is an uncomplicated relationship with a girl," I said as I started upstairs

"Maybe it's the furthest thing from your mind, Caleb, but how about her mind? There is wisdom in what you're hearing tonight, Caleb; try remembering that."

The next day I met Joan at the foot of Mount Fay. She had a picnic basket and a thermos. I hadn't even thought about lunch. In fact I figured we would only be gone a couple of hours. Joan handed me the basket and gave me a little kiss saying, "I'm so glad we are having this time together before I leave. I've dreamed over and over of the wonderful time we had the day before you left."

I was glad too, but a little knot of fear was forming as my mind raced over what was said last night at home. This was a fear that I couldn't talk over with Joan because she was causing it. I said, "Joan, let's hurry up to the ledges. I have to be back in time to take my mother to the hospital."

I took her hand, and we started up the mountain. Joan was strangely quiet as we reached the ledges and sat looking over the valley below. Finally Joan spoke, "Caleb, I thought this was going to be our day, what happened?"

"Well, you know Joan, we just planned this last night, and the family had made other plans counting on me to be there," I answered truthfully.

Joan moved over close to me and put her arm around me and said, "Don't get mad, Caleb, but why do they call you Beverly's Little Virgin?"

"I don't know, Joan. You know that Beverly has earned herself somewhat of a reputation. I think it is because she told the boys that I wouldn't have sex with her." I almost laughed when I thought about what I was saying, because the truth was, that's what she told them. " Now, Joan, remember we weren't going to get into discussions about sex. It's one of our rules. Let's go up to the tower. If we don't waste time I will be able to get back in time."

All the way up to the tower Joan was again silent. In a way I was thankful for that. I don't think I would be capable of the day she wanted. At the top of the mountain by the foot of the tower we sat and ate the lunch Joan had brought. After we finished eating Joan leaned her head on my shoulder and said, "We can't have it back, Caleb, can we? Our ice cream dates, holding hands after school, sitting together on the bus, and that wonderful day we had on the mountain together before you left. I thought we had an understanding that day, and yet when you came home, I didn't even hear from you. I was so hurt, Caleb; I really thought we were so close."

"Oh, Joan, I wish I could explain. All those things you mentioned have meant so much to me over the years. I often think back to our childhood ice cream dates. They were so much a part of my life then. Now, it's different. The world seems to be handing me harder and harder choices and I often feel so inadequate. You know it's different between boys and girls when they get older. I think I love you as much as any girl, Joan, but you don't want to get too serious with a guy like me, who may not be going anywhere in life," I answered.

"Tell me, Caleb," she said, grabbing me and straddling my lap, "would you be sitting here calmly talking like this if we had consummated our relationship the night I lost my pants behind Larro's? Wouldn't we be rolling around on the ground all over each other? What's the matter, Caleb?" she said, kissing and hugging me, with tears rolling down her face. "Is the real reason why they call you Beverly's Little Virgin because you can't commit?" Joan was all over me yelling, "Tell me, Caleb! Tell me, Isn't this all you think girls are good for?"

The craziness and passion was getting to me. Boy, I wanted to show her, but somehow I pulled myself together and pushed her back saying, "Joan, stop it, you stop this right now."

Joan sat sobbing, "So there isn't any you and me, is there, Caleb?"

"Joan, Joan, Joan, I had to stop you or there could have been a you and me, and that would have haunted you the rest of your life. Remember Bob and Katy and all they and their families had to live down?"

"Sure, Caleb, you're going to send your father over to tell my father I raped you. That would be the day." she replied, still sniffing.

I sat down and held her hand saying, "Joan, I want you to be a part of my life, but I'm not ready at this stage in my life to commit to any one thing. It's not that we have to be any less or any more to each other than what we've always been. You own a part of my heart and always have, but I want to keep the rest of it open for whatever might happen in my life. I believe that if either one of us was to commit our whole heart to one person at our age we would grow old feeling we missed something somewhere. I don't want that to happen to you, or me either. Let's always have these days on our mountain not only in our dreams but also as something we can to come back to. Even if we never stand at the wedding altar together, this mountain will always be here for us, and hopefully us for each other."

Joan pulled herself together, stood up, and kissed me lightly, saying, "My knight in shining armor saved me from myself again. Thank you, Caleb."

"You're entirely welcome, Joan. But one warning: I wouldn't try that again. My armor is getting a little worn," I said laughing.

We raced down the mountain with gay abandon just like last time and rolled in the grass in the field below. Joan held me close and smothered me with kisses before she jumped up saying with a laugh. "Sorry, Caleb, almost forgot about your weak armor. Let's get me home; your mother must be waiting for you. Good-bye, our mountain, for now; don't go away. We will be back, because a knight in shining armor has told me so."

At Joan's house, she held my hand quietly for a moment then said, "Caleb, I know there is wisdom in what you said to me on the mountain, and I am ashamed of how I acted. Still since I was a little girl, way back when we started our ice cream dates, I have always thought that you belonged to me. I know, especially after today, how little girlish that was, and I want to thank you for helping me see that. Yet I still need you to promise that the part of your heart that is mine will always be there even if I never walk down the wedding aisle to you."

"Joan, Joan, where are the words to explain? For me, life has been like waves crashing on the shore with each wave carrying a different message. Before losing Josh I never worried; he was always there like a god watching out for me. After we lost him, there was my dark period, then off to work in a man's world, followed by Hanna's surprise and my trip to Oklahoma. Then Dad's accident and all the distressing decisions I have to make that are connected to that. This has created a fear in me, a fear that I will jump in the wrong wave and be smashed to the shore. Still, Joan, I know that nothing could tear from my heart all that you have been to me. I know that isn't a very clear answer, Joan, but my life right now is so full of ifs, ands, and buts. It is the best I can think of," I answered squeezing her hand.

Joan just sat for a minute holding me, brushing my cheek with little kisses. Then with tears in her eyes she said, "Promise me you will always come to me, no matter how confused you might feel, because that was beautiful, Caleb. If you come, like our mountain, I will always be there for you."

Joan's mother came out, loudly slamming the door, and to make sure we saw her she stood by the door watching us. Joan threw her arms around me, kissing me with a passion that steamed the windshield. I wasn't about to struggle; she held me in that embrace for what seemed a very long time. Finally I heard the house door close and her mother went in. Joan let up, saying, "Sorry about your armor, Caleb, but she deserved that."

"Hell, Joan," I exploded, "you don't hear me complaining, do you? But if you're going to do that again let's get the hell out of here."

Joan gave me another little kiss and started to get out of the truck. She stopped and said smiling, "Caleb, can I say you're Joan's Little Virgin now?"

I pulled her back, gave her a kiss and said laughing, "Get in the house, Joan, before you ruin my reputation."

I drove away from Joan's with the same crazy desires that she usually created in me, remembering part of a poem I had just read in one of Josh's books.

Her amorous life was being haunted
Because she thought her love was flaunted
For she had stood steadfast undaunted
Refusing the animal love he wanted

Her mind to this had added terror
To refuse had perhaps been in error
Would he seek another, to be the sharer
Of the kind of love, he found fairer?

Some of Josh's poems made you wonder what he had been involved in or what he was thinking when he wrote them. This one, which I had read just the other night, seemed to have a lot of meaning to what I have been through the last couple of days. Especially remembering Jennie's words about her and Beverly substituting for the passion created by Joan. Man, *that sure doesn't put me in a very good light when you think of it.*

Mother was waiting and a little upset by the time I got home saying, "Caleb, I was getting worried that something had happened to you. You know they don't let us stay with your father long sometimes; I won't have you or Richard here to drive me, when you go to work and Richard leaves for Japan."

"I'm sorry, Mother," I said. "Things got a little complicated between Joan and me, and I wasn't watching the time like I should have been."

As we drove to the hospital Mother inquired about Joan and said, "I hope nothing serious happened between you two. She seems like such a nice girl."

"She is a nice girl, Mother," I answered, "but she wants more of a commitment than I am able to give. I was hoping we could just go on as we always have, but I guess that is not as easy now as it used to be."

"I hope you're controlling yourself with these girls; I wouldn't want a scandal in our family."

"Not to worry, Mother. Joan and I are both known as virgins," I said, thinking again how it wasn't really a lie. *Man, wouldn't she be proud if I could tell her how much control I dug up today?*

When we arrived at the hospital they asked us not to wake Dad or stay long because he had developed a high fever that had just got under control and he was finally sleeping. Mother and I looked in on him but didn't stay because we didn't want to disturb him. The nurse spoke to one of the doctors and told us not to look at this as too much of a setback, that it was not unexpected considering how much damage he had when he came in.

Mother was very quiet on the ride home. I hadn't noticed before how much this was all weighing on her. The weariness was beginning to show in her face and all this trouble was aging her. I said, "I'm sorry, Mother; maybe if I had been on time we could have seen him."

"Don't feel that way, Caleb," she said with a sigh, "even if we had been earlier they probably wouldn't have let us see him. It's just that there have been so many ups and downs with the doctors' reports it's hard to have a lot of hope. When we get home let's not talk about his condition too much. You know the wedding is next weekend, and I want to keep everything as upbeat as possible. I'll call the hospital and see if we can see him later tonight."

"You know, Mother, we talked last time about the possibility of Dad losing part of his leg and how we should be prepared for that. I've given that a lot of thought. As bad as losing his leg seemed; if his leg is the reason for all these setbacks, then maybe it's something we should consider letting him in on. I know it is something that will have to be handled with care; I do believe that we should at least be discussing it," I said hoping it would ease her thoughts.

"You know, Caleb," she answered, "I've had thoughts along those same lines since the last time I talked to the doctor. Still, let's keep this away from the family until after the wedding. Your father insists that we don't allow his condition to interfere with Hester and Richard's wedding. Amazing the difference between this and Eunice's marriage."

"That's just it, Mother. Despite Dad's old-fashioned ideas, he was able to change when he knew all the circumstances. I believe if taking his leg is the best thing to do for his health, he'll respond in the same way," I answered, keyed up because of having this thought come to me.

Mother called the hospital after supper, and they advised that it would be better not to come, as Dad was still sleeping and heavily medicated. The next day was going to be my first day on the job, so I went to bed early, as my day had been really trying.

The next day on the job was actually fairly easy compared to how I had worked with Dad and Harry. My biggest problem was Clem; he was surly and bitter about most everything and not a lot of fun to work with.

I did get a chance to talk to Melvin once in a while on breaks. Melvin was the marker who marked the lumber and took it away from the saw. He was very pleasant and had some good stories about my dad from the old days as he called them. He told me he had been up to the hospital once to see Dad right after the accident and hoped to get back again soon.

There was a boy called Norman who was the mill bitch. I was able to talk to him when we were waiting for lumber. He wasn't really with it too much but he did well at his work. It took me a couple of days to get him to open up, but once he trusted that I wasn't going to mock him or make fun of him he seemed anxious to talk. Though it was hard to follow him at first when he was excited about what he was talking about. What came through in his stories made him pretty much the same as all the boys I knew. He loved fishing, hiking and being alone in the woods with the birds and animals. He told me about some of his experiences while in the woods.

Clem asked me while we were out in the lumberyard why a college-bound kid like me wanted to talk to a retard like him. Clem had been getting more and more under my skin so I said, "Clem, what makes you so cruel? Norman certainly isn't doing you any harm."

"Cruel, am I?" He shouted, "You try living with my troubles, and we will see how friendly you are."

"Look, Clem," I shouted back, "You better than anyone should know that my life is far from being a bed of roses; still you don't see me grousing about everything and everybody, like you."

"Me better than anyone else? What are you saying? Do you think I'm responsible for what happened to your dad? You think I did that to him, the only friend I had when I came home from the war?" Clem asked.

"No, Clem, nobody is blaming you. Dad said it was just an unfortunate accident," I said remembering what Virginia had said about him feeling guilty. "Still you should be able to see that it has presented a pretty big problem in my life."

"Your life? What the hell does a kid like you know about life? You didn't get dragged off to war and have your family desert you. I don't need any kid to tell me about life," Clem answered angrily.

Now I was really mad and I shouted, "At least you came back, Clem; many of the boys, including my brother, Josh, didn't. You make me sick with your 'Poor me,' whining. At least Norman has sense enough to make the most of what he has; that's more than you're doing."

Clem was just putting a stake back in the wagon, and for a minute I thought he was going to hit me with it, but he stopped and said, "That's it! I'm out of here. I ain't working with no smart aleck kid who thinks a retard is a better person than I am. Let's see how you make out now, college kid, when you really have the world on your shoulders."

Clem started back to the shanty. I yelled after him, "Don't forget to get your stuff out of our shanty. I'll give you two days."

"Don't worry," he yelled back, "I'll be gone tonight."

It was close to quitting time so I went back and loaded the last load alone. Norman asked if he could help me when the mill shut down. He helped me stack the lumber and never even asked about Clem. He came with me and helped put the horses up and rub them down. When we were done he asked, "Caleb, do you have anyone to work with you tomorrow?"

Damn, in my anger I hadn't even thought beyond today, so I said, "No, I don't, Norman, but I'm sure after I get my anger under control I can talk Clem into staying until I can find someone."

He said, "You don't have to do that, Caleb, if you don't want to. I have a brother who needs work. He can carry slabs as good as me, and you can teach me how to take Clem's place. Leon Joclin told me he would put my brother to work as soon as he had an opening. If you want me to take Clem's place, Leon is still at the mill sharpening the saw, and I'll go ask him about my brother."

I was still upset with Clem but thought he has been a family friend for a long time, so maybe I should talk to him. So I said, "You go tell Leon what's going on and ask about your brother. I'll go give Clem another chance, and if he doesn't want it, I would be pleased to have you work with me."

I went up to the shanty. Clem was there banging around packing his things. I rapped on the door and said, "Clem it shouldn't be like this. Our families have been friends for a long time; maybe we both need to cool off and reconsider."

"No, Caleb, there is nothing to consider. I have been itching to leave even before your father got hurt. I'm not changing my mind now. I saw you working with that retard so let him take my place."

I wanted to yell back that Norman was more of a human being than he would ever be, but I held my tongue and walked away.

Norman came back to the barn and said, "It's okay with Leon if you want me, Caleb."

"You have yourself a job with me, Norman. I'm so glad you're available to work with me. Now how about your pay rate? We have to decide that before I can officially hire you."

"I will work with you for the same money Leon is paying me, a dollar an hour, if that's all right with you, Caleb," Norman answered

Boy, I thought, *that's considerably less than Clem is getting; maybe his leaving will be a help in more ways than one,* but I said, "That's very good, Norman; I'm kind of new in the financial arrangements of this job. It might be possible that I can do a little better than that. I'll let you know."

That night when I got home everyone was all excited about the wedding plans. Mother had been to the hospital with Mr. Banner, and the doctors told her it would be all right if Dad came home one day for the wedding. I decided not to say anything about Clem. Since I had already replaced him I didn't need to discuss it now. I was elated at the news about Dad and went to talk to Mother about it.

She said, "Caleb, I haven't told anyone else, but you remember talking about Dad's leg and we had better think about that he might lose it? Well, the doctors told me today they were afraid that the time had come. It was decided to let him come home for the wedding and then tell him afterwards. They think it is turning gangrenous. They started treating it with some new powdered drug, but they don't have much hope for it to work. I'm telling you now so you will have time to think about it because we're going to need you when he is told."

I went to my room thinking, *Man, there just is no ending. It's just one calamity after another around here!* I was feeling pretty proud that I was able to handle Clem's leaving, but I couldn't talk about it—now this. *Josh, Oh, Josh, how I miss you. Why can't I see the answers?* One of his poems that was in some papers of his I had read shockingly came to me almost like Josh was answering me.

> *The past is gone,*
> *And though it's true, that we lament*
> *It's as meaningless, as a horse*
> *Who on a ride, is useless spent*
> For when we gain not, from covered ground
> *It's time to search the reason round*
> For lamenting loss, for lack of gain
> Is not the cure, but added pain
> And pain's the cost, the price we pay
> When we race with life, and know not the way

I was kind of scared for a minute or two and then I remembered what Josh had said about the Bennet boy when I didn't want to use his clothes after the fire. He said if you were dead and an angel looking down, wouldn't you want to help somebody? Maybe that's it! Josh is watching out for me with messages in his poems.

The next day was Friday and things went well working with Norman. His brother Bruce did as well as Norman had on the mill bitching job. Norman picked up the knack of handling the lumber quickly and was actually easier to work with than Clem had been. Norman had been quiet most of the day when he said, "Caleb, how about the shanty? Is it still Clem's?"

"No, Norman," I answered, "The shanty belongs to my dad, and it looks like Clem has already left. It looks like I'll be spending some time there, because someone has to take care of the horses. I don't know what I'm going to do about tomorrow. My sister is getting married, so I guess I'll have to drive up early in the morning and then back again at night."

"I didn't think about you using it," Norman answered. "I just thought if it was going to be empty maybe Bruce and I could stay there. We are losing the place where we are staying, and the only place my mother can get is too small for us all to stay with her. I thought maybe we could rent the shanty until we could find something else."

"I'll tell you what, Norman," I said, feeling smarter about hiring him all the time. "If you think you boys can take good care of the horses when I'm not here I would let you use the shanty for nothing."

"Oh, Caleb, that would be so good, and you don't have to worry about the horses. We took care of a team one of our neighbors used to have for years, and he was very particular. I can even get brought back here tonight so you won't have to worry about tomorrow," Norman answered, all smiles.

After work we checked out the shanty to make sure Clem was gone. The last thing I wanted was to have him come back drunk and find Norman there. Clem had stripped the shanty of everything he owned and then some, so I knew he wouldn't be back.

So I said, "I guess we have a deal, Norman. Are you sure you can get back here tonight all right?"

Norman said, "Don't you worry about the horses. I'll be here for them even if I have to walk back."

When I got home Emma and Jason were making an archway with crepe paper out of one of the doorways. Mother had everyone cleaning and decorating the house for tomorrow. It had been decided that Homer and I would go get Dad early in the morning using Richard's car. Richard was going to take the truck back to Oscin that night. He joked about how his partners would be surprised at his new vehicle.

The next morning when Homer and I picked Dad up at the hospital they brought him out in wheel chair and helped us get him into the car, then folded the chair and put in the trunk. Dad seemed so happy because he was going home even though it was only for a day. They had his leg padded and strapped up with a leather cover, Homer joked with Dad saying his leg looked like a papoose. We talked about the job, and he asked how Clem was taking care of the horses. I didn't want him to know what happened so I just said, "The horses are being cared for almost as good as you used to do it, Dad."

"I have been thinking, Caleb; maybe early tomorrow we can swing over there on the way back, and I can see them. I don't see any reason why we can't; do you?" he asked.

"Sounds like a good plan to me, Dad, but it might be better to tell Mother about it tomorrow."

When we got to the house, Dad insisted he could make it on crutches, so we put the wheel chair inside and helped Dad get up the steps into the house. The minister from Oscin was already there, and after everybody had welcomed Dad the ceremony was started. Nellie escorted Hester through the archway and handed her to Richard. They went through their vows and "I do's" with the minister, and he pronounced them "man and wife." Funny, with all the fuss and preparation for this, it seemed to be over very quickly. After the ceremony we had a big feast, and Richard and Hester had to leave. We had tied some cans to Richard's car and decorated it with streamers.

He laughed when he saw it and said, "Didn't you boys forget something? You're going to have to come to Oscin to drive this back, Caleb."

Homer said, "Can I go too, Richard?"

"I guess that's up to Caleb; if he isn't planning on picking up any of his girlfriends I don't see why not," Richard answered.

Mother, Emma and Nellie had tears in their eyes by the time they were ready to leave. When we went out to the car Richard threw me the keys and said, "You drive, Caleb; I'm an old married man now and need all the help I can get."

Hester whopped him upside of the head, saying with a smile, "What do you think, Caleb? Maybe we should take him to the old man's home, and then I could go out cruising with you to find a replacement."

Homer laughed and said, "You know what, sis? Maybe you should wait until he gets you signed on to his retirement money."

We all got in the car and I drove to Oscin, laughing and joking all the way. There wasn't any doubt in my mind about Hester and her choice for a husband, even if he had been married before. Richard's partners, who were shipping out too, were waiting in Oscin to drive them to the airport. Homer and I kissed Hester good-bye and for the first time today I felt the sadness of her leaving.

I went to shake hands with Richard, but he gave me a big bear hug, saying, "Now, Caleb, you take good care of your family, and if at any time you are in financial trouble you let me know. Now I want to hear you promise that."

"You don't have to worry, Richard; I'll keep you and Hester informed, especially if I need money."

Homer was all for going cruising around Oscin after they left. For his sake I drove around for a while. We stopped at the ice-cream place he had heard the barn boys talk about where they used to pick up girls. Homer immediately struck up a conversation with some girls that were there, but my heart wasn't in it because of the thought of Dad losing his leg. We had a sundae, and I lingered awhile for Homer's sake, then said, "We really have to get back to Sterling, Homer. Mother will be waiting for us; remember, Dad's only home today."

When we got out to the car Homer said, "I know we have to get back, Caleb, but you have to promise me that you will bring me back soon. You know, since you had that trouble with the cops Mother doesn't let me go to Oscin with the rest of the boys."

At home Mother was having a hard time with Dad. He was insistent that he could manage the barn on crutches. She had convinced him to wait for us and was angry that we had taken so long. We helped Dad out to the barn; he did surprising well on crutches for someone who had never used them.

He seemed to come more alive once we reached the barn, saying, "You know what, boys? I don't see any reason I can't stay home and recuperate. Look how well I'm doing already."

He wanted to go down to the pigpen but, Homer said, "Not today, Dad. You're going to need a little more practice with those sticks before you travel on ground that rough."

Dad said, "All right, but it's smooth enough from here to the chicken coop. At least let me see if I can gather an egg or two."

I could see that being out was good for Dad after he had been cooped up in the hospital. I felt bad to think how disappointed he was going to be when he went and got the news from the doctors. Dad managed to find a couple of eggs. Jason took them in, and we stayed out until it was dark. By then Mother had started fretting so we all went in.

We sat around talking until bedtime. Nellie and Jason couldn't seem to get enough of Dad. I guess that old adage, "Absence makes the heart grow fonder," is true. Mother had not allowed the younger children to go see Dad when he was in the hospital.

We had brought one of the small beds down from upstairs for Dad, and Mother said, "All right, everyone. It's time we all got to bed. Caleb, I will try to get Dad in by myself. If I have any trouble I'll call you."

Dad said, "What the hell do you think? I'm so decrepit that I have to have my sons do everything for me?"

Mother said, "Now, Henry, let's don't get ornery. It has been a long day for all of us."

Mother must have been right, because I fell into a deep sleep right away. I was wakened in the early morning before daylight with Homer shaking me and saying, "Caleb, Caleb, wake up! Something bad has happened. Mother just went rushing downstairs, and Dad is turning the air blue with his cursing."

Homer and I pulled on our pants and raced down stairs. Dad was sitting on the floor in the kitchen still cursing. Mother was beside him sobbing, "I knew we shouldn't have let you come home, Henry, I just knew it."

The floor was covered with blood, and Mother was trying to stop Dad's leg from bleeding. I said, "Homer, you bring the car up to the door. Mother, you wake Jason and Emma and get them down here. I'll see if I can stop the bleeding. I took my belt and wrapped around Dad's upper leg and tightened it, which cut the blood flow.

Dad, who by now had stopped cursing, said, "Hell, Caleb, let me bleed to death. I'm not good for anything anyway."

"Knock that off, Dad," I shouted. "Our only problem here is you are trying to rush the cure too fast. In time you'll be as good as you were ever were."

I tried to check where all the blood was coming from. It looked like he had broken something in the bottom of his foot somehow. It looked like all the blood was coming from there. Homer was back with the wheel chair and with all of us there, we were able to get Dad into it. It was a hassle getting the wheel chair to the car, but we got him into the car and with Mother in back with him and Homer in front with me we rushed to the hospital.

At the hospital the nurses came out with a rolling stretcher, and we got Dad on it. He was pretty weak by then. The doctor in the emergency room checked Dad out and ordered a blood transfusion. After examining Dad he came out and said, "I am not familiar with his case but he is stable now, and I will contact the doctors who have been working with him and seek their advice on what I should do."

About an hour later he came out and said, "He's resting comfortably now. I'm a little bit confused; they said that his lower leg was so bad that they were making plans to remove it. I know they'll go over my report with me, but my findings seem to contradict what they are telling me. I don't want you to get your hopes up, because I am only an intern, and your doctor's evaluation is more educated than mine."

Dad was out of it again so the nurse said there was no use of our staying, just to call in the morning after our doctors had made the rounds.

The next day when Mother called, the doctor told her they were mystified about how much the circulation had improved in his leg. They decided they would cancel the operation and wait to see what happens. They believed it was a combination of the new medicine they were trying and the bleeding that made the improvement.

I went to bed that night thinking, this has been a hell of a home coming, but it looked like the Carney family had more than one guardian angel looking out for them.

CHAPTER FOUR

For the next few days it was touch and go with the doctors about Dad. It wasn't that they were unhappy that Dad's leg had improved; it was more that they wanted to understand how. None of the doctors who had originally examined the leg or had been called in to attempt to save it could believe what was happening. Still the bottom line, at least for the family, was Dad was going to be able to keep his leg. And the final consensus on the doctor's part was that it was a combination of the powder they had tried and the bleeding.

I had been taking the truck to work and Mother, who could drive but was unlicensed, managed to get a couple of the women in town who had licenses to go with her to the hospital. They didn't mind because they were able to do some shopping while Mother was at the hospital, though they all went in to see Dad too. One day Mr. Banner who rode with Mother convinced her she was ready to take a driving test.

I went to see Dad in the evenings every couple of days and you could see his strength returning more and more each time. The doctors said that after a week or so of rehab in the hospital, Mother would be taught how to care for him. After she understood how to take care of his problems, they thought he should go home for a while, even though he might need more surgery.

I had been working at the mill with Norman and I couldn't have designed a better partner. It may have been true that Norman was a little slow in some areas but he was an excellent worker. After we had worked a few days together and he trusted that I wasn't going to mock him he talked to me about his life and how hard it was dealing with some people. He didn't seem to be unintelligent, though you could see he hadn't had much formal education. His main drawback was that he was slightly cross-eyed and had a startled look whenever you asked him a question. I suppose that was why people were so prejudiced toward him and why he lacked a formal education. I thought about the things that Edgar used to stress and how Norman had mastered living with his disability without being bitter. How I wished I had the strength they had for living with life's hardships. It made me realize all lessons aren't learned in school.

One morning when I arrived at work Norman was all upset. He came out of the shanty barn stuttering so I could hardly understand him. "Caleb, I tried, I tried everything I knew, but one of the horses is so sick we can't work her."

"Easy, Norman! Take it easy!" I said, though scared myself. "Let's have a look."

Molly wasn't down, but she was leaning against the side of the shanty barn so hard I was sure it would collapse. "Look, Norman, get your brother and grab some planks from the mill. Lean them on the outside of the barn and brace some small logs against them. Maybe we can keep the barn from falling."

While Norman and his brother were doing that I slid in beside Molly. Her skin felt hot to the touch, her eyes were blurred, and her head was drooped down. I really didn't know what to do; I had never seen a horse that sick. Just as I came out of the barn, the Leclat crew started showing up.

Seeing Norman and his brother bracing the barn Mr. Leclat said, "What's up, Caleb? Your barn falling down?"

"No, Mr. Leclat," I answered. "It's Molly, and she is so sick she is leaning on the barn to stay on her feet, and I don't think we could get her up if she falls."

Mr. Leclat came right over saying, "Let me have a look, Caleb."

After looking Molly over he said, "You need a vet, Caleb. She has some kind of bad fever, and she needs help fast. I'll send one of my boys back to get one for her. She won't be working for a few days at least, so why don't you take one of my spares and hitch with your Roxie so the mill can keep running. We aren't going to do Molly any good standing around, so we might just as well get to work. Besides, you might run up quite a bill for the vet so you should keep the money coming in."

Norman and I had a real hard time with teaming Roxie up with a different horse. Norman used the same quiet voice and steady commands I had seen my father use when he first teamed Molly and Roxie. We had the team under full control by the time of our first coffee break. The vet showed up about then, and Norman said, "You go up, Caleb. I can manage to load most of what's in the pit, and Bruce can help me with what I can't."

I ran up to the barn where the vet was already in the stall with Molly. He prodded her some and opened her mouth spending a long time checking it. Finally he said, "If you are the owner I have bad news and good news. The bad news is this horse has a bad fever. The good news is that I have run into this several times in the last few months, and it is curable. She won't be any condition to work for a week or so, but after that she will be okay. We're not sure what causes it, but it doesn't seem to spread very easy, so the rest of the horses here are pretty safe. I have some medication that you'll have to force down her for a couple of days, but as soon as she starts eating you can just mix it with her grain."

I helped the vet force the medication into Molly, and he showed me what doses to give twice a day until it was all gone. Instructing me to call him if she didn't improve in a couple of days, he gave me a bill of thirty-five dollars. I only had twenty-one on me but he said he knew my father and could trust a Carney, and he drove off.

Norman was strangely quiet most of the day. After lunch I asked him if he felt all right. He said, "I'm awful sorry, Caleb, that I let the horse get sick. I'm not sure what I did wrong. I want to do good on this job because it helps for Bruce and me to have the shanty. If I lose this job then Mother won't have a place for us all."

I put my arm around his shoulders and said, "Norman where did you get the idea that you were at fault? The vet said there is some kind of fever going around with horses, and he doesn't even know how they get it. Whatever happened to Molly had nothing to do with anything you did."

"Are you sure, Caleb?" Norman asked "I have been so worried I was going to be fired. You remember I told you Bruce and I used to care for the neighbor's horses when we were young. One night one of his horses got real sick, and he had to shoot it. He blamed Bruce and me and fired us both, even though he wasn't paying us much it hurt. I really liked that horse and cried when they had to shoot it."

"You know what, Norman?" I replied. " I know that feeling. I injured a horse once because I was stupid, and it had to be shot. My guess is that you didn't have any more to do with his horse getting sick than you have with Molly's sickness. You certainly don't have to worry about getting fired, besides the vet said Molly will be all right in a week or so, and I am going to need your help in treating her."

After work Mr. Leclat came over and checked Molly, he said, Caleb, I have a stanchion and belt that I use sometimes on a sick horse so it won't lie down. Maybe we should use it on her for a couple of days."

Norman and Leclat helped me get Molly's medicine down, and we positioned the stanchion to help support her. Norman said, "Don't you worry, Caleb; I will be with her all night if I have to."

"I don't think you will have to do that, Norman. If you check her throughout the night a few times I think that will be enough," I answered.

I left the job thinking, *Without Norman staying at the shanty I would have to spend the night here myself.* I wondered even then if maybe it would be better if I came back later tonight. When I got home Mother was all excited she said, "Caleb, your father is doing so well that they are definitely going to allow him to come home next week. She said they didn't want him climbing stairs, so as soon as Homer, Jason, and you are here together I am going to move our bedroom down to the front room."

Emma came in saying, "Great news about Dad, huh, Caleb? Oh, by the way, there is some mail for you on the counter by the door."

I found the mail. It was from Shaq. I didn't expect to hear from him, at least not so soon.

Dear Caleb,

I know that what I am about to ask is an imposition, but with Etta I sometimes don't know where to turn, though, I must say that what ever you discussed with her the last couple of times you two were together has worked magic on her disposition.,
Anyway here's the story. Etta, despite her antics, did very well when she was in school. Before her blowup with her boyfriend, she had inquired about attending at a few colleges. She has just received an invitation to an all-girl college near you. They are offering her a terrific deal. I believe it has to do with some kind of quotas. They want her to come there for a three-day interview-orientation type of deal. The catch is the only inexpensive way for her to travel is a two-week deal. My imposition is, I was wondering if it was possible for you to have her stay at your house for the extra time. I know

*asking such a favor from a friend isn't a true Indian way, but I so want her
to get a different life for herself than where she is heading. I will understand
and still remain your friend if you can't do this, but I felt I had to try.*

Your Friend from Oklahoma,
Shaq

Man, Etta coming here! I still had dreams about her beauty and wondered
if I could have avoided her temptations if I had stayed in Oklahoma. Of
course, even then I had to keep remembering what Shaq had said about the
Indian way of dealing with someone who seduced one of their girls. The
trouble with Etta was the way she looked and behaved. She was the seducer,
though she had calmed down after the first time I went out with her and Shaq.
Lord knows what would have happened if we had met under different
circumstances. I knew that if I were going to invite her I would have to get
Mother's permission and prepare my family. *Lord, Homer is going to do a tailspin
when he sees her if she stays here. Emma, she is something different to consider. I
think most of her antics are just teenage bluff; still I wonder what effect Etta might
have on her. My head tells me the smart thing to do is tell Shaq we don't have room
for her. Yet my heart, or is that the rest of my body, is excited about seeing her again.*
I decide that it would be easier to discuss this with Mother when Homer and
Emma were present. At the supper table I said, "I have a special request that
I would like to talk to the family about right after Homer gets home from the
barn tonight."

Mother said, "If it concerns Jason and Nellie I have them in bed usually
before Homer gets in."

"That's all right, Mother; it isn't something that would concern them so
much it is as it will Homer and Emma. I really need a decision tonight so I can
answer the letter I received today."

Later that night after Homer came in, we all sat at the kitchen table, and
Mother said, "We are all here now, Caleb; I hope you don't have to leave or
anything. We are really going to need you to keep things going when your
father comes home."

"No, Mother it isn't that," I replied quickly. "The letter was from a friend
of mine who I worked with on Harry's jobs. He has a sister, Shaguietta, who
has been invited to interview at Smatters College over in Northborough. The
interview is only for a few days, and the best travel accommodations worked
out to be for two weeks. What Shaq was asking was if it was possible for her to
stay here the extra days."

"Well, Caleb, what's the big deal? You know we would welcome a friend of yours for anything like that," Mother said quizzically.

"Yah! both Emma and Homer chimed in. "What's so special that we have to have a meeting?"

Mother shushed them saying, "We all know Caleb well enough by now to know it's something more than having her come here that's bothering him, so let's hear him out."

Man, I was at a loss as how to explain Etta, but I had to try, so I said, "Etta, that's what everybody calls her, is part Indian and a very beautiful girl. She had a boyfriend that she had known since they started school in the first grade. About the time she graduated from high school there were some problems between her boyfriend and her family. Her uncle ran him off, or maybe it's better said, scared him off, and he left town and Etta's life for good. Because of this Etta rebelled and has been giving her family a hard time, especially about boys."

"Oh!" Emma exclaimed, "You mean like Beverly?"

"Wow!" Homer said, "and she is coming here?"

"No, not like that," I said with my fingers crossed. "It was more staying out late running with a crowd that upset her parents and embarrassing her brother every time she got a chance. I went out with her and Shaq, as a favor to him. We went to a dance hall, something like the one Banner's run for the kids in town, only for a little older group. The first time it was pretty much of a bust; she danced with most of the boys there and fought with most of the girls. I wasn't going to go again, but Shaq said she asked for me, so I went a second time. This time I got to talk to her a lot, and she stayed pretty calm. By the third or fourth time we went she was acting pretty much a lady. My guess is that Shaq thinks she will be all right with me and my family."

Mother said, "You go right ahead and invite her, Caleb; after all, if she is troubled, then being here might be a help to her and her family."

Homer said, "You got my vote, Caleb, especially if she is as beautiful as you say she is."

Emma said, "Mine too, Caleb—sounds like maybe I can learn a few tricks."

Mother gave them both a little slap, saying, "That's just a taste of what you'll get if either one of you acts up."

Later I wrote Shaq.

Dear Shaq,

I was surprised and happy to hear from you. The family is waiting anxiously to meet Etta. It would probably be helpful if you explain to her that country life is quite different from what she is used to. After all, here at the farm we still have an outhouse, even if it is at the end of the shed. I know there are many things here that might be shocking to her. It might be a good idea if she visits my sister Eunice, Harry's wife. She would be more than willing to talk to her about rural living. Please let me know what her schedule will be so I can make arrangements to pick her up. I would be free most evenings, but Mother can get her if she comes during a working day. She will love my mother because she knows all about young girls and how to respond to them.

I am working in my father's place at the sawmill and find it more enjoyable than building, though I miss you and some of the other men we worked with. Say hey to them for me. My hope is that maybe by next year I can return to Oklahoma and college. When that happens I will look you up.

Your friend from Massachusetts,
Caleb

I woke up next morning with a start. Lord, with all my excitement about Etta I forgot all about Molly. I had planned to go back that evening to check on her. I hurried breakfast and rushed to the mill. Norman was at the shanty barn when I arrived. I said, "How's Molly, Norman? I intended to come back last night, but ran into a little problem that needed a family conference and completely forgot her."

"Not to worry, Caleb," Norman answered. "She is doing better, and I stayed here at the barn all night with her in case she needed me."

"Norman, you're the luckiest thing that has happened to me since I came back from Oklahoma," I said putting my arm on his shoulder. "If anything had happened to Molly it would have devastated my father." I checked Molly out, and she didn't seem as warm as she was yesterday. I said, "I guess we better give her a dose of the medicine the vet left Norman."

He said, "I had Bruce come and help me do that just a little while ago, so we can wait until tonight now."

We hitched Roxie up with Leclat's spare horse and went to work at the mill. All day I tried to get through to Norman how much I appreciated his taking such good care of Molly and the rest of the horses. His only answer was it was no big deal, and he liked horses and was glad someone trusted him enough to let him work with them.

Molly got better everyday and now Norman was walking her around at least twice a day and sometimes more. After four days Leclat thought we should put her back to work, but Norman said no. I laughed and said, "I guess our resident vet knows best; he is the one who has been taking care of her."

That night when I got home Mother said, "Caleb, Eunice called today, and there is kind of a problem. Shaq took too long sending you that letter that there wasn't time to answer yours before Etta had to leave. He talked to Harry, and Harry had Eunice get in touch with Etta, and she will be on her way today. She is going directly to the school, and when she is done there she will call here. She made sure she had Eunice's number and ours too, in case she finds it hard to call us. Eunice said that as she understands it, she is to be at the school three days and allowed one more day after her orientation if she needs a room. That should make it a Saturday when she is to come here. I'm glad of that, because you can pick her up, besides I really don't want to have to drive that far, especially in Northborough."

Wow, I thought, *only five more days before Etta gets here! Man, I will never forget the first time I saw her, not only her beauty but the way she undulated down that walk wasn't something any red-blooded boy was going to forget.* I guess I must have had a gleam in my eye, for Mother said, "Now Caleb, I've been thinking about what you said the other night about Etta. I believe that you did the right thing in telling us a little about her, but I've been wondering if I am going to have to have a little talk with you about how to behave."

"You should not worry about me, Mother; it's true that Etta's looks are something that is exciting to most boys; but remember, I'm known as the virgin of Sterling."

I knew I had put my foot in my mouth by Mother's expression. After she had taken a deep breath she said, "Caleb, what kind of nonsense are you talking about? Why would anyone say such a thing?"

"I'm sorry, Mother," I stammered, "that just kind of slipped out. It's something the boys at the barn used to tease me with; it really doesn't mean anything."

"I tried to tell your father you were too young when you went to work with those boys. From what I hear they never got their minds very far away from the gutter they worked near. Your father would always say, 'Now, Helen, boys will be boys, and you have to let them grow up.' I suppose he had his point, though, because even with all the scrapes you got into it never seemed to cause any real harm. Nevertheless, let's make sure that Etta's visit doesn't turn into one of your escapades," she said as she turned away.

Mother's little talk made me see that I really needed to get my thoughts straight about Etta. *Josh, you never told me what it was going to be like.* What sex I had experienced was pleasing, but it never played on my mind like this before. At this stage the best I could hope for was that Etta wouldn't throw her sexuality around like she did the first night I met her.

Next day it was back to work and more trouble. Leclat had a horse sick and needed his extra horse that we had been using back. Norman was very upset that we had to put Molly back to work but we lucked out and there were mill problems so it was a low production day and Molly seemed to take being back to work okay. As it was a slow day for us Norman and I had more time to talk.

He said, "You know, Caleb, it seems as if you have something more on you mind than just Molly today."

"It's nothing to worry about, Norman," I answered. "It's just that a girl I knew in Oklahoma is going to be staying at our house for a week or so, and I'm concerned how it's going to work out."

We made a couple of trips out to unload the lumber before Norman said anything more. Then he said, "What's the trouble with that, Caleb? Is it the sex thing that's bothering you?"

I was looking at Norman, thinking, *Now where do I go with this?* when he said, "You know, Caleb, looking like I do, I learned very early on to control myself about that around girls. So I imagine that if she's someone you've been with you will have to have control too."

"What do you mean, Norman, been with?" I asked, trying to get a grasp on where this was going.

"You know, Caleb, did you to do it?" he said with a grin.

"No, no Norman," I exclaimed. "It's not like that; we didn't do it. I only went dancing with her a couple of times."

"Then what's the trouble, Caleb?" he said, laughing. "She fill you with such a desire that you can't get her off your mind? Must be some woman!"

I looked at him, startled, thinking, *If he can see that no wonder my mother was worried.* "Do you really think a woman can do that, Norman?" I asked

"Probably, Caleb, probably, but I think you know that better than I do right now," he chuckled

Luckily, Bruce came over to talk to Norman and they spent the rest of the day arguing about something so I didn't have to continue discussing sex with Norman. I got to thinking about Clem calling him a retard and I thought *he has a lot more sense about life than many people I knew.*

The next few days went faster than I had anticipated. Thursday night when Homer came home from the barn he said, "Caleb, I have to tell you something. I guess maybe I talked up your Etta more than I should have at the barn. I was just doing it to tease the boys about her being your raving beauty. Tonight Jennie called me aside and asked about Etta. She seemed upset, something about you going from one rock to another. Then she said, 'You tell Caleb that no matter what, he still has a good friend. What the hell, Caleb? Have you got your hooks into all the girls in Sterling?"

"No, Homer it isn't that. Jennie was a big help to me after we lost Josh, and we developed a dear friendship," I answered, wondering myself what this was supposed to mean. I had a great affection for Jennie, but I knew she was right that our futures weren't meant to be together. Still, this did give me an idea.

The next morning at breakfast with Homer I said, "You know what, Homer? Why don't you ask Jennie if she can get free to ride with me Saturday to pick up Etta?"

"You know what, Caleb?" Homer answered back. "I used to think you were a little bit crazy sometimes, but now I know it. I had planned to ask if I could go, but Old Golly Moses needs me in the field Saturday. I could understand taking Emma or even Mother, but Jennie? If the boys at the barn are right, there is more to you two than either of you ever let on, and you're taking her to get the girl you had in Oklahoma? Seems to me that you're just asking for trouble."

"Just ask her for me, will you, Homer? Never mind trying to evaluate me with the barn's gutter philosophy," I answered as I grabbed my lunch and left.

Friday night Homer said, ,Jennie wants to go Caleb, but she can't get free until after ten in the morning so she understands if you can't wait. Now you have an excuse to change your mind about putting the two of them together."

"I still want her to go, Homer, so I guess I'll drive down to her house and tell her myself," I said as I hurried out to the car.

Jennie wasn't home, so I left her a message that I would be there at ten Saturday.

The next morning I was at the milk house a little after ten. Jennie came hurrying out and got into the car saying, "It was good of you to invite me, Caleb. Listening to Homer this is some raving beauty you're picking up to day."

"Well, Jennie," I answered, "Etta is a striking girl, but I think Homer was just building something up for the benefit of the boys at the barn. I wanted you to come so she wouldn't feel uncomfortable being alone with me. You have to understand, even though she is part Indian she has been raised in the city, and country life will probably be a shock for her. I thought that as my good friend, you could help me fill her in a little."

"So that's it, huh, Caleb?" she replied. "I'm to come along as kind of a teacher. Gee, listening to Homer I thought I had to be here to rescue you from a beautiful, wild, seductive woman," she said laughing.

We were several miles out of Sterling before it dawned on me that Jennie had a strong odor of the barn about her. I was so used to it over the years that it wasn't anything I'd given any thought to before. Now I was unsure if I had really thought through what asking Jennie to go could mean. Though these thoughts put a little knot in my stomach, I pushed them aside and of course I didn't say anything. When we reached the college campus we had to ask a couple of times before we found the dormitory where Etta was staying. Since this was an all-girl college there were many pretty girls, and some of them were dressed pretty provocatively.

Jennie said, "So, Caleb, this is what it's like on a college campus? No wonder you and Jake were so excited about going off to college."

"I don't know about the college in Oklahoma, Jennie, because I never got a chance to attend when they were having classes, but I guess it's true that college students are a little more ahead of the curve than kids in the towns like we grew up in," I answered just as we found the right dormitory.

Etta was standing outside waiting with a half a dozen people—mostly boys—hanging around her. She was all that I remembered and then some, and I heard Jennie take in a breath when I pointed Etta out to her. I parked and said, "Come on, Jennie, let's go greet her."

Jennie said, "No, Caleb, please don't make me. I'm way out of my element here. Remember, I'm one of the barn girls. Can't you tell by the smell?"

I sensed her embarrassment and went alone, thinking, *Homer's right—I must be crazy to get caught in this.* I wasn't sure what Etta I was picking up, and here I was putting Jennie and myself in a potentially embarrassing situation.

Etta seemed to be having a good time, slightly flaunting her looks for the hangers-on. I hailed her, and she said, "Caleb, how good to see you again! Did you come to get me in a horse and buggy? I've been looking forward to this great country life that your sister Eunice told me about."

"No, Etta," I said trying a laugh, "I'd have had to stop and shoe the horses a couple of times if I had tried to drive them this far."

When I reached her she gave me a gentle hug and a little kiss on the cheek, whispering in my ear, "Get me out of here, will you, before I blow a fuse at this bunch of fawning fakers."

I took her bag and led her to the car and introduced her to Jennie as she was getting out of the car. Etta took Jennie's hand and said, "Let's both sit in the back; that way we can have a little girl talk without bothering Caleb."

As I drove off Etta said, "Do you know how lucky you are to have a boy like Caleb, Jennie?"

Jennie laughed and said, "Don't get the wrong idea, Etta; he's not my boy. I'm not sure he is anybody's boy, though there is a girl named Joan who he's chased after since first grade."

"I'll be damned, what kind of a girl would run away from Caleb?" Etta asked. "Why, when he was in Oklahoma all the girls were after him. Caleb, didn't you tell her how crazy I got with you the first time I met you?"

"Oh, come on, Etta," I said laughing, "you know very well it's a boy who goes crazy the first time he sees you."

"Well!" exclaimed Jennie, "Looks like I've been bamboozled again! Here I was thinking that I had to come and save Caleb from some beautiful, strange girl he was afraid to meet alone, when all the time you sound like you are old friends."

"I don't know about the old part of that, Jennie," Etta said, "but Caleb is a good friend who has helped me and my family immensely in the short time we've known him. You know what, Jennie? I think we've shook Caleb up enough. Tell me, is it true this town you come from is so backwards you just find a big tree for a bathroom? Shaq, he's my twin brother, told me Caleb wanted to warn me how backward it was here before I came. I think he forgot I was part Indian, and Indians lived in the woods for years before there were houses in America."

I held my breath for a full minute before both Etta and Jennie started giggling and then I realized I'd been had. While they were laughing together it occurred to me that Etta had sized up the situation and was handling things better than I would've ever thought. They joked and kidded about life and especially how clueless boys were about life.

I finally broke in saying, "If you two don't stop picking on me, I'm going to put one of you up front so I can whack you. Let me tell you, Etta, it's a good thing you're part Indian, because when Mother finds out how you're treating me, you might have to sleep in the woods."

They both laughed, and Jennie said, "I don't know about the woods, Caleb, but when your mother sees what Etta looks like, you and Homer'll probably be sleeping in the barn."

"Oh," Etta exclaimed, "is Homer as cute as Caleb, Jennie?"

"I don't know how I should answer that, Etta. Maybe not cuter, but he is known as the kissing champion of Sterling," Jennie said, laughing.

"Now, you two stop it," I said rather angrily. "Don't tell me, Jennie, that you have joined Homer's kissing club, too?"

"Why, Caleb, what's a girl to do when her main squeeze goes off to college? Join a nunnery?" she said among squeals of laughter from the back.

"Why, Jennie!" Etta said coyly, "Were you two lovers?"

My heart was in my throat wondering what Jennie was going to say, with all this hoopla going on between them. One thing for sure, Homer was right, even though this isn't what he thought it would be, it looks like I shouldn't have brought Jennie.

Jennie broke off her laughter saying, "Not quite, Etta, not quite. You see, Caleb is known as the virgin of Sterling, or more accurately, Beverly's virgin."

"Wow!" Etta exclaimed, "I have to meet this Beverly. What does she do—cast a spell over boys?"

I pulled the car over and stopped, saying, "That's it; if you two can't stop then I'm going to leave you here beside the road."

"Oh, Caleb, you don't want to do that! Why, Etta wouldn't be a minute getting a new ride with her looks. Still, we don't want you to be embarrassed by us coming home without you, so we'll be good. Besides, Caleb, I thought you brought me along to keep you safe from Etta," Jennie said with a knowing smile on her face.

Etta said, "We'll be good, Caleb. I didn't think our little fun would bother you so much. You know, I haven't had another girl to laugh like this with in a long time. I guess we did get carried away. Besides, Caleb, ever since I knew I was coming I've been dreaming what kind of tryst we'd have when we met. Then you show up with your not-quite lover. What's a girl to think?"

I started the car as both of them chorused, "We're really sorry, Caleb." But I could see them still giggling in the rear view mirror. We were almost into Sterling, and though I had planned to have Jennie come to the house with us I decided to leave her off first. Jennie asked to be dropped off at the barn. When we got there Etta said, "Is this where you work, Jennie? Can I go in and see what you do?"

I was just about to say we really didn't have time, when Jennie said, "Sure, Etta, it'll be fun."

We toured the milk house first, and I thought, *Well, this won't be too bad,* but as we came out Jennie said, "Would you like to see where Caleb and I met while we were strippers, Etta?"

"Well, I don't know, Jennie," she answered. "Do you strip as a team, and is this the wild country life I was warned of?"

Jennie laughed and said, "No, Etta, what we did was follow the automatic milking machines and strip whatever milk was left in the cows by hand."

I said, "Etta really isn't dressed properly to be walking around in the barn, Jennie."

"You're probably right, Caleb; maybe it's best we do it some other time," she said, pointing to Etta's shoes.

"You have to promise to bring me back, Caleb," Etta said, "or I'm going to go in now."

"Okay, I promise," I said, thinking, *If she goes in now she'd come out smelling like Jennie when I take her home.*

"I know what!" Jennie shouted, "she should come some night when we're milking."

"What a wonderful idea, Jennie," Etta answered. "That way I can see what this stripping is all about."

We were just about to leave when Old Golly Moses showed up saying, "I came to take a look at that separator that you been having trouble with, Jennie," he spotted Etta and said, "By Golly Moses, Jennie, you didn't bring me a new worker dressed like that did you?"

Jennie laughed and said, "No, Mister Muldon, she's a college girl doing a little slumming."

"Too bad. The boys would've liked to have her for a helper," he replied with a smile.

As we left the barn Etta said, "Caleb, I'm sorry if Jennie and I got too carried away, but I sensed a lot of tension in both of you. When Jennie started kidding you I thought it was best to keep it going. I hope all your friends are as nice as Jennie. She is so open and not at all like city girls. Most of them would even hide the fact that they had a job, while Jennie seemed more than happy to show me where she works. It must be great to be as sure of yourself as she seems to be."

I had never thought much about that aspect of Jennie; still when I think of our history together it kind of makes sense. The way she had handled our affair, with truth and honesty and with the unemotional hard facts, had allowed us to stay friends.

"I wasn't so much hurt, Etta, as I was scared. That wasn't the kind of talk that I'm used to from girls. You know, even though we had our last couple of nights out when you were amiable, there is still the history of the first time we met. I am glad you came, but I wouldn't be telling you the truth if I said I wasn't worried."

"Caleb, you have my solemn promise that I shall be the most demur little city girl you ever met all the time I'm here. I understand your worry, but I've given a lot of thought about our encounters, and I know now that I was wasting my life before. Since I owe you and Shaq for helping me see the light, I've promised Shaq and myself that my behavior will be exemplary while at the college and here," Etta said emphatically.

At the house Emma, Jason, Mother and Nellie were all waiting. Emma and Jason came out to the car to see if they could help with the suitcases. When Etta stepped out of the car, Emma exclaimed, "My God, Caleb, she is absolutely beautiful! You didn't do her justice when you described her."

For the first time since I picked her up, Etta was at a loss for words. So I said, "Meet my sister, Emma, Etta. You'll get used to her. She doesn't hide her emotions very well."

Etta took Emma's hand and said, "I am very pleased to meet you, Emma, and I think that was a very welcoming greeting."

I introduced her to Jason who, though quiet, looked as thunderstruck as Emma. We went into the house to meet Mother and Nellie. Mother was the soul of graciousness, but Nellie held her hand for what seemed like a long time before saying, "Welcome to the Carney household, and Emma was right; Caleb, didn't do you justice." As Nellie turned away, she gave me a quizzical look as if to say, *What do you think you're doing?*

Mother said, "Emma will show you your bed. She's going to share her room with you."

Etta said, "That sounds nice, Emma. We can get to know each other during my visit. Right now I need to use your—ah—facilities. Caleb has warned they are somewhat different from what I'm used to. Will I need help?"

Mother said, "Emma will show you."

Emma seemed just a little bit hesitant, so Nellie said, "Let me, Mother," while taking Etta's hand and leading her out to the shed.

Mother formed a big "Wow!" with her lips and said, "Caleb, I won't have any tom foolery about Etta from you boys, or else!"

Knowing that Mother's "or else" was a dire threat I could only answer, "Mother, you can rest assured that there won't be any," thinking, *It will be easier now considering Etta's promise.*

When Homer came rushing home to eat before going to the barn to do his milking, Etta, Nellie and I were touring the farm. Jason had just brought the cow in to milk, Etta was adamant that Jason show her how to milk a cow. It was a good thing she had changed because she was having a hard time managing the milk stool. Jason was up to the task though; he got a grain sack and sat down beside her, deferentially showing her how to use her hands. It took her a while, but Etta finally was able to produce pretty steady streams of milk. She was so proud and when she gave the job back to Jason, she gave him a little kiss on the cheek. Jason grew a little red but managed not to drop the milk pail during the exchange.

Afterwards Etta said, "Caleb, is that what they do at the barn when they are stripping?"

"They milk in the same way, Etta, except the milking machine gets the most of the milk before they milk the cows," I answered, thinking maybe now that she knows what it is that Jennie and Homer do, I won't have to take her to the barn as I promised.

We must have been in the hen house or at the pigpen when Homer came in because he came out of the house and was getting ready to grab his bike and leave when Etta came out of the cow stall. Homer just stood there holding his bike with one hand staring at Etta.

"I take it you're Homer," Etta said, giving a little swirl of her body. "Like what you see?"

I thought Homer would be at a loss for words but he said, "Pretty much, Etta, I was just evaluating to see if you could join my club, but maybe you're too old," as he was riding his bike out of the yard.

Nellie shouted, "Homer, you come back here," as he rode away.

Etta said, "It's okay, Nellie. I guess I had that coming. I'm sorry, Caleb, I won't let that happen again—old habits are hard to break sometimes."

"Don't worry Etta, Homer can hold his own most of the time. Besides, he'll soon be telling the boys at the barn about his wild encounter with the most beautiful woman they'll ever see. That's what they talk about most of the time down there: their conquests." I saw the light in Etta's eyes and thought, *Damn, I shouldn't have mentioned the barn to her.*

Etta said, "Tell me, Caleb, this milking thing, is that what Jennie does too, working right along with the boys?"

"Well, she fills in when they're short of help now, but she used to work every day in the barn, she and her sister, too, when I worked there." Just then Mother called us in to eat, saving me from any more questions.

After supper I drove Mother to the hospital. Etta stayed with Nellie and Jason and Emma. I called Emma aside before we left and told her to be vigilant when Homer got home. She laughed and said, "Jealous already, Caleb? I'll be here; don't worry. Nellie has already told me about Homer's and her meeting outside."

Mother was quiet most of the way to the hospital, but finally said, "Etta is sure some different than most girls, isn't she, Caleb?"

"I know she's different from girls around here, Mother, but you have to remember it isn't just that she's part Indian. All the girls in the city are much different than the girls in Sterling and the towns around here. They're brought up in and live in a completely different world than country girls do, though I have to admit that not many of them have Etta's looks," I said, kind of fishing for where Mother was going with this.

"I'd have felt much better if Hester or Eunice were still home. It's just that Emma still acts more like she was a young teenager than a full-grown young lady. Lord knows that I've tried with her, but she still has a rebellious streak and sometimes acts like she was still thirteen. I don't believe having her teemed up with a girl like Etta for the next nine or ten days is going to be helpful." Mother said with a sigh.

"I don't think you have anything to worry about, Mother. I believe that as soon as the newness wears off for Etta and the rest of us, you'll find her acceptable as a companion for Emma," I said as we pulled into the hospital parking lot.

I was pleasantly surprised to see Dad sitting up in a chair, though I'd heard he was making great progress, this was the first time I had visited him when he wasn't bedridden. He greeted us with a hearty, "Hello there," and a big smile, saying, "Caleb, it's good to see you. From what I've been hearing I thought you might have run off with some moving-picture beauty. It's good to know you haven't deserted your dear old dad."

Mother laughed and said, "I have to tell you, Henry, this Etta is sure to turn the heads of most young boys, but from what I hear we don't have to worry about our Caleb."

In the back of my mind I had this fear about what kind of trouble I had caused when I let it slip about being called a virgin to Mother. Now it looked like a good thing.

Dad just laughed and said, "Well, I guess I won't be any worry when I come home on Wednesday, Helen, since I'll still be on crutches for a few months."

I hadn't thought about Dad coming home at the same time as Etta was here, but it was evident that Mother had because she said, "Well, as long as she is safe from you I guess we can train her to be a nurse along with the rest of us. I believe she is a good student. I heard Jason had her milking in just a few minutes when he milked the cow tonight. From the looks of her I think she'd be better as a nurse getting an old man's blood flowing than she would at being a milk maid."

Dad said, "Let's take a walk down and see if we can get a drink at the cafeteria. I'm not sure if we can this late, but it's time for my exercise anyway."

I wasn't too surprised that Dad handled the crutches so well, but he seemed so much stronger now. Mother had told me he had been working hard to build up his strength so he could come home. The cafeteria was closed, but there was a coffee machine, so we sat in one of the waiting rooms and had coffee.

Dad asked, "Well, Caleb, how are things going at the job?"

I felt that Dad was strong enough to hear the truth, so I told him about Clem having a fit and leaving and about hiring Norman, and how Norman had been so good at caring for the horses. I held back telling him about Molly being sick, as it wasn't something he ever had to know.

Dad said, "It is just as well, Caleb. I was afraid you were going to have trouble with Clem. He's been going downhill more and more lately. A couple of times I was on the verge of firing him myself. I didn't do it because I felt sorry for what the world had handed him. Still, he was his own worst enemy, and I didn't see any way to help him if he couldn't see that."

It came over the intercom that visiting hours were over. We walked Dad back to his room where a nurse was waiting saying, "Say good night to your guests, Mister Carney. It's time for your leg massage, and we don't want them to hear you screaming."

Dad answered, "You know, you can't make me scream any more, Nurse Nell, or have you designed some new torture for tonight?"

As we were driving back to Sterling Mother said, "Caleb, I never knew you were having such a hard time at work. You never said anything. I can't imagine that Clem doing anything like that to our family after all we have done for him."

"You know, Mother," I answered, " I stayed home to help, and it wouldn't have been very helpful if you had to worry about my job as well as about Dad. I'm not angry with Clem; he has some personal problems that he is finding hard to deal with. The truth be known, Mother, I am better off with Norman, and he even costs us less than Clem."

Mother was quiet most of the rest of the way home. Just before we got to Sterling she said, "Caleb, I don't want to belabor the fact, but I really sense there is more to Etta than what you've told us."

"Not really, Mother, I couldn't tell you much more about her than I have. I worked all the time I was in Oklahoma with her brother, and he asked me to go with him and his sister to a dance. I thought he was just being nice because I was a stranger there. We went out together only three times. I have to admit, the first time was pretty bizarre, but after that, things were pretty normal. I guess it was because she was still having a hard time with her family because of her boyfriend that first time. I think that Shaq, that's her brother, thought I might help out with her situation. I really didn't want to go with them the second time, but Shaq seemed so desperate that I went anyway, and it worked out okay. I know she is strange to us, but I think she sincerely wants this visit to go well, so I don't think we have to worry," I answered hoping desperately that I was right.

"I hope so," Mother answered. "Now it looks like your father is going to come home on Wednesday. I know you can't stay home from work, but I might need some help."

"I was worried about that too, Mother, until I saw how well he was doing with his crutches," I answered. "I think you'll be all right if you bring Homer with you. The Muldons can spare him for a day; besides, he'll be in school the week after next, so they will already have planned for him to be gone." Saying that, the thought crossed my mind that that way Homer won't be alone with Etta. *Whoa, Caleb, get a hold on yourself. Stay away from that kind of thinking; things are going to be hard enough for you.*

When we arrived home, Etta, Homer, Jason, Emma, and Nellie were all sitting in the living room playing a board game. As we came in Etta got up and said, "Mrs. Carney, you have some of the nicest children I ever had the opportunity to visit with. Not only has Jason showed me how to milk a cow, Nellie has been teaching me a new board game. Emma and I are having a grand time talking about our experiences, and Homer has been the perfect gentleman while explaining how a big diary farm works. You must be very proud of your children."

"I usually am," Mother replied. "I'm especially pleased that they've made you feel comfortable here. I was worried with all I had to do with their father in the hospital how I would have time to make you feel welcome."

"You don't have to give me another thought, Mrs. Carney," Etta said. "Think of me as another one of the children, and if I step out of line you should box my ears too or do whatever it is that made your children behave so well."

I thought, *Watch it, Etta; don't pour it on too thick. Mother is very good at judging people.* Looking at Mother I could see that she was pleased with what she had heard, so I was relieved. Homer had a kind of puppy-dog look, like when it's trying to please its master.

We all sat around talking for a while until Mother said, "I think it would do all of us good if we went to church tomorrow. We have so much to be thankful for with your father coming home and Etta being here."

We all knew that when Mother expressed herself that way it really was an order, so we didn't have to respond, but Etta said, "That's a great idea, Mrs. Carney; it would give me a chance to meet more country people. I am finding it very exciting being with this family."

Sure, I thought, *she's excited; wait until the men at the church see her; then we'll see excitement.* Instead I said, "Good idea, Mother; it will give Etta a chance to experience more of what country life is like while she is here."

Emma said, "I think it's time for us girls to get our beauty sleep. Are you coming, Etta?"

Homer and I went upstairs shortly after they left, and as we entered the room, Homer let out a deep breath saying, "Man! Caleb, you danced with her? It must've tingled your nerves some!"

"I admit, Homer, the first time I saw her it was a pretty traumatic shock, but after you get by that, she is just a girl," I answered.

"Well, she might be just a girl to you now, but to me that's some girl." Homer sighed as he climbed into bed.

Sunday at church Etta spent her time with Mother, Emma and Nellie and though I saw some eyebrows raised, especially by the women in the congregation, Etta was the essence of a lady. She was talking to everyone and asking questions about life in the country and telling them how lucky they were not to have to live in a city. Mrs. Banner was so taken with her; she asked Mother if the family could join her for dinner at the Inn. Mother was hesitant at first but seeing that the girls were excited about it she agreed. I told them that I had promised Norman I would be over to the job site Sunday afternoon to check on a sick horse, but I thought it was a great idea for Etta to go.

After we arrived home, Etta waited for me as I parked the car and said, "Caleb, are you avoiding me, or is that just an excuse not to be with all these women?"

"Now, you know I wouldn't do that, Etta. I just felt you were comfortable enough on your own so I could take care of some things at work," I said, thinking, *I know Norman doesn't need me, but it's best that we're apart as much as possible while she's here.* "Etta, if you're uncomfortable with my family, I can rush to the job after dinner if need be."

"No, no, Caleb, I'm not at all uncomfortable with your family. In fact, so far I am very impressed with all of them," she replied, "it's just, I kind of got the feeling today that you were avoiding me."

"The truth is, Etta," I said, carefully choosing my words, "I believe that we should be careful not to let anyone think we're too close. My family thought at first we were an item, and that was a worry for them somehow."

"An item, Caleb?" she questioned. "Don't you mean lovers? I know now after being here, that that is out of the question for us, but I have to admit the thought crossed my mind after the second time we went out."

"Oh, damn! Etta, don't even hint at something like that. I don't think you have any idea what a girl like you arouses in a boy and the thoughts they sometimes get just seeing you. It would be bad news around here if everyone started to think you were my girl; you must understand that," I answered

"I understand, Caleb, and don't worry. I'll keep my promise to you, and it isn't hard, because I really, truly like your family, and I'm sure that there are enough things for me to learn here to keep me occupied, even without you," she said, walking into the house.

I knew that I didn't really have to go see Norman but I didn't really cherish the idea of spending all day with Etta and the family. It wasn't that I didn't want to be around her, I did, it was just I felt safer if I wasn't. Oh, damn, I can't even think straight. Maybe if she hadn't thrown herself at me so wildly the first time we met my emotions might be different. I left in the truck so Mother could have the car. As I was going through town I spotted Jennie so I stopped.

She said, "Caleb, I didn't expect to see you again until Etta left. Why, I'm surprised you even stop to talk to a Sterling girl anymore."

"Look, Jennie," I replied, "I didn't think this up, you know. I'm only doing a favor for a friend back in Oklahoma. Etta and I are not an item, and if you were my friend you would be more helpful. I have to go back to the mill. Would you care to go with me?"

"I would be glad to, Caleb, on two conditions, one—that you get me back in time for the evening milking, and two—that you are not expecting me to cure any pent up desire you might have," she said with a low laugh.

"I'll get you back in time, Jennie, and you have never needed anyone else to help me have a desire for you that way. You should know me well enough by now to know I will keep my promise. Besides," I said, "you certainly don't fear Beverly's virgin, do you?"

Jennie got in the truck, and we went to the mill site. Norman had everything under control and seemed surprised to see me, saying,"What's up,

Caleb? Don't you trust me? I would think by now you would know I am capable of taking good care of the team. I even have a job on weekends taking care of Leclat's teams."

Jennie said, "Don't worry, Norman. Caleb is only here to avoid being somewhere else. He has this beautiful girl staying at his house, and he can't keep his mind on anything else when she is around. So he is escaping by coming here as an excuse. I just happened to be an afterthought."

"Oh, yeah," Norman said, "he did say he thought having such a beautiful girl around was going to be hard on him. I tried to tell him that beauty was just a mind thing, and a girl is a girl, beauty or not."

"Jennie!" I shouted, " I thought we were to be friends, and I picked you up because I needed a friend. You made a mockery out of our friendship when we picked Etta up; now you're at it again."

Norman looked at me kind of dumbfounded and said, "Caleb, you know, I'm no expert on girls, but any damn fool should know when you put two beautiful women together with a man they both like it, means trouble for him."

Jennie laughed and said, "I'm sorry, Caleb. I'll be more careful before I shoot off my mouth again, but you know there's a grain of truth in what Norman says. As much as we have been to each other, I bet you never described me in words as beautiful as you use talking about Etta. Come on, Norman, let's take a walk and let Caleb cool off."

Norman and Jennie took a walk down to the mill site and left me there at the barn. I went in to check Molly out thinking, *sometimes I can't believe how dumb I can be.* Jennie and I might have started out being close because of our grief at losing Josh but it had become much more than that before Jennie decided it had no future. Girls! Ever since my onset of puberty they have made my life an enigma. I certainly wasn't brought up to believe that their biggest contribution to men was sex. Still that is my prevailing thought every time I see a pretty girl. Josh never said whether you grew out of this or not. Maybe that's what his poem about tempering fire was about, now how did that go?

Passion's fire has slowly ashed
And grayed the imposing will
If only they had worked to wait for love
The fire would be burning still

Passion's fire can temper love
And help to make it true
But fire without the shield of love
Can just make dust of you

True love is not about to lose
And be cast at passions feet
But it's true of life, when in love
Passion you shall meet

Conquered passion, is loves tempered strength
Which banks the fires so well
Well, passion with just lust not love
Is a devil's trip through hell

I know that Edgar had told me I had to grow up to be myself and stop thinking I needed to be Josh. Still I would be foolish not to use his legacy as a learning tool.

Later as we were driving back to Sterling, Jennie said, "Caleb, I didn't meant to upset you, but you have to understand that experiencing someone like Etta isn't easy for me."

"I know, Jennie," I said. "I'm sorry about blowing up. I was hoping when I saw you today you could help me plan something we could do while she is here."

"Well, she seemed to really want to see what we do at the barn. I know the boys will go ape, but she is more than capable of handling that. I know how hard that might be on you, so I was thinking, why not let her come in with Homer one evening. We know Homer will love that, and since he is at the barn before you get home it will look all right. You could, of course, come to the barn on your way home if you think you have to. Oh! Something else I was thinking," Jennie said with a twinkle in her eye. "You said you took her dancing. Banner's still opens the dance hall for young folks on Friday nights. I bet she would be a big hit there. You really have to stop thinking about just yourself in this, Caleb. Let's show her what life here really is. You know she seemed to be enjoying herself when I showed her the milk house. I believe we can impress her more by being ourselves than any put-up job."

"Okay, Jennie. I see the purpose in what you're saying. So let's start with the barn thing, as soon as I can get it set up with Homer. I like the idea. Thank you, Jennie," I said giving her a little kiss.

The family spent a late evening at the Banners, so I was all alone when I got back home. I checked to see if all the chores were done and went for a walk around the property. Looking under the barn as I came back I remembered the horse, Old Tom, and how I had caused his demise by trying to be a great teamster like my father. Funny how you think you have put those things out of your mind, then something you see causes them to come rushing back.

It was almost dark when Mother came driving back with the family and she said, "You should have come and joined us when you got back, Caleb."

"I would have, Mother," I answered, "but I knew it was after supper had been served, and you know Mrs. Banner. She would have insisted on feeding me, and that would have been uncomfortable for everyone."

Etta, Emma, and Nellie hurried into the house all excited about something they had planned. Mother said, "Jason, you see to the animals," as she followed the girls into the house.

I told Jason I had taken care of everything and asked if he had seen Homer. He said, "Homer had to go the barn right before we ate. Seems that Arny wounded himself cleaning his rifle. Damned if I know how he could have done that!"

I told Jason I thought I better check and see how bad it was. "You tell Mother I've gone to the barn."

They had finished all the milking when I got there, but Jennie was still in the milk room. I went in saying, "Jason just told me about Arny. Is it bad?'

Jennie said, "No, he isn't hurt bad, just nicked in the shoulder by the bullet. I told him he was getting too careless with that gun. He'll be good as new in a couple of days. He was more scared than hurt."

I hung around until Jennie had finished cleaning up the milk room and gave her a ride home. We sat in the car for a while at her house talking.

When she left she kissed me warmly. "Poor Caleb; your libido must be racing all the time lately. If I wasn't so envious I would almost feel sorry for you," she said as she got out of the car.

I drove around a while before heading home. When I got there Etta and Emma were in their room, and Jason and Nellie were already in bed. Mother was in the living room.

She asked, "Was Arny hurt bad, Caleb? I understood it was just a flesh wound. And how is Molly? I didn't realize she was sick. You know, Caleb, you are going to have to learn to share with your mother what's going on in the business so I can help."

"Weren't nothing important, Mother," I answered. "She caught a bug of some kind. The vet said he had seen more than a dozen horses like that in the last few weeks and knew right away what to do for her. We rested her for a few days and used one of Leclat's spare horses, but Molly is fine now and back at work. I just felt I have been putting too much on Norman's shoulders; that's why I had to go back and check today."

"Well, it's too bad you couldn't have been with us today. Your Etta just seems to fit in naturally everywhere we go, and she's such a beauty that the men can't keep their eyes off her. I still have a feeling that there is more to her being here than meets the eye. You're not holding back some big surprise for us are you?" she asked.

"Mother, the only surprise is that she is here at all, as far as I am concerned. It really is just as I told you. We met a couple of times, and I really didn't think I would ever see her again. I'm glad you find her easy to take, Mother, because her brother was very good to me when I first started working for Harry. And Mother," I said as I left to go upstairs, "she is not *my* Etta; she is the sister of a dear friend of mine."

Homer was already sleeping, so I couldn't talk to him about Etta going to the barn with him. I hadn't thought too much of the idea at first, but after thinking about it I could see it had its possibilities.

Homer and I left about the same time in the morning, but I didn't want to broach the subject with Mother around. No telling what Homer would say at first. Things went well at work the next day, though Norman was insistent that I was making a mistake in not seeing that Jennie wanted more than friendship from me. That night Emma, Etta, and Nellie went to a church group for young girls. I would have liked to be a fly on the wall at that meeting. I had a chance to talk to Homer about Etta going to work with him, and he was ecstatic and practically danced a jig, singing, *I'm in heaven, I'm in heaven.* I reminded him that it wasn't heaven; it was a smelly old barn, and Jennie was to meet him outside and walk in with him.

Just before we went to sleep, he said, "Caleb, I know how hard this all is for you with Dad, your college, and all. So I think you should know that we are all very proud of you. You know, when Josh left he said we would have you here for us, and when it has really counted, you have been. So thank you not just for loaning me Etta, but for being my big brother."

"Thank you, Homer. Being compared to Josh is quite a pickup," I answered, "but Etta's not mine to loan. You'll find out she is her own person."

The next night the girls had something else planned so Homer made a date with Etta for Thursday night. Dad was coming home Wednesday, and he wouldn't be working anyway. Homer came home from work later all upset; he hadn't mentioned to Old Golly Mosses that he needed Wednesday off, and the Muldon's had planned to move their young stock from their summer pasture to the pasture at the Coors barn before the summer help had to go back to school. They were already short handed and were afraid they might have trouble driving the cattle without him.

Mother said, "I probably can handle it alone, Homer; don't be so upset."

The girls were just coming in when I said rather sharply, "No, Mother! Dad's more important than Muldon's damn Heifers."

Emma said, "What's wrong? Something happen to Dad?"

"No, no," Mother answered, "it's just that the Muldon's need Homer tomorrow, and we had planned for him to help get Dad home."

"And that's just the way it's going to happen. Since when have the Muldons taken precedence here over our family?" I said loudly

Mother said, "Caleb, you know the Muldons have been good to us, and the money you, Josh, and Homer have earned there have always been a big help to us as a family, so it is only fair we consider them."

Etta said, "I don't want to butt in where I'm not wanted, Mother Carney, but you know Emma and I could go with you. We are big girls, and besides I worked as a candy striper at a hospital in Oklahoma so I can probably be as much help as Homer."

Mother laughed and said, "You know, they say the simplest solution can often be seen from the outside. Etta, thank you, and you can drop the 'Carney' and just call me 'Mother' if you wish."

Etta walked over to Mother and gave her a big hug saying, "I would be more than pleased to be your daughter, Mother, but I don't want you to be stuck having to explain having such a dark-skinned daughter. So I will stick to Mrs. Carney in public."

We sat around talking until it was bedtime. Mother went up, and Emma said, "You ready, Etta?"

"No," Etta said, "I'll be up in a minute. I need to talk with Caleb. Well, Caleb, how am I doing? You know I don't think I need you to plan everything, so we are never together. It kind of hurts when you act like you don't trust me."

"Please, Etta, don't think I planned everything that has been happening. I did suggest to Homer you go to the barn with him because by the time I get home and eat, they are all done, and besides, you will be with your cohort, Jennie, so I'm more worried about Homer," I said, thinking I was getting to see

Mother's hand in some of the nights that Etta was busy elsewhere. "I tell you what, Etta, they opened the dance hall at Banner's for the young group Friday nights. Would you like to go to that with me?"

"Yes, yes," Etta said, "but there is something else. Nellie has talked to me about the magic of your mountain, and I have read some of Josh's verses about it. Before I leave, I would like it if I could go there, just you and me."

Oh, boy, Etta and me on the mountain! I thought as I mumbled, "I'm sure we can work that out too, Etta."

Etta crossed the room, brushing against me lightly, and gave me a little kiss as she left for her room, saying with a smile, "Now we don't have to worry anymore, Caleb, since we're practically family.

Wednesday when I got home Dad was there and he was excited and happy to be back. Mother was laying down the law to him about what the doctors said he could or could not do. She said, "Henry, you have to promise me that you are not going to do something dumb like you did before. The doctors said you have to have patience. Your body had so much damage it is going to be a long recovery period. So the better you are at doing only what you are supposed to do, the quicker you will be able to return to work. That means getting your body healthy enough so they can re-operate on that leg. We don't want another accident like you had when you were home for the wedding."

I thought I had better change the subject here, because if Dad found out his accident was what saved his leg, there would be no holding him down. So I said, "Boy, Dad, am I glad to see you home! Now these women will have somebody to pick on besides me."

Dad laughed and said, "I don't know about you, Caleb, but with women like your Etta around I wouldn't be complaining. You know, when I left the hospital she took over as well as any nurse I ever had there. I tried to hire her, but Mother said we didn't need a nurse, and Etta said Oklahoma was calling."

"Well, Dad, she does have to get back if she is going to go on in school. She has decided that Smatters College near here is too snooty for her, so she has decided to go to a college in Oklahoma. Besides," I said laughing, "if we provide you with nurses like her you might not want to get better."

Emma came in and gave Dad a big hug saying, "Don't tell me Etta's got you drooling over her too, Dad?"

Mother said, "Emma, you watch that mouth of yours, and get out there and get the supper on the table. I tell you, Henry, that girl needs a good spanking sometimes."

Dad laughed and said, "If she does, Helen, I think we waited to late to do it. I certainly am in no shape to do it now."

After supper we sat around talking. Everybody was thrilled to have Dad back with us. Etta beguiled us with stories of Oklahoma and how it was on the Indian reservations when she and her family went to visit relatives there. Nellie spent most of the evening holding Dad's hand or rubbing his back. Jason was full of stories about things that had happened around our little farm since Dad had been gone. All in all it turned into an enjoyable evening for us all. When Mother announced it was time for Dad to get to bed, we all hated to leave.

Etta asked Mother if she needed help with Dad's bandages or getting him to bed. Mother laughed and said, "I hope not, Etta. I think he's had enough excitement for one day."

Etta, Emma, and I were in the living room when Homer came in. He went in to see Dad and helped Mother get him into bed, then came out to see us. He said, "You ready to take over for me tomorrow night, Etta? I told the boys that I wouldn't be in tomorrow night but had found a replacement. Jennie is going to introduce you around as my replacement before I come in."

Emma said, "My God, Etta, you aren't going to the milk barn with those gutter rats are you? Mother would never let me go there."

"Now there was a problem that we had never thought of," I said. "Mother probably is going to have a fit when she hears about this."

"No, it's not." Etta said, "I mentioned it to Mother, and she told me that it was a dirty, smelly place when you're not used to it and that some of the boys that worked there are pretty crude sometimes. I told her about meeting Jennie and how I really wanted to see where and how she, Caleb, and her boys had worked. She told me that I had proven to her I was capable of handling things on my own, and if I really wanted to do this I should."

Homer said, "You know, Emma, three of your brothers have worked there. Are you calling us gutter rats?"

"Oh, Homer, you know as well as I do," Emma replied, "that most of the so-called barn boys have bad reputations, and they get called a lot of things."

Etta who had been taking all this conversation in with a grin exclaimed, "So, that's why they call Caleb Beverly's virgin?"

Emma gasped, and Homer started stuttering, "It wasn't me, Caleb; it wasn't me."

Etta held her hand over her mouth saying, "I'm sorry; it was just something Jennie said to me about Caleb, and I was wondering where it could have come from."

I wasn't sure but if I were to have to bet on it I wouldn't have bet she was sorry from the glint in her eye. So I said, "Look, all of you, I don't know how this became public gossip. It was just a nickname the barn boys gave me when I worked there, and no, I don't know why it still is said. One thing though," I said as I headed upstairs, "I don't want to hear it used around here again. Do you all have that?"

When I got home from work Thursday night Dad called me in and said, "Caleb, did you know about this foolishness of Etta going to work in Homer's place tonight?"

"It's okay, Dad; it's just Homer's little joke on the boys," I said. "When I picked Etta up at the college Jennie Sledge was with me, and she talked about the barn and how I had worked there. Etta asked if she could come watch sometime. What could I say? I couldn't very well say it was no place for girls when Jennie was still working there. Etta ended up making us both promise that we would make sure she did before she left. I wouldn't worry about her, Dad; she is very capable of handling those boys at the barn."

"I was more worried that Homer had mixed up in some tom foolery down there than I was her," he said. "If my memory hasn't failed me, it seems that you got in your share of mischief when you worked there. More than once I had to talk your mother out of making you quit."

"You don't have to worry about Homer, Dad; he was always a little smarter than me about staying out of trouble," I answered, "Besides this is something that Jennie planned, not Homer."

I was tempted to rush down to the barn right after supper, but I knew Homer wouldn't be pleased with me if I did, so I waited impatiently for them to get home.

Nellie came over and held my hand for a few minutes and said, "Caleb, remember our little talk on the mountain before you left this spring? I have a premonition. Do you want to know what I feel?"

Lord I wasn't sure if I should let her talk or not, but remembering her advice about it, I said, "Am I going to like it or not, Nellie?"

"I'm not sure myself, Caleb, but I have this very strong feeling that you and Etta are going to become very, very close somehow. I wish I could see it a little better than that, but every time I'm in the room with you two I feel that very strongly."

Homer and Etta came in just in time to keep Nellie from getting any deeper into her feelings with me. They were both laughing, and Homer said, "Caleb, I wish you could have been there when Jennie walked in and said,

'Hey, everyone, I want you to meet Homer's replacement.' John was just moving his milking machine to the next cow. When he saw Etta he dropped the milk container, and milk went everywhere, and he just stood there, bug eyed. Arny couldn't see us, but as he came behind John, cursing at him for spilling the milk, he just stopped in his tracks and stared with his mouth wide open. Leon Muldon, who had come to run the other milk machine, came into the barn and said, 'My God, what the hell is going on here?' Then he turned and looked at Etta, and there they were all three of them, staring. Finally John stammered, 'Why didn't you tell us, Uncle Leon, that you had hired someone like—like—like that?'

"'Hired someone like that! Are you crazy?' Leon shouted. 'I'm not that dumb. You boys wouldn't get anything done with her around.

"Etta smiled and said, 'Oh, that's too bad, after I have practiced so hard for this job.'

"Leon said, 'Hired or not, I can't believe you're able to be a stripper.'

"John said, "Man, I can believe it. I can surely believe it. It would be my wildest dream.'

"'Okay, okay,' Leon said. 'The joke is over. Jennie, you get her out of here, and you boys get busy.'

"'Oh, that's sad,' Etta purred. 'I did so want to be successful in my first job.'

"I thought that was the end of the fun, but Leon said, 'All right, all right! Grab a pail and start stripping.'"

Homer continued, "I watched as Etta following Jennie's lead, went and got a pail and a milk stool, and man, to my surprise, started milking."

Etta said, "That was so much fun that I want to go back again."

"No way, Etta!" Homer said. "Leon told me if I ever did anything like that again, he would fire me."

Mother came in to see what all the laughing was about. They told her how Etta had actually milked several cows. Mother laughed and said, "So that's why you went with Jason every time he milked the cow, Etta? That must have been a sight to see you working with those boys. Homer, you go in and talk to your dad. He seemed upset about you today."

Etta said, "Caleb, let's take a little walk. I need some advice about tomorrow night."

We went out and walked across the field. Etta at first held my hand, then let it go, saying, "You know, Caleb, things are so different here. It has been so much fun getting to know your family and friends, I almost wish I could stay. Don't get excited—I said almost. I was just wondering if the boys I meet tomorrow are anything like what I met tonight?"

"Not all of them, Etta; but if those boys know you are going to be there, they will probably come too. Still, from what Homer said, you can handle them," I said with a laugh.

"You know, Homer said that back when you worked there, there was always something going on. All kinds of parties, even with the girls that worked there, and some of them were drinking parties. How did that go? Is that when you got your nickname?" Etta said, taking my hand again.

"Damn it, Etta! Didn't I tell you I didn't want to hear that again?" I said yanking my hand away. "Let's get back to the house before Mother starts calling us."

Back at the house I went to my room, angry with myself for the way I acted, but glad I knew enough to get back to the house before she got to me.

The next day at work I was so preoccupied with going to the dance that night that Norman finally said, "Did you come to work today Caleb or just send your body?"

"I'm sorry, Norman," I answered, "I am just tied up with everything that is going on at home."

"It's that girl again, isn't it?" Norman chuckled. "Why the hell don't you just ask her to go to bed with you and get over it?"

"Damn you, Norman," I shouted, "What makes you think you know so much about what I'm going through?" I saw the stricken look on his face and said, "I'm sorry, Norman; you're probably right, but is it that evident?"

Norman said, "Maybe not to everyone, but Jennie told me that your Etta was the sexist thing on wheels, and she expected you might have a heart attack if she stayed around too long. So it's my guess that's what is on your mind; how much longer is she going to be here, anyway?"

"She has to catch a train in Northborough at four on Sunday. Norman, do you think you can put up with me that long?" I asked

"Hell, you're not planning on hiding here 'till then, are you? If I was you I would throw me out of the shanty and bring her right over here until at least train time." Norman laughed.

"Damn you, Norman. That's just what I would like to do if I thought she would come, which she wouldn't," I answered, thinking of course that Mother would have a thing or two to say about that.

"You know what? That girl, Jennie, thought Etta, had the hots for you, and it bothers her quite a bit. Come to think of it, if that Jennie was mine, I would be careful what I let show about other girls," Norman said earnestly

"Why is it everybody refers to Etta or Jennie as *my* girls? I don't have any girl as mine right now, and I'm not sure I ever will," I shouted.

Norman said, "I guess we better just shut up and get back to our work."

Riding home that night I thought how close Norman had been to the truth. I was letting my desire tear me apart, when all I had to do was ask if help was available. The biggest trouble with that was I was afraid the answer either way would be too much for me. Well, at least he hadn't guessed how mixed up my emotions really were. *Lord how I wish I could run to Josh; he always had the answers. Why, God, why did you have to take him?*

When I got home the girls were all excited about going dancing. Emma who had gone a few times had quit going but said she wasn't going to miss tonight. Homer was going to rush home from the barn and join us later. Nellie had even asked to go but Mother said no.

Dad said, "Looks like your big night, Caleb. Aren't you afraid the competition will get too intense?"

I laughed and said, "Dad, there are going to be three of us Carneys there. You know there isn't much that can compete with that."

He laughed and said, "You may be right, Caleb, but I expect every available boy in town to be there tonight and some that aren't; don't you?"

"That's why I am bringing my troops, Dad," I said as I was leaving. "You have to remember that Mother has made Etta one of the family, too."

That night when Etta, Jennie, Emma and I entered the dance hall, there was a split moment when everything except the music stopped. Then you could see the girls urging the boys back into motion. It was one of those moments in life that always stay indelible in your memory.

Reilly who happened to be home that week must have heard from the barn boys about Etta because he stepped forward and said, "Caleb, aren't you going to introduce me to your lovely friend?" After the introductions, addressing Etta he said, "Would you do me the honor of dancing with one of Caleb's oldest friends?"

Etta held out her hand, and they swirled out onto the floor. I thought he must mean oldest in age because I didn't feel too friendly to him right then.

Jennie said, "Well, Caleb, are you going to spend the night glaring at the other boys or dance with me?"

Remembering what Norman had said about Jennie's feeling towards me I said, "I'm sorry, Jennie; it was just the shock of seeing Reilly after all this time."

"C'mon, Caleb, I'm Jennie, remember?" She said seriously, "You haven't stopped drooling since we picked Etta up. When are you going to be man enough to do something about it?"

"That's not true, Jennie," I answered, surprisingly adding, "and if it was, what would you have me do?"

"Ask her, for God sake, and get it off your mind," she said, swinging me around, "Or do you have to wait for a girl like Beverly who asks you?"

"You know damn well, Jennie, that Beverly isn't the only girl that asked me," I said loud enough to cause a flurry with the dancers close to us.

Jennie slowed and suddenly held me tighter saying, "Whoa! Caleb I'm sorry, let's just keep dancing and forget what we were saying."

We danced together until there was a pause in the music and as we went to the side a boy that I didn't recognize asked Jennie to dance. I thought it wasn't hard to forget about Etta when Jennie held me that close and warm. By the time I located Etta she was already dancing again with Reilly. I was looking around for Emma when a girl vaguely familiar tapped me and said, "Aren't you even going to ask Little Betty to dance?"

Trying to place her I said, "Why, Betty, I heard you were in town, and I was looking for you so I could ask you."

However little Betty was, she certainly wasn't little in development. Though short, she had a striking figure. We danced quietly for a few minutes when she said, "Caleb, I'm crushed. You don't remember me, do you?"

"I'm sorry, Little Betty. I have been raking my memory, and I can't seem to place how I could have met one as cute as you and forgotten her. Shall we play fifty hints, or would you like to fill me in?"

"Think: best friend, Karl Hart, Little Betty," she said, as we whirled around the dance floor.

I held her away from me and took a good look at her face and said, "Of course, Karl's little sister. Forgive me, Betty, but you know there is a big difference between that little girl I knew and the one I'm holding in my arms right now."

She laughed and said, "As long as I'm finally in your arms, I can forgive you. I have had a crush on you since ever since you and Karl got together, but you never seemed to notice."

The night seemed to fly by. I danced a couple of more dances with Betty and a couple of other girls that I couldn't recall from before. They would just show up and say, "My turn, Caleb." I couldn't ever seem to catch Etta, so off I would dance with them. Emma even caught me once, saying, "Quick, Caleb; let's dance," she needed to avoid someone who she evidently didn't want to dance with. Jennie and I danced again, and she held me close and personal during the slow dances but finished each time with, "Just as friends, Caleb, just as friends." My last dance with Betty; she danced with abandon and with a little more wiggle than was called for.

She asked, "Can we date sometime, Caleb? Do a movie or something?"

I told her, "I think that would be fun when you're old enough, Betty."

She laughed and said, "Caleb, you are hopeless, aren't you? I'm almost as old as you. Think about it. Karl was a couple years older than you, and I was only about three years younger than him. Now can we date?"

"It looks like I'll be home for quite a while, Betty, so I'll look you up. I think it would be fun." Just as we finished the dance, they announced last string of dances for the night.

As I turned away from Betty, Etta was right there, saying, "Introduce me to your friend, Caleb."

I introduced them, and Etta said, "Hope you don't mind, Betty, but it is my custom to have the last dance with the man who is taking me home." Betty didn't answer, but there was fire in her eyes as she turned away.

"Picking them pretty young tonight, aren't you Caleb?" Etta asked as we swung out onto the floor.

"She is just the sister of Karl Hart. He was my best friend here in Sterling, Etta. Funny, I was thinking the same thing about her age, but it turns out we are practically the same age."

"Good thing," Etta said, laughing. "I thought the way she danced with you she might be jail bait."

After the last dance I went to the bar and got some sodas, and Emma, Jennie, Etta, Homer, and I sat in the park for a while. When we were ready to leave Etta gave Jennie a big hug saying, "I'm so glad I met you, Jennie. I will be leaving this weekend, and I want you to promise me you will take good care of Caleb."

Jennie said, "You know, Etta, you are so much more of women than just your beauty. I want you to know that knowing you has added to my life. Still, I don't believe you added enough to it to make me capable of taking care of Caleb. He needs mothering, guidance, loving, and a constant vigilant guard to keep him out of trouble."

"Well," Etta said, "he has a Mother to Mother him, a father to guide him, so I guess you just have to love him and pray he grows up."

After Jennie was dropped off everyone was quiet until we had reached the house. As I stopped the car Homer said, "Jezz! Etta, don't you think you girls were a little hard on Caleb tonight? You know it has been hard enough for Caleb having to leave college and come back here without being belittled in front of his family like that."

Etta stopped and stared at Homer for a minute, looking puzzled, then she

111

said, "Is that what you saw Homer? I assure you that was not my intent. Thank you for pointing that out to me. Now I know why all the girls belong to your kissing club; it's because of your insight," she said, grabbing him and giving him a big kiss right on the lips. Homer grew red, then he grew pale and headed for the house. Etta called after him, "Homer, does that entitle me to a membership? Do I get a card?"

"Damn," Emma said laughing, "you are going to be the death of my brothers, Etta. I'm calling it a night. You coming?"

"I'll be right in, Emma," Etta said. "Seems that I have a little apologizing to do to Caleb."

"Well, don't kiss *him* like that, or you'll end up both being an embarrassment to the whole family," Emma said, laughing all the way to the house.

Etta said, "Caleb, I am truly sorry if you feel what Homer said about Jennie and me is true. I am sure that Jennie would be too."

"Ah, it's okay, Etta; it's just sometimes I don't think you girls realize what kind of an effect you have on us boys. Sometimes you cause needs that leave us feeling evil."

Etta walked over to me. After staring into my eyes, she kissed me, much more passionately, at least I hoped, than she had Homer. She walked towards the house saying, "I realize much more than you can imagine," she stopped at the door and turned and said, "Tomorrow is my last day, Caleb. I am going to see your mountain with you, aren't I?"

I spent most of that night tossing and turning. Thoughts of Etta, Joan, Jennie, Beverly, and now Betty were racing through my mind, remembered words and happenings at many occasions. Most boys of my age had steady girlfriends, some were already married, what was it about me that I couldn't commit? Then it dawned on me, how could I commit to someone else when I wasn't sure about myself. My life was being dragged around right now by conditions beyond my control, sort of like my libido is dragging my emotions around about these girls. I must have fell into a deep sleep late because I awoke to Jason shaking me, saying, "Wake up, Caleb; it's late, and everyone has finished breakfast. You better get down there. Etta told us that she, you, and Jennie, were going to explore the mountain today. Nellie was pretty upset that she had not been invited, but Mother told her the young adults deserved some time alone."

I took my time getting dressed, trying to get it into my mind what was going on. When did Jennie get involved in this? Downstairs the girls were in the living room, and I went to the kitchen with Mother, who chatted on while I ate breakfast, about how appropriate it was for Etta to spend her last day on Mount Fay.

I went in with the girls and said, "What time did we plan this trip for Etta? I seem to be a little foggy on the details."

Etta said, "Don't you remember? Jennie usually has to work until eleven but she said to come earlier. Maybe she can get free. Your mother has packed a beautiful lunch for us, so let's start as soon as you're ready. I would like to walk into town anyway, so it will make our arrival at the barn just about right."

Shortly after we had left the house, Etta said, "I'm sorry, Caleb, for pushing this on you, but I was afraid you would not arrange it. I wanted to spend some time with you alone."

"Well, Etta," I said, "I hope you don't think having Jennie with us is my idea of being alone with you."

Etta laughed and said, "I'm sorry about that, too, but I knew it would upset your mother if she thought we were alone all day. I have a very strong feeling that you and I worry your mother enough as it is. I believe she doesn't trust our relationship. At first I thought it was a race thing, but as I got to know your mother I realized it couldn't be that. Still, I sense a misgiving about us from her. That's why I told everybody Jennie was going to be with us."

I had some misgivings about what might happen if someone in the family asked Jennie about today, but the thrill of being on the mountain with Etta overrode any fears of tomorrow. As we walked Etta talked about how even though the college part of this trip had been a bust, she would remember being in Sterling and with my family forever. She asked all kinds of questions about how it had been growing up here. I told her all about going to school and how I first got the job at the barn, and she laughed and laughed about all the jokes we used to pull on each other at the barn. I told her about how Karl and I had spent so much time on the mountain and about the time we had spied on Bob and Kate. She had many questions about life in Sterling and about my brothers and sisters. I talked freely with her about some of our family problems, Eunice running off and getting married, how we still hid from Dad Hester's secret about her marriage to a divorced man.

She talked about her life and how her father had died with T.B. he had contacted at the reservation when she was very young. How her mother and uncles had raised her and Shag, and how foolish she felt it had been for her to be tied to one boy since kindergarten after hearing about my life. Before we even knew it we were half way up the mountain. When we stopped to rest she said, "I'll understand if you don't want to talk about him, but how did Josh fit into all this?"

"I don't mind, Etta," I answered. "It used to be that thinking about him being gone pained my heart too much to allow it to happen. Now when I think of him it is with warmth in my heart, remembering him as a wonderful gift that God had loaned us. Josh was my personal guidance counselor, my leaning post, the one who always had the answers; I was so dependant on him that I was completely lost when he left us. I was in a terrible funk until I met this wonderful Indian chopper who very carefully led me out of the darkness to see there was a Caleb available to the world without Josh to carry him."

"Indian chopper?" Etta laughed. "What is that; some kind of a motorcycle?"

"No, Etta," I answered, "He was one of the men who cut logs when I first went to work with Dad at the mill, a great guy. Let's rest the history and go to the top and climb the tower before we eat lunch."

We reached the top and up in the tower Etta was ecstatic with the view. After spending almost an hour on the last stairs on the tower we came down and ate our lunch. We had already drunk most of the liquid refreshments we had brought, so I led Etta to the springs to get more water. While we were there she said, "Isn't this close to the caves where you said you and Karl hid that day you ran from Bob? Could we go there?"

I led her to the caves, and we squeezed in. It was pretty tight for us in there. I laughed and said, "Guess Karl and I must have been a lot smaller then."

She wiggled her way out past me saying with a little laugh. "I hope you aren't thinking of me as Karl?" Her wiggling past me had me thinking of many things, but none of them were of Karl, so I just smiled. When we free of the caves and back up on the ledges she said, "I would like to go where you saw Bob and Katy. Can we?"

I didn't really want to put myself under such a test, but Etta seemed so attracted to the place of Bob and Katy's story that I couldn't refuse. After we reached the stand of pines, Etta said, "Show me where they were."

I led her to the spot, as best as I could remember it. She sat down and said, "Join me, Caleb."

When I sat down beside her she unbuttoned her blouse, and taking it off, said, "Isn't this where you are supposed to help with my bra?"

Trembling as I helped her out of her bra, our passions exploded so aggressively I believe we still would have had sex, even if there had been twenty naughty little boys watching.

After as we walked back to the trail she said, "Now, what is Beverly going to do for a virgin, Caleb?"

Deep as I was in the fear and wonder of what had just happened, I felt the anger rising. She said, "Wait, wait, Caleb, don't talk, listen. I'm sorry; I just couldn't help that virgin bit. What I really want you to know is that you should feel no obligation or guilt about what happened. I know that Shaq explained to you about my life-time boyfriend and me. There was good reason for my family to be suspicious of us; our petting games started going too far at a very young age. The big problem was that I was more the aggressor than he was, and when my uncle confronted him, there was reason for him to be scared. Looking back now I'm not sure what hurt the most, losing him as my sex partner, or him deserting me. At first my anger had me thinking about becoming the Indian slut of the neighborhood. Shaq saw that coming and blocked me long enough for me to come to my senses. Then you came along and talked about life as you saw it, and as I watched you curb your urges, it helped me grow up a little more. You know, we probably aren't ever going to be together again, so I figured we could have this tryst without really causing too many waves in anybody's world except our own. Even if life throws us together again, I have been watching you and Jennie, and I know you know the art of restraint."

I wasn't sure if all this was making me feel better or making me more crazy, so I said, "One thing for sure, Etta, nobody would have mistaken what happened for rape. Let's run to the bottom of the mountain before we get overwhelmed again."

We made a wild run down the mountain just the way Joan and I had, except Etta was faster than Joan. I laughed as I thought of it, because it was in more ways than one.

At the bottom of the mountain as we collapsed in the grass holding each other, she said, "This has been the best time of my life, Caleb; thank you, and no, I'm not talking about just the sex. I mean, being here with you and your family and having a chance to see into your life the way all of you allowed. I shall be forever thankful."

We lay in the grass for a long time just holding each other and talking about what her visit had meant to both of us. She wanted to know if when I returned to college how much I would miss all this. I talked to her about how it upset me that most of my friends didn't seem to be able to wait to leave Sterling. I told her that as much planning on leaving as I had done, it all including returning here somehow.

115

We heard the town clock strike four and sat up with a jolt, finding it hard to believe that it could be that late. I said, "We should be getting back home. We have to walk back, and I know Mother is making a turkey dinner. I heard her ask you what your favorite meal was, so I know she has it planned for your last day."

"Oh, Caleb," Etta exclaimed, "I don't want to hear those words. I want this to last and last, not end."

"I don't think, as enjoyable as it was lying there with you, that we could get away with living like that forever," I said, giving her a little kiss.

"I know we have to go, Caleb," Etta sighed, "Promise me that you will always remember me and our day on your mountain."

"Easiest promise I ever had to make in my life, Etta," I answered as we started, arm in arm, back home.

At the house we just made it, as Mother wanted dinner earlier enough so Homer could eat with us before he went to the barn. Everyone seemed a little sad that Etta was leaving. After dinner Dad said, "I think I speak for the whole family, Etta, when I say that it has been a joy to have you with us, and we all hope that you can return again for even a longer stay." We all sat around the table talking for a long time after dinner was over. It was as if no one wanted the day to end.

The girls started to clear the table, and Jason, on his way out to do the milking, said, "Last chance for a lesson, Etta. Wouldn't want you to forget how while you're gone."

"I think I better help in here, Jason," Etta replied.

Mother said, "Now, Etta, today is your day, so you do just what you want to do."

Etta said, "Okay, Jason, I guess I better go with you. I really don't need instructions on doing dishes as much as I do milking."

Nellie came over putting her hand on my shoulder said, "Even the little boys, huh, Caleb? What happened today? There is a tension missing between you two."

I held Nellie's hand, thinking, *I am glad not everybody sees things like her,* saying, "Well, we had a chance to talk things out, and we are at peace now with each other." I was going out to join her and Jason but thought better of it and started helping the girls with dishes.

Emma bumped against me and said, "You're looking kind of lost, Caleb. Little break in your heart now that one of you entourage of girls is leaving? I don't know why you're worried. Didn't I see you recruiting Betty Hart Friday night?"

Jason and Etta came in just at that time and saved Emma from getting swatted. Etta said, "I'm going to miss my milking lessons with Jason so much I asked him if I could take him and the cow home with me. He told me he didn't think he or the cow would like the city very much, and it would be better if I stayed here. Please, I don't want to hear any more of that; I came pretty close to adding my tears to the milk as it was."

"Don't say anything more about the tears, Etta," Emma said, "because if you do the boys will want that milk just for them."

This time I did give Emma a swat with the dishtowel, saying, "Let's not make this enjoyable time end with doom and gloom. Let's see some smiles around here." That seemed to break the mood and everyone sat around the rest of the evening telling tales.

We left for Northborough early the next day because Etta had to pick up some things at the college. Everybody wanted to go with us, but Mother said, "I think it should only be Emma and Caleb. That way should be best for Etta."

I thought Mother was still keeping us from being alone right up to the last minute. Etta gave everyone a hug and a kiss, holding my dad tight thanking him for having such a wonderful family. As we finally went to the car I could see the tears forming in Etta's eyes. We drove silently for a number of miles before Emma broke in saying, "If I'm going to be in the way, you two can tell me to get lost."

"Why, Emma," Etta exclaimed, "what do you think I am? Some hussy from the city? I'm hurt."

"I'm sorry, Etta. I certainly didn't mean that," she answered. "It's just, there seems to be such a strong current sparking between you two."

"Emma," Etta said, "I have to confess, I don't mean to use my looks to tease men, so sometimes I am not to blame, though I admit it can be tempting to tease some of them. I'm afraid I subtly flirted with Caleb sometimes, but whatever the effect, he has always been the perfect gentleman."

We spent a couple of hours at the college locating Etta's things and then had to rush to the train station. Etta gave Emma a big tearful hug, saying, "I'm going to miss you, Emma, along with all your family."

Turning to me with tears already in her eyes she held me close until we heard the all-aboard, then, after kissing me passionately, she ran for the train.

Emma put her arms around me and led me back to the car, and we drove back to Sterling, never speaking, both lost in worlds of our own.

CHAPTER FIVE

The first few weeks after Etta had left time dragged one week into another, with work at the sawmill, help around the farm and occasionally a trip into Oscin so Homer could go to a movie. My mind wasn't into the girl cruising I used to do when I came here with the barn boys. I tried to get Mother to let Homer go once in a while with the boys he worked with, but she was adamant that he wasn't going to be tarred with the same brush they were, even if he did work with them. One Friday night Emma talked me into going to Banners for dance night. I was surprised at how young everyone looked.

Half way through the dance Betty Hart came in saying "Well, Caleb, out slumming are you? I have called your house and left a message for you a couple of times. Didn't you get the messages? When I called tonight, Jason said he thought you were at the dance. How come the avoidance? Did Etta leave us poor country girls looking too plain for you?"

That's blunt enough, I thought, *Etta had erased most other girls from my mind.* I wanted to say yes, but instead I said, "Well, hello Betty, did you come here for twenty questions or do you wish to dance?"

We whirled out onto the floor, and Betty said, "Hit a nerve, did I? You sure had a shocked expression on your face for a moment there."

"The truth is, Betty," I answered, "as much of a woman as Etta is, she isn't my woman. She was here because her brother is a good friend of mine, and he asked if she could spend some time with us as a favor to him. We came to the dance here that night because this is about the same kind of dance she and her brother go to back in Oklahoma, and she wanted to try one here."

"How about your day on the mountain, Caleb? Does she go to a mountain like that back home too?" Betty queried

"You know what, Betty? I was glad when I first saw you, because I thought this group was too young for me. Now I find out you're more childish than any of them," I said angrily walking off the floor. I told Emma I would be back for her at closing and left.

Monday at work, Norman asked if we still had that old truck that Clem used to have here. He wondered if he could use it if it wasn't being used. When we stopped for lunch I said, "What's up, Norman? Getting bored way out here with no wheels?"

Bruce laughed and said, "Norman's got a girlfriend. Norman's got a girlfriend."

Norman jumped up and went after Bruce; we broke them up before they had really hurt each other, and Norman left and went back to the mill. When we were back at work and out in the sticking field alone, I asked, "Norman, what's bothering you? It's not like you to let your brother get under your skin like that. You should know by now I am your friend, and you can talk to me about anything."

"Well, what Bruce said is partly right. There is a girl, but not like he says. One weekend about a month ago, this woman named Virginia showed up looking for Clem. She said she was a friend of his and was worried about him. Whoever brought her just dropped her off, and she was here all afternoon. I offered her coffee, and we talked a lot. When she left she asked if I would mind if she came back again. I told her I would be glad to see her again, and she has been back a couple of times since. I think she is eight or ten years older than I am, but I enjoy being with her. I never have much of a chance getting friendly with women because the way I look scares them away, but it didn't seem to bother her."

Wow, I thought, *now what was it Jennie said about her? That she seemed more than just some woman of the night?* I said, "I met her once, Norman, and she did seem nice. Is she the reason you want the truck?" I asked.

"Well, I knew that Clem had it sometimes, and I thought if you weren't using it, maybe I could take Virginia to a movie or something. Now you-you don't have to do this if it's a problem. You have been kind enough about the shanty already. I still-still will want to work for you," Norman stuttered out.

"Damn, Norman, you don't have to feel bad about asking; it is not an unreasonable request. We've worked long enough together for me to know you. I could tell you either way about the truck, and we would still be partners here. As it is, the truck is just sitting at the farm, and we really don't need it much now that Dad's home, and even if we did, I could swap with you and drive it home when we did. That would leave you with a better vehicle to go dating with. How does that sound?" I asked.

For a minute I thought Norman was going to hug me. Instead he said, "Caleb, you-you would really leave your car for me to drive?"

Only when we needed the truck home, Norman." I laughed. "I have to have dating wheels too, you know."

Saturday night as we were planning to bring the truck over to Norman, Mother was worried about Homer making that trip late in the day with no license. Homer suggested we ask Jennie to come along as she had her license. The only trouble with that was she insisted on driving the car with Homer, which left me in the truck alone. When we arrived, Virginia was there with Norman. He came out, all apologetic, saying, "I'm sorry, Caleb; I thought you were going to bring the truck tomorrow."

"There is nothing to be sorry about, Norman," I answered. "I knew why you wanted the truck anyway, remember?"

Jennie was intrigued with the situation, so when Norman offered coffee, and I started to refuse she said, "I would love a coffee before we head back, Norman; thank you for asking."

I looked at Norman and shrugged, and we all headed to the shanty. Virginia greeted us like we were long lost friends and said, "Let me make the coffee, Norman."

We sat around the shanty talking for the better part of an hour before we left. On the way home Jennie said, "I hope the good feeling I had about Virginia was right. I wouldn't want to see Norman get hurt."

Homer said, "What kind of a good feeling, Jennie? Virginia is, or was, some kind of a bar girl that Clem picked up. Now that Clem is not here she is hooking up with Norman. I don't know how Norman feels, but my guess is she isn't the kind of a girl a man should get serious about, so where is the pain?"

"Well, just like a typical barn boy, you can't see anything good about a woman except sex," Jennie said, swatting Homer.

"Whoa, Jennie, we are not at the barn now, and that's my little brother you're talking to. I know that he sounded a little crude there, but tell us why we should see something different. You and I both know that she spent the night with Clem, so what are we supposed to think?" I asked.

"I'm not sure that even if I could explain my feelings I would be able to make a boy understand it. I just felt there was something honest and caring about her when we met before. I might be reading it all wrong, but we both know that just because a woman had sex with a man doesn't mean there is nothing good about her, isn't that right, Caleb?" she said, glaring at me.

"Look, let's not get carried away here. Even if Homer doesn't know Norman that well, I'm sure he only was thinking of what's best for him, just like we do. It's just that the situation leads to questions, and it's evident we don't have the answers, so let's not get mad at each other over it. Okay?" I asked.

After we had dropped Jennie off, Homer said, "What gives between you and Jennie? Story at the barn has you two hitched pretty tight at one time. Seems her anger over Virginia has a deeper personal meaning of some kind."

"There was a time back when we lost Josh that Jennie was very helpful and kind to me. I began to think it was more than kindness, but Jennie set me straight about that and insisted that we could never be more than good friends. I will always be thankful to her, and hopefully we will be good friends for life," I answered, hoping Homer wouldn't pursue the subject.

When we got home Dad said we needed to talk. "I got a call from Mr. Joclin while you were gone, Caleb. He wanted to talk to me about the next job. He is thinking about moving the sawmill, too. I told him that you would have to be my eyes and ears, because I wouldn't be able to walk the new lot with him. You just have to study the terrain and distances the lumber has to be drawn, and we can discuss it together before we commit to a bid. Maybe together we can come up with a better deal than I did on the job you're on now. I know I under bid it a little; we are only making day wages after expenses, and that isn't good business."

"That sounds like a plan, Dad," I answered, "as long as I have your expertise to lean on I'm sure I can gather the right information for you. How much longer does he think we will be on this job?"

"He said he had planned to buy some adjoining timber and spend the winter there, but he couldn't make a deal that would be profitable. He believes they will be done with what's left on that site in a couple of weeks. I know," Dad said, "this puts a lot on your shoulders, but if Leclat does the logging on the new job, he will be helpful, and besides, Joclin has always been a fair man to work for.

As Homer hollered, "Phone for you, Caleb." I told Dad not to worry. I was sure we could manage everything all right. I went to answer the phone. It was Betty Hart. She said, "Caleb, I'm sorry about the other night, but you can't blame a girl for being a little jealous, when she has to compete with the likes of Etta. Why I called is you promise me a date, and I'm holding you to it."

"Tell you what, Betty, I think that's a good idea, but right now I'm tied up in a little family crisis. I can't plan a time, but if I get a chance to get out, would you accept short notice?" I asked

"As little as ten minutes for you, Caleb," she answered excited, " as long as that is a promise."

"It's a promise, Betty. You know I wouldn't lie to Karl's sister. I'll call, but I have to go now," I said, and hung up the phone.

There was a certain excitement about Betty, but I still thought of her as Karl's little sister and felt obligated. My mind was too full of what Dad had told me about the job to worry about girls. Working his job didn't have any fear for me, but being responsible for planning and bidding a job was scary stuff for me. I knew that I had to keep up a good front for Dad. He was getting more and more able to get around, but there were times you could see how hard he had to fight being depressed.

Monday at work the talk was all about the upcoming move. Norman, especially, was upset about it. He said, "Caleb, are you still going to stick the lumber if they move to a new site?"

"I really don't know for sure, Norman," I answered, "Joclin called, Dad, and they talked about the new job, but we are going to have to bid for it if we want it. I won't know until after we see the job and discuss it with Dad before I have an answer. Right now I am not sure even where the job is."

"I-I-I hope it's not too far away from here," Norman stuttered, "I want to be able to stay with you, Caleb."

"Not to worry, Norman; you can always use the shanty as long as you're working for me," I said, wondering why he seemed so upset about moving.

That night when I got home Mother said, "We had a call from Uncle Louis, and he is coming back for a few days. They had a serious problem at the mill with the motor, and it is going to be a week or so before they can get the parts they need. He had been trying to get back since he heard about Dad's accident and was happy for the time off."

I hadn't thought much about Uncle Louis since I had come back, but felt glad he was coming. He and Dad had a lot in common as far as working in the woods was concerned, and I felt this would be good for Dad.

When Dad found out he said, "Caleb, this is great. Maybe Uncle Louis will check out the new job with you. I sometimes wish he was here to stay, but his job is keeping him from drinking, and we couldn't manage that when he was here."

Dad and I talked about the different things you had to be concerned with while looking at a new job until Mother called us to supper. After supper I felt like a weight had been lifted off my shoulder now that Uncle Louis was going to help, as I remembered how many times he had been there for us in the past. I felt in the need of some peer company, so I tried to call Jennie. She wasn't home, so I called Betty Hart. At her house, her mother met me at the door.

She said, "Caleb, I'm so glad you dropped by. I wanted to thank you for all you did for Karl when he was home the first time. He was a completely changed boy when he got back from the trip he took with you and your father's team. We are also glad you are dating Betty. She has been so excited about you since you came back."

"How is Karl doing now, Mrs. Hart? I asked. "I haven't heard from him in a long time."

"He is doing well, Caleb. After he married his nurse they moved to her hometown in New Mexico. He told us in his last letter that they are expecting a baby; imagine, we're going to be grandparents. Let me get his address for you. I'm sure he would love to hear from you."

Betty came out and said, "Mother, he's my date now, not Karl's. Give him a break."

"Wait a minute, Betty, two things we should get straight. First, Karl and I go back a long ways, and I am very interested in what he is up too. Second, even though I want us to be good friends and go out, we aren't exclusively dating," I said, getting a sinking feeling from the look on her face.

As we got in the car Betty said, "Do you shoot all the girls down early like that, or was that just for me?"

"I'm sorry, Betty," I answered, "if you thought I was shooting you down. It's just that I seem to have trouble with girls thinking I have to walk a path they lay out. I didn't want to have to go through with that with you, so when your mother seemed so excited about me dating you I wanted it understood it was casual."

"Forget it, Caleb," Betty said, cuddling up to me. "Where are we going?"

I said, "I haven't planned anything, Betty. I don't want to stay out too late. I just thought I would pick you up, and we'd go get a sundae or something like that, okay?"

123

"Some date, Caleb, but I did agree to anything anytime, didn't I, and a sundae doesn't sound like a bad idea if we can go to the Grove afterwards," Betty said, moving closer.

We drove to Oscin and went to the ice cream parlor where we boys used to go for a sundae. I noticed a couple of girls that I had been to the movies with, and as Betty and I were eating our sundaes one of them came and joined us, saying, "Good to see you again, Caleb. We heard you had run off with some college girl. What are you doing back here? Slumming?"

"No, Mamie. It is Mamie, isn't it?" I asked, "I just picked up a friend of mine from town and came over for a sundae."

"Oh, it's Mamie, all right. I don't think any boy I went to the movies with has ever forgotten me before. Well, the boys did warn me you were different," she said as she left.

"Well," Betty said, "seems your reputation has expanded from Sterling. Did you make as big a hit in Oklahoma?"

"Now, Betty," I replied, "that is just the kind of thing that I tried to make you understand when I picked you up. I am not ready to make a commitment to any one person. Mamie is someone who I met a long time ago, and there wasn't anything between us. The point is, that I don't need a girl who is constantly going to be upset about the way I am or about anyone who I might have been with in the past."

It was just getting dark when we left Oscin and headed back to Sterling. I wasn't comfortable with Betty and thought it would be best if I dropped her off.

She said, "Come on, Caleb; you promised we would go to the Grove. At least let me save face a little bit. Mother would want to know what happened if I come back this soon."

Though I knew about the Grove, I wasn't sure of what the significance of it was to Betty, so I said, "Okay, Betty, I guess we can go check it out."

We drove to a secluded spot in the Grove and parked. She talked about how it had been for her when Karl and I were involved in all our escapades and how hard it was for her when we ignored her. I only remembered her from back then as Karl's little sister and had never really paid much attention to her. She wanted to know what it was that made such a difference in Karl after he went with me that day to the mill. I told her we had spent most of the day talking about the fun we had growing up in Sterling. We had been there for about thirty minutes when she said, "Well, Caleb, aren't you even going to kiss me?"

124

Remembering the way she danced with me the night Etta was there I said, "I was saving that for at your front door, Betty," thinking, *The last thing I need right now is another entanglement with a girl.* The conversation kind of died after that, so I took Betty home.

As I walked her to the door she said, "Is it true what they say about you being Beverly's virgin, Caleb?"

"Do you always have to say things that make me mad when we part, Betty?" I asked angrily. "That is just a nick name the boys at the barn gave me, and now it seems to be all over town." Though the passion of my kiss was anger, I kissed her with the full strength of that passion and abruptly walked away.

The next day when I arrived home from work Uncle Louis was there, and he and Dad had been talking all afternoon. Mother was so happy about how well things were going with them that she had taken the afternoon off and gone shopping. Dad called me in and said, "I am going to try to get Joclin to show the new lot Saturday, so Louis can be with you. If it is the lot I think it is, he already knows something about it, as he worked in that area before."

Saturday came, and Uncle Louis, Joclin, Leclat, and I went to tour the new lot. Though it was in the other direction from Sterling it was still more than twenty miles from our house. The lot itself was a half a mile off a traveled road before coming to its first line marker. Though the road in that far was a little rough you would be able to get in at least to there with lumber trucks. Beyond that there wasn't really any road, though Joclin said the plan was to bulldoze one all the way to the back line of the property. The lot hadn't been cut in many years, and the trees were straight and tall. Most of them were pine. The land sloped most all of the way to the back lot line, sometimes fairly steeply.

Leclat said, "If I'm logging this with horses it will mean that we will have to move the mill two or three times."

Uncle Louis asked where they intended to stick the lumber, Joclin said that hadn't been worked out yet, but he would have answers to all our questions by the middle of next week. We all agreed that it would be great to work with timber that good, but logging and sticking looked like a tough deal because of the terrain.

Back at work Monday, Norman was still upset about having to move. He said, "I have to tell you something, Caleb. Virginia has been talking about moving in with me. I think I would like that, but I told her that there wasn't room for another person in the shanty. Bruce has been yakking to everybody about Virginia being around so much and told everyone about her wanting to move in. Mr. Joclin heard about it and came and told me that he had all those shanties his father used to use and he would let me have a couple cheap, but I have to move them. Leclat offered to loan me a trailer, and I was going to ask you if you would be mad if I used the truck to tow them here. Now I don't know what to do. I can't stay here if everyone moves, and I wouldn't have a job anymore so I couldn't afford to have Virginia stay."

"I'll tell you what Norman. You are just going to have to put off any decisions until I have an answer for you about work. Joclin said he would have all the information we need by the middle of the week. It'll probably be next week before a decision is made on whether or not I am going to get the bid to work on the new job. I think the truck will be strong enough to move the shanties, but if you are going to be moving from here it's better if you wait, so you don't have to move them twice. I think you should take some time thinking about Virginia before you move her in with you, this will give you a good reason to wait," I answered, thinking, *What should I do? Is it right for me to interfere? No matter what I think, what would Josh do?*

"I really don't need time to think about Virginia," Norman answered stuttering. "She-she is so-so good to me, like nobody has ever been in all my life. I know that you all think there has to be something wrong if a woman wants to stay with me. You know what? I don't care what anybody thinks, even if it doesn't last; I have it now."

"Whoa! Norman, don't get upset; we would question this situation no matter who was involved in it. All anyone of us wants is to make sure you aren't getting hurt. None of us know Virginia, and even you can see why this situation would cause talk. Still, if you are happy, I'm sure all of us will be too, and we'll be more than happy to help you get set up at the next job with her." I was surprised at how adamant Norman was about Virginia, but I remembered what Josh had said about Uncle Louis about being divorced and still needing the women, and it kind of made sense.

On Thursday Mister Joclin called us all together and explained about the new job. He said, "I need you to all understand that this is not going to be solely my job. I am bidding it stump to stick but I don't own the lumber or control how it has to be done. They have offered me a good price, but they have stipulations that you all will have to consider. First they've already bulldozed a road to the back of the lot, and they insist that we start the first setting there. They want all the lumber drawn to the beginning of the lot and put on stickers there."

Leclat said, "Are you crazy, Joclin? It's already the first of November and if we are set up way down there, when snow comes it will be impossible to get the lumber out. We always lose time in the winter, we would be better off staying home than having a job way back there this late in the year."

"No, I'm not crazy, Leclat." Joclin answered. "I told them I would present this to everyone concerned and get back to them. I thought it would carry more weight if I had your input before I pointed out the problems their plan causes. This is a good lot as far as the mill and the choppers are concerned, but there are some problems logging it, and it's an impossible situation drawing lumber that far to stick it. My thoughts were we should try to put together a plan on how it could be done and then see if they are willing to pay for the added costs. I agree that it would be dumb to start at the back of the lot first, but they have some idea that we might do the easy part then quit. Caleb, what do you think? "

"I wouldn't know how to put a price on it, but the only way I can see that the lumber can be handled that way is by two crews and probably with trucks, not horses. I think that leaves us out because start-up costs alone would make the price of the job way beyond imagination," I answered, with a sinking feeling. Not only was this going to make things harder for Dad but for Norman's plans also.

"Now let's not all get discouraged," Joclin said. "I want you to all give this some thought and present some prices on each way of doing it. I am sure that I can make them see the light about not starting at the back of the lot. I believe from what I've been hearing, the buyer they have has an agreement with them that they have to start this year, if that is the case I'm sure we have some control on how it is done. One of the things I thought about was that you probably could handle the first part of the lot with just one crew, then if they insist on moving all the lumber all the way out there, we could put a different price on each setting for sticking the lumber."

Leclat said, "That makes sense if we can do it that way, because even with snow we could handle that first setting, and we should be out of there before next winter. Caleb, you tell your dad, if he wants I can come over and discuss this with him."

I left without talking to Norman; I felt confused enough with my concerns without seeing what this would do to him. I tried to have an open mind about what Joclin said, but couldn't see any way we could stick lumber under those conditions and make a living. I was sure Dad and Uncle Louis would say no sense even getting involved in anything that foolhardy.

When I got home Uncle Louis was talking with Dad and said, "What's the word, Caleb? Did Joclin have any information today?"

I told them what he had said, and Dad said, "Looks like we're out, as far as that job is concerned. No way it's going to pay enough to put two full crews on it."

Uncle Louis said, "Let's think about it for a minute, Henry. The way I see it, Joclin is only asking that we price it that way for him with the hope that he can convince them to do it another way. It won't cost us anything to put together an estimate for him, and it might be fun. I am going to be here for a few more days, and I have a few ideas as to how it might be done, and you could help me set a price that would leave you with more than a fair profit. That way, if you get the job, you'll be safe. I think after they see the costs of doing it their way, they will be open to other ideas, so we can plan for them also. What do you think of doing something like that, Caleb?"

"I like the way you think, Uncle Louis, and the fact that you have seen the lot makes it easier for Dad to be able to trust your judgment better than mine. My first thoughts were, there wasn't any way we could do the job, but now you offer some hope. I'll leave the planning to you and Dad and add my two cents after I see what you come up with," I said, thinking how much this was like the old days, having Uncle Louis to lean on.

When Homer came home that night, he said, "Caleb, I have a message for you. Jennie wants to see you tonight if you have time. She is still at the milk house and said she would hang around until eight thirty if you can make it."

I thanked Homer and went out to the car, wondering what was bothering Jennie enough for her to want to see me. When I arrived at the milk house Jennie was just leaving. I said, "Hey, what's up, Jennie? Homer said you would be here until eight-thirty so I rushed right down. I hope you aren't in any big trouble."

Jennie got in the car saying, "Thank you for coming, Caleb. No, there isn't any big trouble. It's just I can't get this Virginia-Norman situation off my mind. I know I don't know Norman very well, but I really like him, and I can picture all kinds of scenarios where he could get hurt real bad. I've been thinking maybe we should go back this weekend and talk to them about it."

"Wow, Jennie. I guess I am not so special after all. It wasn't just me you wanted to save, it is the whole world," I said, laughing.

Jennie gave me a whap upside of the head saying, "Knock it off, Caleb; I thought at least you would be understanding about this. Maybe I just wasted my time saving you, after all."

"Now, now, Jennie, don't get upset," I answered. "I have wondered if there was anything for me to say to Norman about it. When I tried, he told me he was a big boy and didn't need any advice from anyone. He also said that it has been hard for him to get to know girls because his cross-eyes kept them away. He also told me that even if this didn't last, at least he had now, and that was something he might never have again. From then on I decided that I didn't really have a right to interfere in his life."

"I'm glad you tried, Caleb. I suppose you're right that we don't have a right to tell him what to do. I thought talking with him again would help, at least make me feel better about it all. Thank you for seeing me, Caleb," she said, giving me a little kiss as we arrived at her house.

I said, "I'll tell you what, Jennie; I'm not sure how it will all work out, but I might have some news that Norman would be interested in by this weekend. I could pick you up and go up there if you want to go. I won't be able to give you much notice, though."

"That's okay, Caleb," she answered. "I don't have any plans for Sunday, so give me a call if you are going, and Caleb, maybe I did the right thing saving you after all."

Saturday afternoon Dad said, "Caleb, Louis and I have been over and over different scenarios on how we could do that new job and make a profit. I think we have the best of the lot singled out and are ready to talk about them."

I said, "Okay, Dad, I'll be with you in a few minutes. The cow got away from Jason, and I am on my way to help him. I guess she must be bulling; you know what a time we have with her when that happens."

After helping Jason catch the cow I joined Dad and Uncle Louis.

Dad said, "Here's the plan. The way they have it laid out, I don't think we should spend a lot of time on this one because it is so expensive; basically we have set a price to save us if it was done that way, plus an added twenty percent. We devised a plan we believe makes sense of how to do that lot that will be cost effective for everyone. We know it would be a little more expensive to bulldoze a road good enough for the lumber trucks all the way to the back of the lot. Still the cost of going that far with it is much cheaper than hiring us to bring all the lumber out, so our plan is for them to have a sticking field between the last two lots. That way we can handle the job with one team from both back settings. The top setting isn't a problem for us. We have worked out prices for both ways, leaving you the option of cutting our price by five percent if necessary. What do you think, Caleb? Can we handle everything the way we have it planned?"

"I like most of it," I answered, "except the part of the last setting. It seems to me that we will be hauling everything uphill from there."

Uncle Louis said, "We took that into consideration. The back part of the lot isn't as steep as the rest of the lot. That's why our plan has the sticking field closer to that setting than the second one, where you'll be hauling downhill. I am pretty good at judging the distances a team can handle hauling lumber, and I'm sure that this plan will work for them."

I left them, feeling a little unsure about their plans, but I could see that it at least gave us a chance of being able to do that job. The next day I called Jennie and asked her if she was available to go with me to see Norman. I felt that Dad's plan was excuse enough to go see him. Besides I was looking forward to being with Jennie.

When I picked Jennie up she said, "You know, we have the boys at the barn and some of the town talking about us being a twosome. I want you to know, though it's true I have feelings for you, my decision that we have no future still stands, so don't get carried away."

"Why, Jennie!" I said thinking how hard this was, considering our history, "You know what I promised; who is it that you're afraid of, me or you?"

Jennie gave me a little slap and said, "Damn it, Caleb, how did we get so involved anyhow? I always had a thing for Josh, even when I knew he was out of my league. After we lost him, I let myself get emotionally involved with you because I was so low myself I didn't care what happened. When I began consoling you it was with an altruistic motive, but I was so weak myself then I felt fulfilling your need was important."

"I think that fulfilling my needs is still important, Jennie, so anytime you're so inclined I'll try not to stop you," I answered as Jennie batted me. "All kidding aside, Jennie, despite my libido's strong memory of what you have to offer I'll keep my promise."

When we arrived at the job site, Virginia was there with Norman. Norman seemed surprised to see us, so I said, "I have some good news about a new job, Norman, and Jennie and I were out riding around so I decided to stop in and tell you. My dad and uncle have come up with a proposal that we all feel will make it possible for us to bid on the next job. I am counting on you being my partner if we get the job."

"Oh, Caleb," Norman answered, "you know I want to stay working with you, but how can I get to a job so far away from home? Mother used to bring me to work here, but she wouldn't be able to go that far every day."

"I know you won't be as close to your family, Norman, but we will be moving the shanty to the next job, and you can still use that. I don't think you should be driving our old truck back here often, but a trip once in a while wouldn't hurt it. While I'm here, Norman, how about helping me check the wagon out to make sure it's in condition to take the trip to the next job?" I said, thinking leaving Jennie and Virginia alone might be a good idea.

When Norman and I came back to the shanty Virginia said, "I feel as though there is an elephant in the room, so let's all be honest about it. I can very well see why friends of Norman's would be worried about our situation. I am not able to promise you that Norman won't get hurt knowing me, but I hope not. I married very young to the nicest, gentlest boy anyone ever knew. A little over a year ago he died suddenly in my arms. At first I was just sad, then I was full of fear, which finally turned to anger. During my time of anger I did some things I'm not proud of, and one of those things was ending up here with Clem. The reason I came back, was that Clem seemed so sad and sorrowful; the good thing about coming back is that I got to meet Norman. Now Norman and I have become more than just friends. Is it forever? I don't know; some affairs blossom and others become just that—an affair. Norman talked about getting another shanty so I could move in with him. I know this is a tough life, but I believe Norman and I will be happy together. That's why I am willing to join him if it doesn't cause a problem for his job."

I looked at Jennie, and she was nodding her head as if in agreement so I said, "I don't see any problem as far as his job is concerned, and I'm sure we will have permission to set up shanties as the next job. We will be here for at least two more weeks, by that time I should have a decision about what we can or can't do if we get the job. I don't think we should move another shanty here for so short of a time, so it would be better if Virginia waited until we move before she joins you."

"That-that's all right," Norman stuttered, slightly red faced, "Bruce has been staying home weekends anyway, so Virginia can stay with me weekends."

Virginia gave both Jennie and me a hug saying, "I'm glad Norman has such caring friends as you two. When I first met him I didn't know that he had anyone that was close to him. No matter what happens I'll do my best to see that Norman is as happy with me as you two seemed to be with each other."

Jennie said, "We're sorry if we have made you feel uncomfortable, Virginia; thank you for being so honest with us. I've only known Norman from the couple of times I met him here when I came with Caleb, but I really came to like him and am glad he has you for company."

"No apologies necessary, Jennie; I'm glad that Norman has such good friends. Caleb, it's probably a good thing for you that I came along, or Norman might have stolen Jennie's heart instead of mine," Virginia said, laughing.

After we left Jennie said, "That could have been awkward if Virginia wasn't who she is. I'm glad we came, Caleb. I feel better now. There was just something so sweet and innocent about Norman when I talked to him alone the first time we were here that made this situation worry me. Still, I guess a man is a man when it comes to his libido, and like Norman says, he'll have now, no matter what happens later."

Jennie sat close to me most of the way back to Sterling, her warmth created desires I had to fight given my promise.

When we arrived at her house she said, "Thank you, Caleb, for letting me into your world," kissing me so passionately I almost lost it. She ran into the house. I thought, *Damn, how the hell does she think I'm going to be able to keep my word if she does things like that?*

During the next week after Leclat and I had presented our plans and bids, Joclin negotiated with the Brewers who were the owners of the lot and job we were bidding on. After seeing the cost of our first bids they agreed to have the sticking fields where we planned them. They were still insisting that we do the deepest lot first. Leclat wasn't having any of that; he said it would be a disaster being that far back in the woods during winter snows. The Brewers seemed afraid that once the easy setting was done the crews wouldn't do the hard ones. Friday night Joclin called us all together and asked if it would be feasible to do the middle setting first and moving to the front one after. Leclat was all for that, if they cleared a spot at the first setting for the shanties and shanty barns. I reminded Joclin that we had bid different prices on each setting and I didn't think there was any way my dad would change his bid.

Monday, Joclin told us he had reached an agreement with the Brewers, and the job was a go. Norman was all excited and asked if I was still going to loan him the truck to move the shanties. I told him that it was my job to get our shanty moved and I would get back to him about the shanty he was getting from Joclin.

We finished the job we were on Thursday and when I got home that night I discussed with Dad how we would make the move.

He said, "Caleb, since you have the car and truck to take care of, I think either Jason or Homer should move the team. What we can do is have them bring the team this far one day and after the horses have rested here a day drive them to the next job. You will have to tear down the shanty barn and load that onto our truck yourself. I had planned on Clem being there. He has moved it before. I think if you pay close attention to how I put it up, when you take it down you should be able to reconstruct it easily at the new job. I think

132

Leclat would be willing to help you if you run into trouble. I had planned to go with you but Mother and the doctor insist that I give my leg another month before I start using it except in the house."

I said, "You don't have to worry Dad; even if Clem isn't here, I have Norman to help me, and he can drive the truck for us. He has asked if he could use the truck to move a shanty that Joclin gave him to the new job. I know we hire ours moved, but it is too expensive for him. He has a lady friend who is staying with him and his brother, and they need more room. Leclat has loaned him a trailer, so it's not like he is going to load it on the truck; he'll just tow it."

"I don't know if that's a good idea or not, Caleb," Dad answered. "The truck's pretty old, and it would be a hardship for us if anything happened to it. Talk it over with Leclat, and if he thinks the truck will handle towing a trailer, then maybe it would be a good idea to move both of them that way. Then you could keep Norman on the payroll with what you save not paying to move our shanty, and he can help you build the barn too."

After talking to Dad about the move I talked to Jason. He said, "Oh, boy, Caleb, are you really going to let me drive the team home? I haven't driven them very much, but I went with Dad sometimes when I wasn't in school, and he let me drive them on the job before he got hurt."

"We will have to make sure you know the route and where you can rest and water the horses. I will take you up there with me a couple of times before Sunday. I haven't discussed this with Mother yet, but I believe she will think it's okay."

When we went in Mother said, "Caleb, what's this your father has planned for Jason? Don't you think that's asking too much from him? I think Homer should drive the team home. It seems as though all you boys have had to take on men's jobs too young."

"I know, Mother, Jason is young but no younger than I was when I started at the barn, and besides, he really wants to do it. I will be able to check on him during the trip, so I think you should let him. It really is an enjoyable ride, and perhaps Francis or Nellie will want to go with him," I said, thinking maybe it would be good for Francis to become a little more involved with Jason; he spent too much time alone in his room.

I had talked to Jason and Nellie about it but they said that he was always like that and not to worry about it. It seems funny when I think about it how little Francis was involved in family life; I suppose our age difference has kept me from realizing how different he was from Jason or Nellie.

Early Saturday morning Jason, Francis and I were at the job site loading the wagon and harnessing the horses for their trip back to Sterling. Jason was excited about what he called his first real job. As we were loading I instructed Jason about the feedbags and where he could stop and find water.

Francis was silently taking all this in when he came and tugged my arm saying, "Caleb, would it be all right if I handled the reins part of the way? I am not like you, Jason, and Homer; animals always scare me, but I think I could do that."

Surprised as I was about Francis's admission, I was happy that he was open about it, so I said, "I am sure that Jason would appreciate having someone as capable as you helping with the driving, Francis. It is one of the reasons he wanted you to come."

Norman had joined us and was already taking down the shanty barn and loading it on the truck. I went over the route again with Jason and sent him and Francis on their way, telling them we would meet them about half way after we had the barn loaded.

Norman said, "I went over to Joclin's to look at the shanty he is selling me; it is really nice. It is a little bigger than yours, but I don't think it is much heavier. I was wondering if you have an answer about me using the truck to move it."

I told Norman what my father had said, and he was elated saying, "Caleb, I only worked here for a short time before your father was hurt, but I always thought he was a thoughtful person. If we have good luck today we can have the shanty barn up at the new site by tonight, then I can stop at Leclat's and pick up the trailer on the way back here. Leclat is going to be moving his barn tomorrow, and he and his men can help Bruce and me load the trailer. That way I'll be there to take care of the horses when they arrive at the new job."

Listening to Norman planning made me think how much better off I was with him than I would have been with Clem and his surly ways. I said, "Norman, I wish I could be as excited about all that is before us as you are. You make it all sound like fun."

"I have to tell you, Caleb," he answered, "my mother was smart enough to see that I was going to have trouble when I entered the outside world and started school. She prepared me well for the trouble and teasing that I would face because of my eyes. Her most important advice has always been that what mattered most was how you thought about things in your own mind. With her guidance I have learned that there is something bright in most everything if you look hard enough. I know from experience that how true that is, not just in my life but everyone's."

We were only a little over two hours dismantling the shanty barn and loading it and putting in what gear we had that didn't go with the wagon. Norman drove the truck following me, as he didn't know where the new job was. When we met the wagon they weren't quite half way to Sterling, but they were making good progress. Francis was handling the reins, and if he was afraid it didn't show. I knew if we followed Norman's plan to finish the shanty barn at the new site today I wouldn't be home when Jason and Francis got there. I wasn't sure that Jason could handle the harnesses, so I told him to get Homer to help him, and if Homer wasn't home to get Mother without disturbing Dad. Mother had helped me more than once when I first started driving horses, so I wasn't worried about her helping Jason.

After we got to the job site Norman started unloading the truck right away. I asked, "Don't you think we should take a break and eat our lunch, Norman?"

He said, "I ate mine on the way here, Caleb. Let's get this barn built. I want to get to Leclat's before it is dark. He warned I would have a little trouble getting to the trailer."

Dad didn't have to worry about reconstructing the barn. Norman had it down pat, and we were done except for roofing well before dark. I followed Norman to Leclat's; it was a good thing we got there before dark because it took us over an hour of moving things around to get to the trailer. After we had it hitched to the truck I followed Norman for a few miles to make sure it towed all right, then I headed back to Sterling. As I pondered all we had done today I thought again how lucky I was to have Norman and how wrong Clem had been in labeling him a retard.

When I got home and went to check the team out, Jason was in the barn. He said, "Caleb, a funny thing happened with Francis. He was so proud about driving the team I let him drive most of the way. When we got here, and Homer and I had the team unhitched I asked Francis if he wanted to help me brush them down. He started to help me, then it was like he got sick or something, and ran into the house. I felt so good for him today because it has been almost impossible to get him near any animal since he was a little boy. Mother thought that maybe the day had just been too much for him, but I think it's more than that."

I went into the house puzzling over what Jason had said when Emma said, "Caleb, there is a letter for you from your girl, Etta, and boy, does it smell sweet. Any chance I can read it, lover boy?" She said laughing.

135

Trying not to look anxious I swatted Emma and said, "I'll read it later and let you know. Right now I have to discuss some things with Dad."

After talking with Dad about what we had accomplished and had planned, I went to my room to read Etta's letter.

Dear Caleb,

I think of you and your family often. Words can't express how knowing you and your family has influenced my outlook on life. I shall always be sorry about how I acted when I first met you. I know you only came back because Shaq pestered you to; I shall always be thankful to him for that. I have been attending a junior college so I can live at home. This was mostly Shaq's idea; I guess he still doesn't trust me, but I am happy with this arrangement.

I sent a thank-you note addressed to your mother and your family the day I got home. I told her that as much as I loved my family, I would have been proud to have been a part of hers. (Of course there is a little exception to that. I don't think the way you make me feel is sisterly) Of course this is not in her letter, though the way she watched us I'm sure she understood. I want you to thank them all again for me and ask Homer where I place in his kissing club, privately of course. I have tried dating a few times with some of the boys at college. Funny, they don't seem too much in a rush to ask me for a second date. One even told me I was too chaste to be a good college date. I had to look that up to get his meaning. It gave me a good laugh; if he only knew me back when…

I am so glad that Emma came with us the day I caught the train. I am not sure I would have gone if she hadn't been there. It was such a painful goodbye for me; when I held you that last time my heart was crying out, 'Forget this foolishness; grab Caleb and find another mountain.' Without the gift of understanding you and your family gave me, it could have happened, too. Yet as I looked at Emma and remembered conversations I had with Jennie about your being unattainable goods for us, I knew I had to do the right thing and go. I am happy now that I did, but at times I'm still haunted by the ghosts of, "What if?" I hope you don't mistake this for crying on your shoulder. I'm just following the advice you gave me when you were here in Oklahoma about letting my feelings out and not holding it all in.

What happened between us when we were on the mountain, I was just following that advice. I had hoped it was a feeling that I could release without consequences. I know now that isn't true, but at least the consequences are

just that I have created more want, not less. I've had worse pains. As I read
this over I thought I was giving too much away and ought to tear it up myself.
Then I thought, Caleb would understand; it's just his little Indian Girl.

With all emotions,
Etta

After finishing the letter I thought about her ending, "With all emotions."
Just thinking about Etta created enough of them in me to get me shaking.
After receiving this letter from her I would be lucky if I could keep my mind
on anything else but her, after reading it. One thing for sure, I didn't want
Emma or anyone else reading it. Still I hated to rip it up. Sharing a room with
my brothers made it almost impossible to keep anything secret here, so I kept
the letter with me, thinking I would hide it in my car later.

Emma hollered, "Supper's on, Caleb; bring your letter down so we can all
enjoy it; you know she always said she wanted to be treated like one of the
family."

When I came down I said, "Etta wants everyone to know how much her
visit meant to her and that she thinks about the family all the time. Mother,
I don't remember you saying anything about receiving a thank-you note from
her. She said she sent it the day after she got back to Oklahoma."

"I'm sorry, Caleb," Mother answered, "I received it a couple of days after
she left, but everybody seemed so down about her leaving I thought I would
save it for a little while before reading it to everyone. Then I got so busy I just
forgot to do it. I'll go get it now."

After Mother had read Etta's thank-you note, Emma said, "Okay, Caleb,
let's hear yours. I bet it is a little spicier than Mother's."

Mother said, "All right, Emma, that will be enough, if Etta wanted us to
hear what was in her letter she would have addressed it to the family, not
Caleb. We all know Caleb and Etta knew each other before she came here,
and they probably have private things to discuss."

The girls cleared the table and went to the kitchen to do the dishes. I asked
Mother if she understood Francis's problem about the animals. She said, "I
have been talking with your father about that. He has suggested we talk to the
doctors next time we go to the hospital. I used to think he was just afraid of all
animals but I now believe it is something deeper than that. Hester brought it
to my attention that lately it seems he is more ill than scared when he gets
close to most animals."

Jason hollered, "Telephone for you, Caleb; sounds like one of your girlfriends."

Betty was on phone wanting to know if I was free tonight. If I hadn't received Etta's letter I probably would have joined her but wanting to answer it, I told her I was tied up for the next few days working late during our move to a new job. She seemed upset, so I told her I would be free sometime next week and would call her.

She said, "I'll bet," and hung up on me. It was hard for me to understand what I felt about Betty. Part of me still thought of her as Karl's little sister. She had left little doubt that she wasn't that little girl anymore, and somehow that was scary to me.

Homer hadn't come in yet, so I went to our room to write to Etta.

Dear Etta,

I received your letter today and was very glad to hear from you. The family all sends you their best and want you to know that we also gained from your visit here. I asked Homer before about your goodbye kiss and he said he thought he might have to give up kissing other girls, because he didn't want that kiss ever wiped off. What a bad girl you are, destroying my brother's favorite activity. You really don't have to worry though; if what I hear from Jennie is true, he's back in form. By the way, speaking of Jennie, how is it that you two have the right to brand me as unattainable? Jennie uses that line to keep a bed board between her and my libido, so to speak. What's your reasoning? From your letter I felt any nonsense like that between us had been shattered. I understood what you describe about our parting; my mind or at least the part that is connected to my libido was shouting the same message. I really hate believing this, but it is probably better that we are far apart. I often think about the conversations you and Jennie had when I drove you home from the college. Especially when you were talking about my not belonging to Jennie or perhaps any girl. I think of that a lot; maybe it's just my age, but I have a fear of committing myself to any one person or any one thing. Jennie was right about Joan; she and I have been holding hands and eating ice cream since first grade. Joan has often chastised me because of my lack of commitment. That's what kept our situation chaste. (I had to look that up too, but it fits.) I am even ambivalent about wanting to go to college for four years. I love the town of Sterling, but know I wouldn't find it satisfactory if I spent my life here working in the woods, like I am now. I had come to believe when I was in school that a writing profession would be something wonderful. Now without my support system of teachers and friends to encouraging me, I have doubts about my capabilities in that field.

Enough of my whining, Etta; you once asked me about my feelings for Mount Fay. I quote from Josh's poem:

The relentless time can cause no weakening
Of what in my heart she might mean
Older now I find many wonders
That had lied to my youth unseen

When Josh wrote those words I am sure he wasn't describing the kind of wonder we experienced on our day on Mount Fay. I know for sure that will be a day that will forever be etched in my best memories about the mountain. I have often wished we could have been able to confide in each other while you were here. I, of course, understand the dangers that might have entailed so maybe letter writing is a safer alternative for us.

From Beverly's former Virgin,
Caleb Carney

I had planned to leave early the next morning but Dad was up when I came down and wanted to talk. Mother had spoken to me about how antsy he was getting lately. It was especially hard for him now that we were moving to a new job. So I went it over again with him what we had done so far of what we had planned. He found it hard to believe we had moved the team home and moved and reconstructed the shanty barn in one day. I told him that it was mostly Norman who made all this possible because he was so hot on having Virginia move in with him. At that Dad said, "You know, Caleb, I would be careful not to talk about that where your mother can hear you. I am sure since one of the shanties is ours, and Norman works for us, she would have some objections."

"I hadn't thought of that, Dad," I answered. "Good thing I'm having this talk with you; it will save me a lot of trouble, because no way I want to lose Norman. I can't say that her moving in doesn't trouble me some, but I talked to Norman about it, and he is aware of dilemma of the situation. He feels that because of his looks he won't have many chances like this, and he really likes Virginia. I have to admit what I know of her she seems okay. You didn't say much about the decision to start that job in the middle setting. I was a little afraid I jumped the gun and agreed without discussing it with you."

"Well, I have to admit, Caleb, that I was more than a little perturbed that you brought it to me as a done deal, but I would have said yes, too. I had talked to Louis about it, and it was one of the scenarios that we thought was a good way to do the job. Joclin had called me about what was decided; he felt he had to have an answer right away so he wouldn't lose out on the job. The way I understand it, there are some very good stands of trees there, and from the mill's point of view, it is too good a job for him to lose. You know, Caleb, every year there is less and less forest land that hasn't been cut over in the last fifty years. Oh, time for me to do my exercises before your mother gets after me, and you need to get to work," Dad said as he swung away on his crutches.

As I drove to work I thought about what Dad said about there being less and less timber around this part of the country to cut. Even if I had wanted to stay in the logging business it didn't look like a very promising field. Josh said I would understand when I got older. Here I am, almost as old as he was when he was killed, and I still find life confusing.

When I got to the job Norman, Bruce, and some of Leclat's men already had the shanty loaded on the trailer.

Norman was all excited, saying, "Caleb, if we hurry we might be able to get both shanties moved today. If we can do that I told Leclat that I would drive one of his teams to the new job to pay for his help and the trailer."

"I don't know, Norman; that's going to make a long day's work," I answered, "and you know we can't push that old truck too much."

"That's okay, Caleb; I've been waiting for you so you can follow me and make sure everything rides all right. You don't have to worry. I won't push the truck too fast. I'm thankful to everybody for all the help I'm getting. Maybe I am too much in a hurry, but I still know enough to be careful with the machinery," Norman said, looking a little hurt.

It was a boring couple of hours following the truck but the trip went well and Norman sure seemed to know how to get the best out of our old truck without abusing it. When we arrived at the new site Norman already had picked out a spot for his shanty. He had a couple of short logs under the shanty and after unbinding it he chained the shanty to a tree and pulled the trailer ahead enough to let the back of the shanty hit he ground. He stopped and replaced one of the logs under the shanty and then pulled the trailer out from under the other end of it. He said, "It still needs to be leveled up, but we can do that later. Let's go to Jocklin's and get the other trailer."

"I don't know, Norman; it will be well after dark before we can get back here, and then I would have to drive back to Sterling, and I don't want to be that late getting home tonight. I know you are in a hurry and want to help Leclat, but Dad and I thought we could keep you on the payroll with the money we saved by moving everything ourselves, so you can pay him if you have to. Doesn't it make more sense to do it tomorrow?" I asked, heading for my car.

Norman hurried over to the car and said, "Please Caleb, everything towed all right on this trip, so if you just help Bruce and me load the other trailer you wouldn't have to follow us back here; you could go home then. Leclat said he doesn't plan on using this trailer so we could leave it right on the trailer until I have time to get it set up right."

Bruce came over after he finished loading the chains on the trailer saying, "Come on, Caleb, you aren't going to stand in the way of Norman getting back to his pong-tang are you? He's hard enough to stand when he has it."

Norman charged at Bruce, almost knocking him off his feet saying, "Damn you, Bruce, I told you don't ever say things like that about Virginia."

I pulled them apart and said, "Norman, if Virginia stays in a shanty with you I am sure you're going to be hearing things like that from some of the other men. If you can't take it you had better not have her here. Besides, wasn't it you who told me that you had been trained to ignore being teased?"

"I know, Caleb, I know, but Bruce makes me mad. All he does is tease me about Virginia every time he has an audience, and I know that sometime Virginia hears him," Norman answered, near tears.

"Well, Norman, at least this time, he is on your side; he is asking me to help you get your shanty. I'll tell you what, let's go load the shanty. Bruce can ride with me, and I'll have a little talk with him about Virginia. Maybe that will help," I said, wondering what I was getting into.

On the trip to Jocklin's, which was much further than I had anticipated, I talked with Bruce, saying, "What's the problem, Bruce? Don't you want to see your brother happy?"

"It's not that, Caleb. It's just things have changed between us so much since Virginia came. You know, we always only had each other for most of our lives. Now it's so different, he doesn't want me around when she is with us. This makes me mad and scared at the same time, and I say things that cause trouble. You know, Caleb, most of the time people don't want to talk to retards like us, but Norman says you're different," Bruce answered, staring out the window.

"I think I know what you're saying Bruce," I said, trying to respond thoughtfully, "You know I come from a big family, and my brothers and sisters and I have had our difficulties. Now I don't want to hear any more of this retard stuff; the things that you and Norman can accomplish are way above any category like that. Why, just today you have accomplished things that would have baffled me all day. Now, I know you are knowledgeable about sex, and I suppose that with only one shanty Norman would like to get rid of you some times when Virginia was there. That's something all of us boys understand. It wasn't about him being angry with you, it was about getting it on with her. Now with two shanties you won't have that kind of trouble if you use your head and get lost when they need you to. You know if this doesn't last, Norman is going to need you more than ever, so see it for what it is and stop letting your mind make it into a problem between you and your brother."

Bruce said, "I know you're right, Caleb; it is just that it scares me to think I might not always have Norman around. We have always had each other to depend on no matter what was happening in our lives. I know I shouldn't be jealous if Norman has a chance for some happiness, but it isn't just that he has a woman, it's what might happen if he doesn't need me anymore."

We had arrived at Jocklin's before I could formulate a sensible answer, so I told Bruce we would talk about all of this again sometime. He seemed pleased with that, as we joined Norman to load the shanty. We didn't have the equipment or the manpower that Leclat had supplied at the other site, and it was almost dark before we got the shanty loaded on the trailer. After we had it secured and Norman and Bruce had assured me they would be all right on the trip back without me, I headed for Sterling. I was late getting home, and Mother and Dad were worried that something had gone wrong, but I explained to them how Norman insisted on moving the other shanty also today.

Dad said, "You really got yourself a pusher when you hired him, Caleb. I hope he stays until I get back. He sounds like my kind of a man. I am a little jealous at how well you're doing without me, but I am proud of you, son."

Mother asked, "What's this about two shanties? I thought we only had one. Clem has been living in one for a long time, why do you need two now?"

Dad answered, saving me from lying, saying," One of the things that Norman asked for when he came to work for us, was to have his brother stay with him in our shanty. They are both big boys and they have lady friends; they found one shanty confining, so Norman arranged to get another one."

Mother just said, "Oh," and left the room.

Dad gave me a pat on the back, saying, "Keep up the good work, Caleb, and keep me informed; you see, I still can be a big help sometimes."

After grabbing something to eat I went upstairs to bed. I was almost as tired as I was when I first started to work with Dad. I remember thinking isn't there something wrong when help is wearing out the boss just before I fell asleep.

Right after Homer went down in the morning he came back up shaking me awake saying, "Caleb, there is someone on the phone for you. I can't make out what he wants, but he is awfully excited."

Norman was on the phone; he was so upset it was hard to understand him, so I shouted, "Norman, has someone gotten hurt?"

"No-no-no, Caleb," he stuttered

"Then calm down and tell me what the trouble is so I can help," I said rather gruffly.

"It's—it's the truck, Caleb; it quit. It-it is all my fault; I never—never should have talked you into doing this. Now your dad will fire me," he said, still stuttering.

"Look, Norman," I said, trying to calm him down. "No one is getting fired; just tell me what happened, so I can see what needs to be done. Did you have an accident with the truck?"

"No-no, Caleb, it just won't move. The motor runs fine, but I think the transmission must have blown out. Bruce and I spent the night in the shanty and waited for morning to call you. What should we do now? " Norman asked ,still sounding upset.

After finding out where they were and telling them I would be over and we could make a decision after I saw the truck I hung up the phone.

Dad, who woke up when I yelled at Norman, and had heard part of the conversation, asked, "Trouble, Caleb? Don't get to upset if there is; there're always some problems with most every job move."

I told Dad about the truck, and I was surprised that he took it so calmly; I asked if he had ever had any trouble with the transmission on the truck.

He said, "No, I never had any trouble with it, but Clem told me that it was losing oil and needed to be watched. I am sorry that I never passed that along to you. I think it was Leclat who mentioned he knew where there was a truck just like that that I could get parts off from if I ever needed them. After you find out for sure what the problem really is, talk to him about it."

I cut over from Sterling to the route that Norman said they were stuck on, thinking as I drove, how had it happened that I had ended up with the help running the show anyhow? I thought that I was being good to Norman, but

143

now I wondered if I wasn't somehow being conned a little by him. I knew enough about him now that I understood he sometimes used his seemingly backward ways to his advantage. When I arrived where they were, Norman was a mess, pacing back and forth by the truck.

I felt sorry about what I had been thinking and said, "Calm down, Norman; turns out that the truck had a leaky transmission, and because I didn't know about it this was bound to happen sometime. Dad thinks he knows were we can find parts, so stop your worrying, and let's get the problem straightened out."

"You—you don't understand, I—I didn't plan this; it's a ba-bad m-m-mess. It's all o-o-over for me now," Norman said, stuttering as he walked away.

I tried to get him to stop and make sense, but he just kept walking away, talking to himself. I saw Bruce in the shanty and went in asking, "What the hell is the matter with him, Bruce? This might be bad, but it isn't the end of the world. I can't make any sense out of anything he's saying."

"What do you think I'm hiding here for? I tried to talk to him all night, but he is out of his mind about what he did," Bruce replied.

"He didn't do anything, Bruce. I tried to tell him Dad said he forgot to tell me to watch the transmission on the truck because it was leaking, so the breakdown has nothing to do with what he did. How can I get through to him?" I asked.

"No wonder he's upset. You don't know do you? He figured we would be back last night and Virginia had already given up her apartment, so he told her she could move in this morning. Someone was supposed to bring her and her things early today. He thinks she is already there, and he doesn't have a place for her; that's why he is so frantic," Bruce said, studying my face for my reaction.

"Oh, my word. No wonder he is so upset, he thinks he's getting fired and losing Virginia, too; is that it?" I asked.

"Well, what would you expect your boss to do if you pulled a stunt like that? I swear Norman is even nuttier with his plans than ever since he met Virginia. He always has had these wild ideas on how he and I could lead a normal life even if we were a couple of retards," Bruce answered.

I said, "Come on, Bruce; stop this 'retard' business. You two might not be college educated but not many men have the ability that you two have shown since I have known you. Let's go see if we can get Norman back to earth."

Norman was back at the truck still muttering. I said, "Look, Norman, Bruce has it all figured out. We'll go over and level up the shanty that's there.

144

Virginia can set up house keeping while we get the truck repaired and bring the other shanty over."

Norman looked at me with a surprised look on his face saying, "B-b-but how about what I did? Aren't I going to lose my job?"

"Look, Norman," I said using the most exasperated voice I could muster, "I been trying to tell you since I got here that the truck wasn't your fault, so let's cut the blame game and get to work on our problems before Jocklin finds someone to take our place."

We all jumped into the car and drove to the job site. Virginia was already there with her things piled on the ground around her looking worried. Whoever had brought her had just dropped her off and left. She looked relieved to see us and asked, "What happened, did you run into a little trouble?"

"Nothing too bad, Virginia. The old truck blew the transmission, and the boys got stuck on the road all night. We decided it would be better if we got at least this shanty ready for you before we fixed the truck," I answered.

It didn't take us long to get the shanty leveled up and ready to use. Virginia said, "I'm going to be all right here, Norman. I'm a big girl; you boys get back to the truck and get it running, and if you need any help I'm a pretty good mechanic."

I thought, *I am going to have to find Leclat to see about that truck he told Dad about, then get the transmission and bring it back. There really wasn't any need for us all to go,* so I said, "Tell you what, Norman; you stay here, and after Virginia is settled you can do a little more work on the barn. Bruce and I will see if we can locate a transmission. The truck isn't too far from here, and we'll come get you when we find one."

As Bruce and I were leaving he said, "Pretty sharp, Caleb. I think Norman has already forgot that he never told you what he was up to."

"You know, Bruce, when you're the boss, the important thing is getting the job done and not losing sight of what is needed," I replied, feeling a lot better about myself than I probably should have.

I was just trying to figure out whether it would be better to try Leclat's house or try to catch him at the old job site when Bruce said, "You know what, Caleb? I know where there are a bunch of old trucks not far from where we used to live. Maybe he has a transmission that will fit that old '37 Ford of yours."

Bruce knew right where these trucks were. That seemed like our best bet, so I drove where Bruce told me. After we left the main road I was getting rather skeptical about where Bruce was taking me, but we finally arrived at an old farm deep in the woods. A man carrying a shotgun came out of the house saying, "I hope you're just lost."

Bruce got out and said, "It's me, Bruce, Mister Granger; this here is Caleb Carney; his truck, a '37 Ford, blew a transmission down the road a piece, and I thought maybe if you had one that would fit his truck, you might sell it to us."

I didn't think I had made a good choice coming here, because the man just stood there frowning for better part of 5 minutes. Finally he said, "Just might be I have one. I think it is a '38, but it should fit. Now depends on what you're offering whether I sell or not."

Damn, I thought I don't have the foggiest idea of what I should have to pay, but I said, "Depends how hard it is to get to and who takes it off your truck."

"Well, I'll tell you, stranger, my brother has been dismantling those old trucks and storing the parts in the barn for years, plans to get rich on them someday, he says. I'm pretty sure he has what you want up there, but you'll have to deal with him. I'll go get him," he said, going back into the house.

"Bruce do you have any idea what it's worth?" I asked.

"I'm not sure about money, Caleb," Bruce said, "but if it fits, and it's already out it would save a lot of time, and that's worth something."

The man's brother came out. At least he didn't have a gun. He said, "'37 Ford, huh? I just might have what you're looking for, but I ain't giving it away to nobody; gonna cost ya."

"Well, name your price, Mister Granger, and we will see if we can do business," I said, feeling kind of out of place in all this.

He said, "Well, let me see, there probably aren't many of them around, so it's going to be expensive."

I started to say, "How expensive?" when Bruce cut in and said, "Only money Caleb here has got on him is twenty dollars. It can't be any higher than that."

" Oh, I don't know," he answered, "should be higher than that, maybe at least 25 dollars."

Bruce cut me off again saying, "I maybe have 3 dollars in my overalls I can loan him, but that's the best we can do."

"Well, I guess seeing as you're stuck on the road and pretty broke, the good lord would want me to help out. Twenty-three dollars it is."

After we got the transmission loaded in the trunk of the car we carefully drove back down to the main road. I laughed, saying, "I don't know of anybody else smart enough to pull off what you just did, Bruce. I am glad I had you with me, or I might have spent twice as much and been all night getting him to agree to sell to me."

"Weren't no big deal, Caleb," he answered. "I knew what he was after more than the money, was company and being able to feel good about what happened between us. Our job was to help it work out that way. I still have no idea of what an honest price would be, but I knew that 25 dollars would look good to him. He has been taking those old trucks off from people's hands as a favor, and didn't have much invested in them except time."

I couldn't help thinking how different the last two days would have been if Clem had been the one I had to depend on instead of Bruce. Norman had a tendency to get extremely nervous when his plans had trouble, but he was more than adequate in all other ways. It's sad that people sometimes take others' opinions without investigating for themselves. I probably would have allowed Clem's opinion of Norman and Bruce to stand in my mind if I hadn't begun to work with them.

It was well into the afternoon by the time we got back to the new job site so I said, "I guess we will have to wait until tomorrow before we tackle the truck, boys. I have to make arrangements to get the horses on the road tomorrow. Dad wants them rested in their new place a couple days before we have to work them."

Norman was a little angry, saying, "Caleb, you could just drop me and Bruce off at the truck, and if we don't get it finished tonight we can sleep there in the shanty."

"The trouble with that, Norman, is I forgot to load the tools we need this morning. I didn't want to admit it, but I guess you're forcing it out of me. I'll get here early tomorrow, and we should have the truck fixed by noon. I'm sorry, but even if I went home and brought the tools back it would be dark before we could get started," I said, then I drove away.

I wasn't more than a mile from the site when I passed Leclat's crew and trucks on their way to the job. Leclat had hired his teams moved by trailer and moved everything the same day. I wondered if they thought they were going to get their barns up before dark. At home Dad was waiting to hear how things went. He laughed when I told how we had bought the transmission and said, "Caleb, I don't know why I worry about you; it seems that the boys you hired are not just good workers but one hell of an asset to the business. I know that what happened wasn't any fault of yours, but this reminds me how you always seemed to be in some mess when you first worked at the barn, milking."

Mother came in saying, "Caleb, I hope you aren't planning on Jason driving the team over, because I don't want him taking a day off from school."

"I wasn't until now; I had planned on taking them myself and having Norman bring me back with the truck," I answered. "Now I need him or Homer, because the truck's broke down, and I'm not sure when it will be ready. Homer would have to take time off from school and from his job too, so I think it should be Jason."

Mother left, muttering, "Next thing you know you'll be finding a job for Francis too."

Dad said, "Might be a good idea if we did. What's your take on Francis, Caleb? Mother has talked to the doctors at the hospital, and they have suggested he might be allergic to most animals, but wouldn't offer any advice without seeing him. They say it requires a lot of testing, but seeing as he has always been around animals, they think there is a chance he might outgrow it."

"I don't know, Dad. It might be a good idea to at least have him looked at. He was so happy about being with Jason on that last trip, but when he went to help Jason rub down the team he got sick," I answered as I left to go see Jason about making the trip. Jason was more excited about this trip than he was the one before, I guess because he got out of going to school. I went over the route with him and drew him a map to go by.

The next morning after getting Jason off I drove to the new job site to pick up Norman and Bruce and the transmission. When I arrived, our truck and Norman's shanty were already there. Bruce came running over from where they were leveling the shanty, all excited, saying, "What do you think of this, Caleb? Not bad for a couple of retards, huh?"

"Leclat came in right after you left, and one of his boys was interested in the transmission. Seems he was quite a mechanic, and so Leclat said, 'If one of you boys is willing to stay here and work on the barn he can change that transmission better than any of you.' I went with Donald Trent, that was his name, and we had that old truck ready to go just about dark. I drove it back here, and he followed me. He says not to use it much until we add more oil to it; we lost some changing it. He told me that someday he is going to have a garage of his own, and when he does he wants to hire me. That's good isn't it, Caleb?"

"Yes, that's good, Bruce, but I told you stop referring to you and your brother as 'retards;' you two are more resourceful than most men I know," I said, thinking I should thank Leclat.

I went over to thank Leclat, and he said, "Hell, Caleb, I got the best of that deal, Norman and Virginia both worked on the barn; they were worth more than Donald ever was; all he ever wants to do is work on cars and trucks, so I guess we both made out."

After helping the boys finish leveling the shanties, Norman and I walked down to check on where the Joclin crew was setting up the sawmill. Norman took some good-natured kidding from them about him being a married man now. Norman handled it well, telling them he would invite them all to the wedding, but it wouldn't be for a while. After joshing with them for a while we went to find the place that had been leveled out to stick the lumber. It was a bit farther than I had figured it would be, but considering it was downhill from the mill site I didn't see any problem in keeping ahead of the mill when they started sawing.

Walking back, Norman said, "I'm sorry about the mess I caused, Caleb. Bruce says that my head has been in a cloud ever since Virginia showed up. Maybe I'm not thinking right."

"Hell, Norman, what is it with you and Bruce?" I snorted angrily. "I've told you a dozen times that the truck wasn't your fault. If I didn't have you and Bruce helping me it probably would have been sitting on the side of the road for a week. Even with the breakdown, this move has been a snap for me, so you stop your damn worrying and enjoy what we have accomplished. Dad said he was proud of how well we have done; I told him it was mostly you and Bruce that made it all happen. I have thought a dozen times how lucky I was that Clem quit, and you were available to take his place."

"How about Virginia, Caleb?" Norman asked, "Are you upset about her moving in with me?"

"Look, Norman, my job is to see that the work gets done here, properly, and I need happy, contented helpers, are you happy about Virginia?"

Norman said. "I am happy and scared at the same time, Caleb. Virginia seems too good to be true. I never ever saw myself as having a woman of my own."

"Well, Norman," I answered, "I think you are going to find out that nobody ever belongs to you, but remember what you said before: even if it doesn't last, you have now.
So stop fretting about everybody else and enjoy your now just like it was going to be forever."

When we got back to where the barns and shanties were I drove off to check on how Jason was doing with the team. He was almost to the half way mark and was resting the horses and eating his lunch.

He said, "Glad you came by, Caleb. It is kind of boring driving a team all this way by yourself. I tried to talk Mother into letting Francis come with me, but she said one of us missing school was more than enough. I didn't expect to see you back this soon, though."

"We got lucky, Jason; Leclat had a man with him who likes working on cars who fixed the truck yesterday afternoon, and they had it at the site when I arrived this morning. I know what I can do, Jason. I'll go back and pick up Norman and come back. He can take my car, and I'll ride the rest of the way with you. I'll be back in about a half an hour," I said, driving away.

After coming back and joining Jason on the wagon we talked about Dad's accident. I was surprised when Jason said, "I'm worried about how it has changed the family, not just having you back home but the way Mother hasn't been available to us children like she always was before. Nellie, Francis, and I have talked about it. We know that Dad comes first right now, but it still hurts sometimes. I have some problems that I couldn't talk with her about anyway, but I still miss her. I sometimes try to talk to Homer about this damn boy-girl thing that is driving me crazy, but he isn't much help. He keeps coming back to the bulls and the cows at the Coors barn. I don't care about the damn bull; I need to know if I'm going crazy or not."

"Oh! Jason you're not going crazy, you're going through puberty and it can be frightening, I remember well how confusing it was to me. I got a lot of those bull stories then too. I think it is a little bit different for each of us; the trick is getting through it without it creating trouble or fear. Josh used to tell me that it could be a wonderful thing once you understood it. Still he never seemed to be able to make me understand it. I will tell you that it made me think things and want to do things that seemed shameful. Josh said puberty was God's test to help develop our characters, as you become a man. I can assure you, Jason, you're not crazy. What you're going through is natural for all boys your age. I'm not sure if I am any more help than Homer, but please feel free to come and talk to me anytime about it; I'll do my best to help."

I told Jason about how Karl had joined me on my first time driving the team to a job and how our childhood here had been such a help to him after he was wounded during World War II.

Jason said, "I have a friend like Karl too. He is a little older than I am. His name is James Watt, and we have been climbing the mountain and going fishing together just like that."

I said, "Jason, you keep doing things like that with James. Your childhood may not be the best time of your life but it will always be an important part of it. You know, Karl only came back once after that time, but it made what I felt about my childhood so genuine on that trip, it let me see that it was all right that my youth seemed so important to me."

When we reached the job site Norman and Virginia insisted that they could take care of the team and curry them. Norman said, "Caleb, Joclin will be a couple of more days before he is ready to start the mill. I'll take the team with the wagon down a couple of times and drive them over the route we are going to use, just to make sure there aren't going to be any problems. You don't have to come back here tomorrow; that will give you a chance to catch up on things at home."

After getting a promise from both Bruce and Norman that they would find a phone and call me if any problem developed, I left for Sterling with Jason, thinking about all the things that had happened in the last few days. I felt rather good about how I had survived another chapter in my life as chief of the Carney Enterprises.

CHAPTER SIX

Things at the new job site went better than expected, even though Norman and I had to work almost as hard as Dad and I had on the first job I had worked with him. Because the timber on this job was so good, the mill was producing much more lumber than they had at the last job. This was good because of the increased pay, but we certainly felt we earned it at the end of the day. After the first week I talked to Dad about raising Norman's wages.

Dad said, "I been thinking on that; you know, he not only has proved to be a good worker. He is also saving us money because we don't have to worry about the horses when you are not there working. I have been doing some figuring and think we could give him fifty cents an hour more and still come out ahead of the game."

"I'm glad you understand what a benefit Norman is to us. I imagine all this would have been much harder if Clem had been still with us. You know Norman and Virginia go down every night and lay as much bedding ahead as possible. Very seldom do we have to lay any during the day. You remember how we had to practically give up our lunch breaks to keep ahead when we first started sticking lumber together?"

I could see that too much talk about the job was upsetting to Dad because he couldn't be a part of it. So I said, "Dad, did you give any more thought about Francis's problem? I would hate to think that he has been hiding from the farm animals because of some sickness that might have a cure."

"Mother and I have been discussing it." Dad answered. "She is worried that maybe this isn't the right time to get him involved in treatment while I am laid up. We are sure that there will be bills beyond all that has been donated to us since my accident. Struggle as we have through the hard times we have always kept our bills paid. I also don't think it is fair that you are not drawing a full wage, so we are trying to be prudent in all that we do. I have to go and do my exercises now; I'll let you know what our plans are for Francis as soon as we decide."

I left Dad, thinking how hard it has been for him to accept that he had to depend on a son to take his place in the family. It was a severe blow to the strong male image that he had seemed to adhere to when I was younger. I know he would hardly talk to Uncle Louis for a long time after Louis had killed big red, after he had attacked Nellie. Still I had to admire Dad for not becoming angry with the world about the accident like Glenn's father had. There were times when he acted depressed, and that worried us, but the promise that with one more operation on his leg and a few more months of exercising he would be almost as good as before kept his sanity. Remembering what Jason and Nellie had said about mother being so busy with Dad it was understandable where he got the strength to see this through.

Everything on the job went smoothly and we got through November and well into December with little or no snow. Jennie asked me to contact her when I was going to the job site on the weekends to see if she was free. I picked her up one Saturday and I teased her about having the hots for Norman or Bruce.

"Caleb, don't you think it's about time for you to get your mind out of the gutter?" Jennie said giving me a whack. "You're not just one of the barn boys now, you know. I shall be eternally sorry about allowing the affair we had when we were so low about Josh. I know there is no way to erase it in either of our minds, but that isn't the real person I am. I am not a Beverly, though I do understand her desires. By the way, I suppose you know that Beverly has moved to some town in Vermont. I understand she has a good job up there."

"No, I didn't know she had moved. I am happy for her. I hope she finds the man she is looking for and lives happily ever after. I know she will make the right man very, very happy," I said with a laugh.

Jennie smacked me again and said, "I don't know why I put up with you,

Caleb Carney; you're incorrigible. I asked to go because I wanted to see how Virginia and Norman were doing. Before listening to your garbage about sex, I thought that we enjoyed being together, even platonically."

"Whoa with the big words, Jennie; I haven't been to college yet, you know. Wasn't it you who thought I was chaste? Now I have to be platonic while I'm with you. Maybe I am going to have to do some studying every time we date," I said laughing.

"Caleb," Jennie said with tears forming in her eyes, "Don't make this any harder than it is. I want us to be close friends. Considering our history it would be easier just to avoid you, but I feel that Josh's loss put us together."

"I'm sorry, Jennie," I answered, "I didn't mean to upset you. I also think we should stay close friends, sometimes closer than you want, but I'll try hard to keep my promise about sex. In lots of ways we have what Joan and I had for all those years, someone of the opposite sex to discuss things with. I really wouldn't want to think I couldn't call you and ask you to take a ride or go for a sundae or something when I am troubled. There is a need in my life for female companionship in every connotation of the word. I can't promise I won't make you mad or upset but I want you to know that I really care for you in more ways than one."

I was glad when we had reached the job site. Norman and Bruce weren't there but Virginia was. I left Jennie with Virginia and went down to the barn to change a wheel on the wagon, which was the reason for this trip. I had trouble getting the nuts loosened; I don't think they had been off in years. I had to go back to the shanty to get some kerosene to help loosen them, and Jennie and Virginia were having such a deep discussion I don't think they even noticed that I had come back. It had taken me almost two hours to finish changing the wheel, and Jennie had to hurry her goodbyes because we had to get her back to work at the barn that night.

On the ride home I asked, "How was your visit with Virginia, Jennie? Is she ready to skip out on Norman?"

"I don't think you are going to believe this, Caleb," she answered, "but she asked me what I thought about her marrying Norman. I wasn't that surprised because I knew she had a good heart, but I was afraid to answer her too positively because I see some problems. Tell me what you would have said."

I thought about that for a minute before saying, "I guess I would have told her what a wonderful person Norman is. After all, from a man's point of view it looks real good for Norman. What would be your objections?"

"Oh, I didn't object. I questioned her about how she sees Norman and the world that he lives in. I also told her how I worry about Norman getting hurt just like I thought when she first showed up. She said it wasn't a plan, it was just something that had come up between her and Norman, and she wanted my point of view. She said what family she has thinks she is crazy for just being with Norman, so she can't discuss it with them. She seems to be truly in love with him, and you can tell Norman adores the ground she walks on. Love can be the most beautiful and the scariest of things at the same time, can't it, Caleb? I told her if she needed to talk some more I would try to get back, and that I was sure you would be willing to talk to her too. Was that okay?" she said, giving me a hug.

"I'm not sure what I could say, Jennie," I said, feeling kind of edgy at having been put in this position, "but I will talk to her if she wants me to. The last thing I would have thought about when I hired Norman would have been about women or marriage. You have spent more time with Virginia than I have. What's your take on her as a person?"

"I believe that she is what she seems to be—a woman with a lot of passion for life that has seen her hard times and is willing to give of her self to others," Jennie answered. Then after thinking a minute she added, "I think if I talked to her again I would explore her understanding of what life could end up being, married to Norman. I would ask if she thought she always would be happy with what Norman could give besides his love for her. I think Virginia is the kind of woman from whom I would seek advice if something happened in my life that I was afraid I couldn't handle. The feeling I get from her is that not only is she honest and open, I believe she thinks ahead. Why else would she want to talk to us about possibly marrying Norman?"

We rode quietly the rest of the way back to Sterling with Jennie cuddled up close to me. When I let her off at her house she kissed me passionately, saying as she got out of the car, "Goodnight, Caleb, now that Beverly's gone I guess you will have to be my little virgin. Call me if you get a chance to take me to see Virginia again."

I knew that Jennie knew how kisses like that aroused me, and couldn't for the life of me figure out what the hell she was trying to do to me. After finding out Beverly had left town I figured I was safe from that Beverly's virgin nickname. *I think the effect of having Etta here has some how changed Jennie; I know if she insists on that kind of behavior then my promise doesn't stand a chance of surviving.*

The next few weeks at work Norman never mentioned marriage. Since Jennie and I had decided it was best to let him bring it up I had completely forgotten about it until Virginia met me just as I was leaving the barn on a Friday night.

She said, "Caleb, can I have a minute of your time? I know Jennie has told you about our discussion on marrying Norman. I would like to hear your opinion."

Man, I hoped I had avoided this discussion. I punted, saying, "I have been waiting for Norman to open up to me about it, but he hasn't said a word. I think I would feel more comfortable talking to you if I knew his feelings. It has many more avenues to consider than just you two living together. There's Bruce and his family's feelings to consider. I am not familiar with any of them except Bruce, but I understand there are a couple of younger children still at home."

I think Virginia sensed that I was grasping at the straws of the situation and not the meat because she said, "I don't want to put you on the fence Caleb, it's just that Norman has such high regard for you and your family, I thought it was important to hear how you felt."

"I guess the real answer, Virginia, is the whole thing is a surprise, and I need time to assess just what it is I feel before I make any serious comments about it. Jennie, who has come to know you better than me, thinks you are a wonderful person with a compassionate heart and wouldn't ever do anything to hurt Norman. In fact she said if she needed advice about a problem in life she feels you would be a good counselor."

Virginia laughed and said, "I guess that goes back to the old adage—if you want to see how something was made you have to study the mill it went through. I'm a little older than Norman and saw things of life before I got married that no young girl should ever see. My marriage was a wonderful thing. We had financial struggles but up until Jim got sick it was heaven for me. I was lost for a while after he died and struggled but I feel stronger now and I really believe that Norman and I can have a happy and productive life together. Still there is no hurry to get married, though Norman has some misgivings about how we live now, and that is a concern to me."

"Look, Virginia," I answered, "I feel that you are good for Norman, and I'm glad that he has a chance at a happiness that might have passed him by. It just that I really want my comments about the marriage to be informed ones, and I don't think I can do that without his input. I will be more than willing to have a discussion with one or both of you after he decides to let me in on what he is thinking."

As I left heading for Sterling, it looked like we might be getting some more snow, although we have had a few storms there has been little accumulation of snow. This was good because we were hoping to be done with the middle lot before the snow got too heavy. I felt pretty good about talking with Virginia even though it didn't settle anything; at least the dread I felt about having to talk to her about marrying Norman had lifted.

When I got home I went in to give my daily report to Dad, I had discovered that he looked forward to it if I kept it short. I talked about the job in general, not about how well Norman and I were doing because that seemed to bother him somehow. Maybe he thought how easily little Caleb got his old job done. I know sometimes I wondered how much I would have accomplished without Norman, Bruce, the Leclats and Joclins looking out for me. I remember Josh saying, that life is so much easier when you allow yourself to be open to all the possibilities of help that is available.

When I left Dad, Jason said, "Caleb, one of your girlfriends is on the phone and demanding to talk to you."

It was Betty. She was indignant that I hadn't called her. When I tried to tell her I had been too busy to date she said, "How about all the time you been spending with that Jennie? Seems you have plenty of time for her. You have made it quite plain that you don't want a steady girl, but you did promise to call me. My mother has been on my tail because you don't come around. She was so excited when she thought we were dating."

"Whoa, Betty," I said, cutting her off, "I honestly was going to contact you this week. Let's take in a movie this weekend. How about tomorrow night? You pick out a show. I'll pick you up about six."

"Oh, Caleb, I'm sorry I was so bitchy. I'll make it up to you; you'll never be sorry about dating me. I think the movie I wanted to see is playing in Oscin. I'll check on it and be ready tomorrow," she answered.

After supper I went with Jason, checking on things that needed attention around the farm. The pigs were gone; Dad had hired them butchered this year, as Uncle Louis wasn't with us anymore. He thought without him and Louis to do the butchering it was putting too much pressure on us boys. Jason thought we would run short of hay before spring, which would mean I should order more when I bought for the horses later on. There were a couple of the hens that were no longer layers that we marked for the stew pot. All in all it was evident that Jason was doing a good job keeping things up around home. I told him how proud we all were of him and that someday he would make a great farmer.

157

He surprised me by saying, "I don't think I want to be a farmer, Caleb. I don't mind taking care of things for the family now, but I don't see it as a way I want to spend my life. I'm not sure what I really want yet, but I do know it isn't farming."

I said, "That's okay, Jason. I'm still not sure what I want to be yet, and I'm much older than you. I just feel if we work hard at what we are given to do, it will better prepare us for what it is we decide on making our life's work."

"Caleb," Jason asked, "you won't laugh or be mad if I ask you a personal question will you?"

"Fire away, Jason," I answered, "that is what brothers are for."

"Have you ever done this sex thing, Caleb?" he asked, hanging his head.

Man, I thought, *now what do I say?* Stalling for time I said, "Why do you ask, Jason?"

"You remember Beverly Stone who was about your age? Well, she has a sister Elaine who is just a little older than I am, and she is always trying to kiss me. When she does she rubs up against me, and I get the strangest feelings. I was just thinking if this led to sex, I wouldn't know what to do," he answered.

"You know what, Jason? I'm going to tell you what Josh told me," I said, hoping I could satisfy him with that. "He said going through puberty, and that is what's happening to you, is a test, training you in the restraints needed to be a gentleman when you grow up."

Jason was quiet after that about sex, so we went on with our plans to walk the fence tomorrow and cutting some brush back that was creeping into the fields. I went to bed that night thinking I had been lucky with Jason and Virginia not to have to get too deep into our discussions.

Saturday night at six I went to pick Betty up. As she came to the door I had to admit something to myself, that I had avoided her. Betty might be short but she was pretty and had a definite sexual appeal. I suppose I hadn't seen past my desire for Etta that night at the dance.

She gave me a little kiss and yelled back to her mother, "I'm going out with Caleb, Mom; don't wait up for me."

She was all cuddly and talkative on the ride to Oscin, telling me all about the picture we were going to see. Finally I said, "You keep talking about the picture and there won't be any sense in going to see it, Betty."

She said, "I'm sorry, Caleb; I'm just so excited. I've heard so much about this picture, and now not only am I getting to see it I'll be seeing it with you."

The movie was an emotional roller coaster and I had to keep peeling Betty off from me, sometimes because of the movie and sometimes I think she was

158

doing it just to drive me crazy. After the movie I suggested we go for a sundae or something, thinking maybe it would cool us off. Betty was adamant that we should go back to Sterling and go to the grove. At the grove we sat and talked about Karl and how Karl and I had been such good friends and how mad she was I never seemed to notice her. Betty sat close, giving me little kisses, they grew more and more passionate.

I pushed her away and said, "Betty, we should go. If this goes on we are going to get in trouble."

She pulled back and said, "Is Beverly's little virgin afraid of little Betty?"

I shook her and said, "Look, I have nothing to offer you Betty, and if we get involved it will only be physical, and I'm sure that's not fair to either of us."

Betty laughed and undid her blouse and bra saying, "This physical enough for you, Caleb?"

Suddenly the longing left by Etta, the desires that Jennie had created, and the crazy sexiness of Betty all exploded inside me, and we were in the back seat having the wildest sex ever.

After lying in each other's embrace she said, "I loved your physicalness, Caleb, and I bet you found some joy in mine."

After spending another hour or so at the grove I took Betty home. I returned her passionate kiss at the door saying, "Things haven't changed, Betty, about the way I feel. No attachments."

"Maybe there aren't any attachments, Caleb, but I think you'll find after tonight some things have changed," she said, and walked into the house.

I left the Harts with a certain amount of ambiguity about what had happened with Betty. I had made a conscious effort in my thinking that I wouldn't become sexually involved with her. I've had the feeling from when I first met her at the dance that night; she would be trouble with a capital T. Now I have allowed her to get way beyond first base in our relationship. Whether it's yes or no, it seems that God has given the female the upper hand in this sex thing. As I was driving into our yard it was almost like I could hear Josh say '*No, Caleb he only gave them free will just like he did us.*'

The next day I went to church with Nellie and Francis. I found little solace there as the pastor preached about the sins of fornication. After we left church we went to Oscin for an ice cream sundae, I asked Francis if he could tell me more about why he had trouble with animals.

He said, "It isn't like I'm afraid, Caleb. It's just that my head gets all plugged up, and I'm afraid I'm going to choke if I don't get away from them. Nobody paid any attention when I was little. I guess they thought I was scared of

159

animals and would outgrow it. Now I hear Mother and Dad talking about having me examined by a doctor. That scares me, too, but if I could get rid of what causes my stuffiness I would like that."

"I know Dad and Mom are concerned about you, Francis, and as soon as they have decided what is best way to go you will be getting help. They have already talked to some of the doctors at the hospital and are seeking advice about what is the best thing to do," I answered, thinking money shouldn't be a problem in a case like this.

That night I wrote to Hester and Richard in Japan and explained Dad's hesitation about taking Francis for treatment, asking for advice. Next day at work I expected to hear something from Norman, about Virginia and him getting married but did not hear a word about it. For the next couple of days I talked about Hester and Richard, how he had been married before and how they rushed the marriage so Hester could go to Japan with him. Still he didn't utter a word about him and Virginia getting married.

Wednesday night when I got home Emma said, "I saw Jake today at the library and he wants to get together with you while he's home for Christmas break."

I called Jake right after we had eaten supper and made arrangements to pick him up at his house. When he came out of the house I could see that this was a different Jake. Maybe the way he dressed, maybe the way he carried himself, maybe the way he looked more mature, I wasn't sure but little Jake was gone.

As he got into the car he said, "Caleb, we are the luckiest boys alive. I can't tell you how wonderful it is to be in college. I have always believed that I would go to college, but my dreams were nothing like this. I had imagined I would be washing dishes or sweeping floors just to go to college piece meal, now here I am a full-time college student. I have even been invited next year to join two different fraternities. I wish there was some way Old Hanna could see what she has done for me—not only is my tuition paid, but my uncle sends me money every month so I can spend all my time studying. It is like heaven for me, Caleb, and I know when you join me next year you'll love it, too."

"Well, hello to you too, Jake; it's me, Caleb, remember me? I was one of your boyhood pals," I asked with a laugh

"I'm sorry, Caleb," he answered, "I guess I got a little carried away there, but coming back to Sterling just illustrated how far along I am in my dream."

"That's funny, Jake," I said. "Just the other day I was telling someone that just staying in Sterling was my dream. I'm not saying that's a decision, but it sure is one of my options."

"Don't get me wrong, Caleb," Jake said looking startled, "I have no plans to give up Sterling in my life. It is just that Sterling doesn't offer what I am finding for an education in Oklahoma. I may not be always able to live here but my heart always will. And you, Caleb, don't tell me you are thinking of giving up your college education?"

"It is more complicated than that, Jake," I answered. "I wasn't happy about leaving when I went to Oklahoma, and though I made some good friends there I was never at ease. I thought going to college was going to help me shake all that, but when I came back here it was like getting back into my own skin again, and I like that feeling."

Jake said, "Caleb, let's drop that and go cruising. You're beginning to scare me. I'm sorry if I came on like a big blowhard; it's just that coming back brought it all together again."

Jake and I spent most of the next two nights together cruising Oscin and talking about college and old times.

Friday night at suppertime the telephone rang, and Emma, who was always racing to answer, came back and said, "It's Mr. Walden, Caleb, and he wants to speak to you."

I went to the phone wondering what this could be about. I said, "Hello."

Mister Walden said, "Caleb, I know you don't owe me or my wife any favors but I'm going to ask for one anyway."

"That's okay, Mister Walden," I answered, " you know if it's about Joan I'll be glad to do anything I can for you."

"Look, Caleb, we don't know what's wrong with her. She came home last night and went right up and locked herself in her room. She refuses to let us in the room or even talk to us through the door. Her mother is half out of her mind. I suggested you might help, and she jumped at the thought. She wants to know if you can come right over," he asked.

I said, "Mister Walden, let's do it this way. You tell her I called and want to see her, and you told me to wait until the morning because she wasn't feeling well. I think giving her one more night might give her a chance to straighten out whatever it is herself. I will be there early tomorrow. Tell her I have to go back to my job for something and would like her to go with me."

I'm not sure why I had been hesitant to rush over to Joan's; it's just that I had such bad memories from the times I had been there before, I guess. Also, I had agreed to meet Jake because this was probably the last night he would be in Sterling, as his family was going to his uncle's place in Pennsylvania for Christmas, and he was leaving for Oklahoma from there.

161

We had planned to see a movie, but when I talked to him about Joan, he said, "Caleb, let's go to the ice cream parlor so we can talk. I have seen how some of the freshmen became completely unraveled their first time out in the world alone. I am not saying that is Joan's problem, but you know she led a pretty protected life here in Sterling."

I spent the evening listening to Jake; it was almost like he was writing a thesis on what he had seen in his first semester. He told how some students became like babies and their folks were called to deal with it, most of these were taken back home. He spoke of those who became sexually active, others who drank too much and even one who had committed suicide.

After listening to all this I said, "Jake, the first time I saw you on this break, I got the opinion that college was heaven to you. Now you are telling me horror stories about what goes on there. After tonight I not sure that I would even be interested in going back to something like that."

"Look, Caleb," Jake, said, looking concerned. "You know how I want to be a good journalist. We are taught that we must study what's around us and come to an understanding of it before we write about it. Even in grade school I was told I needed to understand my subjects more. I was told that the reason your writing worked so well was that you wrote about what you knew or had experienced. What I talked about isn't prevalent throughout the school. It's just that as a freshman I'm close to these happenings, so that's what I try to comprehend. I told you because I thought it might be of some help with Joan. You should understand that there are many more like me who are ecstatic about being in college."

After leaving Jake off I thought how much this was like the old days when Jake was talking over my head on a subject. I was pleased that he shared his insight with me, though I couldn't really imagine Joan in any of those scenarios.

The next morning I went over to the Walden's. Mr. Walden met me at the door, and he said, "Caleb, she won't respond to anything we do. I am hoping that you know her well enough to get through to her—somebody has to. You are free to use any tactic that you think might work. Please, help us."

"Okay, Mister Walden. Why don't you go up and tell her I am here and see if that gets any response," I answered, trying to think what I could possibly do.

He came back down and said, "Nothing; she won't even ask us to send you away."

I went upstairs feeling kind of strange being involved in this. I knocked on her door, saying, "Joan, it's Caleb. I need to talk to you, and I am not going away until I do." I waited a couple of minutes and got no response. So I said, "Joan, your father has authorized me to do anything I need to do to get to talk to you. So this is what I'm going to do, by my watch if you haven't opened the door in five minutes, I'm going to break it down. I am very serious about this, so if you aren't going to open the door I advise you to be decently dressed because one way or the other I'm going to talk to you."

I waited two minutes went by, three minutes and then four, "Last chance!" I hollered, banging on the door.

"Caleb," Joan answered in a weak voice, "I'll come out, but you have to promise to take me out of the house without my having to talk to my folks. Okay?"

"Give me a minute. I'll try to arrange that, but that door better be open when I come back up," I answered, heading down the stairs.

Mrs. Walden was at the bottom of the stairs listening. She said, "No way is she leaving without talking to us. We're her parents."

Mr. Walden said, "Now, Geraldine, we agreed that Caleb would have a free hand. I'm sure we can trust him to do the right thing for Joan. You come with me. Caleb, please keep us as informed as you can. We're counting on you."

I ran back upstairs, and Joan came out. She was a wreck; she had lost weight and looked like she hadn't slept in a month. "Hurry, Caleb," she said, "get me out of here before Mother gets away from my father."

We ran out to the car and hurried out of the yard with Mrs. Walden at the door yelling. Joan sat as far away from me as she possibly could in the car and said, "Please, Caleb, no questions. Now let's just drive."

"Okay, Joan. I have to go to the job site. It's over twenty-five miles from here; is that okay?" I asked

"I don't know," Joan answered. "Is there anyone there I know?"

"I don't believe there is anybody there except Norman, Bruce, and Virginia. I didn't even know any of them until I went back to work at the mill, so they won't know you. I'm not going to question you, Joan, but we have been sharing secrets and feelings since we were in the first grade. I want you to know I'm here for you in any way I can help."

I talked to Joan about how ambivalent I felt about what I should do about college and what I really wanted out of life. I told her how excited Jake had been about his education when he came home. I hoped that I could hit on something that would get her to talk but seemingly to no avail.

Suddenly she said, "How much further, Caleb?"

I told her about three miles, and she said, "Let's stop for a while, Caleb. I need to tell you something." I pulled over and stopped and turned to Joan. There were tears streaming down her face, so I went to hold her but she pulled away saying, "Don't touch me, Caleb, and please look away from me."

I did as she asked, and between great sobs she told me what had happened. She said, "I was like Jake until the night before I came home. College was like heaven for me; I liked the studies and worked hard at getting good grades. My roommate, who never seemed to study and was always out partying, used to tease me all the time about being a stick in the mud. So on the last night we were going to be there I went out with her and a girl across the hall from us. We went to this nightclub where they had dancing. I danced with a couple of guys that I had met at school. The other girls kept ordering drinks, and I stopped ordering on my second one because I wasn't used to drinking. About half way through the evening both of the girls I was with seemed to have disappeared. A young man came and asked me to dance, and not wanting to seem alone I said yes, and we danced one set. When he led me back to my table he sat down and talked to me about college."

"As we were talking another young man came up. I thought he was about to leave, so I didn't see any harm in him sitting with me. I drank most of the drink I had left but refused when he offered to buy me another, telling him this was my limit. As we sat there talking I began to feel dizzy. He suggested that maybe I needed some fresh air. When we got outside it got worse, and I must have passed out. Next thing I remember is waking up and hearing someone say, 'My God, she was a virgin!' and hearing a door slam. I felt like someone had torn my vagina apart, and I hurt all over. Slowly it came to me what had happened, that I had been raped. I was in some sleazy motel outside of the city. Luckily they didn't rob me, and I was able to call a cab and get back to my room. My roommate had left a note saying she had left for home and hoped I had a good time last night. There was something that felt so callous about that note that I went crazy, and without thinking I grabbed my suitcase and came home. I guess I have been in shock because home was the last place I wanted to be to deal with this."

"My God, Joan," I said reaching for her, "why didn't you call me right away?"

She fell into my arms sobbing saying, "What can anybody do, Caleb? What can anybody do?"

The picture she had drawn exploded in my mind. How could anything like this happen to my little ice cream girl? I felt consumed with fury. Fighting to control my anger and not sure what could be done in this situation, I asked, "Do you want to have the police involved, Joan?"

"No, no, Caleb; my first thought were that I would keep it all quiet and weather the storm myself, but I'm not strong enough. I know I need help, but how do I do that without bringing the whole world into this sordid episode of my life?" she answered, still sobbing uncontrollably.

"Look, Joan, I don't have a ready answer, but you and I can find one if we keep talking about possibilities until we come up with one that you are comfortable with. I, for one, would like to find a way to get my hands on those two guys and make them pay with their lives," I said, feeling the anger beginning to come under control. "Let's get to the job site and take care of my business there; then I'll be free for the rest of the day, and we can go some place to talk this out."

As we pulled back on to the road I noticed that the snow flurries we had been having the last couple of days were getting heavier, and snow was starting to accumulate on the road. By the time we arrived at the job site we were in a full-blown snow storm, and visibility was getting poor.

Norman was just leaving the shanty barn. As we drove up he said, "Looks like we are in for a real nor'easter, Caleb. Leclat said yesterday he had heard on the radio that we might get one this weekend. Who's your new friend, Caleb? She looks like she could use a cup of coffee. Bring her up to the shanty, Virginia already has coffee on."

After I introduced Joan, I started to say no, that we needed to get back, but then I remembered what Jennie had said about going to Virginia if she was troubled with her world.

So I said, "Just as soon as I get that part on the wagon fixed we'll be right up."

"Just leave the part, Caleb, I'll have plenty of time to fix it before Monday," Norman said as he headed toward the shanty to warn Virginia.

Joan said, "Caleb, I am in no shape to meet anyone new, let's just go."

"I really can't, Joan. Norman and Virginia are very important to my job, and Norman takes offense easily. You will like Virginia. She won't probe or ask dumb questions," I answered hoping Joan would accept this.

Norman and Bruce had used one of Leclat's teams and drawn a couple of scoot loads of wood up by the shanty, and Bruce was cutting it up and getting it under cover.

He stopped work when he saw us and said, "Hey, Caleb, see you got a new girlfriend. What happened? You two have a fight already?"

165

I said, "Don't make it any worse than it is, Bruce. She got upset about Jennie, but I think we have it under control for now."

Joan gave me a hit and said, "I want to leave, Caleb; please don't make me talk to strangers."

"They already believe that we have been fighting, so you can get by the few minutes we have to be here without talking if you need to. I'll tell them just one cup, and we have to hurry because of the storm," I answered, taking Joan firmly by the elbow.

Virginia met us at the door saying, "Caleb, what do you mean dragging a girl out in this kind of weather? You'll be lucky if you can stay on the road getting back."

"I know, Virginia, but Joan here has been away at college, and is only home for Christmas break, and I wanted to spend as much time with her as I could, so I talked her into coming with me today. Turns out that maybe I shouldn't have, for more reasons than one. We had a little tiff about what I have been doing since she left. Maybe a quick cup of coffee will make the trip back a little less hostile," I said, forcing a chuckle.

We were at the shanty less than a half an hour. Joan hadn't said more than two words. Virginia didn't press, though I sensed a woman's curiosity in her as she studied Joan. As we left the shanty the storm had grown fiercer and snow had accumulated almost six inches since we had arrived there. We had a hard time getting off the job site because of the roughness of the road there. I told Joan we would be all right after we get back on the main road. About a half of a mile after we reached the main road it was snowing so hard I could hardly see the road approaching a steep incline. I started to try to gain some speed to carry us over the hill.

Suddenly we went into a spin. I couldn't get the car under control, and we landed in a ditch. I got out and inspected our problem. It was very evident that we weren't going to be able to get the car out of the ditch without help.

Getting back in the car I said, "Joan, our only choice is to walk back to the job site and get the truck or a team to pull us out. I would leave you here, but in case anything else goes wrong I think we'd better stick together. It is less than a mile back, and even though we aren't dressed for it we should get back there before the weather really gets to us."

Joan started crying again, saying, "Caleb, I don't want to go back. Just leave me here; I don't care if I freeze to death or not."

"Look, Joan," I shouted, "here's the deal—you're going back. Even if I have to carry you, and if you make me do that, we both will probably end up freezing to death, but I am taking you with me."

166

Joan reluctantly got out of the car, and we started back to the job site. I was surprised at how much snow had accumulated on the road it was already over six inches deep and it was a blinding wind driven storm. Neither Joan nor I were dressed for this but with less than a mile to go I felt we would be all right. The wind was so noisy that we couldn't carry on much of a conversation so I just kept hurrying Joan along. The snow blinded us so that I almost missed the road back to the shanties, luckily there were a couple of good size trees that had been cut near the highway where the road started in or I might have gone right by.

It must have taken us over a half an hour to reach the shanties, by that time our shoes and clothes were soaking and we were numb with the cold.

Virginia came to the door and rushed us into the shanty, taking one look she said, "Norman, you and Bruce take Caleb over to Bruce's shanty and get him and his clothes dried off. Joan can stay here, and I'll give her something to wear. Don't come back for at least an hour. I'll rustle up something to eat for all of us, and then we will decide what can be done."

Norman, Bruce, and I rushed over to Bruce's shanty. Both shanties had roaring fires, so I stripped off my clothes and sat by the stove, shivering, wondering, *What the devil am I going to do now? I wasn't worried about Joan being with Virginia, but here I was supposed to be her big help, and instead I have her trapped in a blizzard with no way to inform her folks about where we are. Worse than that, when she needs was someone to talk too, there isn't any way we could talk in either one of these one-room shanties with everyone around.*

Bruce, who was close to my size, threw me a pair of pants. "Put these on, Caleb; they are half way clean. Then you won't have to set around here naked. Never can tell when Virginia or Joan might decide we need checking up on," he said, laughing.

I don't know why, but pulling on his pants reminded me of when I got all of Russell's clothes the time our house burned down, and I didn't want to wear them.

Norman said, "Caleb, what-what are we going to do? Shall we try to get your car out today or wait?"

"I think that the best thing we can do now is sit still and wait this storm out. Anything else, I'm sure, will just bring us more trouble. We can make that decision after we get back to the girls to talk it over," I answered.

A couple of hours later we were all back in the first shanty eating some of the best bean soup and some kind of home made bread I had ever eaten.

Norman said, "Isn't she something, Caleb? She even bakes on top of that wood stove with this little oven that my mother gave us."

167

Virginia kind of blushed and said, "It's nothing special; when I grew up times were hard, and you had to learn to make do, and my mother at least taught me that well."

Joan who hadn't spoken to anyone, to my knowledge, spoke up and said, "Norman should be proud Virginia. You are not only a gracious host, but this food really is good."

I suddenly remembered that Joan hadn't eaten in a couple of days and marveled that she not only had joined the conversation she was eating. Looking around I thought if her mother could only see this. Shanties are infamous for their lack of utilities, so there wasn't a matching bowl amongst us and Bruce was actually eating out of a can with a serving spoon. It was one of those moments that you just knew would stick in your mind forever. If it wasn't for the burden of Joan's problem I believe this would be a very enjoyable time.

After we had finished all of the soup, and even Joan had seconds, Virginia said, "Here is the way I see it. There is no getting out of here tonight or maybe even tomorrow, so you three boys can sleep in Bruce's shanty, and Joan and I will sleep here. Now Norman, you and Bruce have the clothes for it, so you go down to care for the horses. Get enough wood in the shanties to keep the fires going for a couple of days, just in case. I have enough food to feed us all for a week if I have to. Maybe some of it won't be all that tasty, but it will keep us going."

Norman and Bruce went out; Virginia insisted on cleaning up herself, so I went and sat beside Joan, asking in a quiet voice, "How you making out, Joan? I'm sorry about getting us in this fix. I hope you are not too upset."

"Thank you, Caleb; thank you for taking me out of my world. I know we have a lot to overcome, but now I think it might be possible," she said, surprising me.

Before I could question her Virginia said, "Nothing like a good dramatic storm to get two lovers back together. I'm glad you're still able to talk to each other now."

It dawned on me then that we had covered Joan's silence by saying we had a fight. Then Joan said, "It was just a stupid school-girl thing. I'm old enough to have known better, but seeing Caleb again brought back the old jealousies."

"Well, I'm glad that is all it was, because when I first saw you I thought you looked like you had lost everything you thought was worth living for. That kind of scared me seeing that in another girl's face. I feel so much better now knowing it's just a "Girls will be girls" thing," Virginia answered.

The boys came back and loaded the shanties with wood. We spent well into the night talking and telling stories while the wind-driven snow howled outside.

Finally Virginia said, "I hate to break this up, but you boys will have a hard day ahead of you tomorrow, so you better get to your shanty and get some sleep."

Outside there was an accumulation of snow way over a foot and it was still snowing hard. We rushed to Bruce's shanty.

Once inside Norman said, "You know, Caleb, Joan seems to be sick or something. She hardly says a word, and she looks awfully pale. I can't believe that an argument with you over Jennie would take that much out of her."

"I'm not sure what her problem is, Norman. My friend, Jake, who started college this year, says that many of the first years had trouble their first time away from home and ended up with a depression or worse. With all that has happened I haven't had a chance to talk to her about her problem. I picked her up on the way here because her parents thought I would be good for her. We have been close friends since first grade. She hardly talked on the way here, just cried a lot. That's why we told you the story about us fighting. I thought when we left here I could get her talking and then we got stuck, and here we are," I answered.

Bruce said, "Depressions are bad, very bad. That's why we don't have a father anymore. He got so depressed that he shot himself."

"That's enough, Bruce," Norman cut in. "Caleb don't need to listen to our sad tales."

"It's okay, Norman," I replied. "I would like to hear about you and your family, but maybe you're right; it would be better another time. We should try to get some sleep now. It looks like we are in for a hell of a day tomorrow."

The next morning the snow was up to two feet with some drifts over three. Virginia had prepared us a fine breakfast of sausage and eggs and more of her bread. Somehow Joan seemed changed this morning and even joined in the conversation.

After we were over our morning greetings and were done laughing at the sleeping arrangements at Bruce's shanty, I said, "Joan, I know how worried your parents must be, but until we can get to a telephone there isn't anything we can do about it. The boys and I are going to hitch up a couple of teams and drag the scoots to break the road open from here to the main road. I don't expect the highway to be plowed much before tomorrow if even then; everything depends on when it quits snowing."

"Caleb, don't waste time worrying about my parents. I'm sure they have contacted your family and they have figured out we are stuck here." Pulling me aside she whispered, "There is good medicine for me in what is happening here. Sometime maybe when I understand it better we can talk about it; thank you, Caleb, for bringing me."

I went out with Bruce and Norman. We harnessed Molly and Roxie and two of Leclat's teams, hooked them to scoots and started dragging the road. There were a couple of places where the snow had drifted so much that it was hard for the lead team, so we kept switching leads to save the horses. It was a little less than a half a mile to the highway and by noon we had dragged that stretch three times. The storm had let up some. but it was still snowing enough to be a worry. We stopped for lunch and decided we would take Leclat's biggest team and try to get the car back as far as where our road joined the highway.

Joan seemed even better at lunch than she had this morning. She even laughed at how I looked, saying, "Caleb, you look like one of the men we called rag pickers, that we used to see around the college."

I hadn't given it any thought but the combination of Norman and Bruce's clothes on me must have presented a pretty sight, especially Bruce's barn boots that came up to my knees. After lunch the three of us took one team and a scoot and headed out to where we had left the car. I was lost in the thought that somehow, something had helped Joan more than I ever dreamed I could in such a short time, when Norman said, "That Virginia is some woman, isn't she, Caleb? Look how much better Joan is today. Maybe you ought to keep her here with Virginia as long as you can."

I had noticed a couple of knowing glances between Norman and Virginia while we were eating but had considered it just a part of their affection for each other. "Well, Norman," I asked, "do you know something I don't know?"

"No, Caleb, it's not that; it's just that—that I'm getting to know Virginia, and if you are struggling with a problem, she has a way of getting to the root of it and making it go away," he answered.

"She has such a full time job with Norman's troubles. You're lucky she had anything left to give Joan, Caleb," Bruce said, laughing as Norman almost knocked him off the scoot.

"That may be, Bruce," I replied, "but I thank my lucky stars more every day that Norman came to work with me. If Virginia really has a talent like that, I have friends that would be lined up at her door night and day."

"None of that horse manure," Norman piped in. "I'm happy if Virginia can help a friend of Caleb's, but Virginia is here for me, not the whole world."

By this time we had reached the car, the horses easily pulled it back into the road. It wasn't able to go anywhere under its own power in all that snow, so we towed it with the team back to where the roads joined. Though the storm wasn't near as fierce as it had been, it was still snowing some, and it was quite evident that we weren't going to see any roads cleared in our area until late tomorrow at best, if even then.

We took the team back to the shanty barn and fed the horses and rubbed them down. Norman said, "It looks like you're going to be stuck here at least for another day, Caleb; maybe tomorrow we had better take the teams and break open the road to the mill and sticking yard. I know everyone was hoping we would have that middle setting done before a big snowstorm. Leclat said we would be at least couple of weeks more there, and that was before we had this snow to contend with."

When we got back to Norman's shanty, Virginia and Joan had a big pot of stew ready for us. Joan said, "Caleb, you should see the way she mixes up that bread and lets it rise behind the stove. Tonight she is serving fried bread. I have already had some; it's delicious."

I marveled at the change in Joan the last couple of days from the broken defeated scared little girl I had picked up Saturday morning to one who was excited about fried bread. Mother had fried bread for us many times, but I suppose Joan's mother never made her own bread. By now we had all accepted that we were stuck at least for another day, and that and Joan's seeming recovery made the evening go by almost too fast.

Finally I said, "You know, Norman, I think it's time us scarecrows get back to our roost and get some sleep; tomorrow is going to be another tough day."

Back at Bruce's shanty, soon after we had hung our clothes to dry around the stove, we were all soundly sleeping. The next morning after another of Virginia's hearty breakfasts we again hitched up three teams and dragged the road to the mill and sticking field. After lunch we went back and cleaned the snow from the mill. It had stopped snowing during the night, and outside of a little flurry now and then it looked like the storm was over. As we were coming back up at about three in the afternoon we heard the roar of a big machine coming in from the road. It was Leclat and one of his helpers. They had a big old Reo plow truck pushing a massive V-plow.

Leclat climbed down out of the truck saying, "I was surprised to see your car up by the road, but I'm glad you are here. I was worried about the teams and how Norman and Bruce were getting by in the storm."

171

I laughed and said, "None of us have to worry as long as we have the Edward boys around to take care of things and Virginia to take care of them."

Leclat plowed down to the mill and the sticking field. I guess he figured if he got stuck we could pull him out with one of the teams. When he came back up I asked him if he thought the roads were good enough for me to get back to Sterling.

He said, "I don't think I would try it before noon tomorrow, Caleb. They have every available plow out plowing, but they have a lot of work before all roads are clear. I'll see if I can get through to your folks by phone tonight. I'll let them know you're okay. Bruce tells me you have a girlfriend with you; what's her folks' name? I'll have your folks call them."

After Leclat left we all went back to Norman's shanty. I felt much better about staying now that Joan and my folks would know we were all right. After another of Virginia's wonderful meals and an evening of banter and storytelling we went back to Bruce's shanty to sleep.

The next morning after breakfast Norman and I went down to feed and care for the horses, just as we finished up Norman said, "Caleb, I've asked Virginia to marry me, and we are planning on getting married in the spring; will you come with us and be a witness?"

Norman hadn't mentioned a thing before, and I had completely forgotten that I had been waiting for him to say something about the marriage. "Of course I will, Norman," I answered. "How about Bruce; does he know? I wouldn't want him to be hurt about this. He's worried enough that he's losing you now."

"Oh, he will be standing up for me. Virginia is going to ask Jennie and now maybe Joan, too, if that isn't going to be a problem for you. I haven't said anything to Bruce yet; you know what a blabbermouth he can be. I want to make sure everyone agrees before I let him in on it," Norman replied.

"I'm happy for you, Norman," I answered. "You just let me know the date, and I'll be there. If Jennie and Joan both come I think I can handle it."

After lunch and getting a list for groceries from Virginia so we could restock her larder with all that we had eaten, Joan and I said our goodbyes and left.

Joan was very quiet at first, finally she said, "Caleb, do you believe in destiny? I never gave it much thought before, but if ever an accident in life has meaning, this snowstorm and our getting stuck here has. I'm going to tell you some things that can't go any further, but I need to talk so I can see it better myself. The first night at Norman's shanty with Virginia. I was angry about everything that had happened to me, and us getting stuck there made me just want to die. I had to sleep in the same bed as Virginia, but I was sure I wouldn't sleep. I finally must have dozed off because I woke up to this horrible screaming. At first I didn't know where it came from but as I came conscious I realized that it was me. Virginia was sitting on the side of the bed holding my hand. I completely broke down and started sobbing. Virginia consoled me like I was a child. Finally I told her everything about me being raped. She said, 'You're not alone in the world, Joan; you have a lot of company, and we all have to develop our own way of dealing with it; let me help you develop yours.'

"Over the next couple of days she told me the horrible story of her life. She was molested as a child by an older stepbrother and finally raped when she was only eleven. He threatened to kill her mother if she ever told. This went on until she was senior in high school and her stepbrother was drafted. Then right after she graduated her stepfather raped her. She knew she had to get away, and after seeing a newspaper add for a housekeeper in a small hotel in Vermont, she left home and went to work there. She said she had such opinion of herself she didn't socialize, and most of the time was very depressed. One of the boys who worked for the landscaper that took care of the grounds at the hotel kept teasing and asking her for a date. Finally she said yes, and as they dated, he helped her understand that how you faced problems counted more than the problem itself. With him her life began to have meaning and happiness. Within a year after they met they were married and were very happy together for over five years. That's when he developed an illness and died in less than a month.

"She said she just went crazy and started drinking and running around. Then one night she dreamed he had come to her and said, 'Remember, Virginia, it's how you face life that counts.' Since then she has settled down and thinks she has found new happiness with Norman. All the time I was with her we talked about what had happened to her and how it could have destroyed her life if she hadn't learned that how you face it is what counts. We discussed over and over again all my options, go to the police, press charges, go for rape counseling, tough it out, or destroy the rest of my life. I'm not sure exactly what I'm going to do, but one thing I'm not doing is destroying my life because of it, because that makes the bad guys the winners. If you can bring me back tomorrow she knows where there is a clinic that will be discrete. I can go to and be examined. If you can do that, Caleb, and then bring me to work with you a couple of times to be with Virginia, maybe I can get it together before school break is over. I know this won't go any further than you and me and Virginia, no matter what I chose to do. I trust Virginia, and I remember my father couldn't get the truth out of you with a bullwhip. Virginia says I need to talk about what happened with people I could trust but that I have to be the one who makes my decision. I thank you, Caleb, for being friend enough to force me to come this weekend and for having the friends that you have; even if my being with them was an accident, it was my lucky day."

"I don't know about destiny, Joan," I responded after hearing her out, "I only know that ever since I have been involved with Norman and his brother no matter what happens, with them around it always comes out okay in the end. When Clem quit on me Norman was right there offering me a solution; when the truck broke down Bruce found parts for me and had it all fixed the next day. I was very skeptical when Norman wanted to bring Virginia to live on the job, but where would we be right now if she hadn't been there? My dad keeps telling me how wonderful it is that he has me to carry on for him, when the truth is, I don't know what would have happened without Norman and his family. The truth is Joan, I felt strange about the way things have happened even before this. Destiny, luck, someone watching over us, I don't know what I believe, but one thing for sure, Joan, we are going to take advantage of it in your case. I'll pick you up tomorrow and every day you're here if that's what you want to do. I'm not sure when the mill will be operating again. When it does, we'll have to leave early in the morning. Then you can spend all day with Virginia."

Joan was quiet the rest of the way to Sterling lost in her own thoughts, I guessed, so I didn't try to talk any more. At her house she said, "Caleb, I need one more big favor from you. Can you go in and convince my father to keep my mother from climbing all over me with questions?"

"I can try to do that, Joan, but we better have a story that we both stick to, or it won't work. I know you don't want to tell them the truth, so how about saying you fell head over heels with someone who jilted you for a classmate friend of yours. I know that is a little over the hill for you, but it will probably work. I hate to bring this up, but if there is a woman problem about the rape then you could indicate he caused it."

Joan kissed me warmly and said, "I'm glad you broke me out of my room. Maybe in a while I'll get over being jilted; go warn my father."

I went in and talked to Mr. Walden. He already had been holding Mrs. Walden at bay. I said, "I know this is going to be hard to take, Mrs. Walden, but Joan doesn't even want to come in if you're going to start with twenty questions. I have had my hands full with her all weekend, but if you're patient and wait for her to come to you she'll be all right. It really was only a jilted love thing that upset her; she is eating and sleeping now, and if you keep your patience with her things will get back to normal. I told her I would get your promise. Do I have it?"

"You have my solemn oath, Caleb," Mr. Walden said, taking my hand, "and we both want to thank you for helping us get our little girl back."

I went back and told Joan it was okay. She gave me a big hug and ran into the house. As I drove away I thought, *Nobody is ever going to see the little girl again that Joan was when she left, but if the luck continues the outcome should be a wonderful woman.*

When I got home there was a lot of excitement about all that had happened both at home and where I had been. I filled Dad in on all that had happened at the mill site and told him I thought we would be back in production in a day or so. He said, "I'm glad you decided to stay there. I heard that a lot of people got stuck out in that storm, and a couple of them died from it. It sounds like you have put together a good team, Caleb. I hope Norman will stay with us when I get back."

I laughed and said, "It's supposed to be a secret, Dad, but he is planning on marrying Virginia, so he is going to need the job. I just hope they're going to be happy staying in a shanty on the job, because it makes it so much easier for us."

The next day I took Joan back to Virginia. Not much of the crew showed up to work, and the mill didn't run, so I drove them to the clinic. Physically Joan checked out okay; they gave her information on where to contact rape counselors both near her home and at college and strongly encouraged her to contact the police, though they promised no information about her would ever leave the clinic. On the way back Virginia talked to Joan about getting married to Norman, and they had a grand time planning what the wedding should be like.

The next day all the crews showed up at work and it was decided to finish sawing what logs were already cut and move the mill up to the top of the lot for the rest of the winter. Joan came to the job to be with Virginia three more times and I went to see her every night that she didn't. By the time college started again Joan seemed to have it under control and decided to go back. Her father couldn't thank me enough and even her mother gave me a little hug once.

I received a letter from Hester and Richard, telling me that they had taken care of all Dad's hospital bills and I should see to it that Francis got the help he needed right away. Hester had a job working for Richard's company and like she said before she left her wages would go to Dad. She knew he wouldn't be able to accept that himself so she arranged with Mr. Banner to put her money with the fund that he had started for Dad and pay the bills. Mr. Banner had told Mother to keep giving him the bills until the fund ran out of money. I talked to Mother about Francis, and she agreed that we should make an appointment and get him examined.

After Joan left for college my life quieted down and it was back to the grind of working in the woods in the winter. I went out with Betty a few times, and we always ended up having sex, even when I told myself I wasn't going to let it happen.

I met Jennie a couple of times, but she was pretty cool with me, asking if Betty was taking care of the desires that I let Joan create, like Beverly used to. I tried to get her to go for a ride or a sundae with me, but she would just say, "Are you lonely now Joan is gone, Caleb?" and walk away.

I gave up trying to reach Jennie and even turned dates with Betty down at least once a week. Some times before I would go to sleep at night I would talk in my mind to Josh, asking why I didn't understand better about women the way he had seemed to.

CHAPTER SEVEN

At work the move to the new mill setting at the top of the lot went very well, considering all the snow we had to contend with. This setting was much easier for Norman and me because the sticking field was close to the mill and it was all level ground. Even the snow wasn't much of a hindrance because Norman or Bruce would have the snow packed down for each new row of lumber during off hours in the evenings or the weekends.

Joan had been sending letters for Virginia to my house for me to deliver. I was often curious what was in the letters but had given Joan a solemn oath that I would not read them. As often as Joan wrote, Virginia would ask me to mail her return letters. Though Joan wrote me an occasional letter she never mentioned about the rape; I believe she was afraid someone else in my family might read the letters.

It was the middle of March, and smells of spring were in the air when Virginia asked me to stop at the shanty a couple of days after I had delivered one of Joan's letters. She asked me to leave the horses after work for Norman to stable, because she wanted to see me alone. I thought that it would be about the wedding as Norman said they had set a date for the last weekend in April.

When I arrived at the shanty she said, "I have some good news, Caleb; Joan wanted me to tell you what has happened about her problem. She went for counseling as was suggested by the clinic when she got back to college. After a couple of weeks of counseling the counselor asked if she would be willing to have the police involved; she still said no. The counselors became very concerned because they had ten cases that seemed to be linked to the same two men, and most of the cases were girls from the college. Using an intermediate source the counselors convinced the police that some action needed to be taken. The police had a wired female officer acting as a college girl start frequenting the bars around the college. In about a week the two men picked the officer as a target. Realizing they had probably drugged her drink, she disposed of it and acted dizzy. After allowing them to get her to a motel she arrested them with the help of the two officers who had been following her. Three of the girls who were in the counseling group wanted to make sure the two men got long sentences and decided to testify against them. The men are being held without bail, awaiting trial, and are facing 15-to 25-year sentences. You know of course, Caleb, this is to go no further than you and me. Joan has made her decision not to go public and is recovering nicely from the ordeal. The last thing she needs now is to come home and face gossip about it."

"You don't have to worry about me, Virginia," I answered. "Didn't she tell you her father couldn't get me to talk even with his bull whip? I want you to know, Virginia, how thankful I am that you helped Joan through all this. I was at my wits' end about what to do that day when we got caught here in the storm. Joan had just broken down and told me a couple of minutes before we arrived. During the time we were trapped here you somehow gave her back her life; we talked about it the day we left, and she figured she had experienced some kind of a miracle in meeting you."

"Ah, Caleb, it might have been a miracle that the weather kept you here, but all I did was present her with the truth—that there was life after rape if you allowed it. My history was such that I could help her reach inside her pain and overcome the fears that it was causing," Virginia answered just as Norman asked if he could come in.

"What's up, Caleb?" Norman asked, laughing. "You trying to talk Virginia out of marrying me? Won't do you any good. Bruce has been telling her ever since he has known about the wedding how bad a mistake it was for anyone to marry me. He hasn't been able to change her mind yet."

"No, Norman, we were just talking about Joan and how Virginia wants her and Jennie both to come to the wedding. What do you think? Will I be able to handle that situation? First I have to get Jennie to talk with me again; she has been rather cool ever since Joan was home," I answered.

178

"Now I'm confused, Caleb," Norman said with a grin. "I thought Jennie was mad about that other girl, you know the one you said was so hot, what was her name? Oh, I remember, it was Betty. What are you thinking, Virginia? How can we have a small wedding if you're going to invite all of Caleb's girls? You know, seeing us get married might make them all so mad at Caleb that they will slaughter him. We are going to have to have a little talk about your guest list, Virginia."

Virginia said, "Knock it off, Norman; you've had your little joke. We'll just let Caleb figure out what to do. I just said that if it was possible, I would like them both to come."

I left feeling overjoyed that the men who had attacked Joan had been caught and were going to be severely punished. Norman was sure becoming a changed man. Maybe Virginia was some kind of a miracle worker like Joan thinks. I don't remember Norman being so giddy or talkative before. I guess I had better be more careful about how much of my life I confide to him. I sure wouldn't want him blabbing about me the way Bruce does, about him sometimes.

When I got home, Mother was just coming back from the doctor's office with Francis and she was excited about what she had been told. They figured Francis had some kind of an allergy triggered by animals and there were things that could be done to relieve it. They had sent his blood out to be tested and said there were many more tests that could be done if the cause wasn't found in the blood test. They also gave her some samples of a medication to try him on, saying that sometimes they are lucky enough to guess right and if they have, he will see a difference in a week or so after starting on the medication.

They must have really impressed Francis because he came running out shouting, "Caleb, the doctors are going to fix it so I can be with animals; then I can help Jason and drive the horses for you when you move. Won't that be wonderful?"

I was happy for Francis and hoped that the medication helped so he wouldn't have to keep taking tests. For Mother's sake too, she was busy enough with Dad taking him in every couple of weeks for a checkup. The doctors had set a tentative date in the middle of April to operate on his leg. As near as I could understand it they were going to have to break the bone in his leg in order to straighten it. The accident did so much damage to the muscles in his leg that they decided not to try and set the bone before and the bone healed too crooked to use. The muscles and tendons in his leg have heeled so well they believe that a few months after they operate he will be walking as good as new. Dad has been able to get around on crutches and has been out doors working with Jason around the farm, this has been a great help for both Dad and Jason.

Emma who had been dating sporadically with different boys over the years seemed to have finally found some one who she was happy with. His name was Aaron Little and she met him at Stuarts. She had gone to work there in the office right after Hester left. He worked in the engineering department. She had brought Aaron home a couple of times to meet the family. I hadn't spent enough time with him to really know him, but everyone in the family except Dad seemed to like him. Seems that Dad saw Emma saying goodbye to him a little too passionately one night and had raised the roof about it. Emma had always acted a little too passionately with boys. I often wondered if that was why she changed boyfriends so often. I often thought she either scared them away or got them so hot and bothered she had to dump them to protect herself. Because Emma was older than me I had always thought she was smarter about sex than I was and believed she was more a Joan than a Beverly, but sometimes I wondered. After supper I decided I would write Joan.

Dearest Joan,

I had a discussion with Virginia today, and she told me about the progress you have made; good news, that. We also talked about her upcoming wedding, I know she has already invited you but she asked if I could get Jennie to come also. Jennie was with me the first time I met Virginia, and they became so friendly that Jennie asked that I bring her over to the job site when I went on weekends to visit her. I was wondering what your feelings would be if I asked her. Virginia left it up to me to decide. My problem is that Jennie is hardly talking to me anymore since you were home. I guess I am your same old Caleb, failing to understand why I make girls upset with me. Jennie's own words were that we only had a platonic relationship, whatever that's supposed to mean. All I know is, I only get a little hug and a friendly kiss on the cheek once in a while. I have many girls I consider friends, but outside of you I have never felt they were girlfriends. I still carry a fear of commitment, not just with girls but with other things, even returning to college has its fears for me. I sometimes feel your mother was right. I was just ordained to be one of Sterling's barn boys or a woodsman. I know this sounds kind of crazy, but I feel sort of out of my skin when I'm not here in Sterling. I know I am not supposed to be a little boy anymore, but I guess a lot of me still is. I sometimes think that I stopped growing up after I didn't have Josh here to guide me. I miss being able to talk to him about everything. I know you were always there for me when I needed to talk, but there are things boys can't talk about with girls.

I'm sorry, Joan, I didn't mean to vent in this letter. I'm sure you have much better things in your life to do than listen to a little boy cry. I really had a good week this week; it just seems that writing the word, "Joan" brought out the little boy in me. Oh, for lost time and the memories: they all seem so sweet now.

Let me know your thoughts on the wedding soon. I look forward to seeing you again.

Love,
Caleb

After finishing the letter I went to the kitchen, and Mother said, "Caleb, if you have a little time I would like to talk to you about Aaron Little. I am having a hard time with your father about him. I know Emma is a little too free with her emotions when it comes to boys sometimes. I have tried to explain the trouble she could get into acting like that, but I guess I wasn't very effective. I like Aaron, but your father wants to bar him from the house, and I wondered if maybe you could help me somehow."

"I'm not sure how I can help, Mother, but I'm willing to try," I answered. "What do you think would help most, talking to Dad or Emma? I really don't know much about Aaron, but I will make an effort to get to know him better if it looks like he is going to stay around."

"I don't know much about him, Caleb," Mother said with a smile, "but Emma is sure planning on him being around. She even asked me what I thought about him becoming part of the family. I don't want to make another burden for you, Caleb, but with Hester gone, you are the next oldest to Emma, and you know how Dad is about boys. I am still dreading the day he finds out Richard was a divorced man."

"I'll tell you what, Mother; I will try talking to Emma, and if I don't get anywhere with her, I will talk to Aaron. I might even be able to get Emma to be a little less amorous with him by telling her that."

Emma came bouncing through the door just in time to catch most of my last sentence, and she shouted, "Telling me what, mister smarty pants, Caleb?"

"Emma, I'm glad you came in. I was just going looking for you," I lied, trying to think what to say next.

Mother said, "Yes, Emma, I have just asked Caleb what should be done about you and Aaron. Your father is just on the verge of asking him not to come here anymore."

"Oh, Mother, don't let him do that. I am truly in love with him, and I am hoping he will ask me to marry him. I think he would have already but he has to go back to college for one more semester to get his engineering degree. Please, please, Mother, don't let Daddy send him away," Emma begged.

"Emma, you have to listen for once to what we are saying," I said, jumping in. "Mother and I would like to help, but we can't unless you understand the problem. I don't believe from what I have seen that Aaron is the problem, and neither is Dad or Mother; the problem is the way you act around boys. You have to remember that Dad was a young man once, and he sees the way you act as a danger to you. He isn't mad at you, and he isn't mad at Aaron. He is just a father protecting his daughter from what he sees as potential harm. He saw how you were all over Aaron when you said goodbye one night, and he sees it as his duty to save you. Mother tells me that she has talked to you before about this boy-girl thing, but you didn't listen."

"Come on, Caleb. I'm not a little girl that has to be told about the birds and the bees. If I remember right, it was you who was asking me about that by the horse trough one night not too many years ago. Good Lord, Caleb, we aren't little kids anymore. I'm over twenty-one now, you know," Emma answered angrily.

"I think," I said looking wearily at Mother, "you miss the point. It isn't what you know; it's what you do. The way you hold boys and kiss them gives them the idea that you are willing to go to bed with them. I certainly hope that isn't your intention, but it sure the hell is the message you're sending."

Mother said, "That is a little coarse, Caleb, but he is right, Emma, and you really can't blame young boys for thinking that. Now, Caleb and I are willing to talk to Dad, but it won't do any good if he ever sees you kissing Aaron like that again. I would like to think that our discussion here would help, not just to keep Aaron around but would make you understand that that behavior isn't proper anywhere for a single woman."

"Oh, Mother," Emma cried out, "you can't believe I am that kind of a girl. And you, Caleb, do you believe I'm capable of going to bed with some boy?"

"You're missing the point, Emma. It isn't what Mother or I believe;" I answered, "it's that the way you act with boys seems to send that message. It has always worried me. I well imagine you have got yourself in some pretty tight spots with boys because of it. Most boys are gentlemen, but they can only control themselves so long if some girl is crawling all over them. Dad was a boy once, and it scares him when he thinks his daughter is being too amorous. You have to remember about Harry and the motorcycle kiss he saw years ago."

Emma sat down heavily at the table. For a moment I thought she was going to cry.

Mother went over and put her hand on her shoulder saying, "Emma, I know that hearing what Caleb said is hard, but I have tried to talk to you about this without seeming to reach you. I could never explain exactly what your actions do to boys the way he did; maybe a male point of view, as coarse as that was, was necessary."

"Oh, Mother, I have always known that I had an effect on boys that was dangerous. In the beginning I didn't understand it all, but I'm a grown girl now. Caleb, it is true that I have had my hands full with some of the boys, but I always been able to handle it and dumped the ones that I was afraid I couldn't. It has always been kind of a game for me. I never gave a thought to how it looked to people not involved, and now you tell me I've ruined it with Aaron. You have to help me with Dad; I just know Aaron is the one, and if I can't bring him home what can I do? I don't want to put Dad under any more pressure than he is in, but I swear, if Aaron asked me to run away with him tomorrow I think I would. Please, please, Mother, you and Caleb have to help me," she begged.

"That is exactly what Caleb and I were discussing when you came busting in, Emma," Mother answered. " I asked Caleb if he had any idea about what we could do. He was just suggesting that we talk to you and maybe Aaron too. We hadn't decide on exactly the what or when, but I believe this frank talk is a good start."

"I don't know, Mother, if I can have anyone talking to Aaron like this about the problem. He might begin to think I am not a decent girl if my own mother and brother doubt me," Emma said in a quivering voice.

"We certainly weren't thinking about doing anything like that, Emma," I said, trying to soothe the situation. "I thought that maybe I could have a talk with him about how Father is about you girls and maybe bring Harry and Eunice into the conversation, of course leaving out your part in it. Then maybe it would be a good idea to have him make an effort to get to know Dad and to spend a few minutes with him once in a while. Maybe the two of you together at first and then have him make an effort to talk to him alone also."

"I'm sorry, Emma, that we have been so blunt, but you came in before we had a chance to discuss any tactics," Mother said joining in. "It never was a plan to get Aaron out of the picture. We were just trying to figure out how we could keep this situation from becoming a mess like Eunice got into with Harry. The last thing this family needs right now is to have your father feel like he has to disown another one of his daughters. I'm glad now that you came in when you did. It saved us from having to find a way to talk to you about it."

"I'm glad too, Mother," Emma answered. "I would do almost anything to keep from hurting Dad, but I'm not sure that I could go on if I had to lose Aaron. I realize that I come on too strong with boys, but what started out as a game became a habit. I have never seen it as being something that could tarnish my reputation before listening to Caleb's interpretation. Caleb should have got on my case before now. I'm sure Josh would have if he was still here."

There's Josh again, I thought. *I wish he was still here too; my shoulders aren't near as big as his were. Maybe like Jake says, I live in too small a world, but it seems safer there.*

Still, I said, "Don't worry, Emma. I'll be watching over you like a hawk from now on." Then I left to go out to the barn with Jason.

Jason had asked the day before if I could help him fix the calf pen, we were expecting the cow to calf in the next couple of weeks and he wanted everything to be ready so Father wouldn't be upset. I felt sorry for Jason he had planned to join Muldon's milking crew but without Dad there was too much work around our little farm for him to be spared. He had high hopes that Francis would be able to take over for him if the medication worked. I doubted that was going to happen soon so I supplied him with a little money each week, it left me a little short sometimes but I figured he ought to have at least enough to buy some girl an ice cream cone once in a while. I remembered how important my ice cream meetings with Joan had been to me when I was going to school. Jason wasn't at the barn but he had left the tools and material there so I went to work fixing the pen.

I was just leaving the barn when Nellie came out and said, "Caleb, I need to talk to you about Jason. I had a strange premonition about him and Beverly Stone's sister when I saw them together after school one day. I'm not sure what it is between them, but it doesn't seem good. It's the same thing I felt back when I used to see you and Beverly together. You remember how I told you before that I seemed to sense things before they happen? This feeling about them scares me. I don't want Jason to get hurt or get into some kind of terrible trouble."

Man, I thought, *like I needed this, a sister who needs lessons in controlling herself, another one with sixth sense, and a younger brother fighting the urges of puberty. Was it always like this with you?* I mentally asked Josh, looking up.

"I know you are old enough to understand about puberty Nellie, but what you probably don't know is how hard it is for most boys. All boys have to struggle through those years, and Jason and I have already had a talk about his problem with it. I know we will be talking more about it, and I will do the best I can to guide him away from any trouble."

"Who's in trouble now, Caleb?" Jason asked as he walked into the barn. "I'm sorry I left you to fix the pen alone, but I had to walk the electric fence. It was grounded somewhere, and it was just about dark by the time I found it. Dad realized it wasn't working right, and I told him I would take care of it. It upsets him if he thinks we aren't able to keep up without him; he's always fretting about how I have to do more than I should. I remind him that you and Homer had worked just as hard at my age and it doesn't seem to have hurt either of you any. Now, back to my question, who's in trouble?"

"Well, I guess you will have to tell us, Jason," I answered. "Nellie is worried about you and Beverly Stone's sister, April. She's afraid that you might get carried away during one of your hugging games."

Jason's face turned red, and I realized I had made a mistake in bringing it up in front of Nellie. So I said, "Just joking, Jason, she was just comparing you and April to Beverly and me when we were your age, and wondering if I knew what makes some people go on like that. I told her we would talk about it, and I was sure you were smart enough to stay out of trouble."

Jason, who had been holding his breath, let it all out and said, "You know, Nellie, you are right. I like the attention April has always given me, but lately it has gotten out of hand. Last week we were asked to stay after school, and the teacher read the riot act to us and said if we continued with what she called, 'our amorous displays,' she would have to take serious action. When April asked what serious action meant, the teacher said, having our parents informed, separating us at school, or even having one of us expelled. You really scared me for a moment. I thought maybe the school had contacted Mother. I wouldn't want to be responsible for causing this family any more trouble; Mother has more than enough already."

"We are sorry, Jason; we didn't mean to scare you," I responded. "When it comes to emotions, Nellie has kind of a sixth sense when she is around them; feeling yours, she was just asking me if I thought you were in trouble. I guess she was right, maybe we should have a man-to-man talk about it soon."

Jason left to take another tour around the barn to check things out—more to get away from us, I guessed than it being a duty he usually did.

As Nellie and I left the barn I said, "You know, Nellie, when you told me about your gift last year, I had some doubts, but I don't any more. I want you to promise me that you will always come to me and not keep it bottled up inside you. I don't think you have to worry about Jason; he is going through the age of puberty. It's a tough age, but it looks like he has a handle on it. He has already come to me once, and I'm sure we will talk again, you know, kind of man to man, or in our case, boy to boy."

Nellie said, "You know, Caleb, I have these feelings many times. When Etta was here I could feel the tension between you and her. It seemed much better the last day she was here, but after she left I could feel your confusion and pain. Then at Christmastime when Joan was here I sensed you were feeling a new kind of hurt. I will tell you when I sense a family problem, but you don't have to worry about me, Caleb. I don't fear this 'gift,' as you call it. I think of it as something Josh passed on to me when he had to leave us."

I went in to talk to Dad a few minutes later, saying, "Dad, I just came in from the barn; the calf pen is ready, and Jason found the problem with the fence. Are you looking forward to the operation on your leg next week?"

"I can't say that I'm looking forward to being back in that hospital," Dad answered, "but if that is what it takes to get rid of these damn crutches I'm ready. I'm glad you're giving Jason some time. I often feel guilty about how much he has to do."

"I know, Dad; Mother and I had the same discussion," I said, "but you have to remember that Homer and I started out working pretty young. The difference is we were getting paid. I thought about that and have been making sure he has some money of his own each week. Rather than worrying, you and Mother should be proud that you have brought up boys who can do the work."

"We are proud, Caleb, extremely proud; I just can't help feeling that some how I'm letting the family down. Look at you; you should be away at college instead of slaving in the woods," Dad said, forlornly.

"I wouldn't worry about that, Dad. I'm not sure I was ready for college yet anyhow," I answered. "The stories that Jake and Joan have told me about their first semester in college didn't make me feel as though I had missed anything. To tell you the truth, Dad, even though Eunice and Harry were good to me, and I managed to make some good friends in Oklahoma, I never felt at ease there the way I do here in Sterling.

"I can't picture myself being out there doing anything besides working in the woods, because that is all I have ever done. Back when you started to seriously talk about going to college to become some kind of writer, I didn't think much of it. Since meeting Richard and this Aaron, guy that Emma is chasing, I can see how much a college education can do. And while we are telling the truth, Caleb," Dad said kind of sheepishly, " It made me proud to say you were going to college. I hope that I can get back on my feet quick enough, not just for you to go back but make it possible for Jason and Francis to go if they are a mind to."

"That reminds me, Dad, Mother says you are upset with Aaron and Emma. I know you have a right to be concerned about Emma's flirtatious ways, but you shouldn't take that out on Aaron. Emma has always been a little boy crazy without seeing the harm in it. Mother and I had a long talk with her about her ways, and she seemed genuinely surprised about what an appearance that made to those who saw her act like that. I think it surprised her enough so that she will act more lady-like in the future. I think we should spend a little time getting to know Aaron better, because Emma is really taken with him, so our job should be to make sure he isn't a mistake for her." Seeing this was a little upsetting to Dad I changed the subject, saying, "I have to make a couple of phone calls to check on some things before it's too late; we'll talk again tomorrow, Dad."

I left Dad feeling he had a whole new perspective on life. He seemed much different than the man who had thrown Harry out of our house and stuck to his big red image. It had been over seven months since his accident and many things had happened since then. I imagine Dad had given a lot of thought to the how and why of things with all the time he had on his hands. Though my talking about Aaron upset him some I felt that he was coming to terms with the fact that Emma was a big girl now and she too would soon be leaving us. I felt now he would look at him in much the same way he had Richard. The rest was up to Emma; she had better start behaving herself when Aaron came to visit. I called Betty's house, she had left a couple of messages for me during the week and I had been avoiding calling her back. Mrs. Hart answered and said Betty was out. I told her it was nothing important I was just answering her calls.

She said, "Caleb, you haven't been around lately. I was hoping we would see more of you."

I decided to lay it all on the line and said, "I'm sorry Mrs. Hart, but Betty is looking for a commitment that I am not ready for. So I thought in all fairness to her I shouldn't keep tying up her time. I told her in the beginning I was only looking for companionship. She wants and deserves more than that, so I haven't been coming around so much. I hope she finds what she wants and will always consider me a good friend so we can occasionally get together. Please tell her, her friend Caleb called."

After hanging up, I thought, *I've written Joan, called and relieved my conscience a little about Betty, I might as well try Jennie,* so I called her house, and I was in luck, because she answered the phone.

I said, "Jennie, now don't hang up. I have a message from Virginia for you. She wanted to know if you could come over to the job site to see her this weekend."

"Sure, Caleb," she answered. "I'll start walking now. Maybe I can get there by this weekend."

"Well, that's the thing," I said, adding to my deception, "We are having some problems with the harnesses, and I was going back Saturday to work with Norman on them. I thought if you could squeeze it in, you could go with me to see Virginia."

"Speaking of squeezing, Caleb, I hear that Betty is dating some guy from Oscin. Is that why you're calling little Jennie now?" she said, kind of spitefully.

I had planned to keep my temper, but the combination of dealing with Emma, Joan, Betty, and now Jennie was too much, so I said, "Look, Jennie, I am trying to do Virginia a favor. She wanted to talk to you about the wedding, but if you don't care, neither do I." Then I hung up.

Friday night Homer said, "Caleb, what the devil have you been doing to Jennie now? She asked me to give you a message; she said if you are capable of being a very quiet gentleman you may pick her up at the barn at ten in the morning, if you can have her back by four in the afternoon. You must be completely blind if you don't see that Jennie has a thing for you. When you had Etta here it was hard for her; of course, a girl looking like Etta was hard for all the girls in town, too. Then Joan comes home and you disappear with her, and now there are stories about you and Betty all over town. You, of all people, should know that the Grove isn't a very secret place for rendezvous. You know the boys at the barn used to talk about you acting dumb; sometimes I'm not so sure it was an act. Jennie wants me to let her know your answer in the morning. No matter what you decide, Caleb, I want you to know that underneath Jennie's bravado, there is a warm wonderful woman, and she deserves to be treated better."

"Whoa, there, Homer," I answered, "Jennie is the one who has insisted that our relationship be platonic. There where times I thought we were closer than that, but she insisted we have no future and that we should not pretend otherwise. Besides that, I have told all the girls that I dated that my life right now is too unstable for me to be tied to any serious relationship. You tell Jennie I will pick her up, and I'm sorry that I hung up on her; it wasn't her alone that got to me, it was a combination of problems with girls that made me act so stupid."

"I'll tell her, Caleb," Homer answered, "but I won't mention the other girls. I'll just say you were in a stupid mood that night. I understand your not wanting to be committed to any one girl; what I don't understand is how you always seem so deeply entangled in their lives. I might have kissed seventy-five percent of the girls in town, but I couldn't tell you much about any of them. Look at you, Joan, Jennie, Etta, Betty, and even Beverly, though I have to say despite all the ribbing you get about her, Beverly seems to be less trouble for you than the rest of them. It seems that each of the others owns a piece of you or maybe it's you who think you own a piece of them. Whatever it is, you are going to have to find a way to deal with it, or you're heading for real trouble. If you're lucky, Dad will be able to take over the business this fall, and you can escape at least the three that are here by going to college."

"Man, Homer, you don't paint a very pretty picture of your brother's love life. I certainly don't see it the way you do, but you surely have given me a new vein of thought. I know it's true that most of the girls do confide in me about their private thoughts and life; I assumed that was normal in boy-girl relationship," I answered.

"Maybe that happens when a couple are approaching a serious relationship or marriage, but I don't believe it should in casual relationships. I am too tired to spend any more time trying to straighten out my older brother's love life. I'm going to bed. I'll tell Jennie you'll be there tomorrow," Homer said as he went upstairs.

I picked Jennie up at the barn at ten the next morning. She came out, and jumped into the car, and said, rather coolly, "Glad you could make it, Caleb. I have been wanting to see Virginia again. Thank you for thinking of me."

Still confused about our problem and remembering what Homer had said, I answered, "You're entirely welcome, Jennie," and drove out of Sterling.

We were over half way there when I remembered that I had hung up on her so I said, "Jennie, I'm sorry about hanging up on you the other night. I was having a bad day with a lot of problems, and I guess I was looking for a shoulder to cry on when I called you, and when it wasn't there, I overreacted."

"That's just the point, Caleb," she replied, "it seems that the only time you

189

call me is when you need something from me. I never get a call asking me to just join you for a sundae or something just for the fun of it. It's always something to do with you or your life."

I said, "I'm sorry that you feel that way, Jennie; I thought since ours was only supposed to be a friendly relationship, that was what friends were for. You should know I would be there for you if you ever called me. Homer gave me a lecture about how dumb I was about girls. I don't know whether he is right or not, but because of our agreement I try not to think of you as a girl, just a friend."

"So, that's it, Mr. Carney; if I'm not going to be like Beverly or Betty I'm not even a girl in your eyes. I'll tell you what; we don't need to talk anymore, and it will be safer for you."

Damn, I thought, *maybe Homer is right. Well, to hell with it; I can stay as quiet as she can.* So we rode the rest of the way to the job without speaking.

When we arrived at the job site, Norman seemed surprised to see me, saying, "What's up, Caleb? I didn't expect to see you before Monday; you and Jennie out slumming?"

"Gee Norman, I was sure I told you that we needed to repair the hanes on one of the harnesses, and I would be back today," I answered as Jennie got out of the car and headed for the shanty.

"Oh, damn, I forgot all about that; I'll go tell Virginia that we'll have to wait to go shopping until after we get that done," he replied, following Jennie.

Damn, I thought, *I'm piling one lie on top another; I have to find a better way of handling the girls in my life than that.* I went down to the shanty barn and started inspecting the harnesses. Much to my surprise there was significant wear on the hold-back straps on both harnesses. I remember now Norman mentioning they were showing wear when we were at the middle site hauling loads downhill.

Norman came down and said, "What the hell have you got yourself into now, Caleb? Jennie was practically in tears when she got into the shanty with Virginia. I tried to tell Virginia that we couldn't go shopping right away, but she just shooed me out. Do you have some kind of a plan to bring all of your girlfriends to Virginia to get them straightened out? I hope you're not going to mess up my wedding with these battles."

"I really don't know what the trouble is, Norman," I answered. "Jennie has always insisted that our relationship was just as friends; now she seems all upset because I dated a few other girls."

"Boy, and people call me dumb. I tried to tell you the first time I saw you two together she was more than just a friend. First there was Jennie, then Joan, and that Etta that I didn't get to see, and oh, yes, the one you're making out with, that was Betty, right? And now it's Jennie again. What were you thinking, Caleb? That nobody has feelings but you? Think about it a minute, Caleb. What are these girls supposed to think?" Norman asked, looking at me with one of his quizzical expressions.

"I don't want to hear any more about my so-called girlfriends," I shouted. "I didn't promise any of them anything except a good time when we were together, and I have tried to live up to that."

"Oh, sure, Caleb; you get them to fall in love with you, and then you walk next door and ask their best friend or worse yet, their enemy to go out with you, and you think that's okay?" he asked

"Enough, Norman. I said. I was done listening to all this crap. My brother climbed all over me last night about these girls. I've heard enough for one day. Let's get back to the harnesses," I said, trying to change the subject.

Norman could see I had reached my limit so we spent the next couple hours planning where to get hold back straps and talking about the job. Virginia called that she had a lunch ready and for us to come up to the shanty. Jennie seemed more at ease, I was careful not to get in direct conversation with her; she joined in on the banter and conversation about their coming wedding.

Virginia had already approached Jennie about having her and Joan both at the wedding. I guess it was a girl thing because Jennie was all for it.

Virginia said, "Joan will be home the last week of April, Caleb. Norman and I have contacted a pastor near here, and he has agreed to marry us at his chapel on the Saturday of that week. Bruce has arranged to have a hog roast here for everybody who wants to join us. There are only going to be a few of us at the wedding, but the Leclats and Joclins and all their crews are coming to help us celebrate here afterwards."

Jennie said, "That sounds like so much fun. I will have to make sure to get that day off from the barn. Speaking of that, Caleb and I have to go. I have milk-room duty, and I am supposed to be there by four o'clock."

As we drove off Jennie said, "Caleb, I'm sorry about the way I am with you sometimes; I know that we are supposed to just be buddies, but sometimes that is not enough for me. Virginia says that you can't help being you any more than I can help the way I feel, but I should be honest with you. Losing Josh was what brought us close together, but what happened was an emotional accident on my part. After seeing how wrong what we were doing was, I thought I could just walk away from it and still be your friend. That hasn't worked for me; somehow my heart became more involved than my mind. I'm telling you this because after talking to Virginia I can see it is only fair. I am not asking for anything from you. I know telling you all this makes me vulnerable, but it is better than fighting myself and you all the time."

"I don't know what to say, Jennie," I said, thinking, *Man, Homer and Norman are right.* "I can only tell you that I have a strong affection for you, and if I'm cool sometimes it's because I don't want to destroy what we have. I don't think of any girl as just a sex partner but you do create desires that I have to put down. I have to tell you, Jennie, that I do not have a commitment with any girl, nor do I want one. I have too much of a problem with who I am and what I want to do with my life to be committed to someone else's. I know it probably is selfish of me at my age to feel I can play the field without hurting anybody; I never mean to."

Jennie cuddled up to me like she used to and said, "Well, as long as I have a chance, until some other prince charming comes into my life, I guess I can deal with it. Like Virginia said, enjoy what you have, because life will take its own course."

As I left Jennie at the barn she kissed me hard and held me much too long, before jumping out saying, "Remember, it still stays platonic."

When I arrived home, Francis hollered from the barn, "Hey, Caleb, come and see this."

As I walked into the barn I was hit in the face with a stream of milk, and there sat Francis, milking the cow and laughing not only at the milk on my face but at my expression of seeing him milking. "Francis," I said, now laughing with him. "When did this happen? Are you cured?"

"I don't know if 'cured' is the right word," Francis answered, "but after seeing the doctor the last time he suggested that I try getting close to animals to see how the medication was working. I have been working with Jason now for about a week, and so far I haven't had any stuffiness. I always wanted to be able to milk like you and the rest of the boys, so Jason showed me how. Pretty good aren't I? I hit you right in the face first try."

"I'm not only proud Francis, I'm so happy for you. I bet Jason is glad to have you as a helper. This is going to make it easier for all of us. Dad was getting worried that we had to rely too much on Jason to carry on the work here at the farm. One thing, though, Francis, I wouldn't let Dad or Mom know about your good aim; they might see it as wasting milk," I said, laughing, as I left the barn.

Mother was in the kitchen and said, "I can see by the milk on your face you have seen Francis milking. I hope what has happened is permanent. The doctors say that the medication he is on now probably can be reduced. They say that in some cases children outgrow something like he has, but they can't promise that. They told me that when they reduce the medication if he has trouble again then they would have to try something else. I guess all patients that have this problem aren't the same. I pray he will be all right, he is so happy to be one of the boys."

"I know, Mother," I said, washing the milk off my face. "He was laughing like crazy when he squirted me and seemed so proud of himself. I hope the doctors are right about him outgrowing it. Speaking of doctors, how are the plans coming for Dad's operation?"

"It's all planned. He will be going back to the hospital in two weeks. They want him there for a few days before the operation. If everything goes right they will operate on the last Friday in April. He is really looking forward to having it done so he can throw away those crutches. You should go and talk to him before supper. Sometimes he feels left out of things," Mother said as she turned back to her cooking.

I found Dad in the parlor. He was reading one of the Zane Grey westerns. He looked up and smiled saying, "Wouldn't be nice if all of life could be as concise as they are in his stories."

I talked to Dad until Mother called us to supper. We talked about how good it was to see Francis able to work with the animals. I told him all about Norman's wedding plans and how Bruce was going to have a pig roast for a reception. He was just telling me how much fun a pig roast could be when Mother called us for supper. I had just sat down to the table when it dawned on me that the wedding and Dad's operation were going to be only a day apart.

While Emma and Nellie were helping Mother wash the supper dishes, I went in the kitchen with them. I told them about the wedding and how it was going to be the day after Dad's operation. Emma immediately wanted to go to the wedding.

Mother said, "No, Emma, these are Caleb's friends and companions from work and no place for a young, unattended young lady. I think, Caleb, that you are working up one of your guilt complexes that is going to ruin the wedding for you. I knew from hearing you talk to your father there was going to be a wedding, and if I'm right in what I think, then it's a good thing there is. Now you don't have to worry about your father as long as he knows why you're not there. He not only will be comfortable with it, he'll happy for you. I would imagine that the first few days he wouldn't want many visitors anyway.

I hope you all understand that this is a major operation, and it will probably take a few days before he is anywhere near himself. I am probably going to need more help from everyone when he comes home this time than I did last time. I know he hides it well from all you children but he has become very depressed about his situation lately. Emma, I want you to stop dreaming about weddings, and Caleb, you go to your friend's wedding and enjoy yourself."

As I was leaving the kitchen, Emma joined me and asked. "Did you talk to Dad about Aaron, Caleb?"

I talked to him, Emma," I answered, "I think he will be all right if you control yourself a little when he is around. Have you gone with him to talk to Dad yet?"

"No, he is a little afraid of Dad, and even when I suggested I would be with him he was reluctant. Caleb, will you go with us when we go to see Dad?" she asked, giving me a hug.

"Next time Aaron is here after I have talked with Dad to see how he is, I'll go with you. You have to remember what Mother said. This is no time for the family to have another surprise wedding. We have to keep the family as stable as possible until Dad is better," I said walking away, as Emma was trying to tell me how hard it was for her and Aaron. The last thing I needed to hear about right then, was my sister's love problems.

The next couple of weeks seemed to fly by. Francis was able to still help Jason around the animals even after the doctors reduced his medication. That took a lot of pressure off from all of us, because it was becoming plain that we were asking more of Jason than a boy his age should have to do. At work with Norman and Bruce it was all about the wedding.

Bruce was all fired up about the pig roast he had been back to a couple of old mill sites and picked up all the dry hardwood knots and pieces he could find that would add to the flavor of the pork. He had a big pile of oak, cherry, hickory and even some apple and other fruit tree woods. He had cut them all into a size that would make them easy to handle and was busy with Donald Trent designing a fire pit and spit to turn the pig on. He had made arrangements with a farmer near by to buy half of a hog that had weighed around three hundred pounds. The farmer would be butchering it a few days before the wedding. Bruce already had about a six-foot square pit dug about eighteen inches deep for the fire. Donald made the stand for the spit at his home work shop and brought it piece by piece to Bruce as he got it made.

When they finally had it assembled it was a pretty impressive site. They had stanchions on each side of the pit with slots cut in them with a brass bearing fitted in the slots. They had an aluminum bar about two inches square that was ground round on the ends where the fitted in the bearings. One end of this bar had a crank welded to it, so they could turn the pig. This spit was a thing of joy to Bruce. He dragged everyone who came by over to see the pit and tell them how it was going to work. I wondered what Clem would have thought of the Edward boys now, if he saw all of this. Now that Norman was marrying a wonderful woman and Bruce was managing such a huge responsibility as a pig roast. It came to me to me then, how silly we sometimes are in taking someone else's opinion of someone without getting to know that person ourselves.

The time went fast. On Wednesday afternoon Dad went back to the hospital. Joan came home on Thursday. I only talked to her a few minutes that night because I had promised Jennie I would pick her up when I went to see Dad and we would go out for a sundae afterward. I made arrangements for Joan to go with me Friday night.

Dad seemed in good spirits when Jennie and I visited. He said, "This is no place to spend an evening with a pretty girl like Jennie, Caleb; you two run along. Your old man is going to be all right." We stayed and talked to Dad about an hour and then went looking for a good place to have a sundae.

When we found a place and had ordered, Jennie said, "Your dad seems pretty strong for someone who has to face what he has to tomorrow. I would be scared to death."

"He's scared, Jennie; it is just his way not to allow anyone else to know it; it wouldn't be manly, you know," I answered.

It was after ten when we arrived back in Sterling, so I took Jennie home. She said, "I know Joan is home, Caleb, and I promise I won't make a scene when we are together at the wedding." After kissing me passionately she ran for the house laughing.

When I picked Joan up Friday she was full of the excitement of college, much like Jake had been. We went to the hospital, but Dad was still out of it from the operation. Mother, Emma, and Aaron were there.

Mother said, "There isn't any use of all of us waiting here, Caleb. Why don't you take Aaron and Emma home? I'll stay until your father wakes up."

Emma argued that she should stay. Mother, sensing that if she did everyone would want to, demanded we all leave.

After we had dropped Aaron and Emma off and headed for Oscin, Joan mentioned her trouble when she asked, "I know this sounds accusatory, Caleb, but I have to know, does anyone else know about what happened to me?"

"No, Joan, no one except Virginia and me," I answered. "The only one who I've talked to is Virginia, and we both know she wouldn't tell even Norman. I think she must have told you that we talked about it, but only to each other. She even picked times when Norman wasn't around. I imagine she told you that she has invited Jennie to stand up for her with you at the wedding, hasn't she?"

Joan laughed and said, "That's not all she told me, Caleb. Seems you've been up to your old tricks, getting girls upset with you. I know that Jennie will be with us tomorrow, and I don't have any problems with that. Though we were never close friends, I like what I know of her. She is a little older than we are; I always thought she had a big crush on your brother, Josh, but I guess that would go for most all of the girls in Sterling that knew him."

"Looking back, Joan," I replied answering her innuendo, "I know that I was foolish, not just in our relationship, but how I thought about girls. I guess I haven't changed that much. I have strong feelings about you; I also enjoy being with Jennie and some other girls. The way my life is now I'm just as afraid of commitment as I have always been. This college thing, I feel that I need the education if I'm ever going to be able to work at anything beyond farming or logging. Still I am not comfortable when I'm away from Sterling. I had a good job in Oklahoma, I made some good friends, my sister and her husband were wonderful to me, but I was never at ease. I felt like a round peg in a square hole, which was bigger than me, afraid I would never fit in. Now I am tied up with the family's problems. I know it's not forever, and I still have a few years to use the money for college that Old Hanna left me but part of me says, forget about it and stay here. I feel almost as insecure about my life now as I used to when I had to confront your mother as a barn boy."

"Wow, Caleb, some part of you is still refusing to grow up, isn't it?" Joan said, putting her arm around me. "I'm not sure that it is a good thing, but it is one of the things I loved about you all these years. We are all scared of change when we have to leave our nest, for some it is easier, but it's a struggle that can either make you or break you. My advice to you is to get back out there in the big, wicked world and struggle with the rest of us. If you fail, then this entire world will be there for you to fall back on, but if you don't try then you will live the rest of your life wondering if you could have made it. I am glad that you still feel free to talk to me about your feelings. I know no matter what ever else happens in my life I shall be grateful that I had someone like you to come to. When I came home the last time I don't know if I could have gone on if it hadn't been for you and your friend, Virginia."

Joan and I hadn't gone any place special. She wanted to visit some of the barn boy's haunts in Oscin so we had rode around having a soda in one place an ice cream or a sundae in others and finally had ended up parked by the swings in Sterling. We sat there reliving our youth in Sterling until the clock in the church struck midnight.

I said, "I guess we had better call it a night, Joan. We have to leave early tomorrow, the wedding is at ten a.m., and if we aren't early enough Norman will blast us."

I drove Joan home. She was trembling when she kissed me goodnight, then she jumped out of the car and ran into the house saying, "Goodnight, Caleb, see you around eight tomorrow morning, and thank you for being you."

Aaron was just leaving when I got back home. Mother's car wasn't there, and I was worried what that meant.

Emma was waiting by the door she said, "Mother called and said that Dad was conscious but still incoherent, so she is going to spend the night. The doctor's told her that it wasn't unusual for someone who underwent an operation like his to take a few days to get back with it, and not to worry. She asked me to tell you that you were to forget about the family troubles tomorrow and go and have a good time at the wedding. She said Dad had spoken to her about you and he was worried that you didn't get out enough for someone your age; besides that he was excited about the pig roast and anxious to hear how it went. I still don't know why she wouldn't let me go to the wedding, too."

I was too tired and confused to go into all that again with Emma, so I thanked her for filling me in and went to my room. I lay in bed thinking about all that happened, when it came to me that Bruce had said he and Donald were going to start roasting the pig around midnight. I could just imagine Bruce beside the pit of burning embers cutting slices in the pig's hide, stuffing the holes with garlic and onions. He has been so excited about roasting that pig I sometimes thought he had forgotten it was his brother's wedding.

I must have fallen a sleep when, as been my habit lately, I was mulling over all my dilemmas with Josh in my dreams, because the next thing I knew Homer was shaking me saying, "Wake up, Caleb, wake up. I have to leave for work, and you asked me to wake you before I left."

The phone rang just as I got downstairs. It was Mother. She said, "Dad has improved some since last night, and tell the others I will be home by late morning."

I asked if she would need me to come back early. She said, "No, Aaron and

197

Emma are going to be at the hospital right after I leave so you won't have to worry about anything."

After talking to Mother I ate breakfast and left a note on the table about Dad for the rest of the family. As I was pulling into Jennie's yard to pick her up I remembered how she was laughing when I dropped her off Thursday night. I hoped that wasn't an omen of what might happen today between her and Joan. She was waiting for me and came right out. Climbing in, she gave me a little kiss on the cheek, saying, "How was your date last night, Caleb?"

"Not good, Jennie," I replied, "Dad was still unconscious when we got to the hospital, so we stayed with him until Mother made us take Aaron and Emma home. Then Joan and I went for a ride, and then we parked for a while so I could cry on her shoulder."

Jennie seemed subdued by my answer but finally said, "Caleb, I want you to remember that no matter what our relationship is, my shoulder will always be available for you to cry on. I know that it must be hard for you right now with your dad's condition making it impossible for you to plan about college and what you want to do with your life. I'm really sorry for the way I treated you, when I should have been there for you. I will keep my promise, Caleb; there won't be any trouble from me today, and you can lean on me anytime you need to."

We stopped to pick up Joan as she came to the car I said, "Joan, this is Jennie, and Jennie, this is Joan, just in case you haven't officially met."

Joan laughed and said, "Oh, we have met but never this formally before, that was nice, Caleb. It must be hard having two of your part-time girlfriends together with you for a whole day."

Jennie said, "Easy, Joan, I just finished promising him I would be the soul of rectitude today; after all he is going to be among his friends, and we wouldn't want to embarrass him, would we?"

"I have to admit that it's tempting; you might have to remind me once in a while, Jennie, but I'll try to be a good girl," Joan answered, still laughing

They both got into the back seat and started slyly comparing notes about me. So I said, "Look, Jennie, if this is going to be another harassing like you and Etta gave me, then wedding or no wedding I'll take you both back home."

"Etta? Jennie who is Etta?" Joan asked, "another part timer like us? Tell us, Caleb, how many are there anyway?"

"Not to worry, Joan," Jennie answered, "Etta was just some girl from Oklahoma that was the sister of one of Caleb's Indian friends who he babysat at his house while she was here looking into some college. That's all it was, because Caleb told me so. Boy, she was some squaw though. With her build she had all the boys in Sterling, except Caleb of course, on their knees, begging her to look their way. Enough about Caleb's harem for today; we'd better concentrate on Virginia and the wedding while we still have a chance to go."

The rest of the way to the job site they talked about what they were supposed to be doing at the wedding. Virginia had told Joan in a letter what it was going to be like and she explained it all to Jennie. I was glad they had stopped teasing me, even though I knew it was meant to be only in fun. I was getting a little angry with them.

When we arrived at the site, Bruce and Donald were turning the pig on the spit. Bruce hollered, "Come and see, Caleb, come and see how great this is working."

The girls ran in to see Virginia and I joined Bruce and Donald. He had a right to be proud though the pig had a ways to go before it was fully cooked. It looked so evenly browned that I wondered if Bruce had been there turning it all night. There was a pleasing aroma in the air of garlic and onions and a fire of the assorted woods burning next to the pit that supplied them with coals to add to the pit when necessary.

I said, "Bruce, you have really outdone yourself. I can hardly wait to get back to eat; now don't go inviting everyone that comes over here or they won't want to leave and come to the wedding."

"Don't worry about that," Donald said, "You, Bruce, and the two girls are the only ones going to the wedding, and the party is here. You don't have to worry, though; Bruce made me promise: no one gets to eat this hog until Norman and Virginia have the first bite."

At about nine-thirty the five of us loaded into my car, and we drove to the little chapel in Florence. There we met the pastor, who requested a few minutes in private with Norman and Virginia. The chapel was a house built sometime in the seventeen hundreds that had been converted to a house of worship.

At ten thirty exactly, we all stood at the altar as the pastor bestowed the blessings of the church and state on their wedding vows. At one point, Norman stuttered so badly the pastor had to ask him to repeat his vows. He looked like he was going to faint, but Virginia put her arm around his shoulder and he slowed down and was able to enunciate the rest of his vows without the stutter.

When the pastor asked who gives this woman, Bruce nudged me with his elbow so I said, "I, Caleb Carney, as one of her closest friends do."

After he had finished the vows, the pastor said, "Now, Norman, you may kiss your wife."

Norman still looked rather shaky, but Virginia grabbed him and kissed him passionately.

After we left the chapel everyone except Bruce was quietly enmeshed in their own thoughts but Bruce just bubbled over with excitement, saying, "Imagine that, my brother is really married, and to a wonderful woman. Who would have ever believed it? This calls for the greatest celebration ever, on to my pig roast."

Virginia leaned over the seat and kissed Bruce lightly on the cheek saying, "This was the best part for me, Bruce, but I know that I am going to enjoy all that you and the crews have prepared for Norman and me. Not every girl gets a chance to have a pig roast for a reception or has such a wonderful bunch of woodsmen to celebrate it with. Thank you, Bruce; Norman and I are both delighted in what you have done."

When we arrived back at the job site the men from the different crews were already drifting in, all of them brought dishes of some sorts to go with the pork and of course plenty of beer and booze.

Bruce wanted introduce the new Mr. and Mrs. Edward right away, but Joan and Jennie talked him into waiting until we got ready to eat and more people had arrived. The girls went into the shanty to change and I joined the people who were gathered around the pit that was cooking the pig. Leclat's full crew had come; some of them brought their wife's and children. The mill hands and the Joclin family were here.

Brian Melwin, who was head of the crew that cut the logs, was there with a couple of his choppers. He came over to me and said, "Caleb, I met an old friend of yours today. You remember Edgar who used to work for me, don't you? Well, he said to say hello for him and to tell you he would be over this way soon and would like to see you again. I tried to get him to come today but he said he had other engagements."

I hadn't thought about Edgar for some time, hearing from him again brought back good memories of how he had helped me after we lost Josh; it was too bad he couldn't come today.

It was already after twelve noon, and some of the boys were starting to feel their beer and were hollering, "Where is the bride and groom, and when are we going to eat?" Bruce and Donald had built a long table out of planks from the mill and covered it with a roll of paper that they scrounged from somewhere.

Bruce came out and quieted the crowd, and then Jennie and Joan came out and started pouring wine from gallon jugs into paper cups at the table.

After everyone had a cup of wine Bruce went to the shanty and brought Norman and Virginia to the table, raising his wine he said, "It is my honor to introduce for the first time Mr. and Mrs. Edward!"

Everyone cheered. Joan and Jennie seated the Edwards, and Bruce and Donald, using thick gloves moved the pig, still laced, to the bar onto a set of stanchions that they had arranged by the table. Bruce carved big chunks of meat from the pig and put them on the table, Donald carved them up smaller, and Jennie and Joan served the Edwards, then everybody grabbed plates and served themselves.

Bruce's smile grew wider and wider at all the "ohs" and "ahs" heard from those eating the pork. Even Joan, who was at first was skeptical about something cooked that way was seen going back for seconds. When I got a chance to talk to Bruce I admitted I had never tasted better pork.

There were great varieties of food, and there was pork enough that everyone could have all they wanted. Someone pulled out a fiddle and started playing and received a roar of approval. A call went up for Norman to give a speech. I think most of us knew that Norman would break out stuttering if he tried.

Virginia rose to the occasion raising her wine glass she said, "Norman is much too emotional right now to talk. He is overwhelmed, not just because we are married but because all of you took the time to come and honor our day. So eat, drink, and be merry, and let's make this a celebration we will never forget."

Joan and Jennie had joined me and when we finished eating we walked around and I introduced them to some of the crew. I received some teasing about having two girls, being as most of the crowd were men, and a couple of the men were a little bawdy. I could see that it was bothering Joan, so we took a walk down to the mill sight, and I explained my job to her. Jennie tied to sooth Joan with a, "Men will be men" speech, but seeing that wasn't going to help, I said, "We had better get back and spend a little time with Virginia and Norman. We are not going to be able to stay too late because I have to go to the hospital to relieve Mother today."

Joan said, "I would like to go with you, if it's okay, Caleb. I'm leaving to go back to college Monday night, and I would like to spend a little time with just you before then."

Jennie put her arm around Joan and said laughing, "That's okay, Joan. I'll loan him to you for tonight." I think she sensed Joan had a problem besides this party.

Joan seemed to brighten up, saying with a laugh, "That doesn't seem fair, Jennie. I should get more than one night. After all, you will have him all to yourself after I'm gone."

"Oh, if that was only true, Joan," she answered, "You're forgetting Betty, Etta, and Lord only knows how many others."

I shouted, "That's enough. You two remember, this is Norman and Virginia's wedding day, not get-Caleb day; besides you both promised."

We got back to the party and joined the bride and groom. Virginia was admonishing Norman not to overdo his drinking. Bruce was shining like I had never seen him. Everybody was congratulating him on the pork and asking when he could do it again. Someone had made a little platform for the fiddler near a level, clear spot, and some of the couples and children were dancing.

Virginia said, "Come on, Caleb, help me convince Norman we should at least have one dance."

Norman said, "All right, but only if Caleb dances, too."

I was looking askance at the girls when Jennie said, "You dance with, Joan, Caleb, and I'll get Bruce to dance with me."

We all joined the group with the fiddler and asked for a slow dance. Bruce was putting up a fuss about dancing, so one of Melvin's young choppers came over, and taking Jennie's hand, said, "May I save Bruce?"

Norman was having a hard time at first, but with Virginia guiding him he soon got into the swing of it. The fiddler went from the slow waltz to something a little faster and at the end of three or four dances we all were flying around the little clearing. A couple of the men asked to cut in with Joan, but I told them we only had today together and I didn't want to share her. Jennie on the other hand was having a ball. She enjoyed dancing and had swapped partners a few times, though I noticed she ended up dancing with the same chopper she started out with.

Joan and I danced four or five more dances during the afternoon. I figured it might cause trouble with Jennie but she was having such a high time she hardly noticed. At around four thirty I told the girls to say their goodbyes because we would have to be leaving soon. Jennie didn't want to leave, pleading for just one more hour.

While we were talking, Gene Aldrich, the chopper who she had been dancing with, came over saying, "Caleb, if she wants to stay I'll see that she gets back to Sterling."

I was about to say, "No way," when Bruce, who had been listening, said, "It's all right, Caleb; I can vouch for Gene, and if it will make you feel better, I'll ride back to Sterling with them."

I was about to argue that when Joan elbowed me and nodded her head yes. So I said, "Because I brought you here, Jennie, I feel responsible for you. This is nothing against you, Gene, but I want you all to promise that Bruce goes with you."

Gene said, "Not a problem, Caleb; I'm glad that Jennie has a friend like you who cares."

Jennie gave my check a little brush whispering, "Thank you, Caleb. I haven't felt this free since I first went dancing with you."

Bruce and Donald had put what was left of the pig on ice, keeping a chunk hanging over what was left of the fire for people to have, as they wanted it.

To my surprise Joan said, "Let's go have another piece of Bruce's pig and a bite to eat before we leave, Caleb."

After getting the food, when we sat at the table, Joan said, "Is it hard for you, Caleb, seeing Jennie in another man's arms?"

My first inclination was to say no but I thought better of it. So I said, "In lots of ways it is, Joan; it's like watching a beloved sister exploring her womanhood outside of the family."

"Beloved sister, my foot, Caleb!" Joan laughed. "I bet you to have been far more intimate than that. I get the feeling you two are bedded lovers."

This time for Jennie's sake I lied, saying, "The truth is that we probably would be, if I had my way, but Jennie has always insisted that our relationship has to stay platonic."

Even though it was Joan who brought the subject up, I could see by the way she quivered talking about sex she was probably reliving some of her horror.

So I said, "Let's find Norman and Virginia to say goodbye and be on our way."

Joan was quiet until we were about half way to the hospital. Then she said, "That's the way it should be isn't it, Caleb? Norman and Virginia's wedding—a rousing party, Jennie finding someone she is comfortable with and wanting to stay. All of that is life, common life; I wonder if I can ever feel that it is okay for me to feel that way again. I know that you and your friends live in a different world than I have. Still, even when it gets a little rowdy sometimes, it's just people being honest with themselves and the world they live in, enjoying what God has given them. Thank you for bringing me into that world, Caleb. Last time I believe it saved my life; this time it is trying to tell me what living is."

"I think that what you have seen in this group is a part of my life, but it certainly isn't all that life is. Most of this group doesn't have formal educations because they grew up in a world that didn't require it. The world keeps evolving, and Jake has always said that wars have a way of speeding that up. What that means is that our generation has to become more educated to keep up with it. So as much as sometimes it seems so much simpler to hold on to the old ways, those who do, get left behind. We at the Joclin mill are a good example of not letting go. Most of the mills today are using Cletrac Tractors to do their logging and trucks to stick lumber while we still use horses. When I am working with these men and involved in their world I am very content. Then when I see all that is happening in the world I have a longing to be able to overcome my fear so I can find my place out there. I know I am where I need to be right now because of the family trouble. Still I am so comfortable where I am now, I sometimes doubt that I will develop the courage needed to leave when I have a chance."

Joan snuggled up close to me saying, "You are going to have to grow up enough to shake Sterling out of your system, Caleb. There is so much out there in the world that you'll never experience here, and if you are going to write, you need to see it, feel it, and taste it, before you can write about it. I know well there are things to fear out there, but I learned from your friends that you can't let some individual horror of life take away the beauty that is left."

By the time we reached the hospital Mother had already left, and Dad was sleeping. Mother had left a note with the nurse in charge for us, which read:

Caleb, your father is running high fevers; the doctors are puzzled by them and are waiting for some test that won't be back until Monday. They have him heavily sedated because he fights everything when he is fully awake. It is not at all like him to be so hard to handle, but they say it is common with high fevers for patients to act out of character. They told me I should go home because they plan to keep him sedated that way most of the time until the test comes back. They will allow you in his room but don't become depressed at what you see; he is helpless as a baby right now. The doctors said his condition isn't that uncommon after some operations, it is just that they are not sure about the why of his high fever. Mother

After reading the note I decided I wanted to at least step in and see him. I told Joan she didn't have to go in, but she insisted. Dad looked awfully pale and weak. He had a mask over part of his face that was hitched to a tank; I guess that was to help his breathing.

204

Though he was motionless he seemed to be breathing regularly. I held his hand silently praying he would fully recover. I stayed like that for ten minutes or so and then said, "We might as well go, Joan."

Joan bent over and kissed Dad on the cheek saying, "Thank you, Mr. Carney, for having a son like Caleb."

Worried as I was about Dad when we were leaving the hospital I couldn't control the thoughts about what losing him would mean to me. There would no more indecision about what my future would be. As the oldest boy I would be expected to provide for the family. These thoughts created as much fear as thinking about leaving Sterling did. Josh used to talk about growing mature enough to be happy with who you are. He even wrote about it.

Who am I? I wish I knew
And could really get it right
I know from history, I'm different now
From what I'll be tonight
It's not the heights or depth of what I've been
Or what I'll someday be
I'll know today, I've been a success
If I'm happy being me

"What is that from, Caleb?" Joan asked.

I didn't realize I had been actually reciting the poem as I was recalling it. So I said, "Sorry, Joan, I didn't realize I was thinking out loud. It was just a poem of Josh's that came to mind that seems to fit my thoughts."

"I have heard that Josh wove magic sometimes with his poems. Do you think I could see some of them sometime? Would you do that one again right now for me, Caleb?" she asked, cuddling up to me again.

After I had recited it again, Joan said, "There is such truth in that poem. You know, for a little while today I allowed what happened to me to start to ruin the day. Still, by the time we were leaving, I felt just like Jennie; I wanted more of the good feelings that were starting to develop as we were dancing. As I watched Jennie taking advantage of what was there instead of moping because of what wasn't, it made me feel more alive. I know it may be ages before I can feel comfortable around any man except you, but you and your carefree friends are proving it will be possible. Caleb, I know it can never be like it was when we were kids, but promise me that I can always come to you. I know now after seeing your need I want to be there for you."

It seemed good to be able to discuss things with Joan again but she was right, we weren't kids any more and adult problems seemed so much more of a heavy burden. I know my heartache about my father and the family and my aims in life or lack of them are subjects Joan can be helpful with. What I need also is someone like Josh to help me weed through the Ettas, Bettys, Joans and Jennies in my life. I know from experience it not a safe subject with Joan.

Joan hadn't wanted to hurry back to Sterling so we found a soda place and went in to have a sundae. We spent about two hours there, talking about old times both wishing we could go back there and escape the horrors of now. Realization set in on the ride back to Sterling.

So I said, "I know tomorrow is your last day home, Joan, but I am going to have to go back to the hospital tomorrow. I will try to get back in time so we can take in a movie or something."

"Oh, Caleb if you are going to be alone, let me go with you. Let me help ease the burden in some way. Maybe I can somehow be as much help as you were for me. I don't know how, but at least you will have someone to talk to. I found that was a big help for me even when I thought I didn't want anyone near. We can see a movie after if there is time, but a least we will be together longer," Joan answered.

When we arrived at Joan's house she held me tight kissing me lightly on each cheek. As she ran to the house I sensed that this time she hadn't shivered while she held me.

When I arrived home I checked in to tell Mother things were much the same when I left the hospital. I crawled into bed and slept until almost noon.

Nellie was in the kitchen when I came down. When I asked why someone hadn't wakened me, she said, "Mother told us to let you sleep. She and Emma left around ten this morning, Aaron is going to pick Emma up there, and Mother said for you to come when you can. Jason and Francis are out working in the barn or the garden. How was your pig roast, Caleb? Sounds kind of barbaric to me."

"It was some of the best pork I have ever eaten, Nellie, and it isn't any more barbaric than you cooking chops on the stove. After all, it wasn't like we roasted a pig alive."

I wanted to explain it better than that to her, but I wasn't in the mood for anything like that then. I bolted down some toast and coffee and went out to tell the boys I was leaving, and then I went to pick up Joan. Joan's father came out to the car before I could get out.

He said, "Caleb, we want you to know how sorry we are about your father's troubles. We have asked for prayers at our church for him. We also want you to know how grateful we are for all that you and your friends have done for Joan. I know our history hasn't shown it, but at least I know now you are the best kind of friend a girl like Joan could have."

Joan came out and cut him short saying, "I hope Dad isn't out here threatening you with his whip again, Caleb. I asked him not to bother you, but he beat me out here."

"No, Joan," I replied, "he has been just telling me how much he appreciated that I introduced you to my world and all the characters in it. I think he thinks I am better company now that I'm not a barn boy anymore."

Seeing the look on Mr. Walden's face as we pulled away, I thought maybe that was a little strong, After all he was really thanking me, I made a mental note to do something about the anger I still held for Joan's parents.

Joan and I were quiet on the trip to the hospital, both of us at the time with our thoughts tied to different worlds.

Mother was still there when we arrived and met us outside of Dad's room saying, "He's awake, Caleb; sometimes he is incoherent, but he has been asking for you."

The three of us went into Dad's room, and he said, "That's the one, Helen! I told you it wasn't a dream. She kissed me last time she was here."

Mother started to try to shush Dad up, but Joan said, "Why, Mr. Carney, don't tell me you have to fake being asleep to get a kiss?"

"No, no," Dad said, "it wasn't like that. I've been having some really strange dreams, and I always tell my wife in case they are real, and I don't know it. I told her some beautiful girl I didn't know had come in and kissed me on both cheeks last night, and it seemed so real. Then when you walked in you looked just like the girl in my dream."

Joan surprised me by walking over to Dad's bed and kissing him on the cheek and asking with a laugh, "Do you remember it like this, Mr. Carney?"

Mother looked a little shocked, after all Joan had never been associated with my family and really didn't know her. I suppose that seeing Dad so happy about the kiss she saw it as a way to help.

I knew Mother wasn't jealous but just perplexed, so I said, "Isn't that something, Mother? We spend all day with him and he doesn't even remember us. Then some pretty girl comes in and kisses him, and he remembers that. The last thing that happened when we left last night was Joan kissing Dad on the cheeks. Maybe the doctors are using the wrong medicine. I think I'll have a talk with some of his pretty nurses."

Mother said, laughing, "I'll take care of all of that kind of medication. The last thing I need is competition from young girls like Joan."

We spent a couple of hours with Dad. Though he drifted in and out some, for most of our time there he was pretty much with it. When we left I felt better about him than I had the night before.

Joan said, "It will be a couple of hours before it gets dark, Caleb; let's drive back to Sterling and climb Mount Fay."

I didn't think that was too good an idea considering the time of year it was, but I wanted Joan's time she had left used to suit her, so I said, "I'm not sure we can make the top or not before it gets dark, but let's give it a try."

When we got to Sterling I opened the gate and drove through the pasture to the bottom of the mountain trail. We didn't talk much going up, as we had to rush to get up there and back before it got too dark.

At the top I said, "Joan, thank you for being so good with Dad. You really made his day, and to think I almost talked you out of going to the hospital with me."

So far I had purposely avoided trying to hold Joan since her rape, worrying it would bother her. I put my arms around her and kissed her on the cheek telling her, "That's for Dad."

She didn't pull away, just stood there letting me hold her for about a minute before pulling away and saying, "Come on, Caleb. I'll race you back down."

About half way down Joan stumbled and sat down. At first I thought she was just breathing hard but then realized she was crying. Sobbing she said, "It'll never be the same again will it, Caleb? The magic is gone; even your mountain cannot bring it back for us this time, can it?"

I sat down and held her; she clung to me and sobbed. "Don't sell my mountain short, Joan. It has rescued me more than once. You remember I spent two whole days up here after we lost Josh. I felt it had failed me then, but just when I was about to curse it, the mountain wind brought me Josh's voice asking me to let him go in peace. One thing I can promise you: the mountain will always be here for us," I said, holding her closer.

Joan squirmed around to face me saying, "No man or mountain will want me now, Caleb."

I took Joan's shoulders and said, "You listen to me. The mountain doesn't care about that and no man except me knows, so you can erase those crazy thoughts from your head."

"How about you, Caleb? You know; do you want me now? If I remember right, there were times I think I would have, but we didn't."

208

"Look, Joan, I have to fight right now not to take advantage of this situation, but that's not going to happen, not now, not like this. For us it has to be something special. I've known that ever since the night you lost your panties. So let's get back down the mountain so I can run off some of this want I have for you," I said, standing up to go.

Joan stood up, kissed me wildly, and started running down the mountain. I didn't catch her until she had reached the car. I grabbed her, and she held me close.

I kissed her passionately, saying, "That's enough of this, Joan; let's go to Oscin and see a movie."

When I brought Joan home after the movie, we just sat and held each other for about ten minutes without talking. Then Joan kissed me softly saying, "I'll write to you, Caleb; please answer." She left the car, running for the house with tears in her eyes.

When I got home I checked with Mother. She said, "Dad was resting comfortably when we left, and the doctors said they should know more about his fevers tomorrow."

I went to my room and crawled into bed, physically and mentally exhausted from my weekend. In my prayers I asked God to give me the wisdom of Josh that I might make sense out of my whirling world.

The next day at work Norman was rather sullen but Bruce was wild about all the excitement that had happened after I left the party Saturday.

He came out of the shanty as soon as I got there shouting, "Caleb, you should have stayed; you really should have. We had a wild time after you left. Donald and I put the pig back on, everyone ate again, and we finished it all up. Somebody brought out a jug of white lightning, and some of the boys were getting drunker. The fiddler played even after it was getting dark, but most of the men who had brought their women folk were getting dragged out of here, so there wasn't much dancing except Gene and Jennie. I'm not sure what happened. I guess someone got a little fresh with Jennie, Gene got mad, and a hell of a fight started. Norman and I broke it up, and I told Jennie it was time Gene and I took her home. She wasn't in a mood to go, but Virginia talked to her into going. Gene and I took her back to Sterling where she only gave Gene a little kiss on the cheek and ran into the house.

"When Gene and I got back here the boys had piled wood on the fire pit and had a big roaring fire going. They were all sitting around the fire drinking. Norman and Virginia had gone back to their shanty. There were the usual drunken arguments and scuffles, finally someone said, 'We have to start a

209

shivaree,' and everyone started cheering. I didn't know what that was, and I don't think half that crowd did, because somebody asked, 'What the hell is that?' Donald, who was pretty drunk by then, shouted, 'Come on; I'll show you how it's done.' We all marched down to Norman and Virginia's shanty and started marching in a circle around it, all hollering and banging on everything we could find. Man, what a hullabaloo.

"We kept this up, going around and around the shanty. Once in a while we would hear Norman swearing at us, but we didn't stop. I don't know how long we had been just marching banging and hollering when somebody began singing bawdy songs; others soon joined him. Finally Norman came to the door with his shotgun and fired two shots in the air, shouting, "The next time I shoot, it's going to be at one of you sons of bitches if you don't stop.' The boys kept right on singing.

"Virginia came out and took the gun away from Norman and said, 'That's not the way, Norman.' She took Norman by the hand brought him out and sat on the steps and began singing right along with the men, offering them more drinks as they marched by. This went on for quite some time before some of the men began staggering off into the brush and falling asleep. Finally when there were only a few of us left we went back to check on the fire, and when the rest of them started to fall asleep. I went back to my shanty. The next day I made a lot of coffee. There were men crawling in out of the brush until almost noon looking for ways to get home. That was a party to end all parties, wasn't it, Caleb?"

I had to agree that it might have been interesting to be there, but I was somehow glad I wasn't. I was especially glad that Jennie had gotten out of there before it got to rough.

Norman didn't say a word until we were alone out in the sticking field. Then he said, "Some damn wedding, huh, Caleb? Damn bunch of rowdy drunks singing and hollering until almost dawn. I think I might actually have shot some of them if it hadn't been for Virginia. That damn Bruce! To hear him talk, he thinks he has pulled off the party of the year or something."

I could see that Norman was still in a foul mood. I could understand in a way, but I said, "Lighten up, Norman; these men are your friends, and you should have known how pig roast for a group of woodsmen was going to end up. There was nothing personal in what went on; it was a celebration of your wedding in the way they always celebrate. Hell, you're lucky nobody thought to try and tip your shanty over. My Uncle Louis told me about that happening once at a wedding party he was at. You shouldn't be angry with Bruce. Having

Virginia come into your life was hard on him. The party has made him feel like he was more a part of your new family. Don't take that away from him. I guarantee you one thing, Norman; in years to come you will tell the story of your wedding party many times with pride, so don't lament it now."

"Ah, I know, Caleb. It's just that I wanted it to be something nice and sweet for Virginia, and it ended up a drunken bash. Then I got a tongue lashing from her for shooting the gun. You know, you sound like Virginia; maybe you two are right. She says I should be proud of such a party. Thanks for talking to me, Caleb," Norman said as he put the stakes back in the wagon.

By the end of the day Norman was beginning to see the fun side of the party, which was a good thing because all the men teased him every time they got a chance. He was even joking with Bruce about it just before I left.

I went straight to the hospital from work anxious to hear what the doctors found out about Dad. When I arrived at the hospital Aaron and Emma were just coming out. I could see she had been crying. "What happened?" I asked. "Is Dad worse?"

Aaron answered, "It's kind of bad, Caleb; the doctors got the test back, and he has been diagnosed with break-bone fever. Some of the doctors have doubts, but the lab is insistent their test is right. The prognosis is bad: six or seven weeks of high fevers, joint and muscle pain, bad headaches, and a long recovery period. Though this fever isn't unheard of around here, the doctors can't imagine how your dad could have contacted it."

Emma held me, crying. "Oh, Caleb, how much more can Dad take? He was having a hard time being incapacitated before! What will he do now?"

"I don't know, Emma, but let's deal with one thing at a time," I answered. "I'll go in; maybe I can get more information."

When I saw Mother she looked beat. I held her for a minute, saying, "We'll get through this, Mother; maybe it isn't as bad as Emma said."

"It's bad, Caleb, real bad. Another doctor just examined your father and came and told me that in his opinion, the lab tests are right. What are we to do?" Mother asked, holding me tighter.

A nurse came by and said, "If you want to see your father, you had better go in now; the doctor has ordered medicine that will keep him comfortable, but he will probably just sleep."

We went in, and Dad was still awake saying, "Where is that little kissing angel, Caleb? You too jealous to bring her back?"

"No, Dad, I'm afraid she has left us both. She went back to college today, but she sent her best to you and said you'll have to do with Mother's kisses until she gets back."

We stayed with Dad until he slowly drifted off. The nurse said he wouldn't be awake again for ten or twelve hours. Mother and I drove back to Sterling. I hadn't seen Mother in such a state since the time Josh died. At home Emma had made a meal for the family, but Mother went right to her room. Nellie wanted to go to her, but Emma said no, maybe tomorrow would be better.

We all sat around the rest of the evening quietly lost in our own thoughts. When I went to bed it came to me in a jolt. Six or seven weeks of fever is a long recovery period. I went to sleep thinking, here it is May and college starts in a little over three months. I woke in the middle of the night with Homer shaking me. I had been dreaming. Josh had me by the shoulders shaking me saying, "You can do it, Caleb; you have to do it for me." Homer said I had been hollering, "No, no, no, Josh, you have to come back!" over and over again.

CHAPTER EIGHT

They kept Dad at the hospital for almost two weeks after the operation, trying different medications to control the fevers. When he finally came home he spent most of his time in the living room and sometimes when we talked to him it was almost like we weren't even there. This was hard on all of us but I think was hardest on Jason. He had become used to Dad coming out with him and helping or at least supervising the work around the farm.

Mother had told us that the doctors had warned that between the medication and the fever he could become moody, though sometimes I felt that his moods were beyond that. Jason wouldn't give up though, everyday he would go in and lay out a schedule of what needed to be done and ask Dad about it. There were occasions when Dad would respond to this and help Jason with the planning but Jason never could get him to go outside on his crutches with him no matter how hard he tried.

Francis was doing well on the medication and was able to work with Jason with the animals, which made it easier for Jason. Still, Jason seemed to have a special need for Dad. I believe it had developed while Dad was teaching him how to take care of things at the farm. I could well understand that happening, remembering how gracious he had been with me when he had to shoot the horse Tom, because of my stupidity.

Things were going well at work. Norman and Bruce made it easy for me as they took care of the horses and everything else that needed to be done when we weren't working. What a blessing it has been for me having those two caring for things at work. We had plans to move down to the lower setting by the first of July. The setting we were on was too big to finish by then, so we would have to move back here after we finished the lower lot. We knew that it would take us more than four months to finish up down there and we needed to be out of there before it snowed.

Mr. Banner, in talking with Mother, had convinced her that there was money enough in the Carney fund he controlled to have a nurse come by to help with Dad. This made life so much better for her because on some of the trips back to the hospital Dad fought going and it took so much out of her. The nurses that came handled his mood swings in stride, telling Mother it will get better, that this was to be expected in his case. When Dad came home from the hospital before, several of the men in town had visited for a while, now only Mr. Banner and Pastor Jones visited with him regularly. Dad had never been much of a socializer so I'm not sure that was a problem for him, besides with the five of us still living at home, we tried to keep his time occupied.

One evening at the end of May I got a call from Betty. She said, "Caleb, I have to see you. It is urgent. I know what you told Mother about us. I respect that, but I need some help. You owe me at least that."

I told her I was free that evening, and I would pick her up at her house at eight. I couldn't imagine what it was she needed from me, but I felt she was right in believing I owed her something. Jason had asked me to look at our cow. He thought she needed treatment on a cut she had on her udder. After supper I went with Jason to examine it. It looked like a barbed wire or a brier cut that had become infected. We got some alcohol and a clean cloth, and washed the wound clean, and applied bag balm. I told Jason that it should be all right in a week or so if we kept it clean.

After leaving the barn and cleaning up, I went to pick up Betty. She came out just as soon as I pulled into the driveway. Jumping in the car she shouted, "Get out of here fast, Caleb."

I could see her mother coming out the door, so I drove off like she asked, saying, "What the hell, Betty; are you fighting with your mother?

"No, no, Caleb don't talk, just drive. Let's go to Oscin and grab a sundae or something," she answered.

I could see she had been crying and was in no mood to talk, so I drove to Oscin, wondering what the hell I had got myself into this time. When we got to Oscin she had cleaned her face up before we went into the ice cream parlor to get sundaes.

Even after finishing our sundaes, I could see she was in no mood to talk about her problem, so I asked, "How's Karl doing since he ran off with his nurse?"

She kind of laughed, saying, "They are doing well; they bought a new house and are expecting their first child." Then the tears started again, and she said, "Let's get out of here, Caleb."

Back in the car I said, "What has you so upset, Betty? You called and asked for my help. I can't help if I don't know what's wrong."

Betty cuddled up close to me, saying, "Caleb, you do care for me, at least a little, don't you?"

"Of course I care for you, Betty. It's just I'm not ready yet to settle down with any one girl. Life is too complicated for me right now," I answered.

"Complicated," she exploded, "complicated, let me tell you about complications, Caleb. I'm pregnant."

I felt like I had been kicked by a horse and was holding my breath, trying to deny the pain. *Oh, my God, what is she telling me? This was my baby? My mother will kill me if she hears something like that. Life, as I know it, will be over.*

Trying to regain control of myself and said, "Betty how could this happen?"

"Oh, God, Caleb. You know how it happens; my problem is not how, but who," she said, sobbing. "That's why I was running from my mother. She was calm when I told her I was pregnant and said we would work it out somehow. She asked me who. When I told her I wasn't sure, she exploded. The timing makes you only one of three possibilities. My first thoughts were that I would blame you, so you would have to always be a part of my life. After relishing that thought for a while, I knew I couldn't ever do that to you. I know that Eric, the boy I have been going out with lately, would accept it as his, but the timing is not right for him. The truth is, Caleb, that I don't want to be married to any of the other boys it might be."

As hard as I tried I couldn't slow down the crazy wild thoughts whirling through my mind. Betty and I married, no more college, no writing career, facing Mother and family—on and on the thoughts came, tearing at very heart and soul of all my dreams. Numb as my mind was, I reached out and held Betty close to me. I know I needed to say or do something, but my whole being was just drained of all energy. Then I remembered something Josh had asked me about believing in angels when I felt unable to wear the clothes of a classmate who had died, after I lost all mine when our house burnt. If he was there looking down on me as an angel then, like Josh said, wouldn't Josh's angel be looking down on me now?

I know it wouldn't be with approval but at least maybe some guidance. I could never prove that Josh's angel reached out to me, but soon I felt comfortable enough to talk to Betty in a soothing tone, saying, "Betty, there is a lot we have to do before we get into who's to blame. Number one is making sure that your health is being taken care. What doctor did you go to?"

" I haven't been to a doctor, Caleb. I just got courage enough to tell my mother today."

"Then you are not even sure that you are pregnant?" I asked.

"I'm over two months late with my monthly, Caleb. Even you ought to know what that means," she said, breaking out crying again.

"Easy, Betty," I said, holding her tighter, "I didn't mean that the way it sounded, but I do believe that before you show or the news gets out we had better see what a doctor has to say first. If nothing else, it might help establish a more exact time. I promise you this, Betty, no matter what happens I will stand by you."

"I knew I could count on you, Caleb; forgive me for wanting more from you than you want to give," she replied, cuddling up closer.

Betty was in no hurry to go home, so we drove around until almost midnight.

When we finally arrived at her house I said, "Betty, you are going to need your mother, so why don't you tell her that your, "I don't know," was only that you were not ready to talk about 'who' yet. I know what conclusions she will probably draw, since you called me before telling her. That will be all right as long as it doesn't get out, and I don't think it is something your mother will be talking about for a while."

Betty held me tight and said, "I knew you would help me, Caleb, and I will see a doctor as soon as I can get an appointment." With that she kissed me goodnight and ran for the house.

I guess Josh's ghost must have deserted me after I left Betty off because all my doubts and fears began swirling through my mind again. I tossed and turned all night, and Homer shook me awake a couple of times saying, "Stop your screaming, Caleb. You're waking the whole damn house. Mother has enough on her hands with Dad, without worrying about you, too."

The next day at work Norman asked, "What the hell is bugging you now, Caleb? You act like somebody loaded the whole world on your shoulders. Did your father take a turn for the worse, or is it trouble with your harem again?"

"No, it's not my dad," I answered almost confiding in him, remembering just in time how he had used my confidences before. "It's just all the uncertainty of my life right now. I have to reapply for college if I'm going back this fall, and I still don't know if my father will be able to handle things then. Of course the Joan- Jenny-Etta-and-Betty thing gets confusing some times; still, you can't think of that as a bad place to be, can you?"

"You know what, Caleb?" Norman said with a laugh. "I know that I teased you about bringing all your girl friends to Virginia for guidance, but I think maybe you should have a talk with her yourself."

The day dragged on, with my mind still full of trepidation, and though I hoped I had helped Betty with my assurances, I certainly hadn't assuaged my own feelings about what might happen. By the end of the day, after Norman had chastised me for my mood several times, I began thinking seriously about talking to Virginia. After all, she had been a big help to Joan and kept it all to herself.

After the mill had closed down and Norman and I had unloaded the last load of lumber, I said, "Norman I think you're right; if you don't mind taking care of the team I would like to talk to Virginia."

Norman laughed saying "I don't mind, Caleb, but I think Virginia should set up office hours and charge you for her time."

While Norman tended the horses I went to see Virginia at the shanty. She seemed surprised to see me but said, "Come in, Caleb; what brings you here, and why the long face?"

All of the sudden this didn't seem like a good idea, and I felt guilty about burdening Virginia with my troubles. So I said, "I'm just here to placate Norman; he thinks I need a mood change."

Virginia laughed and said, "Well, what's bugging you? Spit it out. I can't promise you anything except a good ear, but sometimes that's all it takes."

Despite my intentions not to say anything, I blurted out all that had happened with Betty.

Virginia didn't look shocked; she just studied me for a while and said, "Your big problem is that Betty isn't the one for you, right, Caleb?"

"It's not a matter of the right one, it's just the status of my life right now is so confusing, and this is like the hammer that nails my life down in an unplanned way. Then there is the fact that she doesn't know whose child it is."

Virginia was quiet for a minute before saying, "I've never met this Betty that I can recall. Would it be possible for us to meet?"

217

"She has never been here. Virginia. Tomorrow is Friday, but if you think that will help I can bring her Saturday if she is free. Should I tell her why?" I asked

"No, Caleb, I think we had better just play it by ear. She might not want to trust you if she knew you had told someone else. You just bring her for the ride like you did the other girls. I'll decide if I should talk to her or not after we meet. I hope you haven't told Norman about this. He sometimes finds it hard to keep secrets," she said just as Norman came walking in.

I shook my head no, as Norman asked, "Did you set up a pay schedule for Caleb, Virginia? After all, if you are going to be his adviser you should get paid, don't you think?"

"Knock it off, Norman," Virginia replied. "All Caleb needs is someone to talk to that doesn't tease him all the time, like someone else I know."

I left the shanty feeling somewhat relieved that I had been able at least to talk to someone about it, though it dawned on me that Virginia hadn't offered me any consolation.

I called Betty Friday night, but her mother said she wasn't home and slammed down the receiver. A few minutes later Nellie came and said, "Telephone for you, Caleb."

It was Betty. She had heard her mother cursing me and called me back when her mother left the room. I asked her about riding to the job site with me, and she readily agreed, saying she couldn't talk long and to be at her house by eight Saturday morning, before hanging up abruptly.

When I pulled into her yard the next morning, Betty again came running out of the house, with her mother in the door shaking her fist at me shouting. "How could you, Caleb Carney? Your best friend's little sister!"

I drove off as soon as Betty was settled. She looked kind of haggard. I supposed it was because of the pressure she was living under, but she said, "I wasn't sure I should go today, Caleb. I'm feeling ill. Mother says it's just morning sickness, and it serves me right. Still, if this is morning sickness, why does it last all the time? I just have to get away from Mother for a while. She swings from being very concerned about me to being extremely angry."

We drove slowly to the job site, as every bump seemed to hurt her. I asked if maybe she should go back and see a doctor. She said, "No, I have an appointment Monday with our family doctor. I will be all right until then."

It was raining and damp when we arrived at the shanty, and I told her it would be best if she waited there with Virginia while Norman and I took care of some things at the barn. She didn't object, so after introducing her to Virginia, Norman and I left.

Norman said, "So this is Betty. Wasn't she supposed to be the hot one you talked about? She looks terrible, like she has the flu or something. Are you sure she should be out riding around?"

"I didn't know she was ill when I called her last night. I tried to get her to go back after I saw her, but she insisted that she would be okay."

Norman and I had been at the barn just shooting the bull for about a half an hour when Virginia came down and said, "Caleb I'm taking your car and taking Betty to the clinic I go to. She needs to see a doctor right away. She said she had an appointment for Monday, but I don't think she should wait."

Remembering the clinic and what they had done for Joan I said, "It's okay, Virginia, if you think it's needed I trust your judgment. Do you want me or Norman to go with you?"

"No, the poor girl is having woman problems, and she would just be embarrassed if you two were along," Virginia answered as I handed her the keys to my car.

Norman and I went over to Bruce's shanty. Bruce dug out a couple of bottles of home brew that he had stashed under his shanty and poured us each a glass.

Norman said, "I don't think you have to worry too much about drinking this, Caleb. We drank two or three bottles some nights without feeling it, so I guess it isn't very potent."

The homebrew wasn't half bad, though sitting there drinking it reminded me how sick I had been the first time I drank any. Of course I was only about ten years old then, and probably had drunk a lot more than a couple of glasses full. I told Bruce and Norman about that night, and they laughed about my older brother Josh making me stick my finger down my throat so I would throw up. I told them about Uncle Louis and how he had helped us keep Mother from finding out I was drunk and not just sick. We spent the afternoon spinning tales of our youth until Virginia came driving into the yard.

She came into Bruce's shanty and said, "Caleb, you come with me. We need to talk. You boys stay here."

I went with Virginia to her shanty.

Betty was still sitting in the car. She said, "Listen close to what I'm going to tell you, Caleb. Betty needs to get into a hospital. She isn't pregnant. She has a big cyst or tumor on her ovaries. They didn't want to explore closer than that at the clinic. They insisted she needs to be hospitalized today. They have instructed Betty in what to say at the hospital so they will take her. You have to take her to the emergency room and tell them you have a very sick friend

219

in the car. She will carry it from there. They will have to notify her folks, but it might be better if you can beat them to it. Just tell them that she developed a lot of pain and passed out on you, so you rushed her to the emergency room. Now get out of here and get going, and don't let her talk you out of it no matter what. They were very emphatic at the clinic that she needed have this taken care of right away."

I was frightened at how pale Betty looked when I got into the car. Weakly she said, "Caleb, you don't know how glad I am that you brought me here today and that I met Virginia. She is a wonderfully compassionate person."

I drove as fast as I dared to the hospital. Betty slipped in and out of consciousness on the way. At the hospital I didn't have to make up anything. I was scared and ran in for help. Nurses came out and loaded Betty on a wheeled stretcher, she was conscious enough to tell them what she had been advised to at the clinic and after they had her in a room with a doctor they started calling other doctors. They asked me about family, and I said I would call them. I got Mrs. Hart on the phone and she started to berate me.

I said, "Please, Mrs. Hart, not now. We need you at the hospital. Betty is very sick."

I heard the phone drop and doors slam, and informed the hospital personnel they were on their way. They asked me how old Betty was, and I told them I wasn't sure exactly but around twenty. They said that was good because they had her permission to operate and could go ahead if her parents didn't show up in time. They were just wheeling Betty into the operating room when her parents showed up. Mrs. Hart ran over to her and talked with the doctors.

She came back looking rather pale and spoke to Mr. Hart. "They feel they need to operate right away because of some nerve involvement that could cause permanent damage."

"What about the baby?" he asked.

"They said she was never pregnant, that a tumor was causing the problem that made her think she was," Mrs. Hart answered, giving me a dirty look.

An intern came out and explained that it was going to be a long operation and she would be out of it for some time in the recovery room afterwards. Mrs. Hart said, "Well, I guess we don't need you around anymore, Caleb; you can go. We'll take care of things from now on."

Not feeling comfortable around the Harts, and knowing Betty wouldn't be conscious for hours I decided it was best, so I left without saying anything.

It was late afternoon when I got home, and Homer was just leaving for the barn. He said, "Glad you got back, Caleb. Jenny told me this morning to ask you to meet her at the barn around six tonight."

I thought it would be nice to be with her even if I couldn't tell her everything, so I told Homer I'd be there.

Later at the barn when Jenny came running out I said, "What's up, Jenny?"

"Nothing's up, Caleb," she answered. "I haven't seen you for a while and thought it would be nice to go for ice cream or something. Besides, if I wait for you to call, I'll know it's because you're in trouble again. I thought it would be nice to be together sometime without the terrors of your harem."

So much for discussing my problem with her, I thought, saying, "Speaking of my harem, I heard Betty had an emergency operation today. Do you mind if we stop at the hospital and say hello?"

"What was it that Etta said about you?" Jennie asked. "Oh, I remember, Caleb will never be without turmoil in his life until he settles down to one girl. You know, at the time I didn't give that thought much credence, but lately I begin to see what a smart girl Etta was. I heard that you were out with Betty Thursday night until the wee hours in the morning. No way you would know if you knocked her up then or not, so what happened? A fouled-up, illegal abortion?"

We were just leaving Sterling, so I pulled a u-turn and headed back to the barn. Stopping there I said, "When Homer told me you asked to see me I was looking forward to being with a friend who cared, but I can see that was a dumb mistake, so you can get out and forget I showed up."

Jennie started to get out, then jumping back in and held me tight, saying, "I'm sorry, Caleb, please don't dump me like this. I have suffered through Beverly, Joan, Etta, and now Betty. I don't mean to let my feeling ruin things for us; it's just working with the barn boys and hearing all the nasty talk about you and your harem gets to me. Please forget what I said in my anger, and let's go see how Betty is doing."

Grudgingly, because I knew in my heart that I didn't want to lose our closeness, I said, "I don't know if I can forget it or not, Jennie, but for both our sakes I'll try. Still, you of all people, know that most of the barn talk is bull, and you shouldn't be thinking it's fact. If I had been involved in half the sexual fantasies that they dreamed up for me, there would need to be two of me."

Jennie cuddled up to me saying, "I'm sorry, Caleb, truly sorry. Please forgive me."

We drove to the hospital with us both lost in our own thoughts and pain, without speaking. As I parked at the hospital Jennie said, "I think it would be easier on both Betty and me if I didn't go in, Caleb."

I just nodded, thinking she was showing some sense in this at least. I went to the desk and asked to see Betty Hart. They asked if I was her brother; when I said no I was informed that on doctor's orders she was allowed to see family only, but that she was in satisfactory condition.

Back at the car Jennie said, "That was a pretty short visit. Is everything all right?"

"I guess everything is okay. They said she was in satisfactory condition but only family was allowed in to see her," I answered, trying to keep the concern from my voice.

It didn't fool Jennie, for she said, "Look, Caleb, we can get together some other time. Why don't you take me back to Sterling?"

"I don't know what to do, Jennie. When I heard you wanted to see me I felt, what a gift it was having you for a close friend. When I heard your tirade about me and my harem, that balloon busted real quick. You may be right about me always being in trouble, and the truth is I am right now. So maybe it is better that I don't trouble you, because I can't talk about it anyway," I answered.

"Please, Caleb, if being with me helps at all, I want to stay with you. I'm sorry about my outburst of jealousy. I am trying not to have feelings for you because I know they can't go anywhere. I thought for a while that Gene Aldrich and I would become an item. We went out a few times before I decided he wasn't the one for me. I truly want us to be close friends but it does hurt sometimes to think I have no hope for anything more with you. I'll understand if you want to be alone, Caleb," she said as she cuddled up close to me.

I didn't really know what I wanted to do. Jennie had gotten to me with her little confession, and her mention of hope reminded me of one of Josh's poems.

> Always reserve a bit of hope
> To mask the recurring fear
> That life has reached its final scope
> And what remains is year to year
> When dreams remain a smoky mist
> Trail and stairs unbuilt to reach their height
> For without hope, what remains is this
> A hollow shell fraught with fright

Remembering that, I said, "Jennie, the only hope I could give any girl right now would be false hope. I think that would be the worse kind. My hope is we can work out our feelings so we can always be close friends no matter what happens in our lives. I'm sorry that I always seem to be in trouble, but I hope that we are friends enough so that we can turn to each other when it happens. I know you were looking forward to a night when we could just be together because that's what we wanted; if we keep plugging along I'm sure it'll happen sometime. Now let's forget all this and go get that ice cream."

We drove to Oscin and ended up at the same ice-cream parlor I had been at with Betty Thursday Night. The girl at the counter raised her eyebrows, saying, "Back again, huh? You going to make this one cry, too?"

Startled I said, "The lady I was with the other night had received some bad news, and as her friend I thought a little ice-cream outing would be helpful to her. It wasn't me that caused the tears."

Jennie looked at me with a quizzical look on her face, but she didn't say anything. I was happy for that, as the last thing I needed right now was a third party asking questions. We finished our sodas without ordering ice cream and left as soon as we could. Outside Jennie said, laughing, "What the hell, Caleb? Another one of your harem?"

"I don't even know her name, Jennie. I guess she has seen me there so much over the years she thinks she has a right to get involved. What I told her was pretty much the truth. Betty called and asked me to come and pick her up. She had a problem that I promised not to talk about. I thought coming here would help take her mind off it."

"One question, Caleb. Did the problem have anything to do with her being in the hospital?"

"Maybe in a way, Jennie, but I'm not saying anything more. Remember, I told you I promised to help, not spread gossip," I answered rather curtly.

That seemed to upset Jennie because she was quiet on the way back to Sterling. Once at her home she kissed me lightly and rushed into the house. No one was around when I got home so I went to my room and soon fell into a deep sleep.

Homer shaking me woke me up, he was saying, "Caleb, Caleb, stop your screaming. Man, I'll be glad when you go back to Oklahoma so I can get a good night's sleep."

I got up late Sunday morning and Mother asked, "What's troubling you, Caleb? Homer said you were having wild dreams again last night."

"I don't know why that happens, Mother. I guess I'm just wired wrong or something most of the time. I'm not even sure what I've been dreaming about," I answered, hoping Mother didn't dig any deeper. I knew from experience that Mother was a lot more perceptive than we used to imagine.

"I have some good news for you, Caleb. Dad's out in the barn with Jason," Mother said with a big smile on her face. "I don't know when I have ever seen Jason as excited as he was when Dad announced that he wanted to see what Jason was up to out in the barn. They have been out there together for over an hour now."

"That's great, Mother," I said, rushing outside. I had felt that Dad was making progress the last couple times I talked to him but this was more than I expected. Jason was showing Dad the cut the cow had on its udder. I heard Dad tell Jason how proud he was of the way he had taken care of everything. Funny how even at my age I felt a twinge of jealousy that I wasn't Daddy's little boy.

Shrugging that off I went into the barn saying, "Well, isn't this a surprise? Dad, it's so good to see you outside for a change."

"It's good to be out, Caleb," Dad said smiling, "I thought it was time I climbed out of that dark hole before you boys became so efficient that I wouldn't be needed around here anymore."

Jason gave him a little pat on the back saying, "We will always need you, Dad; black hole or not, we will always need you."

I spent the morning helping Jason around the farm. Dad tired after being with us for a couple of hours and went back into the house. Francis who had been checking the fence line for breaks came and joined us just before Dad went in.

He was as excited as Jason about Dad being out with them, saying, "Isn't it great to see Dad out of the house? Jason said that when Dad is better, then he and I can do the chores, and maybe he can get a job at the barn with Homer."

"I think it's wonderful, Francis. I was surprised when Mother told me he was out here with you two. Still, I wouldn't rush him too much just yet, though the doctors said after his fevers had run their course he would recover from the operation pretty fast."

Dad joined us when Mother called us for lunch. Mother said, "I haven't seen this many smiles around here for a long time. I take it that your father approved all the work that you boys have been doing?"

Dad smiled and said, "Helen, I not only approved of all they've done but it dawned on me what a wonderful family we have. I had the belief that our world would fall apart if I weren't out there pushing it. I am proud to admit that I was mistaken. Now for the first time in a long time I'm looking forward to rejoining the boys to help keep things turning."

Francis laughed and said, "Does that mean that Jason can't boss me around anymore?"

Mother said, "Now, Francis, I'm sure Jason was only trying to make sure you knew how to do things and wanted to make sure you didn't get hurt."

Everybody was laughing as I said, "I am going to have to leave this joyful party and go to the hospital. Betty Hart had an operation yesterday. Jennie and I stopped to see her last night, but they only were allowing close family then and said come back today."

Mother said, "Caleb, you tell the Harts if there is anything we can do to help to just call."

I drove off thinking the last thing I need is to have the Harts talk to my mother. Right now I dreaded them even talking to me.

When I arrived at the hospital Mr. Hart was sitting outside smoking. He hollered, "Caleb, please come over and talk to me before you go in."

Reluctantly I walked over to where he was, and to my surprise he said, "Caleb, we owe you a big apology. Betty thought she was pregnant, and when you called us to the hospital last night we thought you had taken her for an illegal abortion that had gone wrong. Now we know she wasn't pregnant, and from what she says I don't believe there was any way she could have been. She assures us that she has never done the things that would have made her pregnant, especially not with you. I hope you can forgive us; you and our son Karl were so close, and you did so much for him after he was wounded, and we still thought the worst of you. Then we find out you were only trying to help Betty. She also told us how your friend, Virginia, insisted that you bring her to the emergency room." Mr. Hart hugged me saying, "Thanks for being there for my children, Caleb, and please forgive us."

I mumbled something about not needing to be thanked and that I understood their anger and fear and left him to go see Betty, thinking, *What kind of a yarn did she spin?*

When I entered Betty's room her mother was there and started the whole apologizing thing again.

I said, "It's okay, Mrs. Hart. I just talked to your husband, and he told me all about your fears and suspicions. It's okay; I understand. After all, I have sisters and parents."

Mrs. Hart started to reply, but Betty weakly cut her short saying, "Please, Mother, will you let me talk to Caleb alone? I'll explain to him."

I could see that Betty's mother was a little put out with this, but she complied and left the room.

Betty said, "Thank you, Caleb, for being my friend, and thank you for having a friend like Virginia. God knows what would have happened if she hadn't talked me into going to her clinic. I needed to talk to you alone before Mother or my father confused you about what was going on. I'm going to be all right in a month or so. Evidently I had a pretty big tumor of some kind, and that was my problem, not a pregnancy. Father wants so much to believe that his little girl is a virgin. I told them there was no way you could have been responsible. He started asking questions about why I thought I could be pregnant. I felt so sorry for him that I told him that I thought it might have happened when I was necking with Eric. When he asked me what I meant by necking, I said, holding each other tight and kissing, using our tongues. He looked so relieved, and even though I knew Mother was suspicious, she didn't say anything. I expect to be grilled by her once I'm well; I'll worry about that then. I'm very tired, Caleb but I needed to make sure you knew what was going on before you talked with anyone. When you go out tell my parents I went to sleep on you, and you'll try to get back later today. I understand you were here last night with Jennie. Bring her with you if you can."

I found Betty's parents in the waiting room and told them she had fallen asleep.

Her father said, "Good. She needs rest after all she's been through. Caleb, once again we're sorry for all we thought and how we acted."

"Don't you two worry about it. I have already forgotten it. The main thing is that Betty is going to be all right."

"The doctors are not too sure about that, Caleb. Betty may never to be able to have children," Betty's mother said as I was starting to leave.

I stopped and said, "She didn't mention that, yet maybe she will. I will try to get back tonight."

As I was getting into my car I thought, *Not being able to have a baby might be a good thing for someone as promiscuous as Betty.* Then I remembered what Beverly had told me about there being girls that had a craving for sex just as much as us boys, and that they shouldn't be condemned for it any more than we were. It made me feel guilty thinking that way about Betty. Still, her having tumors instead of being pregnant lifted a big load off my shoulders, and maybe when she was well, she would think so too.

When I arrived home Homer hadn't left for the barn yet, so I asked him to tell Jennie I would be down about six o'clock to see if she was free to take a ride with me. I didn't mention Betty or the hospital; I thought it better to tell her in person. I went to see Dad, but he was sleeping, so I went out to find Jason and Francis. They weren't around, so I went to the kitchen to see if there was any coffee left.

Mother was there making biscuits for supper. She said, "How was Betty? I called the Harts, but there wasn't anybody home. I expect they were at the hospital, too."

"Betty is doing as well as can be expected, Mother. The doctors say she will be back to normal in a month or so. Her mother and father were both at the hospital when I got there," I answered, thinking, *Boy, I dodged a bullet on that one.*

"Just what was her problem, Caleb? She always seemed to be healthy enough the few times I've seen her. Wasn't it her you were out with just the other night?" Mother asked, looking at me with a frown.

"Yes, we were together Thursday night, and I asked her to go to the job site with me Saturday. When I picked her up she seemed ill; I suggested that she stay home, but she didn't want to. When we got to the job it was raining, so I left her in the shanty with Virginia while Norman and I went to check on the wagon. Virginia came down and insisted I take her to the hospital right away because of some woman problem. I took her to the emergency room at the hospital and called her parents." I had left out the part about the clinic and pregnancy, but I knew I had better fill Mother in on what I dared before she heard it somewhere else.

"Caleb," Mother exclaimed. "Why didn't you say something? That must have been awful for you! You shouldn't keep things like that to yourself; we might have been able to help you if we had known."

I thought, *If they had known the whole truth they probably would have massacred me,* so I said, "Betty and her family didn't want anyone to know until they were sure what the trouble was. It seems that she had some kind of tumor that had to be operated on right away. I didn't know much for sure myself, until I went today. Jennie and I are going to go back tonight to see Betty, if Jennie can get free. They will probably have more of an answer about what happened then."

Father, Jason and Francis were in the barn as I was leaving to pick up Jennie. Jason hollered, "Caleb, come in here for a minute."

I went into the stable where they were examining the cow. "Jason tells me that you showed him what to do to cure the cut she had. He wants you to see how well she has healed. I didn't know you were such an expert veterinarian.

Maybe you are studying in the wrong field," Dad said with kind of a laugh.

"No, Dad," I answered, "I picked up some things working at Muldons, but if anything, working at the barn has convinced me that I don't want to spend my life in a cow barn."

"Well, don't discourage these boys. They seemed to have a knack for farming and farm animals. Speaking of animals, if I feel as good Saturday, I wonder if you would take me over to see my horses," Dad said with a big smile on his face.

I was so excited about how much Dad was improving that I stayed with them a little longer than I had planned and was late picking Jennie up. She was just leaving the milk house when I pulled in.

She jumped into the car saying, "I thought you had forgotten me, Caleb. I was just on my way home."

I told her the good news about Dad and about Betty on the way to the hospital. When we went in the nurse told us we only had twenty minutes because visiting time was almost over. Betty seemed glad to see us, and she and Jennie talked about her operation. I think Betty saw this as a way to let everyone know the truth, or at least the truth as Betty laid it out.

As we were about to leave I held Betty's hand and said, "Mother has asked the pastor to add you to the Sunday prayer list and is going to call your folks to see if they need any help."

Betty smiled and said, "You take good care of Caleb, Jennie. I don't know what would have happened if he hadn't taken me to see Virginia. I might not have made it."

Back at the car Jennie said, 'Out with it, Caleb. What is this really all about?"

"Look, Jennie, Betty called me last week saying she had a problem, so I went to see her. She never spelled out what was wrong, but she and her mother were having an argument when I picked her up. We went to Oscin for ice cream. She was still upset when I took her home so I invited her to go with me Saturday to the job. I knew she wasn't feeling good when I picked her up, but she said she didn't want to stay home. At the job while Norman and I were working on the wagon, Virginia came down and said I should rush Betty to the hospital, so I did. After her folks showed up at the hospital, I went home. I didn't say anything before because that was the way Betty and her folks wanted it."

"Why? Did they think she was pregnant, too, and you had rushed her off to have a fouled-up abortion?" Jennie sneered.

"Truth is, they did, but they, unlike you, were very apologetic when they found out the truth. I can understand their feelings, Jennie, but I don't feel a real friend would think the worst of me every time something goes wrong, like you seem to."

"I'm sorry, Caleb," she answered. "It's just when Homer told me you wanted to pick me up tonight, I was hoping it was going to be because of us. Then I find out we are going to visit Betty. After we get here I find out you had taken her to see Virginia. Is nothing we have sacred? You know, as much as I loved your brother Josh from afar, I never entertained any hope my love would be returned. I guess I let our affair get too intimate in the beginning to be able to be like that with you. I think it's best for me that we stop seeing each other, even as friends."

"You make me feel guilty when you talk like that, Jennie. I know I am an enigma when it comes to relationships, but I have tried to be honest with everybody. I don't want to lose having you around, but if it makes it better for you I understand. How about tonight. What would you like to do?"

"Just take me back to Sterling, Caleb, and stay out of my life," Jennie replied despondently.

She didn't speak all the way back and at her house she jumped out of the car and ran to the house without a word. Not wanting to go right home I drove to Oscin, thinking a coffee and a sandwich would ease my mind. I went to the same place I had been with Jennie and Betty. I ordered a cheeseburger and coffee.

The girl who had accosted me about making girls cry came over and said, "All alone, huh? You look like you're about ready to cry. What happened? Get ditched?"

I didn't respond, just finished my drink and sandwich, and left, not wanting to hear any more from her. Not wanting to go home right away I drove back to Sterling and parked up by the swings. Sitting there brought back all the memories that they held of my youth. So many times it was, "I'll meet you at the swings." The last time I came here to ponder, Jake was sitting in the swings, just trying to recapture some of his youthful memories, the first time he returned from college. Thinking about Jake made me realize that my answers weren't to be found sitting by the swings lamenting my life or dreaming of lost youth, so I went home.

Emma and Aaron were sitting on the porch. Aaron said, "Do you have a minute, Caleb? I would like to thank you for talking to Emma about us. I spent some time with your dad this afternoon like you suggested. I have to admit that I have been avoiding it, but I think it worked out all right. He put me right to work helping Jason and Francis doing some repairs in the barn and then jokingly (I hope) he told me I had better bring some old clothes here, that I probably wouldn't want to shovel manure in what I was wearing."

Emma laughed and said, "If I was you I would plan on shoveling manure more than once if you want to be accepted by Dad. That happens to be a test he uses to judge boys who come around chasing his daughters."

As down as I was, I laughed about Dad's little ploy and said, " You know, Aaron, I have to believe that Dad's ways are a good way to take measure of a man. If you don't think one of his daughters is worth shoveling a little shit for, then you probably aren't man enough to have her for a wife."

Emma still laughing said, "Well, Aaron, Dad's way may be a little blunt. How do you answer it? Am I worth it or not?"

"Emma after work tomorrow I'm going right out to buy a pair of barn boots to leave here with some of my old clothes. Shall I ask your dad where to put them when I come here with them?" Aaron said earnestly.

"No," Emma replied, "I think it would be better to ask Mother where to put them and let it get back to Dad through the grapevine. Dad might think you're mocking him, and that would be a mistake."

I left the two of them on the porch thinking maybe Aaron was going to be an all right as a brother-in-law.

Things went well at work during the week. I visited Betty a couple of times at the hospital and kept Virginia informed on her progress. Her recovery from the operation went well and she was able to return home on Friday. Saturday I took Dad to the job site. He was impressed with how well our lumberyard looked. Much to my surprise the horses seemed to remember him and both whinnied as he approached the shanty barn.

Norman said, "Can you believe that, Caleb? It's been almost six months since he has been near them, and they remember him?"

"I'm not surprised. Dad always had a way with animals and especially horses. When we first got Roxie she was as bald as a cue ball, and he spent hours rubbing her down with sulfur and lard. She really got to know his voice," I replied, remembering how much I had enjoyed my time with Dad back then.

Dad still had to use crutches, and when he asked if it was possible for him to see the mill, Norman said, "Sure, Mr. Carney. We'll just hitch up the team and give you a ride down. We usually walk the horses around a little on the days the mill doesn't run, so it's no bother. Bruce and I will take you down. My wife wants to talk to Caleb, and we need to pick up some wood for the shanties."

I helped get the team out and threw a bale of hay on the wagon for Dad to sit on.

Dad said, "You know, Caleb, we are darn lucky to have those boys working for us. There aren't many workers left like them anymore. You go have your talk with Virginia. I'll be all right with them. You know, I've never met her, so if she doesn't mind, I would like to meet her before we go back."

Dad and the boys left for the mill site, and I went to the shanty to see Virginia. "Caleb, I'm glad you could get away. I haven't seen you alone since Betty was here. I know you have been careful about what you told Norman, but he has said she was doing well; is that all there is to it?" she asked.

"Basically, Virginia, the operation went well, and she was able to come home from the hospital Friday. I haven't been to her house to see her yet, but I plan to tomorrow. Her mother told me the doctors had mentioned she would probably not be able to have children, but that was a worst-case scenario," I answered.

Virginia said, "I'm so glad she agreed to go to the clinic with me. They were very worried about her condition and insisted she be hospitalized. Norman had to take me back there after we were sure she was going to the hospital to tell them. That's how serious they thought it was."

"I'm glad you were there for us, Virginia; it seems as if I'm always bringing you problems," I said, wanting to pour my heart out about Jennie and me.

"Don't feel that way, Caleb. After all, you have been good for Norman and me. Without you we might have never gotten together, and Norman has really gained a lot working for you and your dad. He is so proud of what he does, so you feel free to come to us anytime with anything, and we'll try to help," she said, putting her hand on my shoulder.

"Virginia, remember that you invited this," I said, as I unburdened all of the misery that was involved in my relationship with Jennie. I even confided how in the beginning it had been a very intimate thing. Virginia just let me talk and talk until I got it all out, finishing with Jennie's farewell last night.

Virginia was quiet for a long time. Finally she said, "Caleb, there has to be something about you that keeps these girls around. Norman is always telling me about your harem. I would have thought that it was all some male bull, except I have met three of them and have some sense on how they feel about you. What I don't understand is why they hang on like they do. I understand that you think you're being honest with them, with your "I'm unable to commit" story. Still you must somehow leave them hope that when you do that, it will be them. I'm afraid there is no easy answer for your dilemma; at least I don't have one. Still, if you care for Jennie then stay away from her, even if she calls out to you. It is the only fair thing for her. You owe her that much."

Norman came in and said, "Your father is getting tired and wants to leave, Caleb. I told him Virginia would come down to meet him before he left."

The three of us went down to the shanty barn. Dad was already seated in the car. I guess he didn't want to meet a Virginia on crutches. Norman introduced Virginia as his wife.

She said, "Mr. Carney, it's so good to finally meet you. Norman has told me how sad it was to have someone as good as you have such a terrible accident. I hope the boys haven't made you do too much the first day you're back."

Bruce laughed, saying, "Us make him do too much! We are the ones that had to stop him, and I swear he would have loaded the wagon with lumber if we had let him."

Dad said, "I wouldn't go that far, Bruce, but it was good to be back on a job site. Maybe in a few more days I will be strong enough to come and spend a day here while they are working. Virginia, I am glad to finally meet you. Caleb has been bragging about you ever since he met you. Virginia, you can be proud of that husband of yours and his brother. They are the salt of the earth to us. I am sure Caleb would have held things together until I was able to get back to work, but they have made it so much easier for him. We have to go back before Caleb's mother starts worrying. Hopefully I will see you all again soon."

Dad was cheerful on the way back to Sterling. He even began singing an old western song that I hadn't heard for years, something about morning glories around the doorway and a lost love. Happy as I was for Dad, I felt that the magic I expected from Virginia wasn't there for me, and her ending phrase echoed back to what Betty had said: "You owe me that much."

Was Virginia's message that I had no right to take, if I was unwilling to give? Someday maybe someone will have an answer for me that won't be a riddle. Everybody came running from the house when we pulled in, wondering how it had been for Dad. He insisted on getting out of the car himself then after taking a few steps with his crutches he said, "Everybody gather around. I have an announcement to make: Henry Carney is well on his way back!"

That night at the supper table and long after, there was more joy in the Carney household than had been seen in a long time. That night I went to bed happy and dreamed I was with Josh. He was assuring me that, like puberty, I would live through my dilemmas and all would be right in my world.

CHAPTER NINE

I had decided after my episode with Jennie that I would swear off girls outside of visiting Betty, so I poured myself into work at the job and around home. Dad was progressing well and had been spending part of each day helping Jason and Francis around home. He was concerned about all the manure that was gathering under the barn and had made inquiries about getting someone with a tractor or a horse to haul it out. The Muldons offered Homer one of their tractors and a manure spreader for four hours. The problem was finding four hours when they didn't need it at the same time and Homer would have help to get it done. Homer informed us that the tractor would be available on Friday at noon.

Mother said, "No way that all three boys are going to take off from school for that. They only have a couple of more weeks before school is out. It can get done then."

Dad said, "The trouble with that, Helen, is the Muldons will have extra help when the boys are out of school, and their tractors will be busy all the time. We didn't get the manure moved last fall because of my accident, and now it is piled up to the floor joist, and if it isn't moved soon it is going to cause some structural problems under the barn. It would be nice if we could get the tractor on a weekend, but that's when they have the schoolboys working, and they need all their equipment. I'll talk to Homer and see what he thinks about another date."

The next night as we were discussing the manure problem, Aaron, who had become a regular a couple times a week for supper spoke up, saying, "I can get Friday afternoon off and come help Homer if you would like me to."

Dad laughed and said, "Aaron, I don't want what I said forcing you to do something you don't want to do."

"It isn't that, Mr. Carney. I have had worse jobs than shoveling manure. I spent one summer working on septic tanks, and believe me, some of those jobs could be pretty bad. They owe me time off on the job I'm on now, and I can get off easy. I want to be of help when I can to the family, at least enough to pay for the meals I eat here," Aaron answered.

Mother said, "You know, Henry, he brought barn boots and old clothes here some time ago, and if he is going to marry into a farm family we might just as well get him used to it."

Emma laughed, saying, "He hasn't proposed yet, Mother; let's just see how he spreads manure before we get into that."

Homer took Friday off from school and worked until noon for the Muldons before bringing the tractor and manure spreader home. Mother told me that Aaron was there waiting when he came, and they went to work immediately. She said she never saw the like of it, the two of them trying to outdo each other. Even Dad was impressed at how fast they got that manure moved. She made Dad go out and force them to take a break and have something to drink. They were all finished in time for Homer to take the equipment back when he went to do the milking at the barn.

Nellie told me that later, when Jason and Francis were out in the barn doing their chores, Aaron and Dad were in the yard talking when Aaron said, "I hope I passed the test, Mr. Carney, because I would like to ask your permission to ask Emma to marry me. It will be awhile before I finish the classes I need to get my degree in engineering, but after that I will have a good job, and I could afford to have a home for us."

Nellie said Dad hollered, "Mrs. Carney, you better get out here and hear this. We have another young man wanting to run off with one of our daughters."

She thought Aaron looked kind of scared, but when Mother came out, Dad laughed, saying, "He sure proved he could shovel it. Do we think that's enough?"

Mother said, "Now, Henry, let's be serious. You're scaring Aaron. Emma has indicated that she thought he was the one, but there was something about him returning to college. I would be in agreement if it was going to be a long engagement."

"That's what I just told your husband. I asked him first because I wanted to do this properly," Aaron replied shakily

Dad became serious, and shaking Aaron's hand said, "You know, Aaron, I made a big mistake with my oldest daughter, not trusting her judgment. That caused our family a lot of trouble; I don't want to ever repeat that. You have my blessings to ask Emma, and if she says yes, then I will trust her judgment."

Nellie said for a minute she thought Aaron was going to do back flips, but Mother's hug kept him from doing it. Then as Mother and Dad went into the house Aaron picked Nellie up, swinging her around, and shouted, "I'm going to be your brother-in-law."

That night right after supper Aaron asked everybody to hold his or her place.

Going over to Emma and pulling her chair out, he took a ring out of his pocket. He got down on one knee and said, "Emma, I am going to give you a chance to make me the happiest man in the universe. Will you marry me?"

Emma lit up like the sun, then stopped and looked questioningly towards Mother. Mother nodded her head and smiled.

Emma shouted, "Yes," and jumped into Aaron's arms knocking him on the floor. I guess they remembered our little talk, because they both jumped up and looked at Dad.

Dad said, "Emma, this young man shoveled manure all afternoon like a trooper, and then, smelling like one of your brothers, he came and asked my permission for your hand. I told him I thought that it was appropriate for him to ask, but the decision was yours, and I guess you answered that. Now let's all take up the cider that Mother has passed around, and we'll drink a toast to a long and thoughtful engagement."

After we had all left the table Nellie came to me and said, "Caleb, with all the excitement I almost forgot to tell you; you have a letter."

The letter was from Etta; I went to my room to read it.

Dear Caleb,

College has been good to me, and I feel as if I am a much more mature woman than the silly girl you met way back when. I started college with a

dozen thoughts about what I wanted to be, without one true goal. I worried about this at first but found that I had a lot of company as I got to know my classmates. I seemed to have a knack for chemistry and biology and have been encouraged by my professors to pursue a career in medicine. I am not wholly committed to that as yet but am leaning that way.

As you know, college gets out before the local schools, so next week is my last week. I have interviewed for a job at a laboratory in Lotus, and they have accepted me and want me to inform them when I can start.

So much for my education. The real reason for this letter is that I would like to spend some time with you and your family this summer. I have already told the laboratory that it would be two weeks after my studies before I could be there. If it can be arranged on your end I can be there a week from next Wednesday at two in the afternoon, if it's an inconvenient to pick me up at the train at that time I can get a taxi to Sterling.

There is one thing you should know before you decide, I have met someone at college, and we are practically engaged, so there will be no mountain trips for us while I am there. I hope that we are good enough friends outside of that for you to still want me to come.

Your Oklahoma Indian,
Etta

Man, I thought, Etta back here again that will test my swearing off girls. It makes me happy and sad at the same time that she has found someone, I hope he is worthy of her. Sometimes I wonder if it wouldn't have been easier for me to just accept one of my so-called harem and try to be serious about it. I guess it's true though, what Virginia told me once, that I had no right accepting someone else until I learned how to accept myself. At the time that angered me some but the more I see of my life the more I am inclined to agree with her.

I went down to talk to Mother about Etta coming. Mother said, "Caleb, you tell her she is welcome here anytime. I swear it almost makes me feel guilty how I felt about her when she first came here. I know your dad will be thrilled; he said she was the prettiest and most competent nurse he ever had. I know you will be working that Wednesday, but I can make arrangements to have her picked up at the train."

Later I went to visit Betty to see how she was doing. She seemed in very good spirits and wanted to go for a ride, but her mother vetoed that idea saying, "Young lady, you are going to stay right in and rest until a doctor tells me otherwise."

I was surprised at how well Betty took that, considering how she used to defy her mother so much before. I told her about Etta coming, which was a mistake. She said, "Well, I guess that means I'll just disappear from your mind again."

Not wanting to get involved in what my replying to that would cause, I said, "When's your next doctor's appointment, Betty? Maybe we can make a date to see a movie or something if they say it's all right?"

She said, "I will be going Monday, but there isn't any movie that I want to see until Saturday. Can we make a date for that night?"

Getting up to leave I said, "If you can go, I'll pick you up before seven so we can see the early show."

Betty followed me to the door and kissed me passionately. As I went out the door she said, "Caleb, I hope you aren't planning on bringing Etta on our date, too?"

I was driving off before it hit me. She thought I meant Etta was coming this Wednesday. She was trying to trap me. *Oh, well, no harm done until she knows the truth. Even then, it's on her shoulders, not mine.*

The next week went by fast, considering everyone was anxious for Etta's arrival. Homer asked if I thought she would be willing to visit the barn boys again. I told him she had said in her letter that she had changed, but I wasn't sure what that meant.

He laughed and said, "That probably means no more trips up to the mountain with you." I looked at Homer and said, "Just what is that supposed to mean?"

Homer, still laughing, said, "You know, Caleb, all the time Etta was here there was so much tension between you two I could almost feel it. After you came down from the mountain the day before she left, it was gone. Even Mother remarked on how much things seemed changed that last day. She felt that you two must have aired out your differences on the mountain. I had different thoughts about what got aired out on the mountain, but I just agreed with her."

Feeling it would be a mistake to argue with Homer about Etta, I asked, "How is Jennie these days? I haven't seen her for some time."

"Funny you should ask, Caleb. I brought that up to her the other day, and she said she didn't want to even talk about you anymore. I am not sure what you have done to her this time, but someday you are going to be sorry. Underneath all that bravado of hers, she is a wonderful, feeling person, and you might live to regret not understanding that."

I decided that it wasn't to my benefit to talk to Homer about any girl, so I left him and went outside.

Nellie was out in the yard and said, "Caleb, I hear Etta's coming back. I really liked her, but I worry how you're going to be, having her around. I know it wasn't easy for you last time until the end."

"Nellie I don't want to hear anything about any girl right now," I yelled. "Homer just got through razzing me."

"I'm not razzing you, Caleb; you know how I feel things, and there certainly were things to feel when she was here last time. I just don't want you hurt," she said with tears in her eyes.

"I'm sorry, Nellie," I said, putting my arm on her shoulder. "Homer sometimes makes me mad. I shouldn't have yelled at you for it. I'll tell you what; go ask Mother if it's okay, and we'll take a ride and get an ice cream."

The next day Dad decided to go to work with me. He was off his crutches but still had to use a cane. He had long talks with Mr. Jocklin during the day, and though I didn't overhear them, they seemed pretty serious.

Norman yelled at me a couple of times saying, "What the hell, Caleb, did you just send your body to work today and leave your mind home? That's the second time today you have left the wagon stakes back in the sticking field. You go back and get them this time yourself. Maybe it's time for you to have another session with a shrink. Want me to set up a time with Virginia for you?"

"I'm sorry, Norman, that I'm so distracted, but I got a letter from Etta the other day, and she is going to be here next Wednesday. I'm afraid that has taken my mind off the job," I answered.

"You know what?" Norman said seriously, "You need to get rid of your harem and marry one of them. No, on the second thought not one of them, at least not the ones I know. What you need is someone like Virginia who can help you with that mess that you have in your mind about girls."

On the ride home Dad was quiet. I began thinking maybe Norman was right, and I did need a shrink. I thought that since tomorrow was Saturday, maybe I would drive back and talk to Virginia. Then I remembered I had to take Betty out tomorrow night, and I had promised Jason to help him get some wood in the morning. Still, even knowing how much help Virginia had been in some trying times with the girls I didn't have much hope she had an answer for me.

The next morning Aaron showed up and went to cut wood with Jason and me. Dad had always made sure we had a year's worth of wood cut a year ahead, and he felt since he wouldn't be able to do it this year, we boys should start early. With Aaron's help we cut an impressive amount by one o'clock that day.

As we were coming out of the woods, Emma met us saying, "Mother has had dinner ready since twelve, and she was getting worried."

Aaron said, "Your little brother, Jason, wouldn't let us quit. He kept saying, "One more tree; one more tree."

Jason laughed, saying, "I don't expect to see Aaron that often so I want to get as much out of him as possible."

Aaron cuffed Jason a little on the shoulder, saying, "You are going to see so much of me you'll get sick of me being around."

"In that case, Aaron," Jason replied, "give me a schedule of the times you'll be available so I can plan work for you around here."

"Hold on a minute, Jason; he comes here to see me, not to work," Emma said with a smile.

"Okay, sis," Jason answered, "but remember if he fails you, it's your own fault, because you wouldn't let me test him out."

"Hold on, you two," Aaron said, laughing. "I think I'm good enough to satisfy both of you. Jason, if you can plan it I'll be here for every Saturday morning so we can cut wood. Emma, you weren't even out of bed when we started this morning, so you won't miss me when I'm with Jason."

We arrived at the house, all laughing and joking. Mother said, "What gives? Was working together so much fun that you didn't need to stop for lunch?"

"No, Mother," I said. "Jason knows he is only going to have help on Saturday mornings, so he likes to make the mornings last. I think that from now on, on Saturdays you had better plan on a late lunch for Jason's crew; working with him is just like having Dad back as boss."

After lunch, Nellie, who had gone to the mailbox, came running in saying, "Boy, Caleb, you are getting pretty important around here. You have another letter, from a girl, too."

"It must be from another one of his harem that Homer is always talking about; read it to us." Emma teased.

Mother said, "Now, you be nice, Emma; try to remember how much Caleb did for you and Aaron."

"Whoa," laughed Aaron. "You're telling me he has been running block for us and has a harem too? I think I have to talk more with my future brother-in-law; maybe I'm missing out on something."

Emma smacked Aaron on the back of the head and said, "I hear any more talk like that from you, and maybe you won't have Caleb for a brother-in-law."

As I got up to go to my room Aaron winked and said, "Maybe it would be safer for me if we canceled that little talk, Caleb."

The letter was from Joan.

My Dear Caleb,

I know I should have written you more, but classes have been harder this time. I take my last exam Monday, and I should be home by Wednesday. I hope I can get to see you then. I know it is in the middle of the work week, but coming home to Sterling wouldn't seem right if I didn't get to see you right away. Here at college I am known as the ascetic virgin because I refuse all contact with the boys here. I am not as fearful as I was at first but decided that it was better for me to stay away from the crazy college partying. I don't need their parties anyway, knowing I will always have you to come home to. That is if you haven't run off with Jennie or Etta or some other girl in your harem.

You can never know how many times I have leaned on what you and I had growing up in Sterling. This background, our history, I feel was what made it possible for you to do what you did for me during my troubles. You mentioned in your letter that you were sorry about unloading on me. I want you to know that I plan to always be there for you no matter what the future holds for us.

I will understand if you can't make it Wednesday night, but I remain hopeful.

Love always,
Your Joan.

Oh, man, Etta and Joan both coming the same day! I am beginning to think there is some kind of conspiracy going on in my life between these girls. There was no way to stop Etta now; Mother had already called Eunice and had Harry tell Shaq it was okay for Etta to come. It crossed my mind what kind of hell it might be to have a real harem. The work or maybe the worry must have got to me because I fell asleep and just woke up in time to get dressed and pick up Betty.

This time at her house she didn't come running out so I went to the door. I asked Mrs. Hart if Betty was going to be able to go, and she said, "The doctors have okayed it, Caleb, but she will be a few minutes. She is still working to make herself beautiful for you. Caleb, I want to apologize again for all the bad thoughts we had about you. I talked to Karl about it on the phone, and he said I shouldn't worry, that you were worldly enough to understand."

"Like I told you, Mrs. Hart, I do understand. You know I have sisters, too, and I'm not upset with your family about anything that happened," I answered just as Betty came down the stairs.

Despite her small stature she was what the boys called stacked, and she had on a tight sweater that emphasized that. I heard her mother draw in her breath, but she didn't say anything, and as Betty drew nearer it became evident that she wasn't wearing a bra.

As Betty hurried me out the door I turned and said, "Don't worry, Mrs. Hart; I will have her back early."

In the car I said, "Gee, Betty, don't you think your mother has gone through enough lately without your leaving the house dressed like a call girl?"

"What's the matter, Caleb?' she said, leaning on my shoulder. "Don't you like what you see? After all, if I have to compete with the likes of Etta, I have to exploit what I have, don't I?"

I could feel the anger starting to rise so I waited a few minutes before I said, "Betty, I think I have proved that I care for you these last few weeks, but nothing has changed. Life with you started to become all about the sex, and I didn't want to feel like I used any girl like that; that's why I broke it off. When you called and asked me to come, you sounded needy, so I came as a friend. I want to stay your friend so I can always be there for you and you for me, but not the way it was. You're smart enough to know what kind of an effect you have on boys, and I'm no different from other boys. That's why I stopped going out with you before. If we are going to go out it has to be on my terms. That means no sex, so you have to stop being aggressive with me, or we can't be together."

"Okay, Caleb, on your terms," she answered. "I want us to be more than that, but I really think I understand why we can't. I certainly hoped that it was more than sex that kept you taking me out, but in my heart I knew better. I'm glad that you at least think enough of me to feel guilty about using me for just sex. Most boys would have led me on forever or until something better showed up in their lives. I did some real thinking about myself while I was in the hospital, and I didn't like what I saw. The way I dressed for you tonight is an example of what I didn't like. Caleb, take me back home, and I'll change."

"Are you sure, Betty?" I asked in surprise. "I think it would be better for us if you did because I would probably end up having to fight off the boys with you dressed like that. Still wouldn't it bother you going back now and changing and letting your family know?"

"Caleb, I promised myself at the hospital that I was going to change my ways, and the first time I go out I revert to my old ways. Yes, it will bother me, but after your little talk I realized what a mistake I have made in how I thought about boys. It will be a little embarrassing to go back and change, but they say the first step is the hardest, so I might as well start now. So please take me back," she pleaded, "before I change my mind."

I took Betty back home and waited in the car while she changed; when she came out she was dressed more to hide her figure than I had ever seen her dress.

I asked, "How did it go with your mother?"

She said, "It was funny, Caleb; when I came in she followed me upstairs worried that something was wrong. I told her no, that I had just forgotten something, then when she saw me come back down she just smiled and said nothing."

Betty and I went to a movie in Oscin. Though she held my hand she behaved like a lady. After we went for a sundae the girl who waited on us said, "Not your little sister tonight. I see you have dried this one's tears up since last time."

When we got back to Betty's house in Sterling Betty said, "Caleb, you won't mind if we sit for a few minutes before I go in, do you? I promise I won't try to entice you into anything. I know that what I have been up to, especially with the boys might give me an awful reputation, if it already hasn't. I truly want to change all of that, but I'm not sure how. I know I will have to stop seeing any of the boys that I have had sex with. That is going to leave me a lonely girl for quite a while. I know that seeing me will create some problems for you, but I need someone who I can trust to take me out once in a while. Do you think you can do that for me, Caleb? I know how much I'm asking, so I don't expect an answer right now, just your promise that you will try to do it."

I gave Betty a little kiss as she started to leave and said, "I'll tell you what, Betty. I'm going to be tied up for a couple of weeks. I promise you that before the month is out I will call you for a date. As long as you understand it isn't a girlfriend-boyfriend type of date."

Betty gave me a hug and headed for the house. Driving home I wondered what I had gotten myself into this time. I was the last one to be giving advice to the lovelorn. It occurred to me that Betty could use more time with Virginia, but Norman would probably have a fit if I brought her more trouble.

Mother was still up when I got home and said, "Caleb, we need to talk. Your father has some half-brained idea that he can go back to work soon.

242

Seems as if he has been talking to Mr. Jocklin at the mill and the take-away-and-marker man is getting through at the mill next month. Your father thinks he can do that job okay because he will be working on a level platform. We have to discourage him."

At first the news startled me because Dad hadn't said anything about it riding back from the job when he went with me. I guess that must have been what all the conversation was about when he was talking to Jocklin.

After absorbing this I said, "When is Dad's next appointment, Mother? I would think this is something that the doctors have to decide, not us."

"That's another thing; he has an appointment next Friday afternoon, and he asked Aaron if he could get the time off to take him. He said he wanted to spend some time alone with Aaron. Now I think he just doesn't want me there to talk to the doctors about him working," Mother answered.

"You know what I would do, Mother? " I said, kind of smiling at the thought. "I would let Aaron take him. You can call the doctors about your fears, and I'm sure they will understand. Besides they would want to know what he is planning anyway. It's not like you are going behind his back in a sneaky way, and I'm sure the doctors will keep your secret."

Mother woke me Sunday morning and asked me to go to church with her and Francis and Nellie. Jason had already been working in the barn, and Mother decided he wouldn't have time before church to get the smell off. Sometimes I wondered if Jason had planned it that way.

After church I decided to take a drive around Sterling and ended up at the foot of the mountain. Remembering how the mountain had help me live through losing Josh I decided maybe it would be a good idea if I took my cares and troubles on a hike through its trails. I chose the lower trail stopping at one of the springs to drink.

When I came to the ledges I climbed down to the cave where Karl and I had hid from Bob Woods the day we had spotted him and Kate Curtis just about to make out over in the pines. As I sat there I remembered how scared we had been and how it had all worked out. As I climbed back up walking the trail memories from my past filled my mind. The first day I worked as a stripper at the milk barn, George getting dragged by the bull, our house burning down, Josh dying. As all the tragedies and fears of the past came to mind it dawned on me that you do survive in the end, maybe because there is no other choice but you do survive.

Later as I was sitting on the ledges where I had a good view to the west of the mountain, the wind came up. Listening to it whistle in the trees it was like when I thought I heard Josh's voice in the wind before, saying "Let me go, let me go," only this time it was more like, "Life goes on, life goes on."

Walking down from the mountain my steps were much lighter than the steps I trudged up with. When I reached my car I sat for a while thinking. I should come back here more than I do; it seems like such great therapy. I was feeling much the same way I had when I was a boy and Josh used to help me understand things, maybe Mount Fay was the way he still communicated with me. This mountain was very important to him. He wrote about it often in his poetry, I thought, recalling a verse from one of his poems.

> As a babe I stood at the foot of her trails
> Gazing up at her beauty with awe
> As a young boy I clambered her sides
> Exploring this wonder I saw
> Many a day I spent in her heights
> Her lessons and wisdom to share
> As I studied the trees, the flowers and fauna
> The wild beauty that God had out there
> Now as a man again and again I return
> Her wonders and beauty to see
> She may not be much on the maps of the world
> BUT MOUNT FAY IS MY MOUNTAIN, TO ME

After remembering his poem about the mountain, I thought Josh may not have lived to reach manhood, but he thought more maturely than many of the men I have known. My hiking and the time I had spent daydreaming in the car dwindled away the afternoon and it was starting to get dark. Feeling so much better I drove back home and spent the rest of the day with my family.

The next couple of days went well at work.

Wednesday Norman asked, "What's up, Caleb? Did you go see a shrink like I told you? You seem so much more relaxed than before. I figured since Etta was coming today you would be worse than your usual wreck. I was telling Virginia that she needed to have a talk with you if you didn't straighten out. Have you replaced her with a shrink of your own? Bet that cost you."

"No, Norman I didn't see a shrink; I just went for a walk on Mount Fay Sunday afternoon and had a little talk with myself. I decided that whatever happens with my so-called harem will happen whether I worry or not, so I'm trying not to worry about it," I answered, feeling less sure of myself now that he had reminded me Etta was coming today.

As I drove into our yard that evening after work, I took several deep breaths hoping to compose myself before seeing Etta. When I first went into the house no one was in the kitchen so I had a chance to wash up before presenting myself. Etta and the family were in the living room where she was beguiling them with college stories.

When I entered she crossed the room and gave me a hug, saying, "Look, everybody, big brother's home."

She still possessed the beauty and build that would stir any red-blooded man's libido, and as she held me I thought the last thing I wanted was to be her brother.

Laughing I said, "Like I told Shaq, if you were my sister I would keep you locked in your room so you wouldn't drive men crazy."

I heard Mother draw in her breath and immediately realized I had made a big mistake as she said, "Caleb, what kind of a greeting is that? Didn't I bring you up better than that?"

Etta said, laughing, "It's okay, Mother Carney; it is just kind of a joke that my brother and I and Caleb have between us, and I'm sure he didn't mean to upset anybody."

"Mean to or not," Mother stammered, "I don't want him talking to any girl like that."

Jason broke in saying, "Guess what, Caleb? Etta still can milk a cow just like I taught her last time she was here. Homer has already asked her to go to the barn and help him milk there. She told him she thought she had been banned from the barn. Did you know that?"

I wanted to tell Jason she had been banned because of the effect that she had on the boys there, but decided I had better not in Mother's hearing.

After supper when Emma, Mother, and Etta were in the kitchen doing dishes, I went in and said, "Etta, I'm sorry, but I have other plans for tonight that I can't get out of. Are you going to be okay with that?"

"Not to worry, Caleb; after all I came to see the whole family, not just you, but try not to let the other girls tie up all your time, because I can only stay until Monday. What you can do for me, though, while you're out, is make arrangements for us to meet together with Jennie. I really liked her."

I left to go see Joan, thinking, *That will take some doing since Jennie doesn't even want my name mentioned to her.*

At Joan's house, Mr. and Mrs. Walden greeted me enthusiastically, saying, "Joan will be ready in a minute. She saw you drive in and rushed up to change, saying she would have to teach you to call when you're coming."

I apologized saying, "I'm sorry I didn't, but we had company from Oklahoma show up today, and I just forgot."

"You don't have to apologize to us, Caleb," Mr. Walden said. "You can't know how thankful we are that Joan has a friend like you. Without you, who knows what might have happened last time she was home?"

Just when I started to talk, Joan came down the stairs. Watching her coming down, I realized again that the little Joan of my mind had developed into a beautiful woman. I stood there with my eyes fixed on her, trying to formulate something appropriate to say.

She walked over and kissed me on the cheek saying, "I hope you have something wonderful planned for tonight, Caleb."

"I certainly do, Joan," I answered, to my surprise. "I plan to spend the night with you."

Mrs. Walden said, "You two have a wonderful evening, and Joan, I know you plan to go back and work with your aunt this summer, so don't spend all the time you have in Sterling with Caleb."

When we got out to the car I realized that I hadn't given much thought to what we would be doing to night so I said, "I have the evening open for anything you want to do Joan, so advise me of your wishes."

Joan surprised me by saying, "I know it's a little much to ask, but there is a play in Lansdale that I would like to see, and tonight is the last night. I will understand if you don't want to drive that far on a work night. I heard so much about it from the students at college that I checked to see if it might be playing close enough to Sterling for me to see it. I imagine I might get a chance some other time, but I just thought I would ask you anyway."

Oh, man, I thought, *it's at least thirty miles to Lansdale,* so I said, "I wonder if we could make it there in time, Joan; it's a long drive."

"The show doesn't start until eight, Caleb," she answered. "It's only six thirty now, so we would have enough time if you want to go."

Feeling like I had trapped myself I said, "Like I said, Joan, it's your night, so we do what you want. I'm happy just to be with you."

Joan gave me a big hug and a pretty passionate kiss then we headed for Lansdale. Most of the drive Joan chatted on about her college experiences. Seemingly forgotten were the terrors she had brought home before. I marveled at her for being able to act so normal so soon after her rape experience.

After she had run out of anecdotes about the semester she just finished, she said, "Caleb, you are going to be able to return for college this fall, aren't you?"

"I'm not sure about that yet, Joan. Dad has made some progress and is pushing to go back to work soon. It is doubtful that he will be able to work sticking lumber for a while yet, if ever. Though the family has discussed my going back, we certainly don't have enough information yet to make any decision. I really try not to think about it too much because it depresses me to think I might be stuck in limbo for another year. I'm sure that you understand that my family comes first, and as much as I hate to leave Sterling again, I have acclimatize myself to the fact that I have to play the hand that life has dealt me. I know we have probably talked about it before, but when I'm out of Sterling, I sometimes feel like I'm outside of my skin. I know that's my heart talking, and my mind says I have to leave to gain a better education and go out and take on the world," I answered as Joan cuddled up closer, just as we found the theatre and were looking for their parking area.

We were able to find a place to park close to the front of the theater whose marquee proclaimed: **Samuel Becket's Waiting for Godot Last Show Tonight**. The play didn't get over until after eleven p.m., and on the drive home we were both fairly quiet. Becket's play left us both with deep thoughts of what our lives were. His portrayal of life as a painful experience with the exception of brief intervals of pleasure, mostly in sex, left a deep impact on both of us. It was no wonder it has been written that not since Shakespeare has any writer used such depth and poetry in his creations.

I could well understand it being a subject of conversation in colleges. It was well after midnight when we arrived back in Sterling, and though Joan wanted to talk, after we arrived at her yard I begged off, saying, "I really have to go, Joan. Morning comes early for me during the week. Let's plan something for Friday night."

"Oh, I was hoping to see you tomorrow, too," Joan exclaimed, holding me tight.

"I wouldn't plan on anything tomorrow, Joan," I answered as she was leaving the car. "We have company at home from Oklahoma, and I think Mother has something special planned for the family tomorrow night," I answered, thinking about Etta

Homer woke me the next morning saying, "Wake up, Caleb, and get a wiggle on or you're going to be late for work. What the hell happened last night? I heard you crawling in after midnight. Etta thought you were out with Jennie. I didn't think that was possible, so where were you?"

"I thought everyone knew Joan came home yesterday," I answered. "I promised to see her the first night she was home. She was all hot about seeing a play in Lansdale. That's why I got in so late."

"Caleb, Caleb, Caleb," Homer exclaimed, "I don't know how you get yourself so tied up when it comes to girls. How are you going to explain this to Etta? Not only Joan, but Etta asked me to have Jennie come see her while she is here. Boy, I'm glad I'm the kiss-them- forget-them type. I wouldn't want to be in your shoes."

I rushed breakfast and headed off to work thinking, maybe Homer has the right idea; I shouldn't get so involved in these girls life.

At work Norman, laughing, asked, "What happened now, Caleb? I'm losing you again. Isn't your shrink helping you anymore? You keep making me drag you along every day at work, and I'm going to have to ask for a raise."

Funny that he should mention a raise I thought. Dad and I had been discussing that the other day and had decided it was due but hadn't decided how much we could afford yet.

I said, "I'm sorry, Norman. I had to go to Lansdale last night, and we didn't get home until after midnight. If Homer hadn't shaken me awake I probable wouldn't even be here yet."

"Well," Norman answered with a laugh, "I expected I would have to carry the load while Etta's here. Did you show her a good time in Lansdale?"

"Etta wasn't with me, Norman. I took Joan to Lansdale to see a play she wanted to see; the only night it was playing was first night she was home. I know, I know, I don't want any lectures about my harem. You know I don't plan these things. The worst of it is, Homer told me this morning that Etta wants to get together with Jennie. Etta and Joan are only going to be here for a few days, and Joan expects me to be with her every day she's here. Think Virginia can get me out of this, Norman?" I said with a laugh.

Norman was quiet for a while before saying, "I know what, Caleb; why don't you bring them all here Saturday, and Bruce and I will help you sort them out. After all, it worked for you when you brought two of them to the wedding."

Norman badgered me constantly about my harem until I angrily told him to knock it off. When I got home that night, Homer had already made arrangements for Jennie to come to the house on Saturday. Mother had made roast pork for supper, and after we had all stuffed ourselves Etta and I went for a walk.

She said, "You and Jennie must have had a night of it last night, Caleb; stayed out a little late for a work night didn't you?"

"Please, Etta, don't make this any harder on me," I answered. "I wasn't with Jennie last night. I was with Joan. Joan and I have been very close since grammar school, and last night was her first night home from college. You know, in your letter you made it clear that you wanted me to know that you were going steady, so I figured you, of all people, would understand my going out with another girl while you were here. I promised her tomorrow night too, I hope you understand."

"Oh, I understand Caleb. It's just the way you did it, without telling anyone, and then came sneaking in after midnight. You know, being treated that way might hurt my reputation," Etta replied, laughing. "Seriously, though, Caleb, it's all right; I'm happy that I can just be with your family, and I hope that my visits can continue over the years. Our history will always make us close; we will just have to make sure we don't get too close, so your dating probably will be of help. I thought for a while when I was here before, that maybe we could be an *us*, but I knew that couldn't ever happen; that's why I moved on, and I'm glad you're involved too."

Etta kissed me on both cheeks and we walked back to the house. The family spent the evening swapping stories with Etta about youthful escapades. I felt that some of their stories about the shenanigans that went on at the barn when I first worked there could have been better left unsaid. Etta beguiled us with tales of the times she and her mother had spent on the Indian reservation.

I must have fallen asleep because Mother shook me gently saying, "I think it's time for some of you to go to bed, especially Caleb, who couldn't have got much sleep last night."

I was surprised when I came down for breakfast to find Etta already there. She said, "I am doing the milking this morning because Jason has promised he would walk up the mountain with Nellie and me right after school."

I left for work with visions of Etta milking and walking on the mountain roaming through my mind. Despite our talk last night I couldn't help the sensual magnetism I felt for her. Norman had the team fed and harnessed by the time I got there. Helping him hitch them onto the wagon I thought what a nightmare it would have been if I had had to work with Clem all this time. The workday seemed to fly by fast, I suppose because I wasn't really looking forward to the evening.

When I arrived home Aaron was back from taking Dad to the doctors and he and Emma had plans right after supper to take Etta, Jason, and Nellie to the early movie in Oscin.

Aaron kind of raised his eyebrows, as he asked, "How come you aren't going with us, Caleb?"

"I understand." Etta said breaking in. "My visit was a surprise to Caleb, and he told me before I came that he had other plans for some of the time I am here."

At the supper table Dad announced that the doctors had cleared him to go back to work as long as it wasn't too strenuous. He had been doing more and more around the farm and felt that in a couple of weeks he would be able to put in a full day's work.

I asked him if that meant he thought he could go back to sticking lumber.

He said, "Not right away, Caleb. But I have been talking to the Jocklins, and their take-away-man and marker is leaving soon, and we thought I could do that job for a while. That way maybe I could go back to sticking lumber in time for you to return to college this fall. Jocklin thought that if I couldn't do that, then Bruce could take your place, and he could hire another mill bitch easily."

Mother, who already had talked to the doctors, said, "This is real good news, Henry; we will all be pulling for you, but you have to promise that you won't push yourself beyond what the doctors have suggested."

Later when I picked up Joan, she said, "Let's not go any place special; let's just cruise around town and visit some of the places we used to go when we were kids."

I was surprised and pleased with her request. We walked around town, sat on the park benches, and even visited the secret spot behind the library where we used to hide as kids to eat our ice cream. We walked around the school and ended up at the swings.

As we sat, swinging lightly like a couple of kids, Joan said, "Caleb, I talked to your mom today, seems that your company is that Indian girl that I heard so much about who was here last fall. Story is, she is a knock out, according to all the boys that have seen her; still, here you are with me. How shall I read that, Caleb?"

"Ah, Joan, there is nothing to read. Etta is practically spoken for; she just happens to be the sister of the best friend I had when I was in Oklahoma. I'm still the same Caleb you left, with an uncertain future, unwilling to tie any girl to such uncertainty."

"Well, I'm glad to hear that, because I want you to take me to see Virginia tomorrow, and I didn't want to take you away from anything that was more exciting. I feel I owe Virginia so much, and I want to stay in contact with her when I can. You will be able to take me won't you, Caleb?" she asked.

"Of course," I answered, thinking, *This is good, I won't have to be around when Jennie comes to see Etta.*

Saturday morning Jason hollered up, "Come on, Caleb, eat your breakfast. Aaron's here, and we need to get started cutting wood."

Man, I had completely forgotten I had promised Jason my Saturday mornings. Not wanting to curb his enthusiasm I got up and joined him and Aaron at breakfast, asking Mother to call Joan and tell her I would pick her up around one o'clock.

Just before we had finished cutting wood, Emma, Etta, and Jennie came out to where we were working.

Etta said, "Why didn't you tell me about this, Jason? It looks like fun. I could have helped you."

"I don't know, Etta." Jason answered, "I was never able to get Emma interested, so I figured it just wasn't a girl thing."

Emma laughed, saying, "He's right. I say, leave the boys' work to the boys."

"Well!" Jennie exclaimed, "Where does that leave me? I have been doing your so-called 'boys work' for a number of years. Do I look like a boy?"

"Not in my eyes," Aaron said, as Emma whacked him one.

"Whoa, I hope I didn't put my foot in it and start a fight," Etta said, looking worried. "I have always worked with my twin brother and just thought it would have been fun to be here this morning."

"Don't let it upset you, Etta. We are all close friends here, at least most of us are close," Jennie said, looking at me.

Aaron, sensing the animosity, broke in, saying, "Well, what have we got planned for the afternoon for such a charming crew?"

Wishing I had bitten my tongue I blurted out, "I have to go to the job site this afternoon."

"Oh, that's great, Caleb. I've been wanting to see Virginia!" Jennie exclaimed. "I told Etta all about her, and she said she wished she could meet her. Can we go too?"

"Why don't we all go?" Aaron suggested

Emma said, "Not us, Aaron, we have other plans, remember? Besides I don't think visiting Caleb's job sounds like much fun."

Etta said, "I'm all for it, Caleb; it will be fun to see where you've been working and what you do there."

"Well, Caleb?" Jennie exclaimed, "You're pretty quiet. Don't you want to take your quest and a former girlfriend with you?"

Feeling trapped I answered, "Joan asked me to take her to see Virginia today, but I don't see any reason why we all can't go, do you, Jennie?"

Jennie looked a little put out with me for asking her to decide and said, "Let me call her, Caleb, and she can decide."

I knew Jennie well enough to know that she would ask Joan in a way that Joan couldn't refuse. Still, there wasn't a good way to stop her.

Thinking, *I guess I'm stuck with the three of them for the afternoon,* I said, "That's a good idea Jennie; you can call from the house. We had better hurry up and eat our lunch, or we won't have much of the afternoon left."

After lunch the three of us piled into the car and drove to Joan's house.

Etta and Jennie sat in the back seat, and as Joan came out Jennie said, "Looks like you have the place of honor today, Joan; we are the backup of Caleb's harem today."

She introduced Etta, saying, "I'm not sure if you have met Etta yet; she is his import from Oklahoma."

Etta laughed and said, "I'm glad to finally meet you, Joan. Caleb has often spoken of you and how you two have been companions since childhood. I once had a friend like that, but we've grown apart now. What you and Caleb have is a wonderful thing. May you always have it to enjoy."

"Well, I don't know whether I can call being a member of his harem a joy," Joan said, laughing. "How big is his harem? Is it going to continue growing? I knew Jennie was friendly competition, and heard rumors about you, Etta; who else is there?"

"Caleb has been seeing a lot of Betty Hart lately," Jennie piped in. "What do you think, Caleb? Shall we pick her up too?"

At first I was tempted to do just that, but thinking these girls would be a little much for Betty I said, "I would like that, Jennie, but Betty isn't ready for too much riding yet because of her operation."

The girls started a round robin of discussions about how I was able to keep a harem, laughing and giggling all the time.

Finally I pulled over and said, "I've had it, and if you girls really want to get to see Virginia, you had better cool it, otherwise I'm dumping you all right here."

Etta laughed and said, "All right, we'll be a good harem and stop picking on you. After all, think of the newspaper write-up: "Caleb Carney Dumps Harem, Literally. Three beautiful women are left stranded on the highway. Theory has it that Carney could no longer handle their henpecking."

"I'm not moving until I get a solemn oath from all of you that I have heard the last of this dumb harem business," I shouted

Almost in unison they shouted back, "We hear you, Caleb; we promise to be good."

Though there was still a lot of giggling going on, the girls stopped picking on me the rest of the way to the job site. When we pulled in Norman was just coming from the horse barn. Man, did his jaw drop when the girls came out of the car.

I just said, "Brought some visitors for Virginia."

The girls all ran up to the shanty.

Norman stood looking at me for a full minute before he said, "Caleb, I do believe that you are out of your mind. These girls are all knockouts, but no man deserves them all."

"Look, Norman, I know we joked about bringing my harem here, but I assure you this isn't anything I planned. Etta and Jennie met before, and they wanted to get together while Etta was here. Things between Jennie and me aren't that good, so I thought while they were together I would bring Joan over here to get away from them. Jennie found out about my plans and called Joan and set this up. I'm so mad I even thought of taking off and leaving them here without me, but I won't."

"Damn right, you won't, Caleb," Norman answered. "I know that Virginia would find some way to take care of it, but I really don't want three beautiful women around Bruce too long; do you? Maybe if I wasn't a married man, I would think different about taking on your messes, especially ones like this."

Norman and I went down to the horse barn. After we had been there awhile, Jennie and Etta came down where we were.

Jennie said, "Etta wants to see what it is that you do here when you're working, Caleb. Joan said she has already seen it all and would stay with Virginia. Besides, I think they wanted to be alone for a bit."

We walked down to the sawmill, and Norman explained to Etta how it operated and what our part was in the operation. Norman was doing such a good job I hung back and let him do the talking. Jennie who had seen it all before hung back with me.

Thinking I saw a change in her demeanor towards me I said, "Homer tells me you don't even want to hear my name anymore. Is it that bad, Jennie? I was hoping we could at least be friendly even if you don't want to be seen with me."

"You know, Caleb," she answered, "I've been thinking, if Joan, Etta, and Betty can put up with you then maybe my anger with you is a mistake; maybe today was meant to be. I think I have gained a whole new perspective of our relationship. So if you are capable of coming to see me, when it isn't about some other girl, I think I would like that."

"I'm glad, Jennie. You just have to understand that each of you means something different to me," I said, putting my arm on her shoulder.

"Oh, I get that, Caleb. I'm not so blind as not to see what Etta does to a man, and the rumors I hear about Betty don't leave much to my imagination. Joan is more of an enigma, though there is something different between you two. I'm still pondering that."

When Etta and Norman came down off from the mill platform she said, "Caleb, Norman has just been telling me what your father would be doing if he takes the marking job. Don't you think that is too dangerous for him the way he is now?"

"Mother and I have talked about it, Etta. Rest assured, we are on top of it. I am a little perturbed with Mr. Jocklin for suggesting it to Dad. It will be awhile before he is needed here and we are waiting to see how he does around home. One thing with Dad, you can't push him once he has made his mind up. Mother has decided instead of fighting with him about it now, we would wait and see how he is when the job's ready."

"I'm glad to hear your mother is on top of the situation, Caleb; makes me feel so much better," Etta said as we headed back to Virginia and Norman's shanty.

My plan was to head back to Sterling as soon as I could and break up this trio. When we got to the shanty Virginia was all excited about having us all stay for supper. It put a damper on my plans, but I couldn't deny Virginia the female company; she didn't see much of that out here. Norman and I went to Bruce's shanty. Bruce who had been somewhere out in the woods when we first arrived came in all excited about a beaver dam he had found about a half mile from the shanties.

He wanted us to go back with him, but Norman said, "Bruce, we have company and Virginia has invited them all to dinner, so we don't have time now."

"Wow, Caleb, did you bring one of your pretty girlfriends?" Bruce asked.

"You'll see, Bruce, you'll see," Norman answered for me, "and it's some different this time, too."

Bruce was all for racing over to see, but Norman stopped him saying, "You wait, Bruce. Virginia is cooking a surprise for us and doesn't want us there until she calls."

Virginia called, "Come and get it, boys."

Bruce raced ahead and when we got into the shanty he was just standing by the door staring with his mouth open.

Norman whacked him on the back saying, "Get a hold of yourself, Bruce," before introducing him to Etta.

I think I was as mystified about how Virginia and the girls had set the meal up as Bruce was about the girls. They had taken a couple of planks from the sticking field and put them on saw horses, gathered up what chairs they had and added a couple of nail kegs to make seating for the seven of us. Though it didn't cover all the planks there was an elaborately crocheted tablecloth, probably something that had been handed down through Virginia's family.

Joan and Jennie had been here before, but when Virginia apologized to Etta she said, "Virginia, you are talking to a woman who has spent part of her life on an Indian reservation. I'm right at home like this."

Virginia had made a wonderful stew with dumplings, and everybody asked if there were seconds. We all sat around talking after we ate. I thought how much this is like the tales that Mother used to tell about her and Dad living in a shanty when they first got married. We didn't leave until well after dark, and the girls couldn't say enough about Virginia and my friends at work.

I dropped Jennie off first, and she hugged me and gave me a kiss saying, "It's okay, Caleb; we voted on it, and we all are going to get to do it."

When I dropped Joan off she said, "Caleb I know tomorrow is Etta's last day, so I release you from any promises you made me about Sunday. I will be here until the middle of the week, and I demand your time after that." Joan kissed me rather passionately.

Getting out of the car she said, "Etta, I hope I see you again, but remember, no more than a goodnight kiss," she said, laughing, as she ran into the house.

Etta climbed into the front seat saying, "Caleb, you lead a very interesting life. In a way I wish I was a man and could have a harem."

At first this made me angry, but I realized she was serious, so I said, "Etta, it isn't what it seems; though I have dated both Jennie and Joan, it's not like they belong to me."

"I get the feeling that Jennie would belong to you in a minute if you let her, and how about Betty? I heard some interesting things about her. You're not going to try to tell me you haven't had sex with these girls."

"No, Etta. I haven't had sex with these girls," I answered, feeling that since she lumped them all together I wasn't lying.

When we arrived home, Etta said, "I'll take my goodnight kiss on the steps, Caleb. If we kissed like you and Joan did here, it might be too much for both of us."

Emma and Aaron were there when we got in, so we sat and talked to them until we went to bed.

In the morning Mother said, "I think since today is Etta's last day, we all should go to church and show our thanks for her visit."

Jason rushed through his chores and had cleaned up so he wouldn't smell from the cows; he had taken quite a shine to Etta. She was always telling him how important she thought what he did for the family was. Homer couldn't make it home in time from milking, but everyone else went, including Dad, which was a surprise.

After church we had one of Mother's big boiled dinners at which Etta told what a wonderful time she had being with us. How much she had enjoyed meeting Virginia, Norman and Bruce. She told how Norman had explained each job at the mill especially the marker's job. She made Dad promise her that he wouldn't start that job until everyone thought he was ready.

After dinner, Etta and I went for a walk without talking much. I think we both felt a sadness that was hard to fathom. We walked one of the trails that went beyond the farm, deep into the woods. It was hard for me not to envision what we had enjoyed the last time we were in the woods alone together.

On the way back she said, "Caleb, I'm almost sorry that I am not free when I'm with you, but I have promised myself to another. Now I have this premonition that this may be our last time together. It saddens me, because from day one with you, I have known you were supposed to be my forbidden fruit. Does any of that make any sense to you, Caleb?"

"Oh, Etta, don't talk about sex. You are well aware of what you do to men; why the first time I saw you and you started kissing me in that truck, your brother being there was the only thing that kept me under control. Even now I feel like ravishing you, but we can't let that happen. I feel the sadness of losing something, too, and I wouldn't want either one of us to have to deal with that as our parting. No matter what happens to us in the future, we will always have the wonder of what happened with us on the mountain."

We had reached the edge of the woods just as I finished talking. Etta grabbed me in a passionate embrace, took my breath away with her kisses, then suddenly, releasing me, she ran for the house. I stayed where I was for a few minutes trying to gather myself.

When I got to the barn Dad was standing there. He said, "What happened, Caleb? I just saw Etta running by with tears in her eyes."

"Nothing really, Dad. She is just sad about leaving tomorrow," I answered, rushing into the house to avoid any further conversation.

The next morning when I got up to go to work, Etta was already at the breakfast table.

She said, "I won't be leaving until around noon, today but I want one last goodbye before you go to work."

Mother said, "I hope that doesn't mean we won't be seeing you again, Etta."

"I hope not, too, Mother Carney," Etta said, giving Mother a hug, "but no one knows what lies ahead. I'm just trying to cover all bases."

As I left for work Etta gave me a big bear hug and kissed me on both cheeks without saying a word and I drove to work with the fear and sadness of yesterday still clinging to me. All day long at work everybody there had a different slant on me being with three women at the same time. I was still numb with Etta's parting to respond so I just let them have their fun.

The next few nights I spent with Joan. We took in a movie one night but spent most of our time together just talking. She couldn't get over what she called the sensual beauty of Etta and all but asked me if we had been lovers. I always responded by reminding her what she had said about my being with her the first night Etta came. By the end of the week Joan had left, leaving me without obligations to any girl, at least for a while.

Dad was working around the farm for longer and longer period every day. He even spent a couple of afternoons cutting wood with Jason.

I asked Jason how it was going.

He said, "Dad does all right when he is in the barn or on level ground but has a hard time in the woods where it is brushy and uneven. He tells me that is to be expected at first, and I must admit there is improvement all the time."

I got a call from Jake, who said he was in Lansdale doing some research and would be home for a couple of evenings and wanted to see me.

The next night I met with Jake, and he said, "Caleb, it's so good to see you again. How are things going with your dad? I hope you are making plans to go back to college. There is so much more outside of Sterling to learn."

"I haven't made any definite plans yet, Jake," I answered. "But it looks like Dad will be going back to work soon, and I'll have to start planning."

"Oh, Caleb," Jake said, "that is such good news. I have been talking to some of our old friends and some of them doubted you wanted to go back to college. Something about Caleb's harem."

"I have to tell you, Jake, it has crossed my mind not to go back, but it doesn't have anything to do with that joke about my harem," I answered, trying to laugh it off.

"Tell you what, Caleb." Jake answered seriously. "You had better start looking into getting into college right away. The G.I. bill has allowed many men to go to college who wouldn't normally have been able to go, and the colleges are filling up fast."

Jake and I rode around Sterling talking about old times, and when I left him off he said, "Caleb, promise me you will look into returning to college right away."

I promised him I would, so I called Eunice and had her check into it for me. A few days later I received a package of college entry forms with a notice that the final day to have them in was little less than a month away. I studied the forms to make sure I had all the information I needed to fill them in and went to bed every night worrying when I would be able to feel safe leaving Dad.

CHAPTER TEN

A week after Etta had left, Dad started working at the mill. Charlie Baron who was the marker that was leaving agreed to work with Dad for a week, so he could take breaks when he needed. Dad was stubborn but not stupid, he took advantage of Charlie's offer and worked a couple hours on and a couple hours off for the first few days. By the end of the week Dad was working full time. Though he was so tired at the end of the day that he slept on the way home he seemed pleased with himself.

He still had a noticeable limp but the leg seemed to be taking the work all right. Mother monitored him carefully and said she believed that in a couple of weeks of work he would be much stronger. Despite feeling good about this, it was becoming evident that his leg wouldn't ever return to normal and it didn't seem likely he would be able to climb on and off the wagon so he could go back to sticking lumber.

Remembering Dad's talk about hiring Bruce to take my place and feeling better about Dad's ability to hold a job, I finished and mailed my college application papers. I leaned heavily on the same documentation I had used when I applied the last time. A couple of weeks after I mailed them I received a reply. They were concerned about how I had left them last year without proper notification. I had been considered a no show and my entry fee had been forfeited. I not only would have to pay another fee but they would need a written explanation of my behavior, including proof if it was caused by family illness. They felt that I should understand their need to preserve the few openings they have for those really interested in being educated.

My first reaction was, *To hell with them, I could find another college or not go at all.*

A few nights later at the supper table, Mother asked, "What's with the college, Caleb? You haven't said a word about their last letter."

"I guess they aren't too happy with me because of the way I left, and they are making it hard for me to return. I have been giving some thought about not going back at all," I answered wearily.

"Caleb," Mother said, "I don't want to hear you talk like that. Hanna Cullings would turn over in her grave if you ever did such a thing. If Josh was alive he would have given anything to be as lucky as you are to have full-scholarship funding."

"I know, Mother," I replied. "I have been thinking about all of that, but it is not the same as it was before when I left. I don't seem to have the desire for education that I had when I first went to Oklahoma."

After supper I went out to the barn with Jason. Aaron, who had been at supper with us, followed us out. He said, "I know it isn't any of my business, Caleb, but if you want to talk about your college dilemma, I've been there, so maybe I can help."

"I don't know, Aaron," I answered. "I talked about wanting to go to college long before I knew about Hanna's bequest. Then, when I first found out that my dream had become a reality, it really scared me. Jake, a friend of mine, who also received money from Hanna, was so elated, his joy and excitement was what carried me through last year. Now that Jake will be a year ahead of me in college, and I will be facing my first year alone, things look different. With the college giving me a hard time and all, I got to thinking—why the hell go?"

"Let me tell you why, Caleb," Aaron answered, "I was able to start college because I failed the physical for the draft, and my folks scraped together enough money for one semester. I won a small scholarship and worked in a restaurant kitchen Friday nights and weekends doing all their dirty jobs to pay the rest. The first summer off, I worked for a septic tank outfit installing tanks all day and pumping filthy tanks nights and weekends. I made enough money so that along with my kitchen job back at college, I was able to pay for a second year. I got lucky that year because I was offered a job working with the engineering outfit that I'm working for now, and they paid for my last two years' tuition.

"I haven't enough credits to get my degree yet, so I have to go back part time this fall. That's my college history. Now the reason why you should go on with yours: you're too smart not to see that what you're doing now is a dying way of life. Yes, there will always be loggers and sawmills, but the business is changing. There is new equipment, and new ways are being planned that will make what you're doing now obsolete. I know you will have other options for making a living, but consider this: if I were still pumping septic tanks, would your sister be interested in me? Could I offer her a good life? Would your family accept me the way they do now? Don't stutter trying to say they might, because it's more likely they might not. Think. Why is Hester on easy street with her husband? It's because he has an education. I hear Harry is a little old world, but his business is on the new side of it, and he was well trained before he started to build a business of his own. There are thousands upon thousands of men in college today because of the G.I. Bill. These men not only won the war, they are going to change the world with their education, and I know you don't want to miss being part of that. I'm sorry, Caleb; I didn't mean to get on my soap box, and I just want you to understand what I see."

Jason, who had been taking this all in said, "Wow, Aaron, I'm glad I heard that. I have to believe that there is more to life then just what I see here in Sterling."

"There it is, Aaron, there it is," I countered. "Everyone else is always looking for a way to get out of Sterling, while Sterling and my life here is so much of what I am and how I feel. I told Joan the other night that when I'm out of Sterling it's like being out of my skin. Maybe I am destined to be just a nobody who's happy living in Sterling. I feel now much like I felt when I was reaching the years of puberty with all of its fears and confusion. I know what you're saying about a better future, then again, what if suffering in the present doesn't produce a better future? Haven't you lost everything then?"

"Emma told me to be careful trying to explore your mind, Caleb. Now I understand what she was getting at. I am not a psychologist, but I can tell you this. You are not alone in fearing leaving what's known for the unknown. There is a little of that in all of us. As for ruining the present, I can't see that. My goal of being an engineer made those times working in lousy jobs unimportant, because they moved me closer to my goal. As for the world out there, sometimes it is harsh, but think of the gains. One great analogy from your life is your so-called harem; your Sterling girls are wonderful, but just think, if you had never gone out in the world, would you have met anyone like Etta here? If that doesn't show you there are wonderful things out there," Aaron said laughing, "I don't know how I could convince you."

Jason said, "Caleb, I didn't mean to upset you about Sterling. I like a lot of the things here, and I'm very proud that I have been able to help carry the load after Dad was hurt. Still, I don't see anything in Sterling that I want to spend the rest of my life doing, and I hope to have a chance to go out in the world someday."

Both Aaron and Jason had their points, and I thought that Aaron seemed a little like Josh with his reasoning, but right then I didn't know if they were helping or adding to my confusion.

So I said, "Thanks for talking to me, boys, but I have a date with Betty tonight, and I better get going."

I really didn't have a date with Betty but had been thinking of seeing her. That was the first thing to pop into my mind that would get me away from the hornets' nest I had created. I drove into town and up to the foot of the mountain. I guess I had some thoughts of hiking, but it was too close to dark, so I just set there pondering.

Remembering what Aaron had said about goals I tried to conjure up mine. While sitting there lamenting my situation it dawned on me that that was my dilemma: I didn't have specific goals. It was so evident in all that I did. When I considered my so-called harem, I really had no thought about a future with any of them. Not that they were responsible—it was just the way I approached everything in my life—no real thought or plans for tomorrow.

It was okay to dream about being a writer when I was a kid because kids are supposed to dream. The thrill I felt about some of my writing back then soon departed as I read some of the preparatory reading necessary for college. I still had a desire to write, but I had such a feeling of inadequacy that I hadn't attempted writing for some time. Thinking about writing reminded me of Josh and how he loved to write, especially poetry. I remember when he wrote about needing to write in this poem:

The Poet's Curse

I have this feeling from which I flee
For it would destroy the life of me
With its wanton mad desire
It seems to set my soul on fire

If it were for a woman, perhaps I'd cope
With strength of will, or maybe hope
Or if it was untamed passion, I might seek
Relief from those who walk the street,
But my fate has chosen another plight;
The spirit within me attempts to write

I thought, *There's solace here next to the mountain, remembering Josh's poems; he seems so close whenever I'm here.* In my heart I believed that somehow he would still give me the answer for my problems, like he used to before he died. I'm not sure how long I spent by the mountain, but as I heard the town clock strike nine it seemed to urge me to leave.

I drove by the park as I was leaving, and I saw Jennie sitting there, so I stopped, asking, "May I give the lady a lift somewhere?"

"No, Caleb, I don't need a ride, but if you can refrain from talking about any of your harem, I could use some company," she replied.

I parked by the library and joined Jennie in the park. "Just like old times, Jennie," I said, sitting down beside her.

"Not quite, Caleb; remember our rules: harem or no harem, they still stand," Jennie said as she put an arm around me.

I laughed and said, "I'll remember, Jennie, but don't ask me to stop dreaming about what we had before. Would it be okay to talk about my dilemmas if it's not about girls?"

"That's why we need friends, Caleb," she said with a smile. "I wasn't angry with you about coming to me in need; it was just that it always seemed your need was because of another girl. I couldn't deal with that."

Sitting there with Jennie's arms around me brought me back to when she had held me here after we had lost Josh, and again I poured my heart out to her about college, my fear of writing, what Mother had said, how Aaron had spoken to me, and the heartbreak of hearing Jason put down Sterling. I told her about going to the mountain and looking for an answer from Josh. All the time I was talking Jennie held me tighter, kissing me on the cheek and neck.

Sensing she was arousing me, she pulled back and folded her hands. She said, "Maybe Josh has answered both of us, Caleb. I have been sitting here thinking about old times too. I have a chance for a good job in a milk room on a big farm up in New York State and have been sitting here pondering the pros and cons. I have a great attachment to Sterling, but the thought of growing old here as a barn girl or wife of one of the Sterling boys, with the exception of you, of course, doesn't present a rosy future in my mind.

"I also have a fear of leaving but it doesn't seem like much of a con, when compared to the alternatives I just described. We both have to be more sensible and separate our childish emotions from the reality of our lives. You have the opportunity to get a good education and perhaps become a great writer. Think what Josh would have said to an opportunity like that. The advertisement I saw for the job in New York stated they were looking for a country girl with a dairy background. The job includes room and board, and it is situated near a college. Maybe I could take some classes there. Now, no matter how you draw up your list of pros and cons, the pros have it for both of us."

"I know that what you say about our chances is true, Jennie," I answered. "It's what everybody tells me. Still I have this great fear that I can't handle it out there. Where will I find the courage?"

Jennie held me tight again and said, "Caleb, courage comes when you want something more than you fear what's standing in your way. That's how I have decided to try for that job."

"One thing is for sure, Jennie, Sterling is going to hold less attraction for me when you're not here. Life is so strange; everyone I know is telling me to go on with my life, and my gut reaction is to beg you to stay," I said, wrapping my arms around her.

I'm not sure how long we sat like that. To my surprise the passions I felt weren't all about sex they were more like the caring, comforting feeling I used to get when I held Nellie as a baby.

Finally Jennie said, "We have to go, Caleb. I am due at the barn early tomorrow, and you have to go to work also."

I said, "Okay, Jennie, let me drive you home and kiss you goodnight; promise me you will let me know as soon as you find out about getting that job."

Things went well at the job the next couple of weeks, and Mother was right about Dad growing stronger. He had already advised Mr. Joclin that he should start looking for someone to take his place doing the marking. Mr. Joclin came into the pit with Norman and me one day asking how we would feel about Bruce taking my place and Dad staying at the mill. Norman and I had already been talking about it, and I knew that I would feel better about leaving if Dad didn't have to take my place. Bruce was all for it, and Norman didn't seem against the idea, though he mumbled about having to teach a damn fool how to stick lumber.

Two days after this discussion Mr. Joclin came and said, "Caleb, your dad was very unhappy about me even suggesting such a thing. He said he was man enough to run his own business. I haven't found a replacement for him yet, but I guess I better start looking."

The next day Norman said, "Caleb, Virginia wants to talk to you alone, so right after we finish unloading the last load, why don't you run up to see her? Must be something about one of the girls that you brought around."

I rushed up to their shanty, hurrying, because I knew Dad would be waiting to get home.

Virginia met me at the door, and I said, "What's up, Virginia? Norman said you wanted to see me."

"I do, Caleb. Norman told me about your father not wanting to stay at the mill and how it worries both of you. I got to thinking that, as it seems more a matter of more pride than sense, if there would be a way out? Now this is just something I thought of, so if you disagree it's okay and won't go any further. What if Mr. Joclin was to offer your dad more pay because he was having such a hard time finding someone? Wouldn't your dad be more inclined to stay? I didn't say anything to Norman or Bruce; you know how they talk too much sometimes, but I thought you might find this something you could use," Virginia said.

Just then Bruce came in, saying, "Your dad's looking for you, Caleb."

I left the shanty thinking that she had a good idea, wondering how Virginia thought I was going to get Mr. Joclin to offer Dad more money. Dad was down at the shanty barn with the horses talking to Norman.

He said laughing, "Norman's been complaining that you were spending too much time with his wife. He said he would be glad when you leave for college, and he gets a chance to work with a real lumber man."

Norman laughed and said, "Don't you believe him, Caleb. He might be better sticking lumber than you, but I bet he never brings me the excitement you do when you bring your harem here."

Dad and I went to the car, both laughing, but as we were driving off Dad said, "What's with this harem business, Caleb? You're not getting into something over your head are you?"

"No, Dad," I answered. "At one time or other I have brought four different girls with me when I came here. I brought three at once one time, and that started the harem jokes."

A few days later on the way home from work, Dad said, "Mr. Joclin offered me a very attractive pay increase if I would agree to stay on as his marker. It would allow me to increase Norman's pay, pay Bruce to take your place, and still come out ahead of the game financially. Seems that there aren't many markers available, or at least none that Jocklin wants to hire. I have to talk it over with your mother, but I think I will say yes. Do you think Bruce and Norman will work well together, Caleb?"

"I think they will be terrific together, Dad. They take as good care of our horses as we would. Bruce has even worked with the farrier that has been shoeing our horses since you were laid up, and he has allowed Bruce to shoe some of Leclat's horses. Leclat said he was going to use Bruce from now on instead paying a farrier. I know he would shoe our horses too, if you were there to watch him. If you are happy on the marking job, Dad, I think it's a wonderful idea," I answered, wondering how Virginia had pulled this off.

Mother, of course, was ecstatic about Dad's decision to stay in the mill, as were Bruce and Norman. If Virginia had arranged this with Mr. Joclin in anyway, I never found out. With the help of Jake, Eunice, and Mr. Welch, Hanna's lawyer, the college in Oklahoma finally sent me papers of acceptance. I was slated to start the second week in September.

Eunice thought I should come a week before that and spend time with her and Harry before moving into the college. A few days after that was settled, Jennie called and wanted me to pick her up at the barn.

When I arrived she got in the car and said, "Let's take a little ride, Caleb, nowhere in particular. I just need to talk to you."

Thinking, *If this is going to be serious, what better place to be than at the foot of my mountain?* I drove there and parked.

Jennie was extremely quiet for her, so I put my arm around her and said, "Jennie, whatever it is, I'm here for you and willing to help in any way I can."

"Oh, Caleb," she said, cuddling close to me, "I called about that job in New York, and they said I sounded like what they were looking for, but they didn't want to hire me unless I could come for an interview. I checked, and there are no trains that go close to that area, and the buses around here only run to that area at the beginning and end of college or during a college break. I know if I wait too long I won't get the job, and I have really looked at it as a way for me to start new somewhere. I'm so frustrated by all this; I just needed someone to talk to."

"Well, Jennie, you have picked the right man. You just call them and set up an interview for Saturday, and I'll get you there," I answered, feeling really proud of myself.

" Oh, Caleb," Jennie replied holding me closer, "I wish you could, but I figured the mileage, and it would take eight hours or better to drive it. How could you do that?"

"It will take some planning, Jennie, but you set a time for your interview as close to noon on Saturday as you can, and I'll get you there. I will get Bruce and his buddy Donald Trent to check the car out to make sure it's in good enough shape for the trip," thinking, *I'll be replacing those tires a little sooner than I thought.*

The next day at work I asked Bruce about getting the car checked. He said he would get hold of Donald and see if he could do it the next day.

The next day Donald was there when we arrived at work. He said, "If you're planning a trip like Bruce said, I had better take the car back to my garage and give it a good going over."

That night after work, Donald was there without the car, saying, "I'm sorry, Caleb, but your generator was so bad I couldn't fix it, and I can't get a replacement until tomorrow some time. There were a few other little things that I took care of, but you really should think about new tires."

I told him I expected that. After making arrangements with him to change the tires too, I went back and told Dad, "Guess we will have to drive the old truck home tonight."

Riding back in the old truck Dad said, " Now I really feel like I'm back to work, coming home in the truck like I used to. Tell me, Caleb, what are your real feelings about going back to college?"

"I don't know, Dad," I answered. "I believe getting an education is really important for me but I still kind of dread leaving this life. I had a long talk with Aaron about it, and his take is that things are going to be changing, and this way of cutting lumber is in for a big change. As it is, there are very few mills now that operate the way we do, with horses. Beyond that I think he's right, that if you want to succeed in the coming years you had better have an education. I used to think how wonderful it would be to be able to go to college; now it feels like just another thing I have to do in my life."

Dad was quiet for a while, then he said, "I'm sorry, Caleb, for how my accident screwed up your life. I would have given anything not to have had this happen. I have been watching you, and lately I see what a toll it has taken on you."

"Oh, Dad, don't put my troubles on your accident. At first I was glad to come home. I hated the reason that I had to, but I wasn't sad about doing it. I have enjoyed working with the mill crew and have a great respect for Norman, Bruce, and Virginia. You know something that Aaron said about if I hadn't gone out in the world? I wouldn't have met Etta, but if I hadn't come back, I wouldn't have known them. It isn't your accident that is convoluting my life. It is my trepidation about allowing little Caleb Carney to become a man. A man has to make commitments and live by them, and I'm not sure I'm ever going to be ready for that."

"Life is really not like that, Caleb," Dad answered after being quiet for a while. "Sure, making commitments is a part of being adult but only after you have evaluated the situation enough to know whether it is right of wrong for you. There will be times you commit to something you wished you hadn't, but that is called 'gaining experience.'"

It seemed strange talking to Dad again about my life, but it was good. I rushed out that night right after supper so I could catch Jennie at the barn.

Her face dropped when she saw the old truck, but I laughed and said, "Don't worry, Jennie. The car's all right; it just needed a little more work than I thought, so Donald kept it another day. The boys at work tell me we better plan on more than eight hours for the trip to Lawrenceville, though. Have you searched out a route yet?"

"Yes, the librarian has been collecting road maps, and she helped me map out what we think are the best roads to travel. I don't have the maps, just the route numbers, but Old Golly Moses said he would pick up some maps for us next time he goes to Oscin. I was so excited about going until we mapped it out. It's such a long ways, Caleb; I think it's more than I should ask anyone to do," Jennie answered.

"I don't remember you asking, Jennie," I said, laughing, "When I heard about it I thought this would be an adventure, just like my fishing trips were way back when. I know it will take some planning, and driving for that long in one stretch will be hard, but it's on a Saturday, and if we don't get back until Sunday, it's okay with me. Tell me about the routes; maybe some of my friends will have suggestions."

The plan is to take Route 2 over the Mohawk trail into Troy, New York. Once there go west towards Rotterdam, stay on Route 5 until you get to Route 30, then go north all the way to Malone and take Route 11 southwest until we reach Lawrenceville. I figure that to reach there around noon we would have to leave by two a.m. Saturday morning. I know I don't have a lot of experience, but I can drive, so if we go, I can drive some of the easy driving." Jennie replied, her voice rising in excitement.

"Oh, we're going, Jennie. The more I hear about it, the more exciting it sounds. Uncle Louse worked up in the Adirondacks logging and told how wonderful it was up in those mountains. He worked at some lake; I think it was called Tupper Lake, and if my memories are right, he mentioned being on route 30. It would be thrilling if we were going to be near there to see the things he talked about," I answered, really beginning to feel the excitement of going on such a trip.

The next day was Thursday, and Donald had my car back by the time we finished work. Dad mentioned how much better it seemed to run on the way home. It sure handled better with all new tires. I asked Dad what he thought about my trip to New York.

He said, "I would have worried about it a year or so ago, Caleb, but I have seen you accomplish so much on your own this last year, I am not worried about you going on this trip. Though of course, Mother has her misgivings, especially your being alone all that time with Jennie."

"I know, Dad; she had that talk with me about Etta, but you have to remember that Jennie and I have been friends forever, and we have an understanding about this sex thing."

Dad laughed and said, "I don't think I want to even ask what that might be, taking into consideration there's Joan, Betty, and Etta, and probably others in that equation. I hear a lot of talk at the mill about you and your harem, most of it with them wishing they were you."

Laughing, I said, "I hope you aren't believing their stories, Dad. I told you how that happened. Norman and Bruce spread all that gossip just because I bring different friends with me when I come on weekends."

"Maybe, Caleb, maybe," Dad responded just as we pulled into the yard at home, "but I have always believed where there is smoke there is probably fire."

Right after supper I rushed off to see Jennie to make our arrangements for Saturday. We decided to stick to the routes she had picked out with the librarian, as nobody seemed to know a better one.

She said, "I think we had better leave at one a.m., Caleb; that will give us time if we get off track. I'll pack a big lunch for us so we won't have to stop on the way up. I think it would be better for us to stay up late tonight so we will go to bed early tomorrow night, so let's go to Oscin and have a sundae or something."

I agreed with her, so we drove to Oscin and went to the ice-cream parlor.

The same girl who was usually there when I was came over and said, "My name's Elaine. What can I do for my Romeo tonight?"

Jennie looked at me with raised eyebrows and said, "Unless you can make very good banana splits you can't do anything for him, because he's my Romeo, at least for tonight."

When Elaine went back to the counter Jennie said, "More harem, Caleb?"

"No, Jennie, she just has the wrong idea about me, you know this is where I come no matter who I'm with, and she's just curious. Don't tell me you're jealous?"

"Not really, Caleb, I just need to keep track of the competition," Jennie answered with a laugh.

After we left Oscin, we drove to the foot of the mountain and sat there talking until we heard the town clock strike eleven.

The next morning Mother said, "I don't think it was too smart to be out so late last night, Caleb. Aren't you and Jennie going to be together enough the next two days?"

"We had to make some plans for the trip, Mother, and we thought it would get us to bed earlier tonight if we stayed out later last night. I know this trip worries you, but I'm a big boy now; Mother, and I'll be all right," I answered, heading for the door.

"Maybe you are a big boy, Caleb, but big boys get in trouble too," Mother shouted after me.

Things went fast at work, though I took a lot of teasing about taking off for a weekend with one of my harem. I went to bed right after supper that night. Staying up the night before must have worked.

The next thing I remember was Homer shaking me saying, "Damn it, Caleb, can't you hear that alarm? It's after twelve, and I think it has woken everyone in the house but you. I sure ain't going to miss you keeping me awake after you go back to Oklahoma."

I jumped up and got dressed, downed a couple of Mother's donuts and a glass of milk and drove to pick up Jennie. Jennie came running out carrying a basket and a small suitcase. She jumped in and we took off for Troy. I must have traveled some of the Mohawk Trail before but it seemed funny to be driving through the town Florida when you always think of Florida as a state. We had a little trouble when we reached Troy finding the right way to Rotterdam but we didn't lose much time.

After we had been on Route 30 North for about an hour we drove along a big lake called Sacandaga. This was quite exciting because neither of us had been to a lake that big before.

Jennie said, "There were a lot of lakes like this on the map, Caleb. Do you think we might have time to stop at one of them on the way back?"

"I hope so, Jennie. It would be nice if we could get a boat ride around one of them," I answered, thinking maybe Aaron was right, it would be a shame to only know life as it is in Sterling.

We drove until we came to another lake, called Indian Lake. There was a little park overlooking the lake, so we stopped there and had the lunch that Jennie brought. It seemed funny having a picnic lunch on a table by a lake at six thirty in the morning but we had marked this as more than half way to Malone, and we both needed to get out, walk around, and stretch after driving for over five hours.

I said, "You know, Jennie, even if nothing comes of this for you, I will always glad we made this trip."

"I know, Caleb. I'm enjoying seeing so much of the country, too. Please don't think that I won't make it working there, because I am really looking to change my life," Jennie answered, looking longingly out over the lake.

"Won't you miss me at least a little bit, Jennie?' I said, laughing.

"You know, Caleb, I would have never thought to leave Sterling if I thought there was any 'us' to consider. I know I'm no competition with the likes of Joan and Etta, and it's like I told you—there is nothing or anybody else in Sterling that I want to dedicate my life to," Jennie said, giving me a little kiss just before we got back to the car.

We passed more and more lakes as we drove along Route 30. Jennie drove after we left Indian Lake for a while, so I got a chance to see more of the landscape than I would have driving. We were driving through part of the Adirondacks, and I couldn't help but think about what it must be like to have been working in some of the timber I saw there, like my Uncle Louis used to. Route 30 did go by the Tupper Lake that my uncle talked about; in fact it skirted the whole east side of it. I noticed cabins to rent along the highway and thought it would be nice to stay there for a while. The driving around the lake was a little more hectic, so I took over.

A little while after we left the Tupper Lake area, Jennie fell asleep, and I had already negotiated my way through Malone before she woke up. It was after eleven, so I suggested we find a place to get a bite to eat and rest a little.

Jennie asked "How much longer before we get to Lawrenceville?"

"I think it will be less than an hour," I answered.

We pulled into the next restaurant we came to. Jennie brought her suitcase in with her and had a conversation with the lady behind the counter before disappearing into a rest room.

The lady asked, "What will it be, Mister? The lady left her order, so what's yours?"

There was a haddock dinner on the daily specials so I ordered that. Jennie came from the rest room just about the same time as our dinners arrived. This

271

was a different Jennie from the one I had picked up in dungarees and an old shirt with her head wrapped in a bandana. She had changed into a skirt and blouse, put on makeup, and combed out her hair.

I smiled and said, "Did you see another girl in there? My date went in there when we came in, and I haven't seen her since."

Jennie slapped me upside the head, saying, "You think this is too much, Caleb?"

"I don't know, Jennie," I answered. "I believe they advertised for a farm girl, and farm girls don't look like that from where I come from."

The woman was just sitting down our dinners when she asked, "Are you the one who is going to work at the Jolene Farm in Lawrenceville? Their boys have been bragging how they were going to hire some girl from down east."

Jennie looked a little taken aback, so I said, "She's the one; so what do you think? Will they hire her?"

Sensing Jennie was uneasy, she said, "I wouldn't worry, miss; from what I hear it is already a done deal. The Jolenes are good folks to work for. We get a lot of the family and help in here because we are the closest restaurant to their farm. The only worry I heard, they wondered if you were going to be a clean enough worker for their milk room. This outfit will certainly give a better perception of that than the one you wore in."

After finishing our meal we thanked the woman, and following her directions, drove to the Jolene Farm. As we drove down off the highway, what a sight to behold! Their barn must have been three or four times as big as the Muldon's barn, and it had a smaller barn hitched to it. Across from the barn was a building that looked so clean it must be the milk room. At the house we were greeted by a couple of noisy dogs; though they were loud they seemed friendly and just followed us to the house.

The door opened before we got there and a smiling woman who looked to be in her fifties called the dogs off, saying, "You must be Jennie; come on in. Ed is out in the fields somewhere. He left me to interview you."

After we introduced ourselves I said, "Mrs. Jolene, I'm sure Jennie would be more at ease if I wasn't present. Would it be all right if I looked your barns over?"

"You go right ahead, Caleb, she said. "Make your self right at home, and if you're interested, we could use another strong back around here."

Jennie went into the house, and I went down to the barns. It was easy to see why they had a smaller barn. It was the one with all the milking equipment in it. I had heard of farms having milking parlors but had always doubted it until now. I guessed that they probably were milking over two hundred head. With that kind of production a milk parlor made sense.

Everything was bigger here; the tractors were easily twice as big as the ones we used in Sterling. There were a few big Holsteins on the pasture side of the barn and a few more that looked as though they were ready to calf penned up in a lean-to structure there. It seemed like there were open fields everywhere, with a few patches of woodland that looked like scrub oak.

The stables had automatic gutter cleaners, and all the stanchions were electronically controlled. There was so much that was way ahead of anything I had seen or worked on.

I was so engrossed in studying their equipment I hadn't noticed how much time had passed, when I heard Jennie call, "Caleb, we finally found you! We were beginning to think you were lost somewhere! We have been calling you for ten minutes or more."

I apologized, saying, "I'm sorry, but I have never seen the likes of this, and I've been studying how it all works."

Mrs. Jolene said, "Like I told you, we could use another man here. Stay with us, and you can get to run all this equipment."

"As tempting as that is, Mrs. Jolene, I am due back at college next month, studying for a degree in journalism. So Jennie, what is your decision? Do they want you, and are you sure this is what you want?" I asked

"Oh," Mrs. Jolene exclaimed, "that's all worked out, all that is missing is a way for her to get back here next week. I think there are buses that run from a couple of the bigger towns down your way as far as Malone, and I have agreed to have her picked up there."

Looking at Jennie I could see there was a little doubt showing on her face, so I asked. "There is one thing that bothers me about this, Mrs. Jolene. Why did you have to advertise so far from here for help?"

"Look around the country side up here, and all you see is farms like this. We train young girls to work in the milk rooms, but most of them move on right after they leave high school. There is a lot of competition for mature girls for this job, so we thought advertising around Vermont and western Massachusetts where there were a lot of small farms would be a way of finding someone who would stay with us.

"Jennie seems like a perfect fit. She has worked in a barn and a milk room and claims she doesn't have many ties except family back in Sterling."

Jennie broke in saying, "It's okay, Caleb. She has gone over everything very honestly with me. I am sure that I will be happy here. There was no future for me at Muldons, though I am thankful that I had a job there all these years."

Mrs. Jolene said, " I understand you two have been on the road since one a.m. If you would like to spend the night here before you go back I can arrange it."

Jennie who was standing a little behind her shook her head slightly no, so I said, "That is very generous of you, but we have plans to spend a little time around Tupper Lake. My uncle used to work there, and there are friends of his there we are supposed to visit."

"Okay," Mrs. Jolene said, "but I insist that you a least let me pack you a lunch. It will only take me a minute, and you'll be hungry before you get to Tupper."

By the time we left Jolene's farm it was after three o'clock. Jennie was very quiet until after we had traveled back through Malone.

Then she said, "It's a little scary, Caleb, but it's a done deal now, and I know I will stay with them at least long enough to make it worth their while that they have hired me. Now tell me what's with the story about Tupper Lake?"

"I don't know, Jennie, but when you signaled 'no,' that was the first thing that popped into my head. I'm not sure what to do, but I know I can't go much further without getting some sleep. Do you have any ideas?" I asked

" I know you have a thing about Tupper Lake. Remember, you talked about it on the way up? I saw a lot of little cabins around the lake for rent. I would be willing to spend a night there. One thing though, you have to keep our agreement, our relationship stays platonic," Jennie answered earnestly.

"I'm sure in the beginning that will be no problem for me Jennie, but you have to behave yourself after I am rested. No kissing or hugging, and then I guess I'll make it through, with nothing more than lovers' cramps," I answered, laughing.

We took turns telling stories about our experiences working at Muldons in an effort to stay alert while driving then about half way between Malone and Tupper Lake we stopped at Lake Clear to have our lunch. I told Jennie if that lunch was anything like she was going to be fed at Jolene's, she would weigh two hundred pounds next time I saw her. She didn't hear me because she had fallen asleep in her chair. I decided not to wake her and must have fallen asleep myself, because I dreamed I was chasing after George being dragged by that bull hollering, "Let go, George, let go of the rope!"

I woke up with Jennie shaking me saying, "I'm not sure I want to spend a night in a cabin with you if that's the way you sleep."

"I'm sorry, Jennie," I said sleepily, "I was dreaming about when George got tangled up with that bull when we were kids. I guess because I was thinking up at Jolene's that it was funny I didn't see any sign of a bull around their farm."

We drove to Tupper Lake and rented a cabin. There was only one bed, but without a thought we both climbed in, fully clothed, and went right to sleep. I woke up, startled at where I was. As it slowly came to me I felt for Jennie in the dark. Feeling no one, I rolled towards her side of the bed and found no Jennie.

Concerned I shouted, "Jennie!"

A light came on, and Jennie was there sitting in a chair. She had already changed back into her dungarees. She said, "Lose somebody, Caleb?"

"It was kind of weird, Jennie, when I first woke up. I didn't know where I was, and I was feeling for you to make it real. You know, with my crazy dreams I sometimes wake up wondering what is real. Do you know what time it is?"

"It's three a.m., Caleb. I have been awake for about a half an hour and have been thinking maybe we should leave now; we could stop at the first restaurant we find open for breakfast. We have over six hours before we get to Sterling; this way we'll get home before noon. I know that you have some desire to spend some time at the lake, but I think it's better for us if we leave now. At least that way you won't have to suffer lover's cramps," she said, laughing.

She was right: my plan was to spend some time here, but I knew if I spent three or four hours alone here with her, I probably would end up begging her to forget being platonic. Though some of my thoughts of about the two of us being here alone here were pleasant, that one wasn't, so I said, "Okay, Jennie, if that's how you want to end our first night together, give me a minute, and we can go."

"You know, Caleb," she answered, "there were times way back when, that I used to think it would be nice if we spent nights together for the rest of our lives. Last night after watching you thrash around calling for Joan, Betty, Etta, and God knows who else, I got to thinking maybe I was lucky this was going to be our last night in the same bed."

"I'm sorry that happened, Jennie. It only happens when I'm over tired or stressed out. Homer said he would be glad when I leave for college so he won't have to put up with it any more," I answered, wondering what I had been dreaming about this time.

We had already paid for the cabin, so after I had cleaned up, we left Tupper Lake in the dark.

After we had been on the road about an hour Jennie kind of cuddled up and said, "I'm sorry that shacking up wasn't like you dreamed, but you only have yourself to blame. When I first woke up I thought about snuggling up to you and to hell with the consequences, then you started calling out all those girls' names, killing that idea in the bud. Still, because working at the barn has given me a good insight into how you boys think, I felt a little sorry for you when you woke up and called my name."

With my libido being fine-tuned by recent events, I answered without thinking, "We really don't have to rush home, Jennie, and there are many more cabins along this route?"

Jennie pulled away from me saying, "No, No, No, Caleb! What I was trying to tell you is how wonderful I felt about both of our restraint. Let's not even discuss taking that away from me."

I don't believe Jennie got any sleep at the cabin because shortly after we had stopped and had breakfast she fell against me and slept. We were almost back to Troy before she woke up, even though I had to reposition her a couple of times while she slept.

Rubbing her eyes she said, "I'm sorry, Caleb. I just didn't sleep well last night, and I guess the last two days caught up with me. Taking this job, waking up to find I'm in bed with you, all got a little too much for me, I guess. Then hearing you shouting about all those other girls in your sleep was so unsettling I couldn't get back in bed with you, anyway."

"I can't tell you what that was all about, Jennie, because I don't always remember what I dream about. Maybe being in bed with you and having to be platonic and all, I was crying out for one of them to come save me," I said with a laugh.

I guess I should have kept my big mouth shut because we were all the way through Troy before Jennie spoke to me again. She said, "Maybe we should stop and have something to eat, Caleb. You have been driving for a long time. I think it would be okay for me to drive for a ways now; seems like I remember the roads here aren't too bad until we get back to the Mohawk trail."

We stopped at the next restaurant and had a good lunch, and I let Jennie drive when we left. I guess things were catching up with me, too, because the next thing I remember was Jennie waking me up saying, "I think you'd better take over, Caleb. We are almost into North Adams, and I don't want to drive there."

She had parked by a small diner, so shaking myself awake, I said, "Maybe it would be a good idea if I got a cup of coffee first."

After we left the diner, Jennie was still giving me the silent treatment, so I let it lie until we were only an hour or so from home, then I said, "Maybe we should talk a little about keeping our stories straight, Jennie. You know there is going to be a lot of talk and speculation about us being together all weekend."

"Oh, to hell with them all!" Jennie almost shouted, "Just stick to the truth. Nothing happened, did it? They aren't going to believe anything we'll tell them anyway, so 'nothing happened' is the only answer we need. Caleb, I want to apologize for my anger with you. I had no right. I have told myself from the beginning there would never be an 'us,' and you have as much as told me the same thing. Still, sometimes I want it to be there so much. That's why I get so angry so much of the time with you. I don't really blame you as much as I do myself for not being in control. I thought I had dealt with it, but last night dealing with a passion of my own and knowing the futility of it, got to me, especially when you called out those other girls' names. I think being apart from you with this job is going to be a good thing for both of us."

Considering Jennie's reaction with the last few things I had to say, I didn't answer right away. Finally, I said, "You know, Jennie, I have only said that I wasn't in any position in my life or in my mind to make a commitment to any girl. That doesn't mean that there will never be an 'us,' though I expect you to find your *Mr. Right* long before I am a stable human being."

"I guess that is my problem. You have never really closed the door, so I keep peeking in," Jennie answered. "It would have been better for all of your harem if you had decided on one of us."

This discussion had no place to go so I said, "Have you given any thought as to how you will get back to Lawrenceville? I can probably make the trip again next week if you can't find another way."

"I'll say this for you, Caleb, you are a sucker for punishment. After you didn't gain anything but anger this time, you're willing to do it again for me," Jennie said, cuddling up to me. "I will check into bus schedules around the area and see what they have going to Malone. I really don't want to make you do the trip again."

I was surprised at first to see it was almost eleven o'clock when we arrived in Sterling, but considering we hadn't hurried and had stopped a few times it made sense. After dropping Jennie off, I got home just about the time Mother was getting back from church.

She said, "How was the trip, Caleb? You look like you haven't slept since you left. I'll have Sunday dinner ready in about two hours. Why don't you rest until then?"

It had been tiring, not only the trip itself, but dealing with the issues between Jennie and me was mentally exhausting. So I went up and crawled into my bed and fell fast asleep.

Jason came and shook me awake when Mother had dinner ready, saying, "Come on, Caleb! Everyone is waiting to hear about your big trip."

At the dinner table I talked about how big the farm was and how we had driven by Tupper Lake where Uncle Louis talked about working. I told them that Jennie had taken the job, and we had left the farm so late that we had to stop and sleep a few times on the way home.

Mother asked, "When is Jennie going back, and how was she going to get there?"

"She is working on that, Mother," I answered, "by checking available bus schedules in the area. She hopes to find one that will take her at least to Malone."

"You know what?" Emma said, "Aaron and I could take her back. I think it would be a fun trip." She looked at Mother for reaction.

It wasn't long coming. Mother exploded, saying, "You will do no such thing, Emma Carney. It's bad enough that the whole town will be talking about that Sledge girl running of for a weekend with Caleb. I will not have one of my daughters talked about like that."

Emma started to sputter, but I jumped in, saying, "Mother, I want you to know that 'that Sledge girl,' as you called her, was nothing but a perfect lady during our trip. I can tell you it wasn't due to any credit for your son, because I sure wanted it to be different."

Mother shouted, "Caleb, you may leave this table right now; later when we can be alone I want to talk to you."

I went out to the barn and talked to Jason. He said, "Caleb, even I know better than to say anything like that at the dinner table. What's with you?"

"I know, Jason, I know. That was stupid of me. I guess I wasn't thinking straight. It was just the way Mother said, *that Sledge girl*, that got to me," I answered, thinking, *I bet Jason won't be confiding in me about his puberty problems again, after this.*

"Oh, come on, Caleb, you know Mother never puts anyone down. Maybe you're just too wired up after spending all night with a girl. Sure boggles my mind to think about it. Not even in a bad way, either." Jason said, laughing as he walked away.

Nobody was left in the house except Mother, and I knew I was going to have to face her some time, so I went in.

Mother said, "Look, Caleb, I know that that trip was hard on you, and I also know that you have some serious issues with these girls you're always running around with. I am not going to threaten you or punish you, but don't ever make a mistake like that in my presence again."

I thanked Mother, told her she didn't have to worry, and walked out to the car. Thinking a hike would be good for me, I was headed for the mountain but decided it might be better if I walked the woods around home.

The solitude was good for me. The woods around home never called out to me like the woods on the mountain seemed to. I wandered around for over two hours stopping often to watch the birds and small animals go about their daily business. After I arrived back home I spent some time talking to Dad and Jason at the barn and then went to my room and climbed into bed.

The next day at work everybody wanted to know how my little "tête-à-tête," as they were wont to call it, went over the weekend.

I knew from experience that there was no way of stopping it, so I would just say, "Nothing happened; Jennie's and my relationship is strictly platonic."

Bruce hollered from the pit, "Hey, Caleb! Do you spell that big word, 'S-E-X'?"

Norman hollered back, "Aren't you ever going to learn to spell, Bruce? It's a 'S-E-X-U-A-L.' relationship. Why else would a man need a harem?"

They were still razzing me when Dad and I started for the car after work.

Dad said, "I've been thinking, Caleb, you will be leaving here in a couple of weeks or so, and I haven't driven since the accident. I'll drive for the next few days while you're still here so we can see how I do with this stiff leg."

I hadn't given this any thought before and was glad Dad was on the ball. He had mastered the marking job okay, but he still had other things in life to test.

I said, "That's a good idea, Dad; things have been so busy lately I haven't been aware of how little time I have left here."

That night when Homer came home from the barn he said, "Caleb, we are having a little going away party for Jennie at the barn Thursday night. I think for Jennie's sake you should be there. She has found a bus that leaves from Stanfield early Saturday morning. It goes to Utica first, where she catches another bus for Malone. She didn't want to get in late Friday, so we scheduled the party for Thursday. She wants to know if you could meet with her either tomorrow or the next day."

I met Jennie at the barn Tuesday night after she had finished in the milk house, and we drove up to the foot of the mountain to talk.

279

She said, "As mad as most of the boys at the barn make me sometimes, I still feel sad about leaving them. Work there has become a way of life. That's a big reason why I am taking this job and moving away. I want to think that life has more to offer me. Tell me, Caleb, did you have mixed emotions when you left before?"

"Not just before, Jennie. I am full of trepidations about leaving this time also," I answered earnestly. "I'm worried about Dad, though he seems to be adapting to his problem with his leg well. I think I have more fear this time than I did before, maybe because I have heard more about what college is like from Jake and Joan. It's like I told you before. Sometimes I feel as if I'm outside my own skin when I'm away from Sterling. I know that is a crazy way to be, but it's true; still I know, like you, that there has to be more to our lives than what we have developed here.

"I was told I was young and free and that I wouldn't always have these opportunities later in life. I understand that, so I'm just going to have to push myself to go back out here and try to find other peace to live with. I understand too well what you are saying, Jennie, and listening to you I realize how much more we are alike than you think we are."

Jennie cuddled up to me and said, "Maybe we ought to just stay here together in Sterling and get married and stay like we are instead of going out in the world and searching for a different us."

"Don't tempt me, Jennie; don't tempt me. I have often thought about doing just that," I blurted out without thinking.

Jennie pushed away, holding my shoulders, saying, "Why, Caleb, you mean you thought of marrying me?"

"You have to know, Jennie, that of course that thought has crossed my mind more than once," I answered, shocking myself. "Still, where would that leave us? Even you say you want life to offer you more than Sterling does, and right now that would be all we'd have."

"How about Joan or Betty or Etta? Have you thought that way about them?" Jennie asked.

"Now, Jennie, you're breaking the rules you laid down for us. No discussions about other girls," I answered.

Jennie gave me a little slap but cuddled up to me again saying, "It was a nice thought, Caleb, and I will always cherish hearing you say you thought of marrying me, no matter whatever else happens in my life."

We sat there at the foot of the mountain talking about our dreams and cares until we heard the town clock strike eleven. When I took Jennie home,

I had to admonish her as she was leaving the car, that kisses that passionate were not platonic.

The next couple of days were pretty uneventful. I did receive a note from Joan asking me to let her know a week before I was leaving so she could come back to Sterling and be with me.

Thursday night I went to the barn for the party about the time I figured they would be done working. The partying had already started by the time I arrived. The boys had their usual booze and there were the usual horse collar and cheese snacks. The one thing that was different was that they were set up by the milk house instead of out behind the barn like we used to do.

John and Arthur were still there and of course Homer, the other boy Gerald, was new to me but Jennie introduced us saying, "Gerald, come over here. I want you to meet the infamous Caleb you're always hearing about."

Gerald seemed to fit right in with the boys and drank and cursed with the best of them.

Homer who never joined in the drinking came over after we had been partying for a while and said, "Jennie, I can't stay late, so I have come to claim a goodbye kiss from about the only girl in Sterling that hasn't joined my kissing club."

Holding her out at arms length for a few seconds, he then kissed her in such a passionate embrace that I could feel the envy stirring in me.

Then like nothing had happened he walked away shouting. "See you all tomorrow, fellows."

Jennie was a little taken aback, but finally said, "I wonder if he kisses like that with all the girls in his kissing club?"

Big John said, "Where shall we form the line, Jennie? After all, we are all part of the crew even if we aren't Carneys."

Jennie laughed and said, "No such luck, John; you three are as close right now as you'll ever get to me. Don't forget I've been listening to you brag about and denigrate girls for too many years to ever let you get closer than this to me."

We stayed at the party for a while swapping stories about old times, especially about the time they all got sick on the booze I brought them and how they had taken me on a snipe hunt. As Jennie and I got ready to leave, she relented and gave them all a little kiss on the cheek as they all earnestly wished her well.

As I started for the car Jennie said, "No, Caleb, let's walk. I want it to be like it used to be before, as I leave."

We walked to the center of town and went into the park and sat on one of the benches. We sat quietly for a while just holding each other.

I was afraid for a minute that Jennie was reaching a breaking point when she said, "Remember when we first started sitting in the park, right after we lost Josh, Caleb? I felt so full of pain and emotion then, it is much like that now, not the kind of sadness you have when losing somebody, but feeling melancholy about something you are going to lose forever—a certain indescribable part of your life. Hold me tight, Caleb, and tell me that everything is going to be all right."

I held Jennie tight to me and said, "I can't promise you everything is going to always be all right Jennie but I can promise you this—even if we never make a place in the outside world where we are comfortable, Sterling will always be here for us. There is no doubt that over the years there might be changes, but nothing can ever take away what we have here and now as long as we want to keep it alive in our memories."

We sat there embraced, as one for a long while with tears running down the cheeks of both of us. Jennie suddenly started kissing me all over, including my neck, cheeks, and eyelids. I was starting to lose it and tried pushing her away.

She whispered, "To hell with it, Caleb, to hell with our platonic promises. This could be the last night of our life together so to hell with everything."

"If you're sure, Jennie," I said, "let me go get my car."

"No, no, Caleb, don't give me a chance to second guess myself. Let's go behind the library. It'll be like old times. In case I ever have to live on memories, let me add to them."

Afterwards, we walked back towards the park with her still kissing my eyes, neck, and face over and over again, with tears rolling from her eyes.

Suddenly she turned and walked away, saying, "Don't forget to pick me up at four in the morning Saturday."

I went back to the park bench and sat down, trying to shake the crazy emotions that were rattling my body. I had completely forgotten that I had told her I would take her to Stanford to catch her bus. I hoped that we had ourselves under control by then. Hearing the clock strike midnight and remembering I had to work the next day, I went back to the barn to get my car, and drove home.

The next thing I was conscious of was Homer shaking me and cussing. "Damn you, Caleb! You get the girl, and stay out all night with her and I get to listen to you screaming in your sleep. God help your roommate if you get one in college."

The next day at work, I guess I was dragging some because Norman complained, saying, "What the hell is it this time, Caleb? I figured with most of your harem gone I wouldn't have to put up with your having days like this. What gives? You practicing being a college boy, staying up all night partying?"

I knew he was right, that I wasn't pulling my load, so I didn't answer him, just struggled quietly through the rest of the day. When I got home, remembering that I had to get up at three a.m., I went to bed right after supper. I was awake before the alarm went off, so I got up and made coffee.

As I sat there having my second cup, Mother came down saying, "You all right, Caleb? Seems like you're burning the candles at both ends lately. I didn't like the way you looked last night; it worried me."

"I'm just tired, Mother, and it's hard seeing all my friends moving on in their lives, even when a part of some of us doesn't want to join adulthood."

Seeing that that kind of talk had put a frown on Mother's face, I said, "I know, Mother; it is just a stage you go through growing up. I'll be okay. I have talked to Aaron and my friends about this, and it's very common."

It was time for me to go, so I gave Mother a hug and went to pick up Jennie.

Jennie came rushing out as soon as I pulled into her yard. "I was getting worried Caleb; it's a little after three," she said as we loaded her things in the car.

She was quiet until we were well out of Sterling, seeming to be wistfully studying every street, house, or landmark that we passed.

Finally, she said, "Do you know where the bus stop is in Stanford? I completely forgot to find out before we left."

"We're in luck Jennie," I answered, feeling a little smug. "I know right where it is."

I didn't bother to tell her that I knew because we passed it when Joan and I went there to the theater. We bantered and talked about family most of the way to Stanford neither one of us wanting to face the fact that it could possibly be long time, or perhaps never, when we would be together again. She told me her sister Janet had written; she worked in a doctor's office out on the Cape Cod and was engaged to an intern at the hospital there. They had planned to get home before she left but they couldn't get time off together and now were planning on trying to come and see her at Jolene's farm.

We arrived at the bus station a good twenty minutes early and after getting her things loaded on the bus, she just held me and said, "Don't let me cry, Caleb; help me to be strong."

Holding her and thinking how her intimacy had carried me through the toughest loss of my life, I searched my mind for words to salve her fears, finally saying, "Jennie, you know how we said that there will always be our life in Sterling to lean on? I want you to know that even if there never is a future 'us,' at least for me there will be the 'us' leading up to this day. Standing here now, my heart and my mind are screaming out, *Do something, Caleb, because a great part of you is about to be torn from your arms.* I know I can't ask you to stay, because right now I have nothing to offer, but I promise you this—no matter what it takes, this is not the end of us being together.

"You don't know how much I wanted to hear that," Jennie said, kissing me passionately just as they announced her bus to Utica.

We went to where the bus was loading, with her still holding me tight. It was like she was never going to let me go. Finally the bus driver said, "Lady, if you're going with us you're going to have to let him go or buy another ticket."

With one last kiss Jennie rushed onto the bus with the tears she asked me to stop running down her cheeks. I went out to the parking lot and just sat there, drained from all the emotions. I don't know how long I was there but the parking lot attendant came over and rapped on the window asking if I was all right. I told him I had just suffered an emotional goodbye and would be leaving as soon as I pulled my self together. He gave me a thumbs up sign and walked away.

When I returned to Sterling, I didn't feel much like talking to any one, so I went for a hike on Mount Fay, searching for the solace that I often found there. When I heard the town clock strike twelve noon, I decided I had better go home so Mother wouldn't be worried.

No one seemed to be at the house when I got there so I made a bite to eat and went back to bed. That evening I spent with the family discussing my leaving. Though I had a little over three weeks before I had to be at the college everyone thought I should take some time off from work before I left, so I would have time to say my goodbyes in Sterling and also to go and spend a few days with Harry and Eunice.

On Monday when we talked to Joclin about Bruce working with Norman, he told us that he had a man ready to take Bruce's place any time we were ready. We made arrangements for him to take Bruce's place the following week. Dad thought it might be better if I came for a couple of days to work with Bruce and Norman then.

Bruce scoffed at the idea saying, "Like I need to be taught to stick lumber; now if Caleb would teach me how to have a harem, then I could use his expertise."

I laughed and said, "Guess I won't be much help there, Bruce; all my harem has left me."

Time seemed to fly now that a date for my leaving had been set. Bruce wanted to have another pig roast for a good-bye party, but we talked him out of it. In the middle of the week I got a call from Betty asking if she could see me. I told her if she promised not to keep me out all night I would pick her up Thursday night.

When I picked her up she said, "I hear you're leaving again, Caleb. Weren't you even going to say goodbye to me?"

"I would have seen you before I left, Betty. I'm taking some time off from work next week, so I can see everyone before I leave," I answered.

"You mean you won't be working with Norman anymore?" Betty asked. "I was going to ask you if you would take me to see Virginia before you left. I have never thanked her for all she did for me. I have enough money and would like to take her and Norman out to eat or something like that if it is possible."

"Look, Betty, I think I'm going to be free Saturday. I'll ask Norman tomorrow and see if we can arrange something. Would you like to take a quick trip to Oscin or just ride around?" I ventured as Betty cuddled up to me in the car.

"Let's just ride around, Caleb," she answered, "I have a new beau, and he lives in Oscin, and it wouldn't be good for him to see us together. I have turned over a new leaf, Caleb. I am going to take some night courses to bring my school marks up. I frittered away my last year in high school and couldn't get into any college I wanted because of poor marks. I was angry and said, 'To hell with school,' and just went wild. I know how wrong I've been and hope I can get on track and back to my education."

"I'm proud of you, Betty, and I bet your family is happy about it too. I have no doubt that you can do it. Have you heard anything new about Karl lately?" I asked, thinking that even Betty was moving on.

Just as Betty was finishing telling me about Karl and his new baby boy we were driving by the grove. Betty, noticing me glance at it, said, "For you, Caleb, and old times' sake if that's what you want."

"No, No, Betty, it's not from lack of want, but because I want to help you in your quest," I said, thinking, *I don't want to ever have to go through thinking she's pregnant again.* When I dropped her off she kissed me so passionately that I had to push her away or head back to the Grove. She just laughed and ran for the house.

I spoke to Norman the next day about taking Virginia and him out to dinner.

285

He said, "No can do, Caleb. Virginia has a big dinner planned as a going away party for you. It was supposed to be just the three of us, but some of the men on the job heard about it, and now there are quite a few of them coming. You bring Betty along. I'm sure Virginia can find a quiet moment for her."

That night I called Betty and told her I would pick her up about ten or ten-thirty Saturday morning. There was a short letter from Joan reminding me she would be home Sunday, and she hoped I had saved some time outside of my harem just for her. I knew she was going to be upset when she found out I was leaving Thursday; I was supposed to let her know what my plans were and had forgotten. Betty called back to tell me she was free and would like to go to a movie or something. I begged off, telling her I had to spend the evening with my family.

Saturday morning when I picked up Betty, her mother was waiting for me at the door. She said, "Caleb, I heard you were on your way back to college. I spoke to Karl the other night on the phone, and he wanted me to give you his best. He said to tell you to remember that we will always have the mountain, and to never lose our wild dreams of youth. He said you would understand."

I smiled at the message and said, "I understand Mrs. Hart. Karl and I were great friends growing up and shared everything."

When Betty and I arrived Virginia and Norman's place there were several men from the job there. They had a table set up outside the shanty like Bruce had done at the pig roast.

I got a lot of pats on the back; it was like they were proud that one of them was going to college. Some of the younger ones asked if I was going to start a new harem at college.

Betty laughed when she heard that and said, "Look closely; here you see the last of his old harem, and the reason why. What makes you think Caleb needs to look any further?"

That got the boys all cheering. Bruce came over to Betty and made an elaborate show of examining her, then said, "Well, she's not as tall as some of them, but everything else seems to be in place. You're probably right, little lady; you must rank high in the top ten. Still, some of the others have played him to a standstill and never got him hooked."

None of this seemed to faze Betty. She really enjoyed herself being there with all these men. A while after we had a wonderful meal, the men started drifting home. Virginia dragged Betty off, and I went down to say goodbye to horses, Molly and Roxy. I would be back for a couple of days next week but I wouldn't be driving the team. I realized as I was patting and talking to them how I really hadn't been as close to them because Norman had taken over their care ever since he worked for us.

As I left the team I felt emotional about leaving this part of my life, still I realized if I stayed I would grow to resent it. Betty and Virginia were back with Bruce and Norman when I came back to the shanty and we sat and talked a while before leaving.

Norman said, "All joking aside, Caleb. It has been a pleasure working with you and having you as a friend."

"I'm going to miss all this, Norman, and I want you to know what a Godsend it has been to have you working with us. I don't think I would have had it so easy if Clem had stayed with me. You can count on seeing me from time to time, after all, what am I going to do if I don't have you and Virginia to guide me?"

Virginia gave me a hug and said, "No matter what, Caleb, we will always be here for you."

Norman rather shyly draped his arm over my shoulder and said, "It's been fun, Caleb, and I'm going to miss you."

Bruce took my hand saying, "One thing, though, Caleb, the next time you come, can you bring your whole harem?"

Betty and I were both quiet as we drove away, for which I was thankful because I was dealing with such mixed emotions. As much as my mind told me I needed to move on, I felt a strong feeling of apprehension about the road I was taking. Betty must have sensed my remorse because she hardly spoke until we were almost in Sterling.

Then she said, "They are very unique, your friends at work aren't they, Caleb? What a wonderful world this would be if we all had their compassion and feeling for other people."

"I don't think I ever thought of them quite like that, Betty, but you are right. I have gained much in knowing them," I answered just as we pulled into Betty's yard.

Betty said, "I know Joan is coming home tomorrow, and you are leaving in the middle of the week. Sit and let me hold you for a while, Caleb, and let's not make this goodbye. Please write me, no strings, just as your best friend's kid sister."

We sat and held each other quietly for such a long time that by the third time her mother came to the door, I said, "I guess we have made her nervous enough, Betty; you better go in." Betty kissed me tenderly and ran for the house.

I called Joan early in the morning, but her father said he didn't expect her until early afternoon. Jason was out in the barn, so I asked him if he wanted me to spend a couple hours with him cutting wood to make up for not being there Saturday.

He said, "Great idea, Caleb, let me go tell Mother why I won't be going to church."

Working on the other end of a crosscut saw with Jason reminded me how efficient a worker he had become.

After we had felled a couple of trees and cut them up, Jason said, "I hope that I can go to college like you, Caleb. It must be exciting to go out into the challenges of a completely new world. Don't get me wrong; I know we have a good family here in Sterling, but I can't wait until I am old enough to shake the dust and smell of farming off and take on a whole new world."

"It is good to have goals, Jason," I answered, thinking, *I wish mine were clearer.* "One thing I'm sure of, after watching you take over here after Dad was hurt, you will be successful at anything you try."

When we got back to the house Mother said, "Joan called and said she got home earlier than her father expected and for you to come over as soon as you could."

After I had lunch with the family I left to pick up Joan. I had just got out of the car in her yard to go in when she came running out. She gave me a kiss and said, "Let's get out of here, Caleb."

As we were driving off, she said, "I'm sorry, Caleb, but I didn't want to have to listen to Mother fawning all over you again. It's so hypocritical after her history of treating you so badly."

I wondered if Joan was protecting herself or me. I knew her mother didn't quite believe my explanation about a lost love causing her actions the first time she came home from college.

"That's okay, Joan," I answered; "I don't mind avoiding your mother's probing. What would you like to do today?"

"I feel like relaxing," she answered, "let's go and take in a movie in Oscin. Do you know what's playing?"

"No, I haven't been lately so I don't pay much attention to the ads, but if we are going to make the first show we'd better hurry," I said as we sped out of the yard.

We got to Oscin too late to catch the first show, so we went to the ice-cream parlor and decided if we really wanted to see *Duel in the Sun* which was the movie that was playing. At the parlor the girl that was always commenting about me was waiting on tables, but she didn't say anything, just raised her eyebrows as she took our order.

After we had eaten and were discussing the movie, the waitress said, "You really should go; it's right down your alley—a real tear-jerker in the end."

Joan didn't say anything, but after we had decided to see the movie and were leaving she said, "Nice-looking girl, Caleb; another one of your harem?"

I laughed and said, "No, I have never seen her outside of that store. Do you think I should get her number?"

"I think," Joan said rather haughtily, "it's about time you gave up toying with girls and became more serious about your relationship with someone."

I had forgotten how upset Joan got when I talked about other girls and made a mental note to refrain from that for the next couple of days. We went to see the movie and the waitress was right, it left us teary eyed in the end. I was a little sorry that we had gone to such an emotional show even though I had enjoyed it.

After the show we drove back to Sterling and parked at the foot of the mountain. I'm not sure if it was the movie or not but we did very little talking, just sat there holding each other in the shadow of Mount Fay.

When the town clock struck eleven I said, "I hate to break this up, but I have to go in to work in the morning so I had better be getting home."

Joan sighed and said, "Caleb, I wish I could put in words what I've felt tonight since we got here. I think it must be the mountain, because here I was able to shut the whole world out and feel like we were just little kids again sneaking away to eat our ice cream. Promise me, Caleb, that before you go we can spend a day on the mountain."

"I have been dreading to have to tell you Joan, but I'm leaving Wednesday, and I am supposed to work Monday and Tuesday," I answered as Joan grabbed at me in anger. "Wait, wait, wait! I only said I'm *supposed* to work. Let me see what I can do about freeing up Tuesday for us."

Joan answered coldly, "You had better, Caleb; you damn well better! If you had kept me informed, I could have left my Aunt's earlier. Now take me home."

At her house Joan had cooled down and held me and kissed me passionately. As she pulled away I said, "One thing, Joan, when we go to the mountain tomorrow you have to promise no sexual enticement. I don't want to have to live through what happened last time again."

Joan held me by the shoulders looking kind of hurt, saying, " Don't worry, Caleb; all of that will be left up to you, from now on."

Joan ran for the house as I pulled away, feeling somewhat guilty about being sexually aroused by her. In some funny way it felt like I was cheating on Jennie.

The next day at work it was quite evident that I wasn't really needed. Norman and Bruce handled the sticking job like old pros. I told Dad to bring the truck home because I wouldn't be coming tomorrow.

Bruce said, "Jess, Caleb, I don't know what I can do now that I won't have the truck to use."

"Don't worry, Norman, it's only going to be a couple of days. I know Dad talked about me taking the car to college, but I decided against it," I answered as Norman and Bruce lifted me up onto the wagon.

The mill closed down and Mr. Joclin hollered, "Let's hear it, Bruce."

Bruce took a paper from his pocket and read:

We have gathered here for the Carney boy, all to say goodbye
Still, unlike his huge harem, you'll never see us cry
Oh, it's true, we'll miss you, as you leave us in a whirl
But more than you, we'll sorely miss your bringing all those girls.

There was a lot of hooting and hollering when Bruce finished, and then the men walked by wishing me well as we all were leaving the mill site. I went up to the shanty and gave Virginia another goodbye hug and again thanked Norman and Bruce for being there for the Carney family.

When I got home Mother said I was to call Joan right away.

When I called, she said, "Caleb, I know this is strange, but could you come and have supper with us tonight? Mother has promised to behave herself, and Dad wants this badly. I think he has a guilty conscious about how they have treated you."

I really didn't want to do this but remembering how I had upset Joan before I said, "I'll be over as soon as I can change and clean up, Joan, and don't worry; I can handle it."

Things went fairly well at Joan's house. They asked me about going back to college and Joan told interesting stories about some of her experiences away from home. A couple of times I heard Joan say, "Mother," in kind of a forceful way but all in all I enjoyed observing the situation. After supper Joan wanted to walk around town, so we visited most of our old haunts.

She wanted me to take her to the barn, but I knew that would be a disaster for both of us, so I begged off by saying, "The boys would be all gone by now, and you wouldn't want to wander through that dirt and smell."

The library was closed, but we sat in the park, laughing about the times we had rendezvoused at the library when she was not supposed to talk with me. It was dark by the time we arrived at the school where we sat on the swings and continued our reminiscing.

Out of the blue Joan said, "Caleb, can you really still love me after what happened to me?"

"Of course, Joan. I love you as much as I ever did, in fact probably even more than I ever did," I answered, thinking at least I can say it that way truthfully, hoping she didn't push it any further. She seemed satisfied with that, and we started walking to her house.

At her house her mother wanted us to come in but Joan told her I had to get home and couldn't stay. I was surprised that we were breaking up so early but I wasn't upset about it. We stood outside for a few minutes then I kissed her good night and told her I would pick her up around ten thirty the next morning.

The next morning Mother reminded me that I had promised Tuesday night to the family and to get home early enough to be there for supper. After I had picked up Joan I stopped at the store and bought the strawberry ice cream I always bought for her when we were kids. I knew a little opening in some thick small hemlocks on the mountain that we went to and ate the ice cream. Tears rolled down Joan's face all the time we were eating it.

I said, "This is supposed to be a happy occasion, Joan; why the tears?"

"It's not all sadness, as I have grown older our ice cream escapades have become such a sweet thing in my memory, that when I think of them as gone, it brings tears to my eyes. Thank you so much for remembering," she said, wrapping both arms around me. "I have often wondered, though, if they were as dear to you."

"You know, Joan, my youth is so much of a live thing in my mind lately. I don't want to let any of it go. Emma and Aaron keep telling me that there is so much more to life than what I have experienced. If that means forgetting what we had I don't want to experience it."

"I promise you, Caleb, it doesn't mean your past is gone, because the past has to be there for you to lean on when you need a lift in the future. I found that out in therapy when I was ready to quit life all together."

Worrying that we would end up crying on each other's shoulders if we continued on this path, I said, "What's our first memory to explore today? Shall we head for the tower, go to the ledges, or just wander the trails all day?"

Joan jumped up and said, "Let's do all three. We'll hit the tower last so we can run down the mountain like last time."

We spent a wonderful day on the mountain wandering the trails, picnicking at the springs, talking all the time about our carefree youth. We now could see the funny side of the time we went behind Larros and Joan had lost her panties and her father went around town with his bullwhip looking for someone to blame.

Joan talked some about college assuring me that it would not be hard for me. We finished the day racing down from the tower and collapsing exhilarated in the grass of the field below. We lay there holding hands for over an hour hoping against hope we could keep our mountain dreams alive forever.

The town clock roused me out of this reverie by striking four and I said, "I am going to have to leave, Joan. Would you like to come to our house tonight?"

"No, Caleb, I know you have to go, but I don't want to leave this yet. You go, I'll stay here and walk home later. What I would like to do if possible is go to the train with you tomorrow."

Knowing how she felt I left her there, telling her I would call her about tomorrow. At home Mother had made me a roast pork dinner with a big chocolate pie for dessert. I spent the evening trying to personalize a special goodbye for each of them.

Later when I was in the kitchen getting a drink, Nellie came in and holding my hand said, "You're still pretty scared, aren't you, Caleb?"

Knowing I couldn't fool Nellie, I said, "I hope it doesn't show too much."

She laughed and said, "You know I never tell, but besides feeling your fear, there is something else about you that I haven't placed yet. Did you get engaged or something like that to one of your girls?"

"If I did, Nellie, I don't remember it happening," I said as we went back to the rest of the family. We spent the rest of the evening laughing and joking and hearing tall tales, mostly about me. The next morning I got up early so I could give Dad a hug and wish him well.

He said, "You don't have to worry about me, Caleb; you have left me in good hands. Those Edward boys are a blessing. All I really have to do is take care of my marking job. Norman said to tell you he will come home with me tonight to get the truck back."

After final goodbyes to the family, we picked up Joan and headed to Oscin to catch the train. We had cut the timing pretty close, so there wasn't much time to say goodbye. Mother hugged me and kissed me on the forehead, and then Joan held me until we heard the last all aboard.

As I turned to leave, Mother pushed a small package in my hand saying, "Your father thought you ought to take this."

The train was pulling out before I found a seat. After sitting down I unwrapped the parcel Mother had given me. It was the medallion that Edgar had given me when I had left for college last time. I thought, *How appropriate, here I am, a little more than a year later, in the same fix, listening to the haunting whistle of the train that's taking me away again to an unknown future.*